TRIPLE CROSSING

Also by SEBASTIAN ROTELLA

Twilight on the Line: Underworlds and Politics at the U.S.–Mexico Border

TRIPLE CROSSING

A NOVEL

SEBASTIAN ROTELLA

MULHOLLAND BOOKS

LITTLE, BROWN AND COMPANY

NEW YORK BOSTON LONDON

Mulholland Books/Little, Brown and Company
Hachette Book Group
237 Park Avenue, New York, NY 10017
www.hachettebookgroup.com

First Edition: August 2011

Mulholland Books is an imprint of Little, Brown and Company, a division of Hachette Book Group, Inc. The Mulholland Books name and logo are trademarks of Hachette Book Group, Inc.

Library of Congress Cataloging-in-Publication Data
Rotella, Sebastian.
Triple crossing : a novel / Sebastian Rotella. — 1st ed.
p. cm.
ISBN 978-0-316-10530-9
1. Border patrol agents — Fiction. 2. Organized crime — Mexican-American Border Region — Fiction. 3. Organized crime investigation — Fiction. 4. Undercover operations — Fiction. 5. Mexican-American Border Region — Fiction. I. Title.
PS3618.O8555T75 2011
813'.6 — dc22 2010041796

10 9 8 7 6 5 4 3 2

RRD-IN

Printed in the United States of America

Para Carmen, mi amor
And for Valeria, with love

In memoriam
Enrique Méndez Alvarez
May 12, 1921–June 5, 2011

Till the finger of guilt, pointing so sternly for so long across the query-room blotter, had grown bored with it all at last and turned, capriciously, to touch the fibers of the dark gray muscle behind the captain's light gray eyes. So that though by daylight he remained the pursuer there had come nights, this windless first week of December, when he had dreamed he was being pursued.

From *The Man With the Golden Arm,* by Nelson Algren

Mire la calle.
¿Cómo puede usted ser
indiferente a ese gran río
de huesos, a ese gran río
de sueños, a ese gran río
de sangre, a ese gran río?

From *La Calle* (*Taller Abandonado*), by Nicolás Guillén

AUTHOR'S NOTE

The customary disclaimer is correct: The characters and events herein are fictitious. Any similarities to anyone are coincidental. Et cetera.

Nonetheless, I am also a journalist. I have spent a long time covering Latin America and the borderlands. So for the benefit of those who know the turf, and also for those who are discovering it, I want to set the right tone.

This book is inspired by reality. But a novel gives you the liberty to change and blend, mix and match. Many details of the subcultures of policing and smuggling, of the topography and sociology of the borderlands, are grounded in the present. Others grow out of a past reality that has since evolved. And some aspects are purely fictional.

I hope the result fulfills the mission of a novel as described by the wise Mario Vargas Llosa: "to express a curious truth that can only be expressed in a concealed way, disguised as something it is not."

Part One

OTM

I

FOG AT THE BORDER.

Border Patrol Agent Valentine Pescatore urged the green Jeep Wrangler through the shroud of mist on the southbound road. Hungover and sleepy, he slurped on a mug of convenience-store Coke. Carbonation burned behind his eyes. He braked into a curve, trailing a comet of dust. Jackrabbits scattered in his headlights.

Braking sent a twinge of pain through his ankle. He had blown it up months earlier while chasing a hightop-wearing Tijuana speedster through a canyon. He had intended to snare the hood of the punk's sweatshirt and jerk him to a neck-wrenching stop, confirming his status as the fastest trainee in his unit.

But instead Pescatore went down, sprawling pathetically, clutching the ankle with both hands.

Border Patrol agents gathered around him in the darkness. Tejano accents twanged. Cigarettes flared. A cowboy-hatted silhouette squatted as if contemplating a prisoner or a corpse.

Hell, *muchacho,* time to nominate you for a Einstein award.

Was that a female tonk you were chasing, Valentine? Playing hard to get, eh?

Hey, you're not gonna catch them all. Slow down. Foot speed don't impress us anymore.

The voices in his memory gave way to the dispatcher's voice on the radio, asking his position. Pescatore increased speed, rolling through the blackness of a field toward the foothills of the Tijuana River valley. With a guilty grimace, he pushed a CD into the dashboard player. Bass and cymbals blared: The song was a rap version of "Low Rider."

Another night on the boulevard
Cruisin' hard
And everybody's low-ridin'.

The song had become his anthem, his overture when he headed out into the nightly battle theater of the absurd. He grinned behind the wheel, swaying, mouthing the words. He entered San Ysidro, the last sliver of San Diego before the Tijuana line. The Wrangler cruised past parking lots for tourists who crossed on foot into Mexico, past discount-clothing outlets for shoppers who drove up from Mexico. The area was a meeting point for *raiteros* (*raite* was Spanglish for "ride") waiting to drive north the illegal immigrants who made it through the canyons. He saw figures crouched among rows of parked cars, but he didn't slow down. There were already Border Patrol agents, uniformed and plainclothes, creeping on foot among the cars, waiting for smuggling vehicles to fill up before they pounced. No *raite* tonight, homes. Try again tomorrow.

The restricted federal area near the pedestrian border crossing to Tijuana was illuminated by stadium lights atop steel masts that ran along The Line toward the Pacific. Past the southeast corner of the lot where a Border Patrol van idled, a crew of teenagers—boys in Raiders jackets and low-slung baggy pants, girls in shorts and halter tops despite the chill—trooped through the pedestrian turnstile. The revolving gate made a melodic metallic clatter that reminded him of a calliope or steel drums. The youths were Tuesday-night partyers bound for what was left of the Avenida Revolución nightlife district, a casualty of the drug wars lined with shuttered bars and abandoned clubs. Farther east, a steel river of freeway traffic flowed into the Mexican customs station. Pescatore turned west and drove alongside the border fence. The rusting barrier had been assembled from metal landing mats once used for temporary air bases: military castoffs from the Vietnam era. A secondary line of fortification, a newer, taller fence made of see-through steel mesh, gleamed on his right.

Migrants perched atop the border fence on his left. They bided their time, suspended between nations. They peered down at him. Their breath steamed in the February night. This stretch was known as Memo Lane because rocks often rained down on Border Patrol vehicles, forcing agents to write incident memos.

Pescatore blinked and yawned. Back in high school, a wiseass English teacher had had fun with his name. It means "fisherman" in Italian. And there's the biblical connotation: fisher of men. Which will it be, Mr. Pescatore? Fisherman or fisher of men? As it turned out, in a way the Jesuits would not have expected, Pescatore had become a fisher of men. And women and children. All you can catch. You couldn't make a net big enough to hold them all. Catch catch catch. And throw them back.

The next song began with the baritone recorded voice that greeted callers to the phone lines of the U.S. immigration bureaucracy. Then came helicopter sounds, simulated Border Patrol radio traffic, a fast frenetic beat. A rapper ranted about oppression, Christopher Columbus, migrants on the move. The rapper got all excited accusing the Border Patrol of abuse, rape, murder and just about everything except drowning Mexican puppies.

Pescatore kind of liked the song; he liked to hate it. It reminded him of the ponytailed Viva La Raza militants who were the nemeses of every self-respecting PA. The ones who hid in the brush with video cameras waiting for you to break the rules, who whined about human rights when an agent defended himself against some drug addict or gang member coming at him out of a mob. The song reminded him of the Mexican *Migra Asesina* movies in which Snidely Whiplash–looking Border Patrol agents with machine guns mowed down migrants. Quite a twist on reality: Pescatore had more than once seen aliens, when caught between U.S. agents and Mexican police, run north to surrender.

The words crescendoed into the blast of a shotgun. Throwing his head back in sarcastic euphoria, Pescatore shouted out the refrain: "Runnin'!"

He switched off the music. He coaxed the Wrangler up an embankment, dust swirling. He rumbled into position at his workstation: the front line in the never-ending war of the American Foreign Legion, aka the U.S. Border Patrol: the Tijuana River levee.

The landscape never failed to give him the sensation that he had landed on a hostile planet. The levee slanted southeast into Mexican territory. Billows of fog had come to rest in the riverbed like grounded clouds. The migrants lining the concrete banks of the levee were wraiths in the fog. The levee was almost dry except for a stream trickling among tufts of vegetation in the center: a black brew of sewage, industrial toxins, runoff from mountain ranges of garbage in Tijuana shacktowns. Border vendors sold the migrants plastic garbage bags to pull over their shoes and legs before wading through the muck.

There were dozens of people on the Mexican side. Smoke from bonfires mingled with the haze of dust. The scene gave off an infernal glow: the flames, the stadium lights, the glimmer of the *colonias* speckling the hills of Tijuana.

The voice of Agent Arleigh Garrison, his supervisor, rumbled over the radio.

"Here we go, Valentine. You finally made it."

Pescatore fumbled with his radio. "Yessir. Sorry I was late. I had the problem with my radio and everything."

"Your problem was too many *cervezas* last night at the Hound Dog, son," Garrison chuckled.

"Yessir."

"Ready to catch some tonks? Ready to play? I plan on breaking my world record tonight, buddy."

"Yessir." Although he had cracked more than one head, Pescatore could not quite bring himself to call the aliens "tonks."

"Come on over here. I wanna show you something."

Pescatore pulled up alongside two Wranglers sitting side by side on the north riverbank. He got out to talk to Garrison and an agent named Dillard, a boyish and reedy cowpoke who was telling the supervisor: "Them old boys wouldn't pull over, so I cut on my lights and sy-reen."

And they all rag on me, Pescatore groused to himself, because supposedly I'm the one who talks funny. He caught a glimpse of his reflection in the window of a vehicle: Pescatore was twenty-five, bantam, built low to the ground with sturdy corded arms and legs, thick black curls. He had big wary eyes and flared nostrils. He liked to play with his appearance as if he were on undercover assignments. He cultivated mustaches that made him look like a Turk, a Hells Angel, a bandit. Back in Chicago before he joined The Patrol, he had on occasion grown out his hair like the Mexican soccer players in the parks near Taylor Street. But now he was close-cropped and clean-shaven. Trying to tone it down, play the role and, as Garrison would say, get with the program.

"There's my buddy," Garrison said. He engaged Pescatore in a palm-smacking, knuckle-crushing handshake and let it linger with Pescatore off-balance, as if he were going to yank him forward and shove him down the concrete embankment. "You need anything, Valentine? Coffee? Water? Oxygen? We wanna keep you awake. Don't want you running that government vehicle into a tree."

Pescatore rescued his hand from Garrison's, which was encased in a black glove, and affected a sheepish look. "Oh man, you know I'm king of the road anytime. I haven't been sleeping so good, that's all."

Pescatore hadn't slept well for months, even after the drinking sessions at Garrison's house or the gloomy mini-mall bars of San Ysidro, Imperial Beach and National City. After reading an article somewhere, he had decided that his affliction was caused by all the chases. The article had said the experience of a hot pursuit produced a cocktail of fear, rage and adrenaline that caused chemical changes in the physiology of a police officer. All Pescatore knew was that when he finally managed to doze off, he drifted into a zone between wakefulness and oblivion. The border seethed on the edge of his sleep. Haunting him. Disembodied faces surging up out of the riverbed at him. He would wake up, freaked out and exhausted, afternoon light streaming through the window, to see the green uniform draped across a chair. Ready for work.

"So you oversleep," Garrison said. "You roll in around six for the five-to-one shift. You got your radio problem. You're back at IB getting it replaced. Maybe hitting on that little Lupita works at the front desk. It's eight-thirty and the shift is going by quick. Good thing you got me looking out for you, Valentine."

"Damn right."

"At least you work hard once you're here. Not like some of these slugs."

Garrison had put in ten years in the trenches of Imperial Beach. During the previous ten years, he had served in the U.S. Army Special Forces and worked as a security contractor in Latin America and as a self-described "white hunter" in Africa. He was six feet three. His back and shoulders were slabs stretching the green uniform. He wore his baseball-style uniform cap high over the rampart of a balding forehead.

Pescatore had once seen Garrison deliver a headbutt that dropped a prisoner to his knees. Talk about permanent chemical changes, Pescatore thought, assessing the gray-eyed sniper stare. What had a decade of chases done to Garrison?

Garrison turned in his muscle-bound way and pulled binoculars off his dashboard.

"Guess what," he said. "Your boy Pulpo is back."

"No way, Jack." Pescatore took the binoculars. "I referred him to Prosecutions, they were gonna do him for illegal entry. He got lucky because he jumped in the back of the load van. The aliens wouldn't give him up as the driver."

"Well, he must've slipped through the system. Isn't that a surprise."

"*Pinche* Pulpo."

"What're you gonna do if you catch that turd?" Garrison asked. The bulging gray eyes fastened on Pescatore.

Pescatore hesitated, then said: "I'm gonna fuck him up."

He took refuge behind the binoculars. He pointed them at the crowd on the south riverbank near the spot where man-sized letters painted on the concrete declared in Spanish: NOT ILLEGAL ALIENS: INTERNATIONAL WORKERS. The migrants sat with hunched shoulders, a huddle of hoods, caps and backpacks. They were like spectators in an open-air amphitheater between the two cities, waiting for the action to start. The smuggler known as Pulpo paced in front of a group of migrants, holding court, gesticulating like an old-time Mexican politician, the flames of a bonfire dancing behind him. Pulpo: buff and bowlegged in overalls, a wire cutter or pliers protruding from a low pocket, a red bandanna wrapped around his head, Los Angeles County Jail–style.

"He'd cut your throat and laugh about it, then go home and tell his mother, so she could laugh about it too," Garrison said, close to Pescatore's ear.

Pulpo enjoyed messing with PAs whenever and however he could. The smuggler moved back and forth between Tijuana and San Diego with the ease of someone crossing a street. Pescatore had once seen Pulpo drop over the border fence in plain view of a Patrol sedan in Memo Lane. Pulpo had jogged alongside the fence, his jaunty stride taunting the agents. When the Patrol sedan screeched up to him, Pulpo turned, bounded onto the hood and catapulted himself off it like a trapeze artist. He caught the top of the fence and clambered back over, making an annoyed growling noise as two agents scrabbled at his ankles. From atop the fence he raised an arm in lazy triumph. And a bunch of low-lifes popped up to unleash a cascade of rocks and bricks that shattered the windshield of the sedan and sent a PA to the hospital.

Garrison's cell phone rang. Pescatore kept looking through the binoculars while he listened to Garrison hold a monosyllabic conversation, mostly in Spanish. Garrison's Spanish was fluid, though he had a serious *gringo* accent. Pescatore lowered the binoculars as Garrison clipped the phone back on his belt.

"My guy says it's on for tomorrow," Garrison said to Dillard, who nodded.

Garrison turned to Pescatore. "How about you?"

"Tomorrow's tough for me, man."

"Hmm." Garrison stooped to produce a pack of Camels tucked into the top of a sock. He swiveled away from the ocean breeze, cupped and lit a cigarette. "So Valentine, ready to play the Game tonight? How much you betting? Dillard's down for fifty dollars."

"Oh man, you know I don't want none a that action." Pescatore quickly handed back the binoculars. "Plus I'm short on cash tonight."

"Don't worry, buddy, you can add it to what you owe me. Let's get to it."

During the next hour, Garrison led Pescatore, Dillard and another agent in a series of maneuvers intended to keep back the crowd on the levee, four vehicles arrayed against the oncoming forces of history and economics. Garrison was a scientist of The Line and an artist behind the wheel. He knew just how close to come to the fleeing aliens without hitting them, how fast to run at the fence before swerving. Lights flashing, the Wranglers sped back and forth and down into the riverbed, frantic figures scattering at their approach. The Wranglers stopped short and spun doughnuts, kicking up dust, herding back groups of migrants who whistled and jeered as they retreated.

Periodically the agents tumbled out to catch small groups—probes by Pulpo and his cronies to gauge the defenses. Pescatore and Garrison chased down a trio of runners in tall grass. Pescatore nabbed a teenager who twisted out of his shoes in the mud and stumbled a few yards barefoot. Nearby Garrison had the other two prone on the ground. He gave each of them a kick in the ribs; Pescatore winced at the impacts. Garrison's roar made him sound eight feet tall.

"*Pinche pollo mugroso hijo de la chingada no te muevas o te doy una madriza, joto!* Don't you run when I tell you to stop. Understand, *pendejo?*"

Garrison had explained his philosophy to Pescatore. You have to scream and yell and cuss at them like you're going to tear their head off. That's called command presence. That's what they expect. That's what the Mexican cops do. If you're all quiet and polite, they'll take you for a wussy, Valentine. A PA demands respect. And if they keep running from you, they just signed up for an ass-kicking. Thump 'em if they run.

Back behind the wheel of the Wrangler, Pescatore peeled away from the levee, pursuing a family into a maze of chain-link pens filled with construction machinery. The family of three held hands as they fled among cranes and bulldozers. They looked like the image on the yellow freeway signs that depicted a family of running migrants to alert drivers to the fact that the roads around here swarmed with frightened, exhausted pedestrians who got run over in gory and spectacular ways.

Unlike the girl in the freeway sign, though, the little girl he chased did not wear pigtails, but rather ribbons in her hair and a silver party dress with a jeans jacket over it. For Christ's sake,

Pescatore thought, put a coat on her. It's cold. He cut the lights and sat for a moment by a storage shed. The family emerged, hurrying toward the blue neon of a supermarket in the distance.

He zoomed alongside them, lights flashing, and bellowed over his rooftop loudspeaker: "*Parense ahí, parense ahí! Migración!*"

They froze. Pescatore patted down the father, dumping the contents of his pockets on the hood: cigarettes, a lighter, a plastic Baggie holding weathered identification documents and wadded cash. The father grinned tentatively, lines crinkling a caramel-colored face with long sideburns. A well-groomed dude dressed more for Saturday night than slogging through canyons: cowboy boots, a purple Members Only jacket, gray slacks.

"Tired," the man said in English.

His daughter whimpered in her mother's arms. Pescatore felt bad about making so much noise. He could have whispered out of the window and they would have climbed aboard without a fuss.

"That's OK, baby, don't worry, everything's under control," Pescatore told the girl.

In Spanish, he asked how old the girl was. The mother said she was four. The mother's trim body contrasted with a chubby face. She was decked out in designer jeans, a sweater, boots with some kind of embroidered design. She wore makeup, high corners painted onto her eyes. Her hair, like her daughter's, was arranged with multicolored ribbons. It had been important to this family to dress up tonight. He wondered if it was an attempt at disguise or if they just wanted to look sharp for an expedition to *El Otro Lado.*

The mother whispered to the girl, who had the same round face and shiny black hair and eyes. The girl stared at Pescatore, spilling tears. She clutched a little red backpack decorated with faded images of cartoon characters.

"I'm one of the good guys," Pescatore told her. "Hey, those the Dalmatians? Pongo and Perdita? Cruella De Vil? Woof woof."

He was rewarded with a brief snuffling smile. He escorted them to the back of the Wrangler. He hoisted in the girl first, helped the mother with a carefully applied hand to her elbow.

Then came the moment Pescatore anticipated and dreaded. As the father got in, Pescatore intercepted him. He pulled a wad of bills from his pocket without looking; he estimated it was about twelve dollars. He palmed it into the father's hand down low.

The man looked from the cash to Pescatore, startled. He began to say something and moved his hand as if to return the money. Pescatore waved him off, tight-lipped.

"Take it, *ándale*."

He drove them to a detention transport van. The couple exchanged brief words in the caged backseat. They sat stiffly. The girl leaned forward behind Pescatore on the other side of the steel grillwork. In a chirpy little voice, she sang "Cruella De Vil, Cruella De Vil..."

He hummed along with her. He thought about his insomnia. And about the money. At first, like many other agents, he had occasionally bought a meal or handed a couple of bucks to poignant cases who washed his way on the nightly torrent of misery. But after his trainee status ended, he started giving away money regularly. Every afternoon, he gathered up small bills and change. Although he told himself he wasn't consciously setting it aside, he usually came up with about thirty dollars. He had tried at first to select the most deserving prisoners: ragged Central American women with babies, lone teenagers. But the arcane logic of selective charity wore him down. He stopped differentiating between hardship and despair. As long as they weren't smugglers or scumbags, as long as they didn't resist or disrespect him, he was likely to give them money.

While the prisoners transferred to the detention van, the father said something about how he had studied at a university in Puebla. There was a catch in his voice. In the shadows,

Pescatore couldn't tell whether the man was insulted or trying to thank him.

"De dónde es usted?" the man asked.

No matter how much he mimicked their intonation and expressions, they never pegged him for Mexican-American. They guessed everything else: Puerto Rican? *Cubano? Argentino?*

"I'm from Chicago," Pescatore said, sliding the door shut. "*Suerte.*"

The rhythm picked up. The radio dispatchers called off motion-sensor hits and tips from citizens in measured tones, as if there were some logic or order to this business. "Group of nine crossing at Stewart's Bridge... Group bushing up by the Gravel Pit... Five to eight in the backyards on Wardlow Street."

The count became a cacophony as the night wore on. Garrison directed the PAs' movements from a plateau by the Gravel Pit, where the infrared nightscope was operating. As reports of crossing groups intensified farther north, Garrison dispatched Pescatore to a housing subdivision about half a mile from The Line.

"I'm doing good, buddy," he exulted over the radio. "Got eight already. On my way to my world record. Go help the horse patrol plug up that area by the Robin Hood Homes."

At the main entrance to the subdivision, Pescatore met up with Vince Esparza, a horse patrol agent who had been his training officer. Pescatore stood on the running board of his Wrangler to shake hands with the horseman.

"Valentine," Esparza said. "My favorite loose cannon."

Esparza's L.A. lilt always had a calming effect on Pescatore, even when Esparza was chewing him out. Esparza had a furry mustache and a solid gut beneath his bulky green jacket.

"How's it going?" Esparza said. "You're looking run-down and ragged tonight."

"Yeah, well, you know. Garrison keeps us hopping."

Esparza's face got less jolly.

"That fucker. Hey, you hear about the sniper sightings at Brown Field? They're sending out some guys from BORTAC with M-16s to ride shotgun."

"Must be dopers, huh?"

"Ever since the holidays. I never saw anything like it. Snipers. Dope all over the place. *Comandantes* and politicians getting smoked in Mexico, left and right. And all these OTMs: Chinese and Brazilians and Somalians, people from places I never heard of."

"We been breaking OTM records," Pescatore said.

"I caught me a bunch of Bo-livians last night, for Christ's sake. I was doing paperwork till three in the morning. Fuckin' OTM Central."

OTM meant "Other Than Mexican": non-Mexican aliens who could not simply be sent back to Tijuana. The surge in OTMs had started around Christmas, a few months after a crisis had hit Mexico hard and generated action border-wide. Numbers were up in every category: apprehensions of Mexican and non-Mexican border-crossers; busts of coke, methamphetamine and marijuana loads; assaults, rockings and shootings. The onslaught had put the San Diego sector on the brink of reclaiming the title from the Tucson sector as the busiest in The Patrol.

OTM meant lawyers, interpreters, headaches, paperwork. An especially burned-out journeyman had once advised Pescatore to simply turn and flee if he caught an alien who spoke funny Spanish or none at all. But Esparza ran from nobody.

"You know some *federales* or somebody are making money off those Chinese in TJ," Pescatore said. "Every Chinese alien pays fifty grand, right? That's a lot for the *polleros* to spread around."

Esparza controlled the horse with easy, powerful tugs of the reins, stroking its ears, letting it step in place. He took off his cowboy hat and wiped his forehead with a sleeve. He was thirty-five and had seven years on the job. With the revolving-door turnover of the Imperial Beach station, he was an old-timer. He leaned forward in the saddle and peered at Pescatore, who knew what was coming.

"Garrison got you guys playing that game again?" Esparza asked quietly.

"Yep." Pescatore had one elbow propped on the roof of the vehicle and one on top of the open door. A moving cluster of lights flashed in the fog: a Patrol helicopter on the hunt. He heard the distant thump of rotors.

"Tell him you don't play that shit."

"Vince, he's my supervisor."

"Then switch to the day shift. You need to learn how to wake up in the morning anyway. That *pendejo* is gonna get indicted and bring you down with him." Passing headlights illuminated the journeyman's glare beneath the brim of the hat.

"For thumping aliens? No way. Garrison told me they been allegating him for years. Never laid a glove on him."

"Not just thumping. The FBI and OIG got a big-time investigation going. He's at the top of the list. He thinks he's some big operator. Treats you young guys like pets, his little walking group, prowling around the canyons. Buying all the drinks. Pool parties at his house, chicks from TJ. You ever wonder where all that money comes from?"

Pescatore recalled the start of his training period, the scathing Conduct and Efficiency report Esparza had written up on him. Pescatore had been convinced that Esparza was on a personal mission to kick him out of The Patrol. Instead, the reports got better and his trainer had put in a good word for him at the end of his probation.

As if reading his mind, Esparza said: "Valentine, I told you a thousand times: You're a borderline case. You could be a fine PA if you work at it. But Garrison is a criminal. He is a disgrace to The Patrol. He is bad news. Especially for a kid that's easily led."

Esparza's tone was making Pescatore depressed. He managed a sickly laugh.

"I appreciate the concern, Vince. I'm gonna be OK."

Pescatore ducked into the vehicle to respond to the radio; Garrison wanted him back on the levee. Esparza's mouth turned down to match the corners of his mustache, the disappointed parent, the voice of doom on horseback.

"You take care, Valentine. Watch yourself."

"Alright then."

Midnight approached. Things were getting out of hand. Aliens sprouted out of the brush, flashed across roads, disappeared behind ridges. He captured some farmworkers from Oaxaca, short dignified *campesinos* who spoke to each other in an indigenous language and crouched automatically at the roadside, familiar with the drill. He watched, too captivated by the sight to give chase, as a group of illegal-alien musicians in *charro* attire hurried along a hilltop lugging instrument cases. Two of the *mariachis* carried the bass fiddle together, no doubt late for a gig.

Garrison kept him speeding back and forth, changing directions. The Wrangler shuddered across rough terrain, rattling as if it were going to break apart. A volley of rocks clattered on the roof. The throwers were nowhere to be seen in the fog; maybe the rocks threw themselves. Garrison yelled at the top of his lungs on the radio. Pescatore heard a plaintive chorus of voices in the background.

We're in the hands of a lunatic, Pescatore told himself. Esparza was right. Something terrible is going to happen. He floored the accelerator, the Wrangler hurtling alongside the rusted-brown metal border fence.

Two silhouettes materialized in the dirt road in front of him. Dangerously close. Moving in terrified underwater slow motion, Pescatore tromped the brake. The Wrangler went into a long dirt-spraying skid. When it finally came to a stop, the two migrants cowered unhurt in the blaze of the headlights. They held their hands over their heads. They were women.

"No problem," Pescatore whispered, clinging to the wheel. "Almost ran you over, killed you dead. No problem."

He got out. The women shrank against the fence. Loopy with relief, he found himself affecting the jovial authoritative tone that good-ol'-boy Tejano journeymen used.

"Welcome to the United States, ladies. You are under arrest."

They were apparently sisters, late teens or early twenties. Piles of curls around striking, Caribbean-looking faces. He shined his flashlight at the top of the fence, mindful of rock throwers, then back at the women. Taller than average, long-legged in tight jeans. Maybe Honduran, Venezuelan? They reminded him of a teenage girl he had once arrested in a load van, a pouty Venezuelan sporting sunglasses and platform heels that were completely inappropriate for border-crossing. OTMs for sure. A lot of forms to fill out, but he could get the hell off The Line for the rest of the shift. One of the women wore two sweaters under a cheap leather jacket. Her hands were still raised over her head. As gently as he could, he asked her where she was from.

"Veracruz," she said, heavy-lidded eyes on the ground.

That part of Mexico could account for their looks, but a smuggler could have also coached them. Pescatore ushered them into the vehicle.

"Valentine." Garrison's voice on the radio startled him. "Where you at, buddy?"

"Got two OTMs. Gonna take 'em back to the station and start processing."

"Negative. Need you here at my location. Hurry it up."

"Yessir."

The dirt road wound up and around a hill. Crickets buzzed in the darkness. The tires crunched over rocks. In a clearing at the top of the hill, Pescatore found Garrison, Dillard and an agent named Macías. They stood around a parked Wrangler in the middle of the clearing. They examined it with folded arms, like researchers in a laboratory. The Wrangler was illuminated by the headlights of other vehicles.

Pescatore glanced in his rearview mirror: The two women were transfixed by the scene, fear flaring in enormous eyes.

"Jesus Christ," he muttered.

The Wrangler in the middle of the clearing was crammed impossibly full of prisoners. Men were in the front seat, the caged backseat and the space behind it. They were stacked on one another's laps. The mass of bodies wriggled behind the breath-steamed glass as if in an aquarium, a face visible here, a foot there. The captives pounded intermittently on the windows and roof, blows rocking the vehicle. There were complaints and curses.

The prisoners had become pieces in the Game. Garrison organized the Game now and then when he felt like gambling. The Game consisted of seeing how many prisoners could be stuffed into a vehicle during the course of a night.

Garrison welcomed Pescatore with another vigorous black-gloved handshake.

"I told you," he declared. "I got twelve. Your two gives me fourteen. And then I collect, buddy."

"My two?" Pescatore said, keeping his tone mild. "They're OTMs, I gotta process them."

"Hell with that. Where do they say they're from?"

"Veracruz. But—"

"Hey, take 'em at their word. Transfer your prisoners to my vehicle, Valentine."

Pescatore beckoned his supervisor aside. Garrison grinned at his discomfort.

"Listen," Pescatore hissed, "all due respect, you can't put females in there."

"It's only till the end of the shift."

"Still. It ain't right."

Valentine peered at Garrison in the shadows, trying to figure out if the supervisor really intended on going through with it or was just messing with him. Both scenarios pissed him off. Garrison looked down at him as if he were about to swat a bug.

"Valentine. These people break the law every day. They spit at you. They rock you. And it's all a big joke to them. This is the worst punishment they'll ever get. So don't you wussy out on me now. Get with the program."

Coming up next to Garrison, Dillard made an exasperated noise. "Come on, Valentine, nobody's gonna hurt your girlfriends."

"Who asked you?" Pescatore retorted. "Take a giant step back outta my face."

"Fuck you." Dillard's thin lips tightened. "I don't understand a word you say in the first place, you crazy Chicago asshole."

Partly because he was getting angry and partly to stall Garrison, Pescatore decided to respond as ignorantly as possible. He stepped close to Dillard and cocked his head. He felt a buzzing sensation in his face and hands.

"You got a problem with the way I talk, you hayseed redneck punk bitch?"

Dillard's face contorted. Pescatore blocked his shove, backpedaling. Dillard started after him and Pescatore crouched and slammed him with a gut punch. Garrison got between them. Dillard was flushed and wild, a hand on his belly.

"Now, Larry, you sure you can take Valentine?" Garrison chortled. "He's not big, but he's pretty mean."

Garrison had a loglike arm extended at each of them, without urgency, like a referee about to resume the action. He's not gonna stop us, Pescatore realized. He loves it: the brawling, those poor bastards in the vehicle, the crazy bullshit all night.

They were interrupted by a commotion. Suddenly the Wrangler disgorged its cargo, prisoners bolting in every direction. The agents spun around, yelling.

Pescatore focused on a man who crouched by a door, pulling

aliens to freedom. A bowlegged man holding a pair of wire cutters, his head wrapped in a red bandanna. A man who had sneaked out of the bushes behind four PAs and sprung a vehicleful of prisoners.

Pulpo.

Pescatore lunged forward, pushing someone aside. Pulpo reappeared, closer, grimacing with effort. The wire cutters came whipping around at Pescatore. He snapped aside his head, reducing the force of the blow, but it staggered him. The smuggler ran into the brush.

"I got him," Pescatore said, unsheathing his baton.

Pescatore pounded through the brush and down a ravine. He ran at an incredible, exhilarating, foolish speed. His head and ankle throbbed. It's all your fault, Valentine, he muttered, they got away and it's all your fault. He ran faster, ripping through curtains of fog. He gripped the baton like a sprinter. He noticed liquid trickling down his forehead onto his face. He tasted it: blood.

"I got him," he said into the radio clipped to his lapel.

At the bottom of the hill, the border fence loomed up out of the mist. Pulpo made for a spot where floodwaters had washed out dirt between two boulders and created a gap beneath the fence. Pulpo scuttled through the opening and disappeared. Pescatore dropped, rolled and came back up on the other side of the fence.

He saw Pulpo glance back over his shoulder in disbelief, then plunge into the traffic on Calle Internacional, the highway that paralleled the international boundary on the Tijuana side. An orange-and-brown station wagon–taxi, elaborate script decorating its side, swerved and fishtailed and almost flattened Pulpo. A bedraggled pink bus braked and honked, the croak of a prehistoric animal. Pulpo reached the center median, which was waist high and as wide as a sidewalk. He stumbled, but kept going as Pescatore closed the gap. A truck left Pescatore a lungful of pestilential exhaust.

A group of migrants trudging single file along the median stopped and stared at the agent and the smuggler pelting by.

"I got him," Pescatore told them.

He found the looks on their faces pretty comical. What's the matter? You never seen a U.S. Border Patrol agent chasing a Mexican through Tijuana before? See it and believe it, motherfuckers.

Pescatore realized full well that he had crossed The Line. He had broken the ultimate commandment. He was making a suicide charge into enemy territory. He wondered what Garrison would say. He wondered what Esparza would say. But he felt dizzy liberation, as if the combined effect of the knock on the head and the incursion into Mexico had transformed him. He was a speed machine. A force of justice. A green avenger. He didn't care if he had to run all the way to Ensenada. He was going to catch him a tonk.

Pulpo fled down the middle of a residential street that went south from the Calle Internacional. It was a quiet, unevenly paved, anemically lit street in the Zona Norte area, dense with cooking smells. Rickety fences fronted low houses painted in orange, green and blue. There was a field in the distance, perhaps a schoolyard.

Halfway down the block, Pulpo threw Pescatore another frantic glance. He zigzagged and cut left onto the sidewalk, knocking aside a gate. Pescatore pursued him into a narrow dirt lot between stucco houses, through an obstacle course of junk: bicycle tires, car parts, a lean-to fashioned from the camper shell of a pickup truck propped up with bricks. There was a wooden one-story hut at the back of the lot.

Pescatore caught up to the smuggler just as he reached the open door. He jabbed with the baton, javelin-style, connecting with Pulpo's back below the label of the overalls. It made a satisfying thud.

The blow carried them both through a curtain of beads hanging in the front entrance and into the hut. Pescatore jabbed again and Pulpo went down, yowling, into a mangy armchair. Pescatore raised the baton with both hands to strike. A lightbulb on a chain swung above their heads, spattering images as if through a strobe: a dank cramped living room of sorts, a shrine with a Virgin of Guadalupe statuette, candles, an incongruously new and large television. A radio chattered. The bead curtain clattered in the doorway. Pescatore and Pulpo gulped oxygen in loud gasps.

A tired-looking little woman in sweat clothes had stepped out of the shadows behind the armchair. On her hip she cradled a baby boy, who was bare-chested in miniature overalls. The woman's mouth opened soundlessly. Pulpo had one thick leg splayed over an armrest, the bandanna skewed down, almost obscuring his eyes. They looked as if they were posing for a portrait: the Pulpo family at home.

Silver spots swam in front of Pescatore's eyes. The baton, held high like an executioner's axe, weighed a hundred pounds. He heard scratchy voices on his radio. Agents called his name. A search was in progress on the other side. In San Diego.

Pulpo's narrow eyes were locked on Pescatore's. The smuggler's chest heaved. He remained in the armchair, cringing from the anticipated blow, a goofy incredulous expression smeared across his face. He looked younger up close; the facial hair was scraggly.

Pescatore lowered the baton. He had regained his breath somewhat.

His voice sounded pretty calm, given the circumstances. He enunciated carefully: "*Ahora sé donde vives, hijo de la chingada.*"

Now I know where you live, you son of a bitch.

Pulpo's face rearranged into a mask of contempt.

"*Bienvenido a tu casa,*" he growled. The standard deferential greeting of a Mexican host: Welcome to your home.

Pescatore turned and ran.

As he sprinted with long chopping strides, wiping clumsily at the blood that was obscuring the vision in his left eye, Pescatore thought about the time when two PAs had tackled a belligerent drunk in the middle of the riverbed. During the struggle, the agents had rolled across the international boundary, a moment recorded, to their misfortune, by a Mexican news photographer. There were internal investigations, angry headlines in Tijuana, diplomatic protests. The agents got heavy suspensions; one resigned. And their invasion had gone a couple of yards. At most. If Pescatore got caught, nothing short of crucifixion would satisfy the Mexicans this time.

Dogs announced his flight back down the street, noisy escorts loping alongside. Horns blasted when he darted north through the traffic on Calle Internacional. The troop of migrants on the concrete median had not moved; a sun-darkened gnome in a straw hat shook his head at Pescatore. He heard a distant siren. Could the *judiciales* be coming for him already? The only way those bastards were getting his gun would be to pry it out of his cold dead hand.

The fence looked much taller from this angle. He could not find the hole through which he had gone south. There were no apparent handholds, no hint at how people scaled the barrier so fast every day. He spotted a junked refrigerator propped against the metal. He clambered onto it, tossing his baton and flashlight over the fence into the darkness. He heard hoots, insults and whistles behind him: The lynch mob was gathering. The top of the fence scraped skin off his hands, dug into his armpit. He heard a tearing sound as his uniform shirt ripped on the metal edge. A bottle hurled from behind shattered next to him, showering glass.

With a sob, he flopped over. He dangled one-handed for a few flesh-gouging seconds, then let go. He landed, sprawling face-first, in the United States of America.

Border Patrol vehicles converged on him in the darkness. A helicopter swooped, circling low, the wind and sound magnifying his headache. He rolled to his feet, started to his right, changed direction. A semicircle of flashlights, headlights and spotlights impaled him. An amplified, distorted voice barked at him.

Pescatore sagged back against the fence for a moment. Finally, he stepped forward, into the light. He raised his hands above his head.

2

AS THE RADIO PLAYED the intermezzo from *Cavalleria Rusticana,* Méndez gazed north across the border.

After the night's fog and drizzle, the morning had brought a cold sun. The old maroon Crown Victoria crested the hill before Calle Internacional dipped east out of the canyons toward the Zona Norte and Zona Río. Leobardo Méndez, the commander of a Mexican law enforcement unit known as the Diogenes Group, sat in the backseat of the Crown Victoria. The butt of a pistol protruded from beneath a newspaper next to him. Méndez felt suspended over the panorama, everything clean and sharp and glistening below him.

The road sloped between clumps of migrants and vendors along the fence on the left and palm trees on the right. Farther ahead, the river levee slanted across the border, the remnants of the night's crowds and a few vendors grouped around the ashes of bonfires. Past the levee, a northbound network of ramps, lanes and bridges wound like a knot of snakes into the two dozen lanes of the San Ysidro crossing. The traffic was backed up for a mile from the concrete hulk of the U.S. inspection station: mainly Tijuana commuters bound for jobs in San Diego. The hill of the Colonia Libertad neighborhood, with its terraced streets and rows of tumbledown houses, rose beyond the port of entry.

From his radio came the soundtrack: the wistful strings of the intermezzo.

As the Crown Victoria started down the incline, Méndez spotted Tiburcio the Ragpicker on the U.S. side. Tiburcio advanced—blue cap, duffel bag, Quasimodo gait—across flatland near a U.S. Border Patrol vehicle north of the fence. Tiburcio was a sociological category unto himself: a self-employed transborder scavenger with a green card. He lived in Tijuana. He crossed legally into San Diego at dawn and scoured the terrain for valuable items left behind by the night's influx of illegal immigrants.

It was like an abandoned battlefield, like the desert after the Exodus, the gap-toothed Tiburcio had once told him, red-eyed from fatigue and alcohol. The things I find, Licenciado. Cash, coins, more than you would think. Luggage. Food. Shoes. Sometimes underwear, and that causes me great sadness, Licenciado, because it is often a lady's underwear, and it is often torn, and that means the smugglers and bandits have struck again. I find identification cards, textbooks, letters. Strange things: a trumpet. A toolbox with a beautiful complete set of tools, what kind of poor *naco* thinks he can outrun the *Migra* hauling that thing, Licenciado?

Tiburcio was a feature article waiting to be written. But Méndez never got around to publishing anything about him in his days as a journalist. When Méndez became the head of the state human rights commission, Tiburcio had been full of tips about renegade police, smugglers and narcos. Now that Méndez was a kind of policeman himself, he still checked in occasionally with Tiburcio for news from no-man's-land.

Tiburcio the Ragpicker disappeared below the top of the fence as Calle Internacional leveled off. The violins were building to the whispery finale of the intermezzo when Méndez caught sight of two vehicles of the Diogenes Group parked on a side street in the Zona Norte. He told his driver to pull over. Four of his officers stood around a burly, handcuffed youth seated on the curb, wearing overalls and a red bandanna. As Méndez's window slid down, his deputy commander approached with a quick salute.

"Good morning, Athos," Méndez said. "What are you up to at this uncivilized hour?"

Athos wore a goatee, a black fatigue jacket with the Diogenes Group emblem, and black pants tucked into jump boots. He was not particularly big, but his corded neck, steel-gray mustache and steady stare gave him an air of quiet menace.

"Good morning, Licenciado," Athos said. "I was about to call you. We had an invasion."

"An invasion?"

Athos allowed himself a grin, the web of wrinkles around his eyes creasing.

"A Border Patrol agent crossed into the Zona Norte near the PRI headquarters chasing an individual last night. It sounds like this monkey got all the way across Calle Internacional."

Athos had a habit of calling suspects, witnesses and just about everyone else, except friends and co-workers, "this monkey." It was not exactly an insult; his tone was dispassionate and weary, just acknowledging reality. He was a weathered street warrior who had dedicated thirty years to tactics and training: commanding SWAT teams, teaching at the police academy, guarding public officials. He lived a life of barracks solitude, haunting the headquarters of the Diogenes Group around the clock. His real name was Ramón Rojas. Méndez had a weakness for the works of Alexandre Dumas and considered the Diogenes Group to be his musketeers; he had nicknamed his deputy Athos because of his wisdom and solemnity.

"Incredible," Méndez said. "And your prisoner?"

"Pulpo. A hoodlum and smuggler. Apparently he is the one the *gabacho* was chasing."

Pulpo looked up at the sound of his name, feral and alert. He caught sight of Méndez and became animated.

"Listen, Licenciado, with all respect, this is a clear case of a violation of human rights," Pulpo drawled, his chiseled shoulders and arms straining against the cuffs. "That American is a madman. He almost killed me in front of my family. An international incident! And now these gentlemen, with all respect, are abusing my rights as well. I am the victim, not—"

Athos turned his head to give him a look, teeth gritted, and Pulpo shut up fast.

"Very good, Athos," Méndez said. "We should call Isabel Puente in San Diego right away. Let's continue this at headquarters."

A few minutes later, the three vehicles arrived at the headquarters of the Diogenes Group, a compound on a bluff at the base of Colonia Libertad with a view of the San Ysidro border crossing. Sentries with AK-47s and sunglasses stepped back as an iron gate slid open. The compound was a former safe house that had been confiscated from a drug trafficker. It contained a drab two-story house, garage and a storage building. A Mexican flag flew in the courtyard.

Méndez led the way into the box-shaped storage building, which had been converted into a command center, squad room and lockup. At thirty-nine, Méndez had gray tufts in his hair, angular features that tightened into a melancholy grimace. When he wore glasses, he looked professorial. When he wore contact lenses, like today, his face hardened. He was thin and tended to coil forward when he walked. He had a lupine profile. His attire was typical of Tijuana cops, reporters, academics and public officials all the way up to the governor: brown leather jacket, blue button-down shirt, and jeans.

Opening the door for Méndez, Athos told him the unit had raided a safe house in Otay Mesa overnight and captured a Chinese smuggler with a group of non-Mexican migrants waiting to cross.

"Eighteen Chinese, five Brazilians, two Ecuadorans," Athos said. "And we caught a state policeman who worked with the smugglers."

"Wonderful. Another battle with the state police in the making."

"We found some interpreters at the Chinese place near Sanborns," Athos said. "We are talking separately to the policeman and to the Chinese smuggler. A heavyweight gangster from the looks of him."

The squad room, where the unit held roll calls and meetings, was noisy and busy. Interpreters and plainclothes officers in black fatigue jackets, armed with legal pads, clustered around captured migrants. The migrants sat in chairs with arm-desks that made them look like disheveled college students. The prisoners regarded their questioners in a daze, as if watching another reel in a nightmare. The migrants' clothes were frayed and soiled. Most of the Chinese had short, shapelessly cut hair. The Mexican officers rose or saluted Méndez as he passed.

"Did you get them something to eat?" Méndez asked. The migrants had clearly realized he was in charge; he attempted a reassuring smile in their direction.

"Chinese food."

"Good. Call the priests at the Scalabrini shelter, see if they can house these people until someone decides what to do with them. They have probably spent months cooped up in one miserable safe house or another. Is this batch from Fujian too? Headed for New York?"

"Nobody's saying much, but they definitely came through South America. Like the last group, and the one before them."

A hallway led past two small interrogation rooms. In the first, the Chinese smuggler sat with his hands cuffed in back. The interpreter sat opposite him, a slender Chinese youth in a waiter's white shirt and black pants. His nervous smile suggested he would have much preferred to be waiting tables. No doubt his immigration status was also problematic. Méndez imagined the look on his face when Athos had marched into the Chinese restaurant frequented by the officers of the Diogenes Group and recruited him as an interpreter.

"This is Mr. Chen, Licenciado," Athos said with sarcastic formality, nodding at the prisoner. "He kept saying he wanted to talk to the boss. Mr. Chen, this is the boss."

Looking elaborately bored, Chen swiveled his head toward them. He had a tapered torso under a burgundy sweater that was torn along one sleeve, exposing a snake tattoo. There were bruises on his forehead. His hair was spiked and gelled and he had hipster sideburns. A city-hardened version of the country boys in the next room.

Athos said that the smuggler had resisted arrest, putting on a martial-arts display. There was a note of grudging admiration in Athos's voice. "He was throwing fancy kicks, using his elbows, spinning. The *muchachos* say it took five minutes to subdue him."

Méndez slid into the chair next to the interpreter, who looked increasingly unenthusiastic. Méndez thanked the interpreter for his help. He examined the passport on the table. It identified the smuggler as Tomas Chen, thirty-four, naturalized citizen of Paraguay, born in Fuzhou, China, and residing in the Paraguayan city of Ciudad del Este. The passport contained entry and exit stamps from Paraguay, Brazil, Argentina, Venezuela, Ecuador, Bolivia, Cuba and Mexico, as well as Asian and European nations. Méndez turned the pages one at a time, making it clear he was in no hurry.

"I am Leobardo Méndez, the chief of this unit," he said, looking up at last. "I understand you wanted to talk to me, Mr. Chen."

The interpreter winced as he listened to the response. "He say he glad you finally here. Best thing you can do is let him go. He say this can all be take care of right now."

"Explain that he was arrested under suspicion of smuggling immigrants, criminal association, and weapons possession. Serious federal crimes."

The smuggler spat out sentences.

"He say this can be take care of with money."

"No."

The smuggler leaned forward, sneering. He gestured with his head toward the front of the house as he spoke.

"He say he the boss here. If I give word, all those people in other room will rise up and attack you, he said."

"In Mexico it's considered rude to threaten someone when you are their guest," Méndez said, looking directly at Chen. "You supposedly lived in Paraguay for three years, no? You must speak some Spanish. What do you do in those far-off latitudes?"

The interpreter listened, blushed, and looked down. "He say... he pay fifty thousand dollar to you. The money comes here in a hour if you say yes."

"Tell him to stop insulting us. Tell him he's lucky this is a modern police unit. Otherwise we would treat him to a traditional Mexican interrogation."

The interpreter gave Méndez a beseeching look. The smuggler spoke dismissively to Méndez in words he more or less understood. "*Yo no quiero falar mais con você. Você no sabe que esto es demasiado grande p'ra você.*"

Athos detached himself from the wall, squinting. "What is that gibberish, Brazilian?"

"It's half Spanish, half Portuguese: Portuñol," Méndez said. "Border language, but a border far from this one. Mr. Chen, do you have a statement to make? Too bad, I'd love to hear about these exotic places you've been to. All right, you are being charged with the crimes I mentioned. And also assaulting police officers and resisting authority."

"*Você no comprende con quien esta metiendo,*" the smuggler said in a chiding tone. More or less: You don't understand who you are messing with.

Méndez and Athos left. They glanced through the thin rectangular window in the door of the second interview room. The state police detective who had been caught harboring the illegal immigrants slumped in his chair, a caricature of dejection. Abelardo Tapia, the second deputy chief of the Diogenes Group, sat across from the prisoner. He was scribbling industriously on a legal pad. The bearded Tapia was all shoulders and belly and—despite his reputation as a bone-crusher—good cheer. So Méndez called him Porthos.

"Who is the state policeman?" Méndez asked.

"De Rosa," Athos answered. "One of Mauro's protégés in the homicide squad. Fat and sleazy. This monkey always liked making money. He owns the safe house."

As they watched through the window, De Rosa leaned forward over the legal pad, which his interrogator turned at an angle so the prisoner could read it. De Rosa nodded morosely and scribbled on the pad with his right hand. His left hand was chained to the leg of the table. Porthos beamed and wrote, chatting all the while.

"What is Porthos doing with the pad?" Méndez asked.

"De Rosa is terrified that we are wired for sound," Athos muttered. "But they go way back from when Porthos worked on the homicide unit. Porthos convinced him to give us information off the record. They are writing down the real questions and answers while they talk about trivialities. They've been at it for a while."

The headquarters of the Diogenes Group was a prime eavesdropping target for other Mexican police forces, intelligence agencies and drug mafias. After the discovery of phone taps, Isabel Puente, an American federal agent who worked with Méndez, had recommended a San Diego private investigation firm that did contract work for her government. The Americans did periodic electronic sweeps free of charge. If anyone was bugging the Diogenes Group, it was with the help of the gringos.

"What will De Rosa want for his cooperation?" Méndez asked.

"I think the fat slob would like to avoid the state penitentiary."

"All right. Put him in the Eighth Street Jail instead. Special federal custody."

Méndez went into the adjoining house and upstairs to his office, which had once been the master bedroom. The walls held a portrait of the current president of Mexico, a portrait of former president Lázaro Cárdenas, a crucifix, diplomas, a poster of Salvador Allende, and a poster from a concert by Carlos Santana at the seaside bullring in Playas de Tijuana. The bookshelves contained a mix of English and Spanish titles about organized crime, law enforcement, politics and sociology, as well as literature: Arriaga, Benedetti, Borges, García Márquez, Paz, Poniatowska, Vargas Llosa, Volpi. There was a row of books about the border. There were caps, mugs, plaques and other trinkets from U.S. and Mexican law enforcement agencies. And a matchstick sculpture of Don Quixote and Sancho Panza.

The bay window behind Méndez's desk offered a view of Mexican territory just south of the port of entry: an epic convergence of legal and illegal commerce and migration. Vendors hawked ceramic Bart Simpsons and Porky Pigs and Virgins of Guadalupe. Buses loaded up with legal crossers bound for California's far-flung Mexican-American strongholds. Armed with binoculars and cell phones, smuggling lookouts posted on the multicolored pedestrian bridge spanning the crowded car lanes scanned the U.S. inspectors in their booths to see whom they could outwit—or which of their paid-off *yanqui* allies was on the job today.

Méndez turned from the window and picked up the phone. His secretary told him the state attorney general's office wanted to discuss the arrest of the state police detective as soon as possible. There was also a message to call Araceli Aguirre, the state human rights commissioner.

Méndez went into the bathroom and washed his face. He looked tired; the lines slanting from the base of his nose to the corners of his mouth seemed especially pronounced. Back at his desk, he took a breath and dialed the number of the apartment in Berkeley, California, where his wife and five-year-old son now lived. As the phone rang, he remembered the last conversation: the long silences with his wife, his son's distractedness. He thought back to the grim good-bye at the airport. He hung up without waiting to see if anyone answered.

For the next hour or so, he made phone calls, read reports and scanned newspapers. He listened to the group Molotov and Silvio Rodríguez, the Cuban singer-composer, on his computer's compact disc player. At eleven-thirty, two American journalists arrived for an interview.

Their visit was the idea of a friend at City Hall who had worked with Méndez at a newspaper long ago. The friend wanted the Americans to meet Méndez, to learn about a group of police in Tijuana who were fighting the good fight. Contacts in the U.S. press could be helpful, a shield for Méndez and his officers. On the other hand, they could also cause him grief.

Here's a yanqui who is going to waste my time, Méndez grumbled to himself as he welcomed a television reporter with a Captain America jaw, a beefy frame in a tan sport coat, and a silver helmet of hair that looked labor-intensive. The newspaper reporter, a bright-eyed young woman with frizzy blond hair, wore a shaggy sweater, jeans and hiking boots. She greeted him in confident Spanish, then stayed quiet and watchful while the TV guy made small talk. Her name was Steinberg. Méndez's friend at City Hall had said that she was not the typical American reporter who talked instead of listening and confused being aggressive with being obnoxious.

His secretary served coffee. The TV reporter, whose first or last name was Dennis, appraised the diplomas on the wall.

"I see you went to Michigan," he said in an Olympian broadcast voice.

"Just a year. Graduate studies in Latin American literature. I did the work in Spanish, fortunately or no, so my English is not so good. In reality, it was exile: I had political problems here at those times."

"Go, Blue," Dennis said, pumping a genial fist at him. "Primo football up there, right?"

Méndez's smile wavered. He wondered if the man really thought he had ever attended a football game. For Méndez, Michigan had been an icy wasteland full of fraternity-house brutes, spoiled suburbanites and addled drug users who united on fall Saturdays for a fascistic spectacle.

Méndez told the reporters the history of the Diogenes Group. How it had formed a year earlier because of pressure from Mexico City and Washington to do something about lawlessness in Mexico in general and in Tijuana in particular. How big shots in Mexico City had surprised Méndez by asking him to resign as state human rights commissioner and lead the new unit. How Méndez had resisted because of his aversion to the country's new ruling coalition, which he had derisively called "Jurassic Park" in public statements. How he had reluctantly accepted because of his respect for the Secretary, the high-ranking security official who had proposed the anticorruption initiative with him in mind. The unit consisted of thirty carefully selected officers from the federal, state and city forces, as well as investigators from his human rights commission. U.S. federal agents had helped screen and train the officers.

"As you know, in Mexico the journalists and people of human rights often do the job that should be of the police and prosecutors. So we are not newcomers."

Dennis asked the predictable question about the unit's name.

"Our formal name is the Unidad Especial Contra Corrupción Pública y Crimen Organizado. A horrible acronym. The Special Unit Against Public Corruption and Organized Crime. When we presented ourselves to the press, a reporter said: 'Listen, Licenciado, let's speak clearly: Your mission is to hunt bad policemen, correct?' And I said the first thing that occurred to me. I said that in this city, unfortunately, I look at it another way: We are like Diogenes. We are hunting for honest policemen. We hope to help them, encourage them. And while we do that, since honest ones are hard to find, we will arrest as many dishonest ones as we can. There was a lot of complaints about my declarations. But everybody calls us the Diogenes Group."

Dennis returned his grin briefly. "How can you be sure the cops you chose aren't corrupt?"

"Well, that is relative, no? They came from a corrupt system. Anyway, I would put my hands in the fire for my comandantes. When I was a reporter like you, they were my best... *fuentes.*"

"Sources," the blond woman said. Méndez nodded gratefully. She left off chewing her pen and picked up the pace. "Licenciado Méndez. The case that made your group famous is still pretty interesting to those of us north of the border. I mean when you arrested the chief of the state police in October with the two tons of cocaine and the dead bodies. Could you tell me where that stands?"

The arrest of Chief Regino Astorga of the state police, also known as the Colonel, had been something of a fluke, Méndez explained. Acting on a tip, the unit raided a warehouse, found the cocaine—and the Colonel and his state police detectives standing over three freshly tortured bodies, one of them a boss in a powerful cartel.

"We have confidence that he will be convicted, no matter how influential he is," Méndez said. "That case shows that this city, this country, is capable of change. We came close to war between police forces, but it was worth it."

"One thing," Steinberg said cautiously. "Supposedly the Colonel worked for a new cartel that is pushing out the old groups. What exactly is this new mafia?"

"As well as drugs, we think they are connected to the increase in illegal immigrants from other nations, especially Asiatics and Arabs. In recent years in Mexico we have had an era of drug lords who were vicious, politically connected businessmen, then drug lords who were crazy *pistoleros.* This mafia combines both traditions. It also has unusual international connections. Including elements of American agencies, I should tell you. The new mafia is opening the valves of corruption and violence in a way I have not seen before."

Steinberg gulped coffee, fueling herself. Dennis watched her with mixed resentment and interest. Méndez could picture the interview from her perspective, gauging how hard to push, the questions building on each other.

"But is it really a big mystery who this mafia is? What about the allegations that the Ruiz Caballero family is aligned with them?"

Méndez wished that they were talking one-on-one. He reminded her they were off the record. He said: "Drug lords come and go. But certain elites have enduring power, both legitimate and criminal. They have alliances with gangsters. I can say nothing right now, responsibly, about the names you mention. But that family definitely belongs to the super-elites."

"Listen, I give you credit," Dennis interjected, interrupting the blonde's rhythm, her blue eyes jumping at him in annoyance. "How can you do what you do?"

Méndez wasn't sure he understood the question. "It was difficult to change mentality when I began the job. There was a time when I believed, as Bakunin said, that society organizes crimes, and people only execute them. That all police were repressive and corrupt."

"Yeah," said Dennis, whose eyes had glazed until the word "corrupt." "It's such a cesspool. The police running dope, the government stealing elections—"

"Excuse me, elections?" Méndez said.

"Um, yes."

"Pardon me," Méndez said. "Elections are one thing here that is *not* corrupt. Even despite the recent crisis of government."

"That's well known," Steinberg said forlornly, hoping to get back on track.

"Is it? What does television show Americans about Mexico? It amazes me to watch the news of San Diego. They start: a story about animals in distress. An important topic in the United States. Some dogs got mistreated in La Jolla. A fire burned a stable in, eh, Carlsbad. And by the way, seven Mexicans were shot in Baja. Fifteen Mexicans killed in bus crash. Corrupt Mexicans steal elections. But first, the sports."

"You're exaggerating," Dennis said, his Adam's apple bobbing in discomfort.

"And the corruption. Isn't it curious we know the names of the Mexican drug lords, *nombres y apellidos,* and nothing about the American ones? Who are the American drug lords? Who protects them?"

"It seems to me," said Dennis, "that the big traffickers in the U.S. are Colombians and Mexicans in immigrant communities."

"But it's impossible no Anglo-Saxon names are involved," Méndez said. "Like the traffickers of arms in Phoenix and Las Vegas who sell guns to the narcos of Tijuana. And the legal gangsters: the businessmens who are partners of Mexican companies that launder drug money? American corporations, banks? I remember in New York years ago when they arrested all those Wall Street people and walked them in Wall Street in chains. Marvelous. You should do this every year. A parade, like Thanksgiving."

"They say you are pretty left-wing," Dennis said tersely.

Méndez grimaced, his eyes narrowing. "*Ah sí?* I'm not sure what is left-wing anymore. Señor Dennis, I answer your question: Why do I do what I do? At this point in my life, the most revolutionary thing I can do is to be a policeman. To arrest people regardless of who they are, what power they have. In this place, in these times, enforcing the law has become an act of subversion."

The silence filled with the scratching of the woman's pen on her notepad. Méndez looked at her until she glanced up and smiled.

"I have talked too much," Méndez said. "Thank you for coming."

During the good-byes, he accepted when Steinberg asked quietly if she could talk to him again soon. Having done his part to advance inter-American understanding, Méndez summoned Athos and a driver.

They drove to the Río Zone, the modern downtown east of the Avenida Revolución tourist district. They entered the square-block complex housing the courts and the state police behind a brawny detective with a prisoner in tow. The detective wore a flower-print shirt, denim jacket and cowboy boots. His pawlike hand rested lightly on the long-haired youth's shoulder. The prisoner was not handcuffed. This was the macho style of the state police; they believed no prisoner would dream of running from them.

It was cold in the long drab hallways of the justice complex, one of those Tijuana government buildings with cinderblock walls that generated either an insidious chill or sweatbox heat. Méndez and Athos stepped over regularly spaced streams of water on the floor, leaks from the radiator system.

The receptionist wore a high-necked sweater and scarf along with her miniskirt. Her cheerful greeting contrasted with the glares of half a dozen cops, aides and other officials lounging in the outer office. A standard welcome for the Diogenes Group.

"Ah yes, from the Special Unit. Licenciado Losada is expecting you. And Commander Fernández Rochetti. Please go in."

Deputy Attorney General Albino Losada, chief of the state prosecutor's office in Tijuana, greeted them glumly. His narrow shoulders were encased in a trench coat that was belted against the cold. He had a small mustache jammed up under a pointy nose. He remained standing with his fists in the pockets of the coat. Losada's predecessor had been murdered. His predecessor's predecessor had been arrested with great fanfare, then released and fired. It was Losada's custom to pace behind his desk, giving the impression that he was about to bolt from the room.

Homicide Commander Mauro Fernández Rochetti, meanwhile, reclined in a chair to the left of the desk. He looked more comfortable in the large, sparse office than Losada. Fernández Rochetti crossed his legs in shiny gray slacks and lit a thin cigar.

Here we go, Méndez told himself. At a gesture from Losada, he and Athos sat down.

"A busy morning for you, Licenciado," Fernández Rochetti said. He commanded the homicide unit of the state police, a job reserved for highly paid operatives of the drug cartels. Since the Diogenes Group had arrested his former boss, Regino "the Colonel" Astorga, the homicide commander had come to be considered the shadow chief of the entire state force.

"That's right," Méndez said. "I'm afraid your detective was directly involved in the smuggling ring."

"You can imagine how concerned all of us are here," Losada said.

Fernández Rochetti blew smoke. His voice had a crust to it.

"Perhaps he was set up," he said. "This smells of a setup, as I was just telling the deputy attorney general."

"Let's not be ridiculous, Mauro," Athos said quietly. "What, somebody planted twenty-five Chinese in his house when he wasn't looking?"

Fernández Rochetti arched his eyebrows. Losada said, "Well, the principal issue, Licenciado, is that we want to thank you for the courtesy of coming to see us. And we'd like to discuss keeping De Rosa out of custody. Perhaps a house arrest..."

"I'm afraid that's impossible," Méndez answered. "We have already turned the case over to the federal prosecutor. The best I can do is put him in the Eighth Street Jail."

The argument about custody arrangements went in circles. A

cell phone rang. Losada fished in his trench coat, produced the phone and answered it. Fernández Rochetti turned expectantly. The prosecutor's stutter-stepping intensified.

"Yessir. Yes, thank you. Well, you should really talk to him, he happens to be right here." Losada pressed a hand over the phone and made an apologetic face at Méndez. "This lawyer has been pestering me all day. A pain in the neck. Best if he talks to you, Licenciado. It's a federal matter."

Losada handed the phone to Méndez, who exchanged a glance with Athos.

"Hello?" Méndez said into the phone.

"Licenciado, how are you?" The voice was resonant and mannered. "This is Licenciado Castrejón greeting you, from the law office of Castrejón and Sáenz? At your service. What a pleasure to hear your voice. You and the family are well, I hope? I'm so lucky to have found you there."

"Yes."

"Listen, Licenciado Méndez," the lawyer said. "It turns out that I've been engaged by certain parties on behalf of certain parties in this business of these foreigners from China. I have a matter I'd like to take up with you."

"Go ahead."

"A delicate, complicated situation, Licenciado. The best way I can express myself is as follows: I would be very grateful if we could work out some kind of arrangement by which you could release Officer De Rosa and the Chinese gentleman, Mr., eh, Chen."

"An arrangement."

"Exactly." The lawyer gathered momentum, the words devoid of genuine expression, as if he were reading from a script. "Let me phrase it like this, if you permit me: Certain parties would be interested, if we could secure the release of these two gentlemen, in making a generous contribution to the Special Unit which you command."

"A contribution." Now Méndez looked at Fernández Rochetti, who was savoring his cigar. Sons of bitches, Méndez thought. They're just doing it to see my reaction.

"Yes sir, maybe 'donation' would be the best word. The Diogenes Group is doing such admirable work. What a difficult battle it is, you have my deepest respect in that regard. I read a newspaper story explaining how you have to make do with old cars and radios, secondhand bulletproof vests from the San Diego Police. A real shame. So we were thinking along the lines of a donation: say three new cars and some vests, radios and other equipment. In exchange for the liberty of Mr. Chen and Detective De Rosa. If that sounds agreeable. After all, we know your real concern is drug smuggling, not a few extra migrants."

Méndez lowered the phone for a moment, the disembodied voice droning in his hand. He contemplated throwing the phone at Fernández Rochetti or the prosecutor. Athos sat forward with his forearms on his thighs. Méndez collected himself. Athos had told him that it was best to respond to the mafia in kind. If they are indirect and flowery, you be indirect and flowery. If they curse and threaten, you curse and threaten. Energy for energy.

"Licenciado Castrejón," Méndez said into the phone. "I appreciate the offer, of course. Of course we could always use new equipment at the Diogenes Group. Lamentably, I can't accept it in this context. And let me say, in anticipation of another offer, that I like money. Who doesn't? I probably like money almost as much as Deputy Attorney General Losada and Commander Fernández Rochetti. But I can't help you. The suspects you mentioned are in jail. And there they will stay."

"Well, I'm so sorry to hear that," Castrejón said. "I thought you were a reasonable, sensible person who could..."

Méndez reached over and, with exaggerated care, placed the phone on Losada's desk. The prosecutor picked it up, said a few words and hung up. Méndez rose, trying to look serene.

"It's been a pleasure as always," he said. "Thank you for your time. With your permission."

Losada made an apologetic noise. Mauro Fernández Rochetti cut him off.

"I am concerned about you, Licenciado," Fernández Rochetti said. Moving languidly, he reached out and tapped the cigar on an ashtray on the desk. His blazer cuff rode up to reveal a gold bracelet, gold cuff link, and powder-blue shirtsleeve on a thin wrist. "Enthusiasm and inexperience are a bad combination. They lead to mistakes like the one you have made in this case today. As far as my agency is concerned, De Rosa has been unlawfully abducted."

Fernández Rochetti had a habit of showing his tongue when he smiled, an unsavory touch in an appearance that aspired to be distinguished. He was in his late fifties, silver-haired. He looked like an aging actor from the black-and-white days of Mexican cinema: dark eyebrows, strong profile, soft mouth.

Méndez turned toward Fernández Rochetti. "And?"

"And I have to tell you: My *muchachos* were naturally upset and concerned about their colleague. It took all my efforts to persuade them not to go to your headquarters and rescue him. Imagine how unpleasant that would have been. You can play any game you want, Licenciado. But every game has rules."

Athos stepped close to the homicide commander. Fernández Rochetti reclined, legs crossed. But his eyes flickered up at the man in black and gave him away: Mauro Fernández Rochetti was as frightened of Athos as anyone else in Tijuana.

"Tell your *muchachos,*" Athos said softly, "that any time they feel the urge to pay us a visit, I will be waiting for them. And you know I don't play games."

Athos turned away. Méndez followed his lead.

"Thank you very much, gentlemen," Losada said to their backs.

Athos and Méndez walked rapidly down the echoing, puddled hallway. After they emerged into the sunlight, into the lunchtime crowd emptying from the courthouse, Athos spat into the gutter.

"Quite a day, eh?" Athos said, shaking his head. "That Losada is an instrument of the mafia. An instrument of the mafia."

"And that bastard Mauro is the one that plays him."

"What do you think, Licenciado?"

"They did all that just to provoke me. Things are getting ugly, brother."

Their driver pulled up in the Crown Victoria. As Méndez got in, he saw Athos scan the sidewalk, the police and civilian vehicles, the windows of the justice complex: reconnaissance in enemy territory.

At about 5 p.m., Méndez lay down in the sleeping quarters next to his office, where he often spent the night since his family's departure. He slept and dreamt that a phone was ringing, but he could not find it.

An hour later, his secretary woke him to say Isabel Puente had arrived from San Diego. Méndez patted his hair, frowning in the bathroom mirror at the gray tinges, and smoothed the wrinkles in his clothes. Feeling vaguely juvenile, he slid quickly behind his desk and popped in a compact disc: a trio singing a bolero. "Sabor a Mí."

As was her custom, Isabel Puente made an entrance.

"Leo, how are you? I brought you a gift."

"*La cubanamericana* has arrived! A gift?"

"For intellectual self-improvement."

She advanced with lithe, sure-footed strides, grinning playfully. She had her hair pulled back today like a flamenco dancer, bringing out the feline bone structure, the wide-set eyes. She was diminutive, athletically well proportioned, wearing a snug gold turtleneck and matching corduroy pants. The belt holster peeking out of her down vest was empty; U.S. agents were forbidden to carry firearms on Mexican soil. But Méndez suspected that she was packing her second gun, a short-barreled automatic, in one of her knee-high suede boots or the bag over her shoulder.

As always, he found the greeting awkward. With his male counterparts from U.S. law enforcement, who like Puente were mostly Latinos with cross-border liaison duties, Méndez generally exchanged the standard ritualistic *abrazo* complete with two-handed back slap. That didn't seem appropriate with Puente. They shook hands over the desk. She leaned forward for a hesitant peck on the cheek, her demure look softening her self-assuredness.

But she recovered quickly, pulling a book from her bag and brandishing it at him.

"Here," she said. "This is for you. This is *about* you."

The book was entitled *Manual of the Perfect Latin American Idiot.*

"*Ay,* how thoughtful," he laughed. "The bible of the neoliberal right, no? They decided the calamities of Latin America are the fault of the left. What a surprise."

"It's a classic," Puente said. Her accent in Spanish retained the sugar-mouthed and staccato rhythms of Cuban South Florida. But she was agile enough to mimic the expressions and drawl of the border. "You've got an image problem with my bosses at the task force. They think you're a Communist anti-American. But an honest Communist anti-American, if there is such a thing."

"Their worst nightmare, eh? What I want to know is, why do you hang out with me, then?"

Puente plopped into a chair. "Obviously, I must have a weakness for Marxist *mamones.*"

"Obviously."

"Leo," Puente said, a boot heel starting a soft hammer on the floor. "Have you told your obnoxious leftist friends in the Tijuana press about this incident with the Border Patrol agent yet?"

As sharp as she was, Méndez thought, her Cubanness and Americanness impeded her from absorbing the cultural lesson that it was not polite form in Mexico to get right down to business. A few more ritualistic pleasantries were in order. One day he would explain gently that, around here, it was better to circle in on your conversational target than to charge at it.

"Not yet, Isabel," he said, making a defensive gesture. "I was waiting to talk to you."

"Good. I hate to disappoint you, but it might work out better if we keep it quiet."

"That goes against all my patriotic instincts. Who is this character?"

"We are pretty sure it was Agent Valentine Pescatore," she said. "Ever hear anything about him? He's on the fringe of Garrison's group."

"I would remember a name like that. Another criminal?"

"I don't know yet." Isabel Puente gave an uncharacteristic sigh. "We did a preliminary interview today. He's a street kid, kind of wild, from what I can tell. But not necessarily a thug. I hope if we handle him right, it might be a real opportunity. What did you get?"

Méndez picked up the phone. His secretary tracked down Athos, who had spent the afternoon canvassing the area in the Zona Norte where the U.S. agent had crossed The Line. Athos was eating at Tacos El Gordo.

Méndez pulled his pistol from a drawer and stuck it in his belt. "Let's go meet them. My treat, of course."

Puente wrinkled her nose. She was squeamish about street food. "I'll say this, Leo, you've got an honest operation here. No fancy meals for the Diogenes Group."

"In reality, I'm concerned how it would look to your government. The way things are in your country, inviting a lovely young agent to a nice restaurant could get me accused of sexual harassment, no?"

She appeared to wince; he wondered if he had gone too far. But she grinned and responded: "Saying what you just said could get you accused of sexual harassment."

Tacos El Gordo was on Avenida Constitución in the nightlife district. A revolving police-style light on the sidewalk stand threw whirls of red across the scene. Neon glowed, music pounded in the curtained doorways of nightclubs. Encircling the taco stand were families with kids bundled against the evening chill, *cholos* in hooded sweatshirts, uniformed cops. All devouring food or watching the taco man work his magic, his dark artful hands chopping and slicing with controlled violence. Méndez spotted Athos and two officers spreading their feast on the hood of a car.

"Come on," Méndez said, sweeping open the car door for Puente. "Let's go hear about the adventures of your Agent Valentine."

3

VALENTINE PESCATORE SAT in the sun with his back to the wall, drowning his sorrows in a Woptown feast.

He occupied a table on the sidewalk outside his favorite joint on India Street. He had eaten an Italian beef sandwich with hot peppers, a slice of Sicilian pizza and a cannolo, accompanied by three beers. Now he was having his second espresso to counteract the effect of the beers. He needed to stay sharp.

Little Italy was his private refuge in San Diego, fifteen miles from the border and a world away from The Patrol. Compared with his Taylor Street neighborhood in Chicago, it was tiny. The surviving Italians clung to a few blocks of India Street and a church around the corner. Little Italy was a skeleton, a movie-set streetfront. But he liked the Sicilian bakery, the barber- and butcher shops, the mix of old-school eateries and sleek new establishments for the lunch crowd from the downtown office towers. He liked the fact that the owners were Italian but most of the workers behind the counters were Mexican. Despite his Italian last name, he spoke only the language of the workers. He liked the graffiti of the local Mexican-American gang. They called themselves Woptown. They sprayed the name on the white walls and cement stoops of three-story walk-ups that reminded him of home.

One afternoon he had passed a faded storefront on India Street. Glancing through the open door, he had spotted half a dozen old-time ginzos in folding chairs playing cards at a table in a carpeted, otherwise empty room. A handwritten sign taped in the window read S.D. ITALIANAMERICAN CLUB. The scene recalled the social club where his uncles hung out in Chicago.

The next time he went by the place, the shutters were down. The sign was gone. He never saw any of the old-timers again. He began to think that it had been an urban mirage. Or a dream.

He wished the past two days had been a dream. But the bandages on his forehead and his left hand were real. He entertained notions of getting in his car and hitting the interstate. He wondered how long his ten-year-old Impala, formerly property of the Chicago Police Department and complete with spotlight and monster engine, would hold up. Probably not long. The FBI and Office of Inspector General would track him down at some desert gas station and pile on additional charges for running away.

The only bright spot was that he had attained renegade-hero status at Imperial Beach station. Until the Tuesday-night incident, he had been considered a loner who talked funny—in English and Spanish—and hung out with Garrison's outlaw clique, causing most agents to keep their distance. That changed dramatically after the Pulpo incident. No one said anything out in the open. But he got furtive handshakes and exultant comments from agents such as Galván, who was always trying to set up fellow PAs with a visiting female cousin from Guadalajara.

"Chased that *pollero* halfway across TJ into his *house,* kicked his ass, and made it back again!" Galván had whispered within earshot when Pescatore had arrived painfully early Wednesday morning, as ordered, his head and hand still bandaged. "What kind of *pantalones* does that take?"

Sipping hot espresso, Pescatore smiled weakly. Whatever the outcome of his troubles, it was hard to imagine going back to work. He felt as if he had broken through a wall. He had worried for weeks that Garrison was pulling him into something demented and dangerous. It had been inevitable.

After Pescatore had made it back across The Line on Tuesday night, Garrison was the first to reach him. Lying in a vehicle waiting for an ambulance, Pescatore told him about his pursuit of Pulpo.

"OK, fine," the supervisor hissed. "You're bleeding all over the place, so play it up big. We'll have 'em take you to the hospital. Don't you admit anything about anything, Valentine, you hear me, buddy?"

Pescatore was X-rayed, cleaned up and sent home to take a few days off. But early Wednesday, a supervisor called and told him to come in to the station ASAP. Garrison called minutes later to tell him they all had to tell the same story and write the same reports and not mention the Game or anything else, goddammit.

The Patrol Agent in Charge and his deputies received Pescatore with stern looks. He denied everything and exaggerated his grogginess. Luckily, the cameras in the area where the incident had happened were either defective or had been shot up by smugglers. He got the impression that the brass had no hard evidence to back their suspicions that he had crossed into Mexico, just scuttlebutt. They told him to write a memo and report directly to the Federal Building to be interviewed by Special Agents Roy Shepard and Isabel Puente of the Inspector General's office.

"Isabel Puente? Oh man you are just totally fried," Galván hooted when they crossed paths later at the Coke machine. "She's a menace. She's on a crusade. Some little *malandrín* says a PA slapped him upside the head, she goes after it like the Kennedy assassination."

"Don't spook him, you stupid asshole," Garrison said. He pulled Pescatore aside. "Don't worry about a thing, buddy."

Pescatore glanced around the small station lounge. He

whispered: "Nobody saw it, right? I don't need a union rep, do I? Or a lawyer?"

Pescatore didn't trust lawyers. And he knew the agents' union representatives didn't like or trust Garrison or anyone associated with him.

"Nah. The bosses rode out this morning with this OIG guy, Shepard. They found some old *borracho* tonk by the fence claims he saw you in the middle of Calle Internacional. But he's a wino. They just hope you'll get scared and start babbling."

"Not gonna happen."

At the Federal Building, Pescatore decided gloomily that he should have put on his uniform. He was wearing a gray sweatshirt under a green bomber jacket. It occurred to him that with his bandaged hand and head he looked more like a suspect than an agent. A stern receptionist in the Office of Inspector General, the internal affairs arm of the Department of Homeland Security, showed him into a conference room and told him to wait.

A good half hour later, they came in. Shepard was in his forties, sleepy-eyed, a bit overweight, with blond hair thin on top but longer than usual. He seemed constricted in the beige suit too—more like DEA or an undercover man than OIG. He started talking, but Pescatore was distracted by Isabel Puente.

Especially in the face, she reminded him of the spectacular, unattainable Puerto Rican girls he had yearned after as a teenager, the ones who lounged in halter-topped glory in front of Roberto Clemente High School when he rode the bus through the Division Street neighborhood. The face of a panther. Skin the color of cinnamon; he imagined he caught a scent of cinnamon across the table. She wore a tight gold-colored outfit: a turtleneck, corduroys, high suede boots. She half turned, knees together, to slide into the chair. He took in taut curves and an achingly small waist with a holstered gun on the belt. Damn, he said to himself. My executioner is fine. But she doesn't look happy to see me.

"Agent Puente is a supervisor in our office currently detailed to BAMCaT, the Border Area Multi-Agency Corruption Task Force," Shepard announced.

A supervisor? Corruption task force? That woke Pescatore up in a hurry.

Isabel Puente watched, her chin propped on her hand, her fingertips playing along a smooth cheekbone, as Shepard said: "We've got your memorandum, but you just tell us your account again."

Pescatore ran his injured hand through his short thick curls near the bandages. He said he had come down right away to get things cleared up, even though he wasn't feeling too hot. He repeated the version he and Garrison had concocted: It edited out the Game, the escape of the aliens from the Wrangler, and the chase into Tijuana. He said he had surprised a smuggler trying to spring an alien from a vehicle near the Gravel Pit and pursued him down a ravine to the fence. They struggled. The smuggler struck him on the head and escaped.

"I musta lost consciousness," he concluded, "'cause next thing I knew the helicopter was there, everybody was around me. The fellas used a towel to stop the bleeding and took me to the hospital."

They didn't buy it. Shepard opened fire. Pescatore kept his answers short and polite.

"Mr. Pescatore, how did you injure your hand?" Puente asked without warning.

"I'm not sure. We were wrestling around and there was rocks and glass on the ground. That's probably when I cut it."

"Interesting. The medical report indicates it's a gash or gouge consistent with the hand injuries the aliens get climbing over the fence."

She did not have an accent. But there was something about her consonants, a musical echo of Spanish in her crisp English. The wide-spaced eyes locked in on him like searchlights.

"I didn't go over the fence. He went under."

"And you went after him across The Line," Shepard said, shaking his head at such colossal folly. "Otherwise why did the agents take so long to find you? There are eyewitness statements that you were seen in traffic on Calle Internacional."

"If somebody said that, they musta been drunk," Pescatore said. Puente's eyes enlarged. Bingo, homes, Pescatore said to himself, that's the only witness they got. "Listen, no offense and everything, but are you guys saying I'm suspected of a crime, or breaking the rules, or what? Is there a complaint or allegation here?"

"If you crossed that line, you know it's a crime and a violation of the rules and about the worst thing a Border Patrol agent could do except kill somebody," Shepard said.

"Except I didn't do it. Sir."

"Bullshit."

"I'm not crazy. If a PA even puts a toe on that line, he's fried. Diplomatic protests, investigations, media gone apeshit."

"Is it true you give out money to the aliens on a recurring basis? Especially the women?" Shepard asked.

Pescatore felt truly frightened for the first time. After a moment, he told himself: They're not gonna indict you for that, get a grip. He was about to deny it with every breath in his body when he registered the surprise on the woman's face. Her mask had slipped. Shepard had apparently developed this information on his own. It apparently had a positive impact on Puente. Pescatore wanted very much to see that look on her face again.

He took a breath, aware that he was slouching. "How you figure that? It's not especially the women. Kids too. Families."

"So you admit it."

"Hey man, it's my money, right? I don't got any mouths to feed except me."

"You realize giving money to women you've apprehended creates a problem of appearances out there? Like you expect something in return?" Shepard spoke with melodramatic disgust. "Don't play stupid, son."

Pescatore did not need to exaggerate his indignation for Puente's benefit.

"Listen up, Jack." He leaned forward, a finger leveled at Shepard. "Don't you dare accuse me of messing with women prisoners. I'm a gentleman out there. Ask anybody."

As Shepard was about to escalate the confrontation with some finger-pointing of his own, Puente interrupted.

"We'll concede regarding your charitable intentions, Mr. Pescatore." Fleeting smile. "Let me ask you about something else. Under what circumstances did you leave the hotel security job you had in Chicago before you entered on duty with The Patrol?"

First the money, now Chicago. Pescatore glanced at his watch, hoping to conceal his panic. Even if they had started investigating him a minute after he crossed back into San Diego, it was hard to believe they could have come up with all this stuff already. They had been at it for a while, digging into his past. This was about more than chasing Pulpo into the Zona Norte.

She repeated the question with a severity that made him wonder if her earlier surprise had been an act.

Dry-mouthed, he answered: "I resigned from that hotel because I decided to apply to The Patrol and I got accepted and that was the end of it."

"Interesting. My information indicates that you got fired because you were involved with a ring of doormen and bellhops who were thieves. You got caught riding at three in the morning in a Lincoln Continental that was supposed to be in the hotel parking garage."

"The Patrol looked into my previous jobs and everything," he protested. "They did the background check. Everything was fine."

"That's no defense," she said. "The Border Patrol has hired

too many people too fast. The background investigations are sloppy. People who got fired from law enforcement slip through. People with criminal records slip through."

"I don't have a criminal record, ma'am."

"Because your uncle is a lieutenant with the Chicago Police and he interceded for you. And then he had the nerve to recommend you to The Patrol."

"That's not the way it was."

"But you did get arrested. You did get fired."

She was acquiring a street snarl. Pescatore tried a counterattack.

"I told the cops then and I'm telling you now, I was investigating those guys who were stealing at the hotel. It was undercover. Like a sting."

"Stop wasting my time," Puente snapped.

"What do you want me to say?"

"Start with the truth about last night," Shepard piped up.

"I told you the truth."

"Another thing," Puente said. "Did you intentionally alter your name when you entered on duty? Why were you known as Valen-*tín* in Chicago when your Border Patrol paperwork consistently refers to you as Valen-*tine?*"

"Hey, don't put that jacket on me," Pescatore exclaimed, eager to play legitimate victim. "My correct given name is Valentín. It was The Patrol's foul-up. At the academy they kept calling me Valentine, my paperwork kept coming back Valentine. I complained, but they never changed it."

In fact, after one halfhearted attempt to correct the mistake, he had decided not to draw attention to himself. His unwanted rechristening was somehow appropriate. He became a Border Patrol agent; he became Valentine.

Puente nodded. Pescatore suspected she had tossed him an easy one to change the pace, soften him up. He steeled himself for another barrage. But she put a hand on Shepard's arm.

"Wait," she told Pescatore. She and Shepard got up and left.

Ten minutes later, she came back into the room alone. The angry-interrogator mode had been replaced by a disconcerting calm. She leaned forward over the table and raised her head, accentuating the swell of the rounded breasts against the turtleneck. Her voice was low.

"Listen carefully, Mr. Pescatore. You're currently under investigation for the allegation regarding last night. You're under investigation for lying about your work history. And we're looking at other activities as well."

"Like what?"

"You know what. Now's the time to start thinking like an adult about resolving your problems. For the moment you are under investigation. We will be in touch."

She got up and went out, leaving an invisible trail of cinnamon behind her.

That evening, Garrison had visited him at home. Pescatore lived in a one-bedroom apartment on the second floor of a stucco house in Pacific Beach, an area populated by students, surfers and aging Anglos. Pescatore lay on the couch with an ice pack on his head listening to an old George Benson disc. His gun was on a chair nearby. There wasn't much in the apartment beyond the couch, the stereo, the television and a bed. He had four posters: the Chicago Bulls, the Chicago Bears, Bruce Springsteen and Oscar De La Hoya. The Chicago wall calendar in the kitchenette was open to a photo of the lakefront frosted over into an ice field.

Pescatore lay in the dark when the music ended. He could not see the Pacific from his apartment, but he could hear the soothing mumble of surf. He was thinking about how his arrest in Chicago had triggered a chain of events that culminated in his arrival at the Border Patrol academy in New Mexico. The Patrol was hungry for Spanish-speakers, and his uncle's recommendation helped. You just ran out of favors, his uncle had declared.

Disgrace me again and I'll break your head. The best thing about the Border Patrol is that it will get you the hell out of town.

Garrison's heavy footsteps drummed up the outdoor staircase to his apartment. The supervisor came in loud and hearty, carrying an open beer can. He said he was only going to stay a minute. Somebody was waiting in the car, they were going to the fights. But he made himself at home. He turned on lights. He wandered around, biceps and triceps bulging in a cutoff football jersey, his high forehead furrowed. He grilled Pescatore about the visit to the Federal Building.

Pescatore stayed on the couch. He did not mention the signs of an ominously in-depth investigation.

"So they asked about me?" Garrison said.

"Yeah," Pescatore improvised. "They wanted to know if I ever saw you thump on somebody."

"And?"

"I said I've never seen any PA thump on anybody."

"Good. What else?"

"Mainly they kept browbeating me about did I cross The Line, you know."

After another round of questions, Garrison seemed satisfied. Pescatore tried to nudge along his departure. "Goin' to the fights in TJ, huh?"

"Affirmative. Multiglobo Arena. Next time come down with us. Great seats, buddy. You did some boxing back home, right?"

"Little bit."

Garrison started laughing.

"What's so funny?" Pescatore demanded.

"I was thinking about you whaling on Pulpo. Relax, Valentine. You're not the first PA ever stepped over The Line and got away with it."

"I'm not?"

"Hell no. But you probably did set a record for distance, I'll tell ya that, buddy. Pulpo got a little shock when you dropped in, didn't he?"

Pescatore sat up, grinning lopsidedly through his dread.

"Oh man. I put the fear a God in him forever."

Garrison whooped and swigged beer. "Crazy fucking Valentine. You got potential."

All kinds of potential, Pescatore thought now as he paid for his lunch in Little Italy. Potential to end up fired, in the joint, maybe dead if Garrison gets the idea in his head that I might rat him out.

Pescatore walked down India Street, head down, hands in pockets. He rounded a corner. A Mazda sports car pulled alongside him, low and black. Isabel Puente was at the wheel.

"Mr. Pescatore," she said through the half-open window. "Got a minute for me?"

He peered at her. She wore a gray sweater-and-skirt ensemble and her hair was down, rippling black, shoulder length.

"Are you guys surveilling me?" he demanded, glancing around.

"I thought we might go someplace quiet. Continue our conversation."

"Am I under any obligation to get in this vehicle?"

She hit him with a grin. "None whatsoever."

She drove with relish, handling the vehicle as if she had training at the wheel. He wondered if she had been in another agency before OIG. Usually the internal affairs investigators put in some years in ICE, the Marshals or someplace before they got into the business of locking up fellow feds.

They rode north in silence on the freeway past SeaWorld, past inland beaches and bridges. San Diego was impossibly beautiful: the slender palm trees lining the curve of Mission Bay, the afternoon sun streaking placid waters, the immaculate lawns of hotel resorts. The beauty depressed him. He felt apart from it, rootless, condemned to skim across the surface of the city.

He asked where they were going.

"A place where we can talk," she said.

A minute later, she said: "What are you exactly, Valentine?"

"What kinda question is that?"

Her smile exposed a slight and appealing overbite. "Ethnically, I mean."

"Oh. My father was born in Italy, grew up in Argentina and moved to Chicago. His brothers were there. My mother's family was Mexican."

"That's where you got your Spanish."

"More my father's side. My mother's family came a long time ago. To work on the railroads in Chicago. My mom can't barely speak Spanish, except songs. My neighborhood was Italian, but there were a lotta Mexicans too. And black people."

"Where did you fit in?"

"Good question."

"I'll get this over with, Valentine, so you know the situation." She sighed, her snub profile intent on the freeway. "You almost convinced me yesterday. I should have known better."

"About what?"

"My Mexican police contacts have a witness who saw you in the Zona Norte with dogs chasing you. The smuggler says you beat him down after pursuing him into his residence near Calle Internacional. And they found a scrap of green material stuck in the border fence. Don't bother denying it's from your uniform, because that can be ascertained conclusively. You must've spent a good five minutes in Tijuana. Quite an excursion."

"So you believe the Mexican police."

"These particular officers are meticulous and professional investigators."

"I bet."

She steered down and around an exit ramp.

"The point is, now you're in really big trouble. They could assist our investigation. Or they could press charges themselves, in Mexico, for unauthorized entry and assault on that individual. Theoretically, they could request extradition. It would make a big stink."

He folded his arms. They descended downhill curves, the Pacific shimmering beyond pine trees, and entered La Jolla Village. A short steep grade led into the Cove, a triangular coastal park overlooking rocks and surf and walled by cliffs. She parked in front of a café-restaurant in a historic-looking house set into the base of a cliff.

She looked at him brightly. "Ready?"

"I gotta tell you, I'm not comfortable with this," he said.

"What?"

"One minute you're talking about the Mexicans extraditing me, which is the most fucked-up unfair outrageous thing I ever heard, considering all the Mexican criminals we can't extradite because of the criminals in their government. And then you want to get coffee."

"Look," she said, her door half-open. "I'm being up-front. I'm taking a big chance with you."

"Why?"

"Good question. Come on."

It was past 3 p.m. and the café was nearly empty, which was probably why she had picked it. Reached by wooden steps, the place was big and homey, a fireplace, pictures of old-time San Diego on the mantel and walls, carved furniture. It was not the kind of place he normally went. But it seemed like a nice spot for a date with Isabel Puente.

They sat in a corner with a view of the ocean. They both ordered coffee, and he ordered waffles with strawberries. Puente looked amused.

"I thought you ate already," she said.

"So you *were* surveilling me." When she rolled her eyes, he added: "I always get hungry when I'm scared to death."

Her delighted laugh encouraged him somewhat. She asked

him if he had done some thinking. He said he was not clear what he was supposed to think about.

"What is it you want, exactly?" he asked.

"Supervisory Agent Arleigh Garrison."

He was not surprised. But he nonetheless rubbed his face with his hand, his mind shuffling scenarios.

"Oh great," he said. "You want me to rat him out."

"I'm thinking you might want to help yourself and help us. And do some good, for a change."

"I've done plenty of good. I got a commendation for catching a stickup man in the canyons. I pulled a little kid from a car wreck. I went one-on-ten with some gangbangers in a damn near riot on the levee. You don't know what it's like out there."

She started to say something, caught herself. She said, "I'm aware of your record."

"Then don't talk to me like I'm a lowlife slug."

"Then don't talk like one. This isn't about being a rat. It's about an investigation."

"To get Garrison."

"Unless he's your friend. Unless you're scared of him."

"What happens if I say hell no, then run back and tell him about this?"

Puente's panther smile turned morose, as if she'd rarely encountered such stupidity. "You're not going to do that."

"Glad you know me so good. What's the proposition?"

"You tell me everything you know about Garrison. And then you gather intelligence for us."

"And what do I get out of it?"

"You don't get indicted or fired. Plus compensation. We pay informants."

"You're insulting me now."

"I thought you might say that. Funny thing is, I don't think you like Garrison that much."

"Not particularly."

"Interesting. Why do you run with him and those characters, then?"

"Look, uh, Agent Puente? Isabel? What do I call you?"

She cocked her head playfully. "Whatever you want."

"Anyway, yeah, I hang out with Garrison some. He's my boss. He was Special Forces. Real badass. He watches my back out on The Line. I watch his. We go drinking after work. I don't exactly have a big social circle outside The Patrol. Inside either."

"You feel loyal. And you like to party with them."

"I guess."

"Garrison's a big spender. He throws extra work at you now and then."

"Hey, you probably know more about it than I do. That's the other guys. He has offered did I want to make a little extra cash, though."

"Doing what?"

"Freelance security for this rich Mexican guy. Garrison teaches him and his bodyguards: shooting, tactical stuff."

"What rich Mexican guy?"

"He doesn't name names."

"You don't have a clue who it is?"

"Uh-uh."

His food arrived. Pescatore wolfed down the waffles. He found it hard to believe he was sitting here, the luxuriant blue of the Pacific framed in the window, having a conspiratorial chat with this woman who held his fate in her hands. Isabel Puente never quite relaxed. She crossed and uncrossed her supple brown legs, fiddled with the torn sugar packets, rearranged her hair. Although she concentrated on him, she periodically surveyed the room behind him and the street below. He wondered how old she was. Despite her poise, he guessed she couldn't be more than thirty, about five years older than him.

Presently, she said: "And you never once took up Garrison on his offer?"

"So I guess this is the part where I tell you everything, huh?"

"I guess. Or you can finish your waffles, I drive you back to your car and the investigation continues."

"Look, tell you the truth, I did work for him a couple times, in a manner of speaking."

Puente gave him a nod.

"One time he said he needed some backup. All I had to do was bring my gun and show myself in the parking lot outside Coco's, down by I-Five north of San Ysidro. Me and this other PA, Macías, we waited outside while he met with these two Mexicans. Serious hard-asses. I think they were AFI or SSP, you know. Federal police."

"OK."

Pescatore explained that the meeting in the diner had lasted about half an hour, that they shook hands with the Mexfeds when they left. Garrison had paid him three hundred dollars and forgiven two hundred Pescatore owed him. On the other occasion, Pescatore told her, he escorted a woman who came up from Tijuana without papers. She took a taxi from Tijuana through the lane of a Customs and Border Protection inspector who was close to Garrison. Pescatore met her in San Ysidro, drove her to a high-rise condominium downtown overlooking the Coronado Bay and walked her in as far as the elevator.

"She was early twenties, lots of hair and perfume, flashy-looking. She told me she was from Sinaloa. Garrison made it sound like she was one of his informants' girlfriend."

"So there's Macías, Dillard, you—the PAs that do these 'jobs' for Garrison. Then there's people in other agencies. Here's some individuals I'm aware of."

She recited names as if reading from a report. He nodded. Puente continued: "And he has regular off-duty contact with Mexican law enforcement."

"Mainly Baja state police detectives. And federales. And a couple guys that work for Mexican customs."

"Any contact with Colonel Astorga, the former chief of the state police?"

"No. But Garrison sure was interested when he got busted. He was the comandante with the two tons and the dead bodies, right? The one who got caught by that secret Diogenes unit?"

"Exactly. How about Mauro Fernández Rochetti, the homicide chief in TJ?"

"I heard Garrison talk to a Mauro on the phone one time."

"How about a subject named Omar Mendoza? Late thirties–early forties, jailhouse-weightlifter type. Not a cop, he's a *veterano* from L.A., talks *pocho* Spanish. Street name is Buffalo."

"Nobody like that."

"I imagine the rich guy you mentioned with regard to the so-called security training is Junior Ruiz Caballero? And don't tell me you never heard of him."

Pescatore exhaled deeply.

"Who hasn't heard of him? Seems like Garrison's business down there has some connection with the Ruiz Caballeros, yeah. Garrison goes to the fights, he gets freebies in TJ at the clubs and everything. But Isabel, I don't know. And I don't wanna know."

She shook her head impatiently. "I'm afraid that's going to have to change."

He stared down at the table, feeling trapped. He knew that the Ruiz Caballero family were heavy hitters, not just in Tijuana but in all of Mexico.

"Who said I was gonna help you in the first place?"

"Nobody. But I know one thing: Yesterday, you spent the whole interview lying and bullshitting. Except for one part when you told the truth. When Shepard asked you about giving money to aliens. That was the real Valentine."

He looked up at her and then away, embarrassed and moved.

She said: "Deep down, you're one of the good guys."

"I wouldn't bet on it."

But he cooperated during the next hour, answering dutifully

as she inundated him with questions: names, dates, locations, vehicles. Then she shifted to his "assignment," as she called it, and he told himself, well congratulations, my man. It kinda slipped by, but you've been recruited as an official undercover rat for OIG. Proud of yourself?

She instructed him to get closer to Garrison and the others, accept the offers to make money, and get in on the action. He shook his head.

"What?" Puente asked.

"After this whole crazy thing in the Zona Norte, I had pretty much decided to stay the hell away from Garrison."

"Good. I'd be worried if you told me you felt bad because he's your idol. This way you'll stay sharp and watch out for yourself."

"I feel bad alright. About the whole thing: the IB station, The Patrol, The Line. It chews people up and spits them out."

Her face softened in a way that intrigued him. "I told you, the Border Patrol is an outfit with a lot of problems."

"Yeah, I'm burned out. I still respect the agents, though."

"Respect?"

"Damn right. You deal with the bad guys. But most PAs aren't like Garrison at all. They work damn hard. People think we're stone soldiers out there. Nobody has a clue what we feel. The activists are always whining about us thumping somebody. They care so damn much about the aliens. Hell, does anybody care about the aliens more than us? Does anybody spend more time with the aliens, hold their hands, carry their kids? The activists, half the time they're getting hustled by some thug that convinces them he's a poor *pollo* who didn't deserve a beating."

Puente pursed her lips. "There may be individuals who actually deserve a beating, as you put it. But it's illegal. Period."

"Listen. Say you come up against fifteen guys. Solo. It's hard for you to imagine, but it happens all the time. Say only two or three want to brawl, the rest are regular peaceful Guanajuato Joes. Those are still bad odds. You gotta hit the biggest meanest one and hit him hard, knock him down. So the others know you're not a punk bitch. That's not illegal. And the hoodlums who want to throw hands are the ones making the thump allegations."

"I've investigated excessive-force cases. There were plenty of bona fide victims. Plenty."

Pescatore tried to slow himself down. He could not remember the last time he had spent so much time talking to someone with such immediate intimacy.

He continued, his voice low. "All I'm saying is, the Border Patrol gets a bad rap. The Mexican government has some nerve saying we're heavy-handed. Fuck them. They practically kick their people out of the country: Don't let the door hit you in the ass going north. They abuse them all their lives, all the way up to the border. The minute the aliens cross, the Mexican government's like: 'Hey *gabacho,* you put the handcuffs on that guy too tight! Police brutality! Racism!' Can you imagine if they replaced us with Mexican cops? They'd be like piranhas. Killing and raping and robbing every night. Considering everything, we are damn humane."

"How about Garrison?" Puente said. "Explain to me how that guy got to be a supervisor."

"That's just weird. They been getting rid of Old Patrol guys like that. But supposedly he's got a lot of yank with the bosses at the Federal Building. Related to when he was in the military, you know? Some guys think he's got intel connections."

"He just plays Mr. Big," Isabel scoffed. "Don't you worry about him. What's the matter, Valentine?"

He paused. "The fact is, us PAs have a code: We look out for each other. Nobody rats. And you just signed me up for rat of the year."

Puente paid the check. She suggested they take a walk. They followed a promenade out to the corner of the coastal park. They passed a mother with a baby carriage, a couple holding hands on a bench, eyes closed, faces offered blissfully to the sun. Puente and Pescatore found a secluded spot along a wood railing in the shade. They leaned on the rail, staring down at small waves foaming on boulders. Beaches and wooded residential neighborhoods stretched along the shoreline to the north.

He did not look at Puente as she spoke. She explained how they would communicate, procedures for making contact. "You need to watch your back, Valentine. These people are serious business."

"Tell me about it." He turned and saw that she had put on sunglasses. The breeze played with her hair and her skirt, which had a long slit on the side. They went back to the car.

"What do I tell Garrison about the investigation of me and Pulpo and everything?" he asked.

"We'll spread the word that we suspect you crossed into Tijuana, but we can't prove it. Our Mexican contacts will do the same. You tell Garrison we asked about him. We were interested in cases of excessive force. That'll point him in the wrong direction."

"That's what I told him."

"Valentine," she said as he buckled his seat belt. "What exactly happened in that situation in Chicago with the hotel thieves?"

"Like I said. I got to know these guys, I found out what they were up to. I decided to go undercover on them. But they weren't bad guys, it turned out. After a while I wasn't sure what I was doing, tell you the truth."

"Interesting."

The sun lowered toward the ocean, igniting crimson circles in the water. On the way back, Puente said nothing until they drove downhill into Little Italy.

"I want you to know something," she said. "I was in The Patrol. For a year."

"No kidding. Where at?"

"Nogales."

"How come just a year?"

"Long story. But I wanted you to know. When Agent Shepard got on you about giving aliens money, I thought he was out of line. I understand about the money."

He was so drained that this did not cheer him the way it should have. He said: "I'm glad. I'm not sure I understand it myself."

The Mazda stopped behind his white Impala. The sun blazed in her dark glasses.

"Listen, Valentine," she said. "The doctors told you to rest. You do that. Monday you go back to work and we'll be ready to roll. Good luck."

She shook his hand, all business, like she had sold him a house or something. He did not want to get out of the car. He wanted to prolong the moment with her. And he did not want to be alone to think about his predicament.

"Alright then." He gave her a sheepish raise of the eyebrows. "So I'm in your hands, huh, Isabel? I got nobody to trust but you."

She took off her sunglasses. He had overplayed it, coming off like a bullshitter, even though he had meant it.

Isabel Puente gave him a tight smile. Moving slowly, she rested her hand on his knee. He wanted to enjoy it, but the combination of the touch and the smile was as scary as it was seductive.

"That's right," she said. "So if you let me down, or try to pull something slick, I'm in charge of making you regret it for the rest of your life."

4

There were protesters outside the office of the state human rights commission. They had been joined by Porfirio Gibson and his camera crew.

Méndez sat in the car watching. The protesters presented themselves as families of police officers who had been unfairly persecuted by the human rights commission and gotten fired, making the streets unsafe for the citizens. There were quite a few women and children. But Méndez noticed a number of "organizers": ex-cops or para-cops sporting cowboy hats, sunglasses and quality leather.

Once again, Porfirio Gibson was on the wrong side. Méndez watched the reporter conduct animated interviews with protesters. Their signs bore proclamations such as ARACELI MUST FALL, AGUIRRE PROTECTS CRIMINALS, and HUMAN RIGHTS FOR POLICE!

"Look at this bastard," Méndez said. He patted his driver on the shoulder. "Turn up the radio. It's noon, we get to watch and listen to Porfirio at the same time."

In addition to covering law enforcement for television, Gibson hosted a taped radio program called "Radio Patrol." At first, his nasal Mexico City accent hadn't gone over well. But then he had turned the cop-blotter show into a weapon for extortion and intrigue. He had acquired influential contacts. He got scoops on raids and murders. He led the assault when the mafia decided to go after competitors or crime fighters. His growing audience had helped him expand into television work, but "Radio Patrol" remained an institution.

The program began with a wailing siren and radio chatter. Then Gibson read the day's police reports at top speed with minimal editing. The menu today featured assorted stickups, a car chase near the border, a narco-execution and, almost as an afterthought, a street gang dumping gasoline on a police car and setting it on fire—with the officers inside. Gibson's hard-boiled delivery of the police terminology was stilted street poetry. It described suspects as "short, mustachioed and with the face of a good-for-nothing" or "socially inadapted hoodlums of Sinaloan appearance." Gibson engaged in spirited commentary with his perennially indignant sidekick Beto, who spluttered like Daffy Duck announcing a boxing match.

"Can you imagine, Porfirio? A lady works hard in a pharmacy every day. A good God-fearing woman. And a pair of Sinaloan hoodlums stick a shotgun in her nose and take her money!"

"I'm tempted to grab a shotgun and go look for them myself," Gibson exclaimed. "But that would upset the human rights nuts! Human rights! For subhuman criminals!"

Méndez shook his head. He got out of the car and crossed the street.

Gibson caught sight of him, broke away from an interview and hurried over, his camera crew following like pilot fish. Gibson wore loafers and wrinkled jeans below a well-cut checkered sports jacket and yellow tie. He was growing a reddish-gray beard to camouflage his chins. With a flourish, he tossed his microphone into his left hand and extended his right to greet Méndez.

"The dynamic and controversial Leobardo Méndez, leader of the so-called Diogenes Group," Gibson intoned, but Méndez saw with relief that the cameraman had stopped filming. "Hunting the forces of criminality as always, Don Leobardo?"

"And finding them everywhere, maestro."

"As the former human rights commissioner, would you care to comment on the crisis of leadership at the human rights commission and the very serious accusations by the families of brave police officers left defenseless because they stood up to crime? It seems La Flaca Aguirre is in trouble. Maybe she won't run for governor after all."

"Perhaps later, Porfirio," Méndez said. "You'll be here all day, no? It's not like there are any crimes to cover."

"Good one, maestro." Gibson showed small teeth. "We'll very happily grab you on the way out to ask about the radical crusade against the humble cop on the beat."

The commission's offices were in a building near Boulevard Agua Caliente. A plainclothes officer of the Diogenes Group was posted upstairs in the waiting room, which was crowded with citizens and decorated by posters and photos of indigenous villages, street children, rural marches. Méndez had assigned the officer to guard Aguirre because of death threats.

Returning the nods and smiles of youthful, casually dressed employees, some of whom he had hired, Méndez went to Araceli Aguirre's corner office. It had been his office during his three years as human rights commissioner. Whenever he visited, he had the feeling that he had returned home after losing his way.

Aguirre's teenage daughter did homework at a conference table. Aguirre's toddler crawled around arranging crayons at her mother's feet as she talked on the phone. An aide waited with a legal pad. Aguirre, slender and high-shouldered in a long violet dress, untangled herself from the phone cord to give Méndez a kiss and gestured at a chair. She finished the phone call and told her daughter to have their driver drop off her little sister at a day-care center on her way back to school.

"I have news for you, Leo," Aguirre said when they were

alone. "In times gone by, I would have told you to stop the presses."

"What suspense."

"The conversations with the Colonel have taken an unexpected turn," she began. She rose and went to a window through which the shouts of the marchers in the street were audible. She closed the window and pantomimed relief. "Enough. It's the interminable revenge of the cretins out there."

"Let me say one more time how uncomfortable I am with these jailhouse visits of yours to the Colonel," Méndez said.

"Ay Leobardo, you are a man who is fundamentally unhappy unless he has something to worry about," she retorted. "I must tell you, this thing with the Colonel has blossomed. He calls from the penitentiary every night. He talks and talks. First he asks if he is bothering me, of course. A gentleman. My friend, the torturer and assassin."

"Your husband must be as thrilled as I am. I hope it's worth it."

She got serious. "That's what I'm telling you, Leo. It's worth it. The Colonel wants a deal. He wants, believe it or not, to talk to you."

"To me."

"Although he hasn't exactly forgiven you for arresting him, he has decided that you are a 'man of honor.' Exact words. And he says you are the only person around here with enough clout in Mexico City to help him."

"Incredible."

"He's desperate. He says Junior has cut him off, won't take his calls, rejects his emissaries."

"*No One Writes to the Colonel.*"

"Very funny. He thinks he's not going to last long. So he's ready to talk."

Méndez turned down the corners of his mouth. Because he had been worried about her safety, he had discouraged Aguirre's plan to reach out to Regino "The Colonel" Astorga, the former state police chief captured five months earlier by the Diogenes Group. The Colonel had filed a complaint with the human rights commission asserting that his life was in danger in the state prison. Aguirre had taken it seriously, going to the prison to interview him. She had made a public statement urging the government to ensure his safety. She had kept visiting him and, gradually, had gained his trust.

"Well, Araceli, this is really something."

Aguirre was enjoying herself, practically giving off sparks of adrenaline. Ever since they had been students together, he had wished that she were not quite so fearless. She still looked more like an underfed university student than an admired public official with a bright political future. She wore round glasses. Her short hair revealed her silver earrings, one shaped like the sun and the other like the moon. Only the pronounced circles under her eyes gave her brown, fine-boned face some gravity.

"I want you to hear his story," she said. "Some of it fits with what we already know. Some of it is new. If it's true, this is even worse than we think."

"We would need his testimony to seriously consider prosecuting Junior and his uncle," Méndez said. "What does the Colonel want?"

"He thinks you can get the Americans to save his hide. He fantasizes about their witness-protection program. At minimum, he wants a transfer to a prison as far from Baja as possible."

"That's not easy. When do we see him?"

"Tomorrow. Saturdays are especially charming at the penitentiary."

"Short notice. I know you won't like this, but I think it would be wise to bring Isabel Puente on this little safari."

"*Ay* Leo, please. The *gringa cubana?* That woman is imperious and insufferable."

"You are unfair to my friend Isabel."

"You have a strange weakness for her. The last thing I want is her stomping around in that prison."

"If the Colonel really thinks the Americans can help him, it would be a perfect incentive. And we might be able to get them interested in a deal with him."

Aguirre tapped with a pen. She realized he was right, but she didn't like backing down. He continued: "Even if she doesn't say a word—"

"She better not!"

Méndez relaxed. "She doesn't have to. Her presence will appeal to his appetites."

"Very well. But if anything happens to her, don't blame me. If she plays the pushy *cubana* in there, they might decapitate her and play soccer with her head."

The cold returned Saturday morning, along with gray skies.

In his readings about the U.S. penal system, Méndez had come across the term "extraction." It referred to operations in U.S. penitentiaries when a rebellious inmate barricaded himself in a cell and responded to appeals to reason with threats, violence and hurled excrement. Four guards would put on helmets and body armor, arm themselves with clubs, shields and mace, and charge into the cell in a tactical formation to subdue and "extract" the inmate as rapidly and safely as possible.

Méndez wondered what term the yanqui correctional experts might come up with to describe a visit by the Mexican authorities to an inmate chieftain in the penitentiary of Baja California.

Méndez, Athos, Araceli Aguirre and Isabel Puente arrived at the prison at 11 a.m. They had brought Porthos and two of the largest, meanest-looking officers in the Diogenes Group. Méndez, Aguirre and Puente had a quick strategy session in the car. It mainly consisted of Aguirre giving Puente a stern lecture. Puente sat next to Méndez in back, chewing gum, impassive behind sunglasses. She was dressed down in jeans and a ponytail.

"Forget about American prisons," Aguirre said, twisted around in the front seat. "You never saw anything like this. The inmates have guns. Children live inside. The *capos* build houses, hire servants, bodyguards, whores—"

"I know about the prison," Puente said tonelessly.

Aguirre ignored her. "Don't trust the guards. The inmates will harass you for money. And they will tell you what they would like to do to you. Put up with it. No hard looks. No stupid confrontations. And for the love of God, you're in a foreign country. So no guns."

Aguirre got out, lecture over, slamming the door. Puente reached down calmly to adjust the top of her boot; Méndez looked away when he saw the concealed holster. He did not intend to be the one who tried to disarm Isabel Puente.

"Warm welcome," Puente said.

"You have to understand," Méndez said soothingly. "Araceli has worked hard to gain trust in there. It goes against her principles to bring an American agent inside."

As they crossed the gravel parking lot, Méndez saw that Athos had an AK-47 assault rifle slung across his shoulder. He gave the weapon a pained look. Athos raised his eyebrows over his sunglasses in response.

"That zoo in there is a sniper's paradise, Licenciado," Athos said. "If it were up to me, I would have brought the whole unit. You are putting yourself in the mouth of the wolf in there."

It was visiting day. The lines of families were especially long. Among the features that made the prison unique in Mexico and the world were the hundreds of wives and children who lived inside with the inmates. The families went to work and school and returned each day like commuters, blending with the crush of visitors. The prison had been built as a city jail for five hundred inmates, but it housed several thousand: federal and state offenders, incorrigible convicts and wrongly accused suspects, hit men and purse snatchers, drug lords and drug mules, men and women, the vicious and the hapless, the privileged and the indigent.

A guard with a sallow face, a scarf around his neck and an Uzi strapped over his shoulder let them in. He looked eighteen at most. Another guard stamped their hands with red ink insignias, like a nightclub bouncer. The guard with the Uzi walked them through a yellow-walled office area and told them to wait. The madhouse racket of the prison yard reverberated off tiled floors and cement walls: shouts, children laughing, Vicente Fernández crooning, construction hammers pounding, the bark of a good-sized dog, and three small explosions that Méndez assumed were firecrackers because nobody paid any attention.

Wrapped in a multicolored shawl, Araceli Aguirre stamped her high heels on the tile. Méndez couldn't tell if she was reacting to the cold or the anticipation. She leaned against him with a giggle and whispered, "We might as well just move my office into the prison, we spend so much time here. This is a human rights apocalypse."

The deputy warden led them down a hallway. The noise got louder. In the watch commander's office, two guards studied a bank of video monitors. A third stood by a sliding gate with a shotgun across his chest. The chunky, shaven-headed watch commander slumped behind a desk, blowing listlessly into an empty paper cup. He glanced at them, unimpressed. He nodded at the guard with the shotgun, who unlocked the gate.

The prison yard was reached through a cage filled with relatives, lawyers and other visitors, the red stamps on their hands distinguishing them from the inmates, who were also in civilian dress, on the other side of the chain-link fence. Méndez's expeditionary force advanced to a second gate. They were met by a lanky inmate in a San Diego Padres cap and a leather coat. Méndez recognized him as a former state police detective whom the Diogenes Group had arrested along with the Colonel.

"Rico, you probably remember Licenciado Méndez," Aguirre

said without a trace of irony, as if they had run into each other in a supermarket. "Shall we?"

Four grim-faced prison guards led the way. Whenever Méndez entered the yard, he felt as if he were stepping into a hallucination. It resembled the plaza of a bustling and thuggish village. A basketball court was surrounded by two-story blocks of housing called *carracas* with spiral staircases leading to outdoor catwalks. The walls were painted in green, orange and maroon and decorated by murals of historical figures, religious images, zoot-suited *pachucos,* Aztec monarchs, Border Patrol helicopters swooping over figures running through canyons. Most of the buildings were occupied on the ground floors by ramshackle businesses with hand-painted signs: restaurants, grocery stores, a barbershop.

Years earlier, the prison administration had found itself overwhelmed by an excess inmate population of migrants from all over Mexico. Politics had made the federal government disinclined to lend a hand; the opposition party was strong in Baja, so the mess at the prison had been a perennial weapon for the ruling party of that era. The authorities decided to let the inmates fend for themselves. The inmates created their own businesses and mafias, built their own homes—townhouses that sold for forty thousand dollars, cubicles that sold for two hundred. A microsociety blossomed within the walls. At night, the guards only dared to venture into the internal "streets" the way the police entered the toughest *colonias* of the city outside: in platoons and girded for combat.

It took longer than Méndez had hoped to get to the Colonel. The Saturday crowd was thick with strolling families, timid backcountry migrants, tattered heroin addicts who prowled and scratched and hustled. The phalanx of VIPs caused a commotion. A human whirlpool encircled the human rights commissioner. The inmates shouted her name or simply "Doctora." They jostled close to shake her hand, appeal for help, steal a moment of her time.

Méndez realized that Aguirre was not going to brush them off. She was unruffled by the size and noise of the swarm. She inched forward, the shawl draped over her willowy long-backed frame. She hoisted and inspected a toddler with a respiratory disease. She nodded gravely at the semicoherent patter of a bleary-eyed convict on crutches who wore multiple vests, a watch cap and an Artful Dodger overcoat that looked as if he slept in it. Aguirre was doing her job.

Athos stayed by Méndez, AK-47 at the ready, eyeing the crowd, the balconies and rooftops. Porthos shadowed Aguirre, shoving away inmates violently but surreptitiously, his hands low so the human rights commissioner wouldn't notice. The crowd ebbed and swirled. A group of women shouldered forward. They had an elderly female inmate in tow—bent over, gray-haired, grandmotherly-looking. They wanted Aguirre to see her: Exhibit A for the injustice of it all. Can you believe they arrested this poor old *comadre* for smuggling drugs, Doctora? She was just in the wrong car at the wrong time. Can't you do something for her, Doctora? Aguirre pulled the woman aside, a comforting arm around the frail back in a mangy green sweater. Aguirre and the woman took turns speaking into each other's ears, straining over the noise. Aguirre pulled out a pad and took notes.

Athos sidled up to Méndez and murmured: "Listen, Licenciado, perhaps it would be best to cut short the tourism, what do you think?"

Isabel Puente's look suggested wholehearted agreement.

Méndez shrugged. "What do you want me to do? Every time I came here when I was commissioner, it was the same. They all want you to make them a miracle."

Aguirre leaned over a counter into a wooden hut that was a handicrafts store and, judging from the mattress and bassinet on the floor, a tiny residence for the inmate entrepreneur and his family. The ponytailed owner was an artisan who decorated belt buckles with images of curvaceous women, AK-47s, marijuana leaves. After handing Aguirre a folder containing documents about his court case, he tried to make a sale.

"Perhaps your husband would like another one, Doctora, or one of the gentlemen with you," he said in what sounded to Méndez like the cadences of Michoacán. "This is really a complicated design, I call it the Sinaloan Phantom, the skull with the cowboy hat requires an infernal amount of detail..."

Méndez noticed a scraggly inmate with buzz-cut hair and a cotton workshirt shoving his way toward Aguirre, rasping her name. The inmate wore a necklace with a bullet as a medallion. Méndez did not like what he saw.

"Porthos," he called.

The big commander was way ahead of him. By the time Méndez reached them, Porthos had intercepted the inmate and applied a crushing one-handed grip to his throat. Clearing a path in the crowd with his free arm, Porthos pinned the inmate to a wall beneath a dragon painted on a food stand run by Asian smugglers.

The inmate squawked and gurgled. Porthos tightened his hold. Some inmates laughed, others yelled insults. Méndez cursed. They were like hyenas in here.

Méndez fought his way to Aguirre's side and put a hand on her shoulder.

"Araceli, please," Méndez said. "I would gladly spend the entire day here, but..."

They followed Rico down a narrow walkway behind a cell block to the Colonel's compound. It was a cement yard half the size of a tennis court: two picnic tables, barbells around a weight bench. A slobbering pit bull strained a leash. The open space fronted a two-story block of housing that had been custom-built for a drug lord years earlier and purchased by the Colonel for himself, several of his imprisoned former police officers, and henchmen and servants he had hired from the inmate population.

Two stern inmates in cowboy hats manned the gate of the compound. Two more stood sentry on a second-floor walkway of the building. Like Rico, they wore long coats or bulky jackets. Several did not bother to conceal the pistols in their belts, declaring to the world that the prison had turned reality upside down.

The Colonel himself was on hand to greet his visitors. The dutiful host stood at attention in the middle of the cement patio area, arms spread magnanimously. He was resplendent in a brown-and-gold Fila jogging suit with a brown scarf tucked around his throat and into the warm-up jacket. He was thickset, with a long torso, long arms and disproportionately short legs. He wore a baseball-style cap adorned with the English word "Skipper."

"Doctora Araceli," the Colonel called, and embraced Aguirre.

Then he swiveled toward Méndez, who noticed Athos tense next to him. The Colonel made the most of the moment. He advanced slowly, ceremonially, his hands wide and upturned.

"Licenciado Méndez," the Colonel boomed. "It is sincerely a pleasure to see you. I would like to welcome you. I would like to thank you humbly and profoundly for accepting my invitation and taking the time to come see me."

The former police chief gave him a big hug with the requisite double back slap. Méndez smelled cigarettes, tequila and Old Spice — the same aroma the Colonel had given off the day they had arrested him. The day the Colonel had warned Méndez that Junior Ruiz Caballero would avenge this insult by cutting off Méndez's ears and making him eat them, one at a time.

The Colonel disengaged. His laugh echoed in the compound.

This man is even more of a psychopath than I remembered, Méndez thought. But he's shrewd. He's using us and this scene out here in the open, making people think he has new allies.

"Good morning," Méndez muttered.

Araceli Aguirre leaned close to the Colonel and spoke in his ear, gesturing briefly at Isabel Puente. The Colonel's eyes brightened. With a mischievous smile, he stepped forward, took Puente's hand and bent over it with a flourish.

"Welcome, señorita," he murmured, all gallantry and discretion.

"Thank you," Puente said, attempting a polite smile.

"I invite you all to come upstairs and have some coffee," the Colonel declared. "Please, this way."

The Colonel reached the base of the spiral stairway. He paused. A young woman had emerged from a door on the second-floor balcony. She began a wobbly, hip-swinging descent. Her pointy heels rang on the metal steps. She had billowing, pink-streaked blond hair and a heart-shaped face that looked fifteen years older than the rest of her. She wore a pink windbreaker zipped to her throat and, despite the chill, tight denim shorts over sinewy legs.

The Colonel gave the woman a look of homicidal fury that stopped her cold. She gripped the stairway railing, one foot in the air, hair tumbling. The Colonel turned his glare on one of the henchmen on the balcony. The man hurried over and reached to help the startled strawberry blonde pick her way back up the stairs. He steered her into a doorway and slammed the door behind them, cutting off the strains of a song by Los Plebeyos.

The Colonel wheeled with parade-ground precision toward Aguirre. Her face had registered uncertainty for the first time since their arrival.

With a big smile and a little bow, the Colonel said: "After you. Please."

A recent layer of lemon scent melded with musty and unpleasant smells in the Colonel's windowless quarters. Méndez, Aguirre, Puente and the Colonel sat on wood chairs around a metal folding table in a narrow living room area. There was a television on a high shelf, a portable stereo, a cell phone hooked to a charger, a samurai sword on a little table near the short hallway leading to a sleeping alcove. Whiskey and tequila bottles stood on a tray. A bulletproof vest hung from a hook. A velvet tapestry depicting a colonial church in a country landscape covered one wall; photos of the Colonel with relatives, soldiers and policemen filled another. The Colonel was a career army officer in his fifties. He had been appointed chief of the state police when the theory held sway that the culture of the Mexican military insulated its officers from corruption and made them the ideal reformers to clean up civilian law enforcement.

By some silent accord, the four prison guards remained outside the compound. Méndez doubted that any guard had come through that gateway since the Colonel had moved in. Two Diogenes officers were downstairs in the yard. Athos checked the interior and stationed himself outside the door on the balcony. Porthos settled his bulk onto a low couch near Méndez. Rico stood behind a counter in the kitchenette. A short youth with Mixteco features, wet-combed hair and a Georgetown sweatshirt served coffee. He wore a black thread crucifix around his neck.

"The ironies of life," the Colonel said. "When I was a young captain, I had the privilege of serving as warden at a problematic prison in Chihuahua. I can assure you that by the time I was done, there was order, respect, dignity. And now, I find myself in this inferno. This zoo. *National Geographic* would love this place. In this warped institution you have all the degradation and the degeneracy that our society has come to, my friends. An enormous sea of shit. If you'll pardon me, Doctora. And señorita."

Aguirre nodded, warming her hands on the coffee mug. Puente fiddled with her sunglasses, trying not to touch anything else. Méndez whisked a cockroach off his sleeve.

"I have to get out of here," the Colonel muttered huskily. He had a rather square face. His watery eyes gave the impression that he was perpetually on the brink of shedding sentimental tears.

The bravado of the welcome had faded. The Colonel looked old and haunted in the gloom. He contemplated his outsized hands—the ridges of the veins, the knuckles like knots of bone—flat on the table in front of him. Without looking up, he said: "You must help me, Licenciado Méndez. I know that sounds strange, after our discrepancies of the past. But why delude ourselves? I need help."

"Doctora Aguirre gave me the sense that we could be of mutual help to one another," Méndez said.

"I know you want that snot-nosed little son of a bitch," the Colonel rasped. "That little brat sitting on that hill in Colonia Chapultepec who toys with human beings the way children torture insects. Junior has no conception of honor like you and I, Méndez."

Aguirre rearranged her shawl. She said: "Perhaps you could give the Licenciado an idea of how you could help, Colonel. Regarding the Ruiz Caballeros. As we discussed."

"What a partner you have, Méndez." The Colonel raised his head, brightening a bit. "That's why everybody wants her to run for governor. A real lady. And tough as a soldier."

Aguirre laughed uneasily. Méndez took a long sip of coffee.

"I see this as the first step toward a dialogue," the Colonel continued. "I assure you we don't have much time. Junior's people are closing in. I have reliable reports about two heavyweight *sicarios* among the inmates who have been approached separately. Each has been given an advance payment for my head. Like a macabre competition."

"If it's as bad as you say, then you should act first," Méndez said. "That's the best strategy. That means you trust me and hold nothing back."

"That would certainly be one way of looking at it," the Colonel said. "César!"

Everyone jumped. The short servant appeared.

"Bring the book I was looking at earlier," the Colonel ordered. He leaned toward Méndez. "I can give you a sign of my good faith. I can give you the larger scheme of things. You probably see parts of it already, but not the dimensions, the audacity."

César placed a large and moldering atlas on the table. Scrawled in orange Magic Marker on the cover was a reminder that the atlas was the property of the prison library.

Rico flicked on an overhead light. The Colonel's scalp gleamed through the gaps in his comb-over. He had acquired the air of a field marshal dispensing orders in a battle tent. His veined hands pried the atlas open to a full-color map of the Americas. A thick finger searched out and tapped a spot slightly below the center of South America.

"I assume you have heard of the Triple Border," the Colonel said.

"Of course," Méndez said.

"This is the Triple Border," the Colonel proclaimed, ignoring him. "The place where Paraguay, Brazil and Argentina come together. The Tijuana of South America, you could say. The core of the Ruiz Caballeros' scheme."

The Colonel's hands hovered over the map, little bursts of movement accompanying and diagramming his words.

"Being a student of organized crime, you know that Mexican drug mafias now dominate the world cocaine market. Mexican narcos have taken over areas once run by the Colombians, such as cocaine distribution in the United States and smuggling to Europe. Certain visionary Mexicans have established connections with suppliers in Colombia, Bolivia and Peru, transporters in Venezuela, Italy, Africa. And as you know, the Ruiz Caballeros have decapitated and absorbed the cartels in northwest Mexico. Thanks largely to my help when I was chief of police, modesty aside. Though that ingrate Mauro Fernández Rochetti wants to take the credit now."

The Colonel stabbed the heart of South America again. His mood seemed to swing back toward euphoria.

"But Junior is also developing a revolutionary route, new allies. This could make him richer and stronger than the competition. It is untapped territory. You know more history than I do. If I understand correctly, the Triple Border became a smuggler's paradise during the dictatorship of that general who ruled Paraguay for so long."

"Stroessner," Méndez said.

"That one. A kleptocrat. When he fell, the civilians took over Ciudad del Este. The smuggling business kept growing."

"The government barely exists there," Araceli said to Méndez. "The mafias move an enormous amount of money."

The Colonel nodded graciously. "Billions a year, they say. You still have to pay toll to the Paraguayans, but it is an international platform now. Asian gangs. Arabs. Brazilians, Russians. Pure mafias. The United Nations of crime."

Méndez's eyes were on the map. He decided to jab the Colonel. "What could be so profitable down in the middle of nowhere?"

The Colonel's fist clenched on the atlas. He looked miffed.

"Look. It is what the South American cops call a 'liberated zone.' You have every racket: Drugs. Guns. Fake documents. Money laundering. Contraband. Junior got interested in the place when he found out they were pirating the discs of his damned *norteño* bands faster than the pirates in Mexico. He had some emissaries sniff around. He went down himself. There are waterfalls, jungle parks. Better than Niagara Falls. Junior established alliances with big capos down there. Cautious, experimental. But huge potential."

"When was this?" Méndez asked, intent on the map. He had known that Junior was doing business with South Americans, but not to this extent.

"During the past year. They are starting to move drugs to the United States, but also to Europe through Africa. The market of the future. And migrants here: Chinese, South Americans, Africans. You have seen the results."

"The smugglers and migrants we arrest speak Portuguese mixed with Spanish," Méndez said.

The Colonel's trigger finger aimed at Méndez in acknowledgment, then traced lines back and forth between the Mexican border and the Triple Border.

"That's because Ciudad del Este and Foz do Iguaçu, the Brazilian city across the river, are like one continuous city. The border is an imaginary line, Licenciado. The languages mix together, like everything else. Like San Diego and Tijuana."

"The Colonel says gangsters from the Triple Border are here, Leo," said Aguirre. "The Ruiz Caballeros have used Arab and Brazilian *sicarios.*"

The Colonel nodded vigorously. "They fly in, they kill, they leave. Very efficient. For one job I went to the airport to receive the specialists."

"Which job?"

The Colonel was not accustomed to direct questions, particularly on his own turf. His upper lip drew back against his teeth.

"*Ay* Licenciado, let's just say it was the recent murder of a government official. There have been so many, lamentably. And more to come. César! More coffee for our guests."

As the youth in the Georgetown sweatshirt refilled cups, Méndez wondered if the Colonel had gone to the Triple Border himself; the Diogenes Group knew that off-duty state police accompanied Junior Ruiz Caballero on trips. Méndez wondered how much the Colonel knew for a fact and how much was conjecture. He was framing a question when gunfire erupted outside.

Porthos cursed and put his hand on his gun. Méndez, Rico and Puente followed suit. There were more shots, volleys from an assault rifle somewhere outside the Colonel's compound.

Athos burst in, AK-47 in one hand, a radio to his ear. There was grim satisfaction on his face, as if he felt vindicated that his fears had come true. After scanning the room and reassuring himself the Colonel had not sprung an ambush, he ducked back outside.

Méndez remained in his chair. His body ached with accumulated tension. He saw that Aguirre had her cup encircled in her hands. She sipped pensively. The Colonel sat straight-backed, hands flat on either side of the atlas. He looked as if he had just eaten something distasteful and was being polite about it. No one spoke.

Moments later, Athos stuck his head inside again.

"It came from the main yard," he reported. "Some monkey shooting in the air, celebrating the Saturday. The guards say nothing to worry about. They say they have it under control."

Athos pronounced the last two words with quotation marks around them. He gave Rico and the Colonel a look and withdrew.

The Colonel exhaled.

"Maybe someone was saying hello to our guests," he grumbled. "Anyway, Méndez, I hope I am enlightening you a bit. Now I'd like to talk about how you can help me. Permit me to start by saying I have no illusions. And I want you to know this: One way or another, I am getting out of this prison. Soon."

Hours later, Méndez and Aguirre finished lunch at a little restaurant in a colonial-style shopping mall across a busy downtown traffic circle from the Tijuana Cultural Center. Isabel, who got impatient during extended Tijuana lunches, had joined them long enough to drink a Coke and left. Méndez and Aguirre lingered over cigarettes and coffee, exhausted by the visit to the prison. Their bodyguards sat at the bar watching a Saturday sports roundup on an overhead screen.

Araceli Aguirre took a drag on her cigarette. She had removed her glasses. Her face looked younger, even thinner, the eyes bright despite the circles beneath them.

"I won't argue with you—the Colonel is a perverse beast," Araceli said. "But what do you think he will do?"

"Oh, he will testify if he has to. But he's fully capable of playing both sides, using us to pressure Junior to get him out, or pay him off, or whatever."

"I imagine it's up to your pushy Cuban friend to get help from the yanquis."

"My friend Isabel, who does not deserve insults, will help through the task force. But Mexico City is key at this point. I have to talk to the Secretary about what this means for the investigation, get organized to move fast."

"The Secretary," Aguirre said drily. "Your beloved boss. A creature of the system in disguise."

"Let's not get started. I think he would intervene to transfer the Colonel to a new prison. But the state authorities will try to block it because he has been charged under state law as well as federal law."

"So you are pessimistic."

"Araceli. The Colonel is extremely valuable. The Triple Border connection intrigues me. He's a blowhard, but if he will testify in detail, I do think this is as big as he says it is."

The owner of the restaurant stopped by the table to say hello. He was one of the itinerant Basques who had come to Tijuana to play professional jai alai, then settled there. Méndez was not fond of the Spaniard, or Spain, or what he considered snobby colonial cuisine. But Aguirre had studied for her doctorate in Madrid on a fellowship and developed a weakness for the "mother country." The cozy restaurant, with its posters of far-off mountain villages and fields sectioned by stone walls, did give Méndez a sense of shelter. Especially when he was with Aguirre.

"Did you see Porfirio Gibson's show last night?" Méndez asked. "He's getting nasty with his commentaries. Last night he went after you again. He took a shot at me too, because I dodged an interview."

"I can't imagine that anyone whose opinion I respect pays attention to that buffoon. One day he'll call me a lesbian narco-satanist."

"It's not so much what he says, it's the fact he says it. They are trying to isolate us. I don't have to tell you these are dangerous times. The times of excellent cadavers."

"Of what?"

The lines in his face creased. He kept his voice low.

"It's an expression from the Sicilian mafia wars. It refers to murders of people in power. I'm reading a book about Falcone, the Sicilian judge. There are parallels to Mexico, Colombia. *La vita blindata,* that's what the anti-mafia judges called it. Bodyguards, bunkered courthouses, armored cars: the armored life. Do you know when Judge Falcone said he realized that they were going to kill him?"

Aguirre half smiled. "The gloomier the better, no?"

He continued: "When they went after him publicly. Bureaucrats, politicians allied with the mafia. They tore him down with news stories, anonymous letters. Preparing the terrain. That worried him more than the threats. He said it was a fatal combination: He was dangerous but vulnerable, because he had become isolated. That's what they want to do to us, Araceli. This visit to the Colonel will make it worse."

"Leo," she said sweetly. She put her hand on his. "Don't you think it's an exercise of lunatics, trying to calculate the danger? If we do this, it's *x* amount dangerous. If we don't do that, *y* amount of danger. We do what we do and that's that. Nothing has stopped us so far."

"No one wants to stop," Méndez said. He leaned back, watching a slow-motion replay on the television above the bar: A forward for the Mexican national soccer team attempted an elegant back-to-the-goal scissors kick, his mane of hair swirling. The bodyguards at the bar hooted sorrowfully. A narrow miss.

"At least it's good to hear you talk for once, unburden yourself," Aguirre said. "I am probably more worried about you than you are about me. I talked to Estela last night."

At the mention of his wife's name, Méndez's tone grew cold. "Estela."

"That's right." Her smile was defiant. "She called me. She's worried too."

"She called you."

"My God, Leo, you practically threw her and Juancito out of Tijuana. You lined up the job for her at Berkeley, totally clandestine. And you forced her to take it."

He kept watching the soccer footage. He said, "It was for their own good. It was absolutely impossible for them here. Going everywhere with bodyguards, to school, the supermarket. And it's an excellent opportunity for her."

"She doesn't see it like that."

"All I can tell you is, I am finally able to concentrate for the first time since I took this job. I know they are living a safe, normal, civilized life. Far from here."

Aguirre lit another cigarette.

"I suppose everyone deals with the danger in different ways," she said. "But you have banished your family. That doesn't make their life normal or civilized. You have systematically cut yourself off from everyone and everything. Except the Diogenes Group. You talk about the mafias trying to isolate us. You don't need any help."

"I haven't cut myself off from you."

"Because I am essential to your work."

"I see." Méndez's mouth tightened. "And how do you deal with it, if I may ask?"

"I live my life, for God's sake." She brandished the cigarette. "Why let them control your existence? I have lunch with my husband whenever I can. I spend time with my kids. I certainly don't—"

"Excuse me, but now that you mention it, I meant to tell you I don't think it's wise to bring Elena and Amalia to the office, not with those protester thugs around—"

"Leobardo, you are really impossible!"

"Enough," he said. "This unburdening that you like so much is the modern disease. What's your point?"

"Promise me you'll call your wife and have a real conversation with her. All right?"

"Done."

They talked about their plan for the coming week, the logistics of coaxing the Colonel into testifying before a prosecutor as he had promised. Méndez raised a hand as the television filled with images of a bloodied boxer against the ropes, warding off punches.

"Wait," he said. "That's the fight from Wednesday. Junior made an appearance."

Méndez asked the owner to turn up the sound. There were fans booing, scuffles with helmeted police in a boxing ring, hurled coins tracing shiny arcs through smoke and floodlights. The top-billed match of the Wednesday-night fights at Multiglobo Arena had ended in favor of the champion, infuriating partisans of the challenger. He appeared to have outfought the champion, a long-armed Mexican-American managed by Junior Ruiz Caballero's company. The champion's fans had counterattacked with bottles and folding chairs.

The television showed a crowded hallway, the camera advancing among police, rich kids, sultry women in fight-night finery. Junior Ruiz Caballero appeared, turning back from a doorway to attend to a couple of microphones poked at him between hulking backs. With Junior were two American Las Vegas types in double-breasted suits and a thick-necked African-American prizefighter.

Junior was unshaven and deeply tanned, as usual. He wore a two-toned leather jacket that looked like something out of a music video. The gossip magazines portrayed Junior as a swashbuckling ladies' man; he was good-looking in a baby-faced, degenerate sort of way. He appeared to be going through one of his bloated phases.

Junior Ruiz Caballero grinned hugely over his shoulder at the female reporter.

"We always give the people what they want, that's what show business is all about," he said, using the English phrase. "The people want a rematch, we'll give them a rematch. The people want drama. We'll give them drama."

5

BEFORE HIS PURSUIT OF Pulpo a month earlier, Pescatore had only crossed twice into Tijuana.

The first time was during a trip to San Diego that was part of the nineteen-week training course at the U.S. Border Patrol academy. Near the end of the course, when the trainees had been assigned to stations, The Patrol flew them to their sectors to see the reality waiting beyond the gauntlet of Spanish classes, arcane immigration laws and role-playing exercises with Latino actors impersonating suspects. Pescatore and three other rookies walked into Tijuana, had a drink in the first tourist bar they found and went right back, heads down, sweating profusely, pretending they were not worried about getting lynched if someone realized they were U.S. feds.

The second crossing was with Garrison, Dillard and Macías before Christmas. They got hammered in a noisy basement club featuring raunchy dancers and bartenders blowing whistles. A couple of hard-ass-looking Mexicans showed up and slammed drinks with the agents. Garrison explained that they were informants from his days on The Patrol's antismuggling investigative unit: They were called *madrinas* (godmothers) or *aspirinas* (aspiring cops). The Mexican police used them as all-purpose ass-kickers, snitches and flunkies.

The main thing Pescatore remembered from that night was an Indian woman, one of the street vendors known as Marias, who had knocked on the window of Garrison's Jeep Cherokee on the way back to San Diego. The Saturday-night line of cars waiting to be inspected at the San Ysidro Port of Entry wound for a mile over ramps and under bridges. Pescatore dozed in the backseat, his head against the glass. He awoke to see a dark, rutted face framed by a shawl. The old woman extended a fistful of black strings at him. Lowering the window, he saw they were small braided crucifixes made entirely of thread, with a tiny red bead embedded in the center of the cross. A single thread served as the short necklace.

"You gonna buy one?" Garrison glanced over his shoulder disapprovingly. "That's what the TJ jailbirds wear. You know where those crosses got started? The joint. The convicts pulled thread out of their clothes to make 'em."

"Yeah, well, I think they're cool," Pescatore mumbled, handing her a dollar.

"*Que Dios le bendiga, mi hijo,*" the woman said.

At home, he hung the crucifix from a tack stuck in the cork message board on his refrigerator. And there it had remained.

Until this evening. Pescatore put on a blue denim shirt, black khaki slacks, black Timberland boots and his bomber jacket. He loaded and shoulder-holstered his Glock. He gathered up his wallet and badge and cell phone, took a deep breath and turned off a Los Lonely Boys disc as he headed for the door.

But he stopped at the refrigerator, caught up by the crucifix. He removed it from the tack. He went into the bathroom. He faced the mirror. He lifted the necklace up over his head, positioned it around his neck, and squared the cross on his chest inside his shirt. It was the closest he had come to a religious act in years. There was something about that TJ jailbird cross, about that spectral old lady wreathed in exhaust fumes, that stirred his deepest superstitions. He was going to need all the luck he could get.

Because now he was riding shotgun in the Cherokee. Garrison drove. Dillard sat in back chewing bubble gum. They were off duty, rolling south on Interstate 5 behind a Ford van loaded with a shipment of guns that Garrison had arranged to smuggle into Tijuana. M-16s, .45 automatics, Tek-9s: a smorgasbord of weaponry. A Mexican youth whom Pescatore had never met was driving the van up ahead.

"You all right there, buddy?" Garrison asked. He slowed as the big MEXICO sign above the customs booths of the San Ysidro Port of Entry approached.

"Slow motion," Pescatore said.

Isabel Puente was pleased with his work. His apparent success at invading the Zona Norte and getting away with it had boosted his status with Garrison. They were partying together regularly. He was gathering information on how Garrison furnished intelligence on border defenses to smugglers. He had also found out about a home in Imperial Beach that was a safe house for drugs and stolen goods. And a clandestine first-aid station, as he learned one night when Garrison got carried away whacking a combative migrant over the head with his baton near Stewart's Bridge. Pescatore had accompanied Garrison and the prisoner to the house on a semirural road. A robust cigarette-smoking blonde in a bathrobe answered the door. She was unfazed by the fact that it was past midnight and one of her guests was bleeding profusely. She prepared coffee for the agents. Then she bathed, stitched and bandaged the prisoner's wounds, squinting over a cigarette as she worked.

"It was tripped out," Pescatore told Isabel Puente later during a debriefing at the café in La Jolla. "She must be a nurse or something. We drove this alien back to The Line with his head all stitched up. Garrison brings him to a gap in the fence, tells him to keep his mouth shut. He gives him a little shove back into Mexico. And that was that."

Nonetheless, Pescatore hoped Garrison knew what he was

doing when it came to smuggling a vanload of guns into Tijuana. Getting caught with your service firearm alone meant Mexican federal charges and a go-directly-to-jail card.

The van in front of them was next in line at a Mexican inspection booth. Garrison had said that everything was under control. He had told Pescatore to get with the program and not to worry. But now Garrison looked as if he were about to rip the steering wheel out of the dashboard.

"Where's my guy," Garrison growled.

The blue-shirted Mexican customs inspector was apparently not the guy Garrison had in mind. Pescatore tensed. Entering Tijuana was supposed to be easier than leaving. But Mexican authorities had stepped up their searches of southbound traffic looking for guns, stolen vehicles and trunkloads of drug profits. The last went to money houses that the drug lords crammed floor to ceiling with cash they couldn't spend fast enough.

"Where's my guy, where's my guy," Garrison said.

The van slid forward over the international line. The Mexican inspector stepped to the driver's window, looking imperious. Pescatore hooked his fingers into his door handle, though he knew his stock would drop in a hurry if he bailed and bolted.

Then a blue-shirted supervisor appeared, waving off the inspector. The van jumped forward with a lurch that made Pescatore cringe. Garrison relaxed his strangler's grip on the wheel. Out of the right side of his mouth, he said, "Way too close, Nacho, you shitbrain." Garrison nodded gravely as the Cherokee rolled alongside the supervisor. Pescatore recognized him from a party at Garrison's house.

"*Pásale,*" the supervisor said, touching the brim of his cap in a two-fingered salute.

A series of ramps emptied into a tree-lined boulevard. They passed boxlike office buildings, a McDonald's decorated by clumps of balloons, a giant, ball-shaped, concrete construction that housed the Omnimax theater of the Tijuana Cultural

Center. The first intersection was a crowded traffic circle with a grass plaza in the center containing an abstract statue of what looked like tall wooden spikes. Teenage street performers in clown makeup juggled red balls and stood on one another's shoulders in the traffic during the red light. Three dogs trotted in the crosswalk, single file, as if they had waited for the light to change.

"Eight twenty-five," Garrison said. "Right on time."

He pulled ahead of the van and entered the half-deserted parking lot of a shopping center. Garrison cruised around to a side of the mall near a row of apartment buildings. He drove to the center of the lot and pulled into a slot about twenty feet from a red Suburban. He flashed his headlights. The Suburban responded in kind.

"Uh, ain't we real out in the open?" Pescatore asked, thinking that it was appropriate to come off as nervous. Which he was.

"If you're worried about the *judiciales,* don't be," Garrison said. "They got the perimeter for us."

Garrison pointed out the plainclothes state cops in an Impala at one end of the parking lot and in a Crown Victoria at the other. I guess downtown TJ is as good as anyplace to do an arms deal if you've got the police standing guard, Pescatore thought.

Dillard leaned over the seat between Garrison and Pescatore. His whitish-blond hair was wet-combed, accentuating his large ears. He popped a bubble.

"Here come them old boys," Dillard said.

A car parked alongside the Suburban. It was a vintage, navy-blue Buick Regal with a sunroof and a lot of chrome. Five men got out.

"Buffalo," Garrison said. "Let's take care of business, gentlemen."

"He a cop too?" Pescatore asked.

Garrison turned. "What's going on with the questions, Valentine? He look like a cop to you?"

"It's kinda hard to tell around here."

"Listen: You're on a need-to-know basis. All you need to know is, he's not a cop. He's Murder Incorporated."

The man called Buffalo was shorter than the Border Patrol supervisor, but otherwise just as big. And while Garrison had a stiff Frankenstein-monster quality, the newcomer seemed not only rock-muscled but agile, like a linebacker, like he could chase you down and finish you off in a heartbeat. Buffalo looked as if he had done hard prison time and was ready to do more. His steely "How you doin'" was pure Southern California *barrio.*

Three of the men with Buffalo were not Mexican. The one he introduced as Mr. Abbas was bald on top, long nose, neat black beard. His outfit was casual-sharp: a beige sport jacket, pleated slacks and loafers with no socks. His accent was British mixed with something else. Pescatore pegged him for Iranian or Arab. Behind him were two muscle guys: light-skinned, foreign-looking blacks with athletic builds, loose-armed in sleeveless black canvas vests, gold chains glittering on their chests. They were cousins or brothers; they had the same blunt profiles, short curls and amused gray eyes. Buffalo introduced them as Moze and Tchai.

The youthful driver stood back near the door of the Regal: a squat, long-haired Mexican in a T-shirt that was too tight for him. He hunched his shoulders and seemed unsure of what to do with his hands. His narrow *mestizo* eyes settled suddenly on Pescatore, who looked away.

"All set?" Buffalo said. He and Garrison stood face-to-face with their respective partners arranged behind them; the two bruisers were running the show. There were men in the Suburban, but they did not move.

"Affirmative," Garrison said in a deferential voice that Pescatore had never heard out of his mouth before. "The gentlemen wanna check the material before we go?"

"In a minute."

Buffalo padded toward the brown van. Garrison opened the sliding door on the side for him. They climbed in among crates.

Pescatore looked up and met the intent stare of the driver by the Regal.

Buffalo climbed back out. He nodded at Abbas. The three foreigners joined Garrison inside the van. They poked at the crates—noises of wood, metal, indistinct voices.

The thickset driver by the Regal kept eyeballing Pescatore, who didn't know whether to ignore him or not.

Buffalo walked back from the van to the Regal, got in and emerged carrying a small Adidas bag. The driver put a hand on Buffalo's arm. They whispered for a long minute. Both Buffalo and the driver now stared at Pescatore.

Pescatore glanced at Dillard, a gum-chewing statue next to him on the asphalt. Dillard had noticed the surreptitious conversation as well. Pescatore remembered Isabel Puente's reference to a jailhouse weightlifter nicknamed Buffalo. He thought: What the hell is going on with these guys?

Buffalo walked back to the Ford van and leaned in to pass the Adidas bag to Garrison. Buffalo assumed a spread-legged sentry stance by the van a few feet from Pescatore, hands folded over his belt buckle. He was about forty. He had carefully groomed hair with a bit of a wave to it, a punch-flattened nose, a coal-black mustache that turned down below the corners of his mouth. A tattooed Aztec warrior image crept out of the collar of his leather jacket along his broad neck. Pescatore spotted another tattoo, intermittently visible in the dim parking lot: a teardrop below the corner of the left eye.

Pescatore did not know where to look. It was a balmy night and a soft breeze was blowing, but he felt sweat collect on his forehead.

"'Scuse me," Buffalo said. And then: "Homes. I'm talkin' to you."

Pescatore reluctantly swiveled his head. "Huh?"

"You work the station over by Border State Park, right?"

The voice was low, thuggish, surprisingly mellow. Dillard hammered at his gum, perplexed. Pescatore wondered if there was a reason he should not answer. Buffalo and the others certainly knew he was a Border Patrol agent. He grunted, "Uh-huh."

"My cousin, Rufino, he recognized you."

The young driver perked up at the mention of his name. From across the fifteen feet that separated them, the driver gave Pescatore a nod and, of all things, a sheepish thumbs-up.

His grin made strange by the teardrop tattoo, Buffalo said: "Rufino thinks you're this Border Patrol agent that saved his ass last year when he came up from Guanajuato. He crossed during the floods. Fell in the water, damn near drowned. But you fished him out. It was all he could talk about when he finally made it up to L.A. He's from the *rancho,* you know, he was like: '*Me salvó la vida, fue un milagro del cielo!*'"—Buffalo imitated a singsong border-brother accent—"this and that. Said you gave him ten bucks too. He wouldn't stop carryin' on about it."

Rufino's hair had been shorter then, but Pescatore recognized him. He remembered the incident in Border Field State Park: While a trainee, he had chased the youth headlong into a pool of polluted black water formed by flood runoff from Tijuana. Rufino had swallowed the toxic water and had a violent reaction, throwing up everything inside him, spewing vomit from his mouth and nose. His thrashing put him in theoretical danger of drowning, though the water was only neck high. An agent warned Pescatore to stay out of that pool of poisoned shit. But in he plunged, retching as the burnt-rubber-and-sewer smell slammed his nostrils, and hauled out Rufino. Pescatore had slipped his prisoner the cash later, back at IB station, when both of them were waiting to be tested for amebic dysentery and other exotic ailments. The Mexican had kept thanking him the whole time.

"Oh yeah," Pescatore said, weak-legged with relief, meeting Buffalo's steady gaze at last. He saw the resemblance: Buffalo and Rufino both had dark eyes that seemed to have been chiseled over high cheekbones. "I remember. That water out there in the park is nasty. You aspirate that, it can fuck you up. I'm just glad I was around."

"Rufino is too, *ese,*" Buffalo chuckled. "Dumbass, I told him if he'd called me I woulda met him in Tijuana, brought him up first class, no problem. But he couldn't find me and got anxious, hadda do it his way."

Buffalo extended a hand as if they had not been introduced and gave Pescatore a two-stage street handshake. "My name's Omar. They call me Buffalo."

"I'm Valentín."

"Nice to meet you. Appreciate what you did for my cousin." Buffalo ducked his head discreetly and murmured, "He's still a youngster. And a *naco,* when you get right down to it. But hey: He's family, right? Gotta take care of him. I got him a *jale,* he does some driving for me, this and that. Least he ain't scared of workin'."

Pescatore smiled enthusiastically, not wanting to blow it with any kind of comment. Garrison climbed out of the van. He looked perplexed by the sudden chumminess between Pescatore and Buffalo.

"Omar, you keep an eye on my crazy welterweight buddy over there," Garrison rumbled.

"Good with his hands, huh?" Buffalo said. "Yeah, me and Valentín was just shootin' the shit a little."

Garrison suggested they get going and check out the merchandise. His stare mixed annoyance and curiosity. Even Mr. Super-Mercenary Garrison gets all frisky around this guy, Pescatore thought. You gotta figure Buffalo is bad as they come.

"It took half an hour to get out there," Pescatore told Isabel Puente. "The road to Tecate. There's a turnoff in the mountains takes you to the ranch. The shooting range is in a complex behind the ranch house. They got a soccer field, tennis courts, a zoo. Lit up like the Padres' stadium."

"Garrison knew his way around?"

"Like he owned the place. It must be where he trains them. Him and Buffalo did most of the shooting. The Egyptian tested out a few guns, the fancy machine pistols and whatnot."

"Do we know he's Egyptian, Valentine?" Isabel asked, nibbling her pen, leaning over her notebook.

"Whatever he is. With the black guys he spoke Portuguese. I could tell right away Moze and Tchai weren't American. All they said the whole time was '*Tudo bem, tudo bem.*'"

"Brazilians."

"Sure. They reminded me of the Brazilians we been catching at IB, but tougher. The old-time journeymen say that's like catching a Martian. They never saw Brazilian aliens before."

"Anything else referring to Brazil? Or Paraguay? Did Garrison say where they were from?"

"Nope. The older boss-guy, Mr. Abbas, he spoke pretty good English."

"How did it work? The van with the weapons stayed at the ranch?"

"Yep. Sounded to me like that was just a sample, Garrison has plenty more guns if they want."

"Stolen from the military base up north."

"I couldn't tell you for sure, but I know he's got contacts there. Hey, the sandwiches are ready, I'll get them. Remember, it's my treat today."

It was the day after the gunrunning expedition. For security reasons, Puente had decided to choose a new meeting place to replace the café in La Jolla. Pescatore had insisted on picking it. She vetoed Little Italy because it was too close to the Federal Building. They settled on an Italian deli in Encinitas, a placid beach town on an idyllic stretch of coast. There were just a few tables in a side room half-hidden behind grocery shelves, an appropriately discreet setup.

"Now, let me tell you something," Pescatore said, returning to the table with a well-stocked tray. "This is a bona fide old-school sandwich."

Puente, who had her hair pulled back and sunglasses propped on her head, rolled her eyes and said, "Oh, here we go."

"No, really, you might know about fried bananas and everything, but I'm the expert on ginzo food. This joint and Little Italy are the only places in San Diego County where you can get a decent sandwich. See how fresh the bread is? You don't need no mayonnaise or junk on good Italian bread like that. And the mortadella: It's the real thing, not some nasty plastic Oscar Mayer mutant lunchmeat. What's so funny?"

"You never stop eating, Valentine. I don't understand why you aren't fat as a house. I guess it's because you're young."

"What are you, Granma Isabel?"

"Young-*er,* I meant."

"You're what, a couple years older than me."

"There's a difference between twenty-five and around thirty. Hey Valentine, this is pretty good."

"Told you. Stick with me, baby, I promise you won't starve."

They grinned at each other. He looked forward to every debriefing as if it were a date. The relationship felt like an affair: laughing furtively, whispering, watching over their shoulders. She appeared to enjoy herself, but no doubt that was the way a female handler was supposed to treat a male informant.

"I'm still getting used to the idea that you pulled a thorn out of Omar Mendoza's paw," she said. "His cousin's paw, anyway."

"Garrison didn't say much 'cause he likes to be the big boss, but you could tell he was surprised about that."

"It works out well for us," she said. "You're really doing good."

"I feel good. You were right, it's easier dealing with Garrison now that I'm spying on him."

"You have a knack for undercover work."

"Yeah? I guess I always felt like I was impersonating a Border Patrol agent in the first place."

Isabel laughed. Pescatore felt a charge of exhilaration.

"When Buffalo and Rufino were whispering and everything, I thought I was history," he said. "I thought that humongous throwdown jailbird was gonna march over and crush my skull. But he totally changed when we got to talking. At the ranch he let me shoot this laser-sight pistol. The Buffalo seems pretty cool to me."

"Uh-huh. Remind me to show you his sheet. He started killing people in middle school. He was in a gang in the worst housing project in the San Fernando Valley. The Gardens. Hasn't stopped since. Be really, really careful, Valentine."

Pescatore spent the rest of the lunch telling Puente about the evening's activities in detail. He watched her fill her notebook with careful ornate scribbles, her mouth half-open in concentration. Her legs were tucked up under her, smooth muscles bunched in a short crimson skirt.

"If this was Taylor Street in the summer, now we could walk over to Mario's Italian Ice, sit on a stoop and have a couple of lemonades," Pescatore sighed, digging caffeinated granules of sugar out of his espresso cup. "But around here they never heard of Italian ice. And you'd probably have to drive fifty miles for it."

"You've got a serious case of homesickness," Puente said, pointing the pen at him like a teacher.

"I guess home always seems better when you're far away," Pescatore said, running a hand through his curls.

"I get the idea your neighborhood wasn't that great."

"Yeah. The Italians and the Mexicans and the blacks were always brawling. A three-way hatefest. For me, not hanging with any one group was good sometimes. But other times it sucked. I had to stay in the house or run like hell. I got good at running."

"And boxing?"

"You know about the boxing?"

Puente responded with a look that said "Silly Question."

"I boxed a little. I wasn't exactly great. What about you, Isabel? You never get homesick? You don't go someplace reminds you of Miami?"

Puente smiled. "This is classified, Valentine. I go to a Cuban restaurant on Morena Boulevard. A family place. They treat me like a queen. I don't order, they just give me whatever they think I'll like."

"Sounds great. When we going there?"

"I never take anybody there."

"So I guess when you take me, that'd be a big step, huh?" He said it fast and breezy, caught up in the moment.

"Meaning what?"

"Meaning I hope we go there, that's all." He had decided it was ridiculous not to give it a shot. What was she going to do, fire him? He said: "We could even not talk about work, for once. We could spend the whole night not talking about work."

"Valentine." They stared at each other, both leaning on their elbows. "You're not getting distracted from your assignment, are you?"

"No way. But I'm not gonna hide my feelings, Isabel."

She tilted her head warily.

"Really," she said.

"Can't help it." He grinned apologetically. "That's the way it is."

"I'm not going to hide the way I feel either," she said, her smile disappearing. "Mainly I feel worried. You're my best informant and you're infiltrating this organization better than I thought you would. The last thing we want is distractions. Understand? The better you do, the more dangerous it gets."

At roll call at the Imperial Beach station the following Sunday afternoon, the field operations supervisor and the assistant station chief went through a typical litany: a new overtime policy, more sniper threats, a tip about backpackers who were paying their coyotes by carrying marijuana. The bosses outlined procedures for using on-call interpreters of exotic languages—Mandarin, Arabic—who had been hired to handle all the OTMs. Intel reports said the smugglers had warehouses in Tijuana full of hundreds of aliens from far-off places waiting to cross. And keep the agents in report-writing hell.

Pescatore half listened as they ended the briefing with an alert for three inmates who had escaped hours earlier from the penitentiary in Tijuana during a shoot-out that left five dead. One of the fugitives was the former chief of the state police in Tijuana, the supervisor said: Regino Astorga. Aka the Colonel.

By the time Pescatore registered the name, the agents were getting up from the tables and heading out into the warm and rainy evening. Pescatore knew that Isabel Puente was interested in the Colonel. She was helping her secretive Mexican cop friends on an investigation related to him. But that was all she had told him.

Garrison met Pescatore, Dillard and Macías for a dinner break at Adalberto's, a hole-in-the-wall taco place in San Ysidro. Usually, Garrison high-fived, bullshitted and cheerfully terrorized every Mexican in the place, employee or customer, Americanized or border brother. But tonight he slumped, silent and ornery, next to Dillard in the scarred wooden booth.

"We got an urgent thing tonight," Garrison said. "I need all three of you. Full operational mode."

Garrison ordered them to meet at the parking lot overlooking the beach in Border Field State Park. As the appointed time approached, Pescatore heard Garrison on the radio deploying agents to the east and north. Pescatore assumed he was clearing the way for whatever he had cooking at the beach.

A light steady rain fell as Pescatore drove into Border Field State Park. He waved at a park ranger in a yellow slicker who sat in a guardhouse by the entrance. The road slanted southwest through a grassy field. Sheer hills topped by mansions with satellite dishes and cupolas, the exclusive Playas de Tijuana neighborhood with its beach-and-border view, marked the international line. The rain and mist blurred the bowl-shaped hulk of Tijuana's seaside bullring in the distance. Three Patrol Wranglers were parked in the lot overlooking the southwestern corner of the border.

When Pescatore had arrived in the San Diego sector, a retired agent had told him about what the beach was like in the years before the border fence. On sunny weekends, the retired agent had explained, an unspoken agreement between The Patrol and the beachgoers caused the border to temporarily disappear. Extended families arrived in contingents, some from San Diego and some from Tijuana. They camped out on blankets and towels. Kids chased soccer balls in the surf. Vendors carried Styrofoam coolers and pushed ice cream carts. Musical trios known as *conjuntos* lugged instruments across the sand to perform serenades. All of them breaching the unmarked international line as Border Patrol agents lounged in the parking lot above the beach.

The agents sunned themselves, propped on their vehicle hoods in wraparound dark glasses. They permitted the foot traffic between First and Third worlds as long as no one strayed off the sand or too far north. It was a peaceful scene. Only on rare occasions did some lowlife *cholo* ruin the mood by removing his shirt, hoisting a boogie board over his shoulder as camouflage, and trying to sneak toward downtown San Diego, which rose out of the Pacific like an apparition in the distance.

But then the U.S. Army had constructed a specially engineered metal fence at the state park. The fence extended down the dune, across the sand and several hundred yards into the ocean. And it put an end to transborder weekends at the beach forever more.

Pescatore climbed into Garrison's Wrangler with Dillard and Macías. Garrison was on the phone and smoking furiously. Garrison said the name Mauro and wrapped up the conversation.

"Listen up, gentlemen," Garrison said, peering south through the rivulets on the windshield. "You know this Colonel Astorga that busted out of the penitentiary in TJ? Well, he's coming across in a couple minutes. We're giving him a escort north."

"Here?" asked Macías, who was in his early twenties and had a crew cut. "Be less fuss to have him come through one of our lanes at the port of entry, wouldn't it?"

"This guy's all over the news," Garrison said. "It's too hot for him to show up at San Ysidro or Otay. Macías, I want you out by the park entrance. Anybody shows up, you shoo 'em off. Me and Valentine and Dillard are gonna meet our guy. Door-to-door service."

Garrison said he planned to stash the Colonel at the safe house in Imperial Beach until the end of the shift. Then they would give him a ride north past the Border Patrol freeway checkpoint at San Clemente. Somebody else would take over from there.

Macías departed. Garrison, Pescatore and Dillard sat in the Wrangler listening to the rain on the roof. Pescatore's hand gripped the belt sheath holding his cell phone. He cursed himself for not having called Isabel Puente when he had had the chance. He had resisted his initial instinct that Garrison's "urgent thing" involved the Colonel. It had seemed too brazen, too risky.

Garrison checked his watch.

"Ready?" he said.

His phone rang again. Pescatore slumped, restless, exhaling forcefully. He watched Garrison. The supervisor closed his eyes momentarily as he listened. He muttered one word into the phone: "OK."

Garrison closed the phone and clipped it to his belt. He did not look at Pescatore or Dillard.

"You guys get going down there in Valentine's vehicle," Garrison said. "The Colonel is about five seven, one seventy-five, late fifties. Wearing a fatigue-type jacket and a Pittsburgh Pirates cap. He's with a subject in a Padres cap named Rico. You just put 'em in the vehicle. I'll cover you from my little command post up here, buddy."

His door open, water hitting his sleeve, Pescatore started to ask Garrison where the third escapee was and, more important, why Garrison wasn't coming down to the beach. But as he studied the bulging gray eyes, the controlled savagery with which the supervisor stubbed out his cigarette, Pescatore understood. He's scared, Pescatore thought. That's why he's not taking the lead, shaking the Colonel's hand, the big-shot bullshit. It doesn't make sense—unless somebody just told him it's not such a hot idea to get close to the Colonel right this minute. And if he's scared, I'm scared.

Pescatore steered his Wrangler down a sandy ridge to the beach. Dillard popped bubbles next to him. Pescatore drove slowly south across the sand. He stopped about a hundred feet from The Line. There were fuzzy lights along the fence on the Tijuana side, the shadow of the bullring beyond. The fence was dark and devoid of movement. Rain usually thinned the gathering of migrants and vendors on the beach.

The Colonel was supposed to come through a new hole in the fence. The gap was about the size of a doorway. Floods and erosion had weakened the support of one of the metal panels during the winter rains, and smugglers had knocked it down.

Pescatore glanced back up to his left. He saw Garrison's vehicle over the low stone wall of the parking lot atop the bluff. Pescatore intended to sit in the Wrangler until the Colonel came to him.

"They're waitin' on ya," Garrison said over the radio. "You gotta meet 'em on foot. That's the arrangement."

Dillard got out. Reluctantly, Pescatore followed suit. Rain pattered on the brim of his uniform cap. The moon-striped surf sloshed and crackled on his right.

Stepping clear of the Wrangler, Pescatore drew his gun. He held it next to his leg. It made him feel better.

They walked slowly, Dillard about fifteen feet to his right.

"What're you doin' with your gun out?" Dillard snapped. "You're gonna spook them old boys."

"Fuck them old boys," Pescatore hissed, his eyes never leaving the gap in the fence. "I'm takin' appropriate precautions."

The certainty that something terrible was about to happen settled over him. He felt utterly focused. He stopped, knees slightly bent.

Shadows filled the gap in the fence. Two men, both wearing baseball caps, entered U.S. territory. They made their way down the sand slope to the beach. A third shadow remained in the gap.

The tall one in the Padres cap, Rico, raised a hand in greeting. A coat flapped around him. Pescatore heard Dillard advise Garrison over his radio. Pescatore could see the black *P* on the yellow background of a Pittsburgh Pirates cap taking shape in the gloom, the hard squarish face of the shorter man beneath it. The Colonel. Both of the men in caps had their hands open and extended to their sides as they walked.

A raindrop slid along Pescatore's cheek. Shifting his gaze back and forth from the approaching duo to the fence, he saw the third man make a move.

Pescatore went into a crouch, causing the Colonel and his sidekick to falter. Pescatore started to shout a warning. Gunshots exploded in the gap at the fence.

Multiple impacts buckled the Colonel. He said, "*Ay.*" He pitched forward onto his belly.

Pescatore shouted: "Ten-ten! Shots fired, shots fired!"

He saw Dillard draw his gun, wild and disoriented, and yell at Rico, who had extracted a big revolver from the folds of his coat. Rico was next to the fallen Colonel, whirling back and forth between the agents and the shooter at the fence. When Rico saw Dillard point his gun in his general direction, he sank down on one knee in a practiced and fluid motion. He shot Dillard in the face.

Rico thought it was a double-cross; Pescatore was next. Pescatore bounded sideways to his right, still crouching. He aimed with both hands as he moved.

It could have been the fog, sheer concentration, the spotlights above, a supernatural experience. Whatever the reason, the gunman on one knee seemed to emanate a bright white glow, a halo that caught fire as Pescatore capped off rounds, pumping bullets into him, the shots punching Rico back and down into the sand.

A volley rang out from the fence. Pescatore sprinted, dropped and rolled for the shelter of the Wrangler. He felt bullets kick up sand around him. He wondered if the wetness on his chest and back and arms was rain or blood or both. He rolled interminably, convinced that he was dead. He clung desperately to his gun. He rolled through fragments of memories and images and regrets. He came to a stop against a tire of the Wrangler.

He slithered around behind the tire, halfway under the vehicle. There was sand in his mouth. His ears roared with the shots and his own gasping breath. He sighted over his Glock. He sighted through gunsmoke and rain on Dillard's body, Rico's body, a Pirates cap lying in the sand. He sighted on the bareheaded, fleeing figure of the Colonel.

The Colonel was on his feet again, tottering south. He was heading, insanely enough, toward the very spot where the gunman had fired on him. There were no more shots, no sign of the gunman.

The Colonel went down heavily. He struggled back up. He turned in drunken circles. He had a pistol in his hand now, and he pointed it this way and that. He crawled slowly up the embankment. He staggered back through the hole in the fence from which he had come.

Then came a single, final shot. And the sound of a vehicle departing on the other side of the fence. And the waves and the rain.

Part Two

THE OTHER PATROL

6

THE COLONEL LAY FACEDOWN a few yards south of the gap in the border fence.

Peppered by flashlight beams, the corpse's torso was contorted. An arm was stretched forward, a leg bent double, as if he had expired while trying to swim over the sand. An object protruded from the top of a snakeskin boot: an extra ammunition clip for the Makarov automatic pistol clutched in his right hand. The back of his jacket was stitched with half a dozen bullet holes.

Méndez watched Mauro Fernández Rochetti in action on the other side of the corpse. The silver-haired homicide chief stood beneath an umbrella held for him by his driver, a meaty-faced cop in a cowboy hat known as Chancho. Fernández Rochetti had his two-way radio near his ear, alternately listening to it and tapping the antenna pensively against his shoulder. He rocked forward, his sharp-toed black shoes digging into the sand. His lips puckered as detectives came up to him, delivered terse reports, then returned to their inspection of the crime scene. Which they, as was the custom of the state police homicide squad when it suited them, had done their best to tromp all over.

The deaths of the Colonel, his sidekick Rico, and a U.S. Border Patrol agent had drawn a swarm of international law enforcement. Representing Mexico were the state police, state prosecutors, the Diogenes Group, the federal police, the municipal police and federal immigration officers. The dark van sitting in the cul-de-sac above the beach belonged to Mexico's domestic espionage agency.

In years past, the Mexican Army would have also shown up. But the national coalition government that was in power as a result of the political crisis had withdrawn the armed forces from their frontline role in the drug wars. Some leaders of the coalition said that the military campaign against the cartels had degenerated into brutality and corruption. Some worried, privately, that the military had done too good a job pursuing drug lords and the politicians who protected them. Most political leaders agreed that the presence of troops on the streets did not send the right message at a time of instability.

Nonetheless, the deployment of multiple agencies made it clear that the border shoot-out was a big deal. As did the turnout on the U.S. side. The Border Patrol brass had responded, accompanied by riot-equipped agents of BORTAC, the Patrol's tactical unit. The San Diego Police were there to investigate the homicides. Inspector General agents were there to investigate the conduct of the Border Patrol. The FBI was there on general principle, accompanied by a deputy chief of the U.S. Attorney's office in San Diego. The beach north and south of the fence was a maze of yellow tape, four-wheel-drive vehicles and officers holding flashlights.

"So many bloodhounds," Méndez said to no one in particular.

The Tijuana homicide squad had detained two men. The prisoners sat on the hull of an upside-down rowboat near a cement outhouse. Their hands were cuffed behind them. They looked like migrants or transborder vagrants, one in a ski cap and ratty sweater, the other obscured by unkempt hair. The prisoners bent forward, their heads almost between their knees. Two homicide detectives stood behind them smoking cigarettes and talking about Porfirio Gibson's latest TV show. Whenever a prisoner straightened a bit, the younger detective, who wore a bulletproof vest over an Oakland Raiders sweatshirt, lowered his voice an octave, snarled "Head *down, puto,*" and returned to the conversation without missing a beat.

Méndez shook his head. He approached Porthos. Méndez's deputy had worked for the state homicide squad for five years. He had finally gotten sick of being turned down for promotions while turning down bribes, so he had defected to the Diogenes Group.

"What do you think?" Méndez asked.

His mountainous back toward the homicide detectives, Porthos talked through his teeth. Rain dripped off his beard.

"If I believe my ex-comrades, the Colonel and Rico shot it out with the Border Patrol and lost."

"It doesn't make sense to you," Méndez said.

"Not entirely."

"You wonder how the Border Patrol managed to shoot him seven times exclusively in the back."

"For example."

"You wonder why the Colonel didn't just surrender. He could have asked for political asylum. And he wanted to cut a deal with the *gabachos.*"

"Ah, Licenciado, now you are getting too political for me."

"And the so-called suspects?"

"Please, Licenciado. A pair of sad little drunks who were waiting out the rain with a bottle. This way Fernández Rochetti can tell the press that suspects are being questioned."

"Standard procedure, eh?"

"The script for this one is already written. The neighbors in the apartments near the bullring told us the homicide squad arrived before the shooting was over."

"A Mauro Fernández Rochetti Production."

"Totally."

The homicide squad had automatic jurisdiction because murder was a state crime. Méndez would try to elbow his way into the case. But the crucial investigative momentum was on the side of Mauro Fernández Rochetti, a master at shaping evidence to the version of the facts he felt appropriate.

Looking up into Méndez's stare, the homicide commander raised bushy eyebrows in greeting.

And now for some hostile banalities, Méndez said to himself. He made his way around the corpse, wet sand seeping into his shoes.

"Good evening, Commander," Méndez said.

"Good evening, Licenciado." Fernández Rochetti sounded wary. "How can I help you?"

"Well, one of our investigations is involved. We'll need a complete report from you."

"Of course," Fernández Rochetti said, smiling not quite enough for his tongue to emerge from its lair. "You were so interested in the Colonel."

Méndez glanced at Chancho. The cop in the cowboy hat held the umbrella over his chief with stolid determination, as if demonstrating proper umbrella-holding technique.

"You've got everything all figured out already, I suppose?" Méndez said, trying to mimic Fernández Rochetti's amiable scorn.

"It seems pretty clear," Fernández Rochetti said. "The Colonel got desperate."

"I never thought of the Colonel that way."

"The Colonel was not as smart as he thought. He realized how foolish he had been, making wild accusations about heavyweight people. He organized that butchery today at the prison, broke out and made it as far as you see him."

"Your people arrived very quickly. I imagine they saw something?"

"Just cadavers and agitated Americans."

Méndez noticed Athos, impassive under his black uniform cap, off to one side trying to get his attention. Athos had his

AK-47 slung over his shoulder. Méndez had not seen him without the assault rifle since their first visit to the Colonel the month before.

"A pleasure as always, Commander," Méndez said. He turned to Athos, who pointed at a red Volkswagen Jetta parked above them in the cul-de-sac.

Méndez made his way among rocks and climbed wood steps built into the dune. His cell phone rang in his leather jacket, which the rain was discoloring.

"Slaving away, Don Leo?" Isabel Puente sounded as if she were whispering into her phone beneath a cupped hand.

"Where are you?"

"Close. But on the other side, of course."

Méndez stopped climbing and looked down at the gap in the fence, where riot-helmeted Border Patrol agents exchanged glares with Mexican federal officers, toe-to-toe at the line in the sand. He looked past the body of Rico enveloped in his leather coat, the green lump of the Border Patrol agent's body, and clusters of U.S. investigators in yellow slickers near the Wrangler parked on the beach. He did not see Puente.

"What are you wearing?"

"That's a question that could be interpreted the wrong way." Her laugh was like a chime.

"An innocent question, I swear."

"You can't see me, I'm in the parking lot with the bosses," Puente said, eager and conspiratorial. "Listen, we have to talk. Everything is falling into place, believe it or not."

Méndez reached the top of the steps. A breeze spattered drops in his face. Araceli Aguirre's driver stood by the parked Jetta. Aguirre sat in the backseat. She leaned her head back, stretching her neck. When she saw Méndez, she blew him a glum kiss.

Me and these formidable woman partners I've got, Méndez thought. If I were a gangster, I would worry more about them than the Diogenes Group. What had the Colonel said about

Araceli? Tough as a soldier. And the Colonel hadn't gotten to know Isabel Puente.

"From this vantage point, it looks more like everything's falling apart," Méndez said into the phone.

"Don't be gloomy," Puente said. "Can we get together in about three hours? It will be worth it."

"Where?"

"The same place as the last time the Colonel caused a commotion."

"Done. Thanks."

Méndez hung up with Puente. He got into the back of the Jetta next to Aguirre. After a while, he said: "You must have been at the prison all day."

Aguirre removed her glasses, rubbed the bridge of her nose. He tried to remember when he had seen her look more tired and depressed.

That morning, the Colonel had taken his usual brisk exercise walk around the prison yard. The tape from prison surveillance cameras that the guards rewound for Méndez afterward showed the Colonel striding stumpy-legged in his warm-up suit, accompanied by his pit bull and Rico. Then the Colonel repaired to his quarters.

The diversionary gunfight broke out around noon. The video showed two hit men in cowboy hats passing a joint back and forth as they advanced through the crowd at the Sunday basketball game, tossing away the joint, pistols coming out. A narco slurping an ice cream bar got a fusillade in the head.

By the time Méndez and Aguirre arrived at the prison, there were barricaded snipers, cell-block fires and melees provoked by gangs of addicts whom the Colonel's men had furnished with drugs. The Colonel, Rico and the Colonel's servant, César, were long gone, ushered out a loading dock to a waiting convoy of sport utility vehicles. César was still missing. Méndez and a federal police chief ordered the arrest of the warden and his deputies. The federal police had escorted Aguirre into the prison. She had gone among the inmates, convincing the foot soldiers to return to their cells, negotiating with and browbeating the ring-leaders with the help of their wives. She had eventually restored a semblance of calm.

"Araceli," Méndez sighed. "Are those tears for the Colonel or for us?"

Aguirre looked up with a flash of ferocity, replacing her glasses.

"Because if they are for the Colonel," he continued, "let me say you did everything you could for him. And I imagine he appreciated it, in his way. What he did in the end was in his nature. Astorga was the kind of man who sees any sign of humanity or trust as a weakness to be exploited. He couldn't help himself."

"Perhaps you and I can convince ourselves we did everything we could for him," Aguirre said, looking at the silver-blue fortress of clouds over the ocean. "But as far as I'm concerned, your boss might as well have pulled the trigger."

"Not to defend the Secretary, but I know for a fact that he was trying to get the Colonel transferred to another prison. As you wanted."

"Please, Leo, let's not be infantile."

"Things don't move that fast, believe it or not. Even for the Secretary."

"The Colonel said it. After he gave his testimony, he told me: 'Now it's up to the Secretary. After what I just did, he should send a helicopter and take me away. If he doesn't, I'm a dead man.' "

The escape had been a shock. A week earlier the Colonel had kept his promise and given sworn testimony in the prison to Méndez and a federal prosecutor. He had mainly talked about cases with which they were already familiar. He had made brief and general accusations about the Ruiz Caballeros. Then he cut off the session, saying he would continue only after his transfer to a new prison.

"What's happening down there?" Aguirre asked.

"A mess," Méndez said, thankful that she had held fire on the subject of the Secretary. "The Border Patrol says nothing. The state police are tainting the evidence. The federal police seem mainly interested in the issue of imperialist aggression against our national sovereignty."

"What's the hypothesis?"

"Well, there's the Fernández Rochetti version, which I reject automatically: The Colonel escaped on his own and got himself killed playing Pancho Villa with the Americans. Another possibility: The Colonel convinced Junior the best way to shut him up was to help him escape. Then Junior double-crossed him. And of course, there are many others who despised the Colonel and wanted him dead. What doesn't make sense is the shoot-out with the Border Patrol."

"I wonder if there will come a day in this city when crimes have less than a dozen possible intellectual authors," Aguirre said.

"If that day comes, you might as well move to Ohio or somewhere, because your services won't be needed around here anymore."

Aguirre rolled her high shoulders, shaking off her mood.

"Very well," she said.

"What?"

"I'm going down there."

"Araceli, I really don't think that's necessary. You've had a long day."

She leaned over, kissed him on the cheek, and opened the door.

"I owe it to him," she said. "He was counting on me to save him. No?"

"But it's raining," Méndez protested, pulling out his radio.

"Athos, Doctora Aguirre is coming down to the beach. Send someone up here with an umbrella. Confiscate Chancho's if necessary."

Aguirre managed a weak grin. "You realize that, in a way, all of this helps us. It raises suspicions. It shows that the Ruiz Caballeros are scared."

"I suppose that's good."

"Coming?"

"Not for long. I have a meeting on the other side. I think I'll have something to tell you tomorrow."

When Méndez returned to his headquarters, he received a phone call from Mexico City. The Secretary, who was on a trip to Sonora, had heard about the shoot-out. The Secretary had decided to stop in Tijuana and wanted Méndez to meet with him the next day.

It was 2 a.m. when Méndez, Athos and Porthos climbed into the Crown Victoria. Porthos drove. A carload of Diogenes officers followed them as far as the port of entry, where they crossed into San Diego.

The traffic on Interstate 5 was fast and sparse. But the center median of the freeway was full of illegal immigrants trudging north. Méndez rested his head against the window in the backseat. He watched the ghostly army on the march. Headlights swept the immigrants. The concrete gleamed wet and black beneath their boots and gym shoes. His countrymen covered their heads with hoods, baseball caps, newspapers, plastic bags. Or they simply hunched their shoulders, impervious to the rain, the fatigue, the roar and hiss of metal monsters rushing by a few feet away. The immigrants knew the freeway median was a reasonably safe limbo in some ways: no bandits, no Border Patrol, no rough terrain. Just put one foot in front of the other. Pray the cars stay in their lanes. Try not to think about the moment when you'll have to sprint across this cement deathscape hauling your wife, your kids, your worldly possessions. Maybe the moment can be postponed indefinitely. Maybe you can just keep walking north and the freeway median will take you where you want to go.

Sliding along the edge of sleep, the ragged parade blurring and dissolving on the other side of the wet glass, Méndez thought about the Mexican presidents who gave speeches lamenting the exodus of illegal immigrants from the country. The presidents said the bravery and determination of the immigrants made them Mexico's best and brightest. Méndez had melodramatic visions of hauling the Mexican presidents across the border and exacting poetic justice at gunpoint, forcing them to run with the best and brightest on the freeway in the rain.

Fifteen minutes later Méndez and his men arrived at Isabel Puente's condominium complex, which overlooked a bay near SeaWorld in the Crown Point area of San Diego. There was a guardhouse, walls topped with cameras. They walked into a five-story building with a faux-Mediterranean tiled roof, Moorish archways and curved balconies.

Méndez had visited Puente's home once before, in October, during the days of vertigo that followed his arrest of the Colonel. Her invitation had surprised him. Puente had shared case information with him about the Colonel. And she played him a tape from what she called a "U.S. military subsource wiretap": a conversation between a San Diego drug dealer and a Tijuana police detective about a rumored plan to kill Méndez. On that day he had realized she was a friend as well as an ally.

Athos and Porthos hung back respectfully as Isabel Puente opened the door to her fifth-floor apartment. She practically bounded into the hall. Her hair was tousled and damp. She wore jeans, a denim blouse, gym shoes. Her smile and her voice were exhilarated.

"Listen, Leo, this is delicate," she whispered, her fingers digging into his arm. "I've got Valentine Pescatore in there, the Border Patrol agent. You know."

"The star informant."

"*El mero.* He was involved in the shooting. Right in the middle of it. He's going to tell you the whole thing. But he's not happy about it."

The cobwebs of sleep evaporated from Méndez's eyes.

"Another thing," Puente continued, rapid-fire. "He speaks Spanish, but I think he'll be more comfortable in English. All right?"

"Fine with me," Méndez said with a mock bow. "Your house, your rules."

"No, please, it's your house, you already know that. All of you," Puente said, flashing a high-voltage smile over her shoulder at Athos and Porthos, who stammered their thanks.

The apartment was long, high-ceilinged and divided into three step-down levels. At the end of the living room, glass doors to a balcony overlooked a marina, city lights shimmering on the water, the low forms of moored sailboats. The furniture was dark and minimalist, the carpet thick and spotless. Except for a table full of family photos and a framed pop-art relief of old Havana by an exile artist, Isabel Puente's home could have been a chic hotel suite.

Total solitude, Méndez thought. He had once read a line in a novel about how Americans pursued loneliness in myriad ways: they lived alone, drove alone, ate alone. He remembered weekend cross-border excursions with his wife and son to the supermarkets and home-supply stores of Chula Vista and San Ysidro. He remembered commenting with his wife on the contrast between the shopping rituals. The solitary Anglos hunched behind their carts; the Latino families were boisterous platoons of children, grandparents, cousins. He thought ruefully about his own home in Playas de Tijuana, which after four months seemed big in a way he had never thought possible: the silent kitchen, the dusty toys. His home had acquired its own musty air of disuse. He had known the job with the Diogenes Group would be tough, but he hadn't imagined it would turn him into an American.

Puente led them into a breakfast nook. A youthful Border Patrol agent reclined behind a rectangular marble-topped table, leaning his head against the wall. The agent's short-sleeved green uniform was bedraggled. A stain on his shirt appeared to be dried blood.

"Valentine, this is Leo Méndez, the chief of the Diogenes Group. And Comandantes Rojas and Tapia," Puente said. "Gentlemen, this is Agent Valentine Pescatore."

The agent half rose. He was younger, darker and shorter than Méndez had expected. He had muscular biceps and shoulders and black curly hair. Puente had told Méndez that her informant was of Mexican and Argentine descent. He could have passed for either, but his looks were more South American. With his compact bulk and wide, edgy eyes, Pescatore reminded Méndez of a rookie soccer player or prizefighter, boiling with youth and nerves and aggression.

"A pleasure, *a sus órdenes,*" Méndez said, shaking hands vigorously. "Thank you for seeing us."

"How you doin'?" the agent responded, his voice throaty with street inflections. "I heard a lot about you. I thought it was gonna be one-on-one, though." He nodded curtly at Athos and Porthos without offering them his hand. "I didn't know you were gonna bring the whole team."

Athos and Porthos stiffened. Méndez had never heard Athos say anything more than "Ten-four" and "Nice to meet you," but Athos understood his share of English. And Porthos had gone to high school in Inglewood, California. Méndez tried to think of a diplomatic response, but Puente spoke first. She put a hand on Pescatore's forearm, patient and steely.

"Comandante Rojas is the operational chief of the Diogenes Group, Valentine. The number-two guy. And Comandante Tapia is of utmost confidence. I vouch for both of them. They wouldn't be here otherwise. Why don't you guys have a seat, take off your jackets, make yourselves comfortable. I'll get some coffee."

The Mexicans sat. They did not take off their jackets. The alcove quickly became claustrophobic. Pescatore tilted his head back again. He regarded Méndez from beneath heavy lids. His posture reinforced his tone: He clearly wished the Mexicans would go away. Wild-looking kid, Méndez thought.

Méndez had a visceral nationalistic aversion to Border Patrol agents. Although he did not work with The Patrol, from a distance they reminded him of a species he had come to loathe during his year among the gray skies and gray buildings of the University of Michigan: fraternity boys. They had struck him as crude, swaggering, well-off rednecks with a clannish mentality that reeked of racism and fascism. But Méndez had been mystified to discover that Athos and other veterans in the Diogenes Group did not share his disdain. In fact, Mendez's officers viewed the Border Patrol with a comradely we're-all-cops-doing-our-job attitude. And he knew that, unlike the frat boys of Michigan, the Border Patrol agents tended to be working class and many were Latinos.

Nonetheless, reasonable or not, Méndez had a problem with the Border Patrol. And the young Border Patrol agent clearly had a problem with Méndez and his men, if not Mexicans in general.

By the time Puente had served the beverages, there was an interruption: a pizza delivery. Puente bustled around putting the deep-dish pizza, a plate and utensils in front of Pescatore.

"Valentine was hungry," Puente explained. "He's had quite a night."

Pescatore gave her a smile so affectionate and sheepish that Méndez found it endearing in spite of himself. He looked back and forth between the agent and Puente, wondering if personal factors might be complicating Puente's relationship with her informant. When she had first recruited him, she had told Méndez that it was a calculated risk. As the weeks went by, though, she had sounded unusually enthusiastic about the kid.

Pescatore gestured at the Mexicans to join him; they shook their heads. After he had consumed a slice of pizza, Puente broke the silence with a gentle "So..."

"OK," Pescatore said to Méndez, wiping his mouth carefully with a napkin. "First I gotta say I'm doing this under protest. It's messed up: I didn't even tell my own bosses how it really went down. And now I'm gonna tell you guys. But Agent Puente says I gotta help you out. And what Agent Puente says, goes."

Méndez nodded. Pescatore explained that, an hour before the shoot-out, Garrison told Pescatore that the Colonel would cross the border at the beach. The plan was for the agents to give the Colonel safe passage past The Patrol checkpoint in Orange County. Just before the rendezvous, Garrison received a phone call, changed plans and sent Pescatore and another agent to meet the Colonel at the fence.

"Right then I knew some evil shit was gonna happen," Pescatore said, head down, grimacing. "But I went ahead and walked right into the kill zone. Least I had my gun out."

Pescatore described the gunfight in detail, reliving it, his eyes and nostrils flaring. He was unsophisticated but not stupid, Méndez concluded. The agent had an agile mind; ideas and images spilled out of him. Méndez felt a pang of empathy. He understood Pescatore's stare of frozen ferocity. It was awe at his survival. Awe that he could sit here eating pizza and describe the first time he had killed a man as if recalling how he had hit a home run.

Méndez's first and only gunfight had taken place in Playas de Tijuana when he was still human rights commissioner. A skull-faced drug addict in a ragged poncho had confronted him outside his house as he got out of his car: a death mask materializing out of the night behind a .38. They struggled. The assailant stumbled. Méndez broke away, ducked around behind the car and drew his own gun. They traded fire across the hood. Méndez killed him, emerging unscathed probably because the gunman had a headful of heroin. The police called it an attempted robbery. But Méndez believed that someone had sent the hapless attacker to eliminate him, or at least scare him. They succeeded in the latter.

Méndez noticed that Pescatore was talking more to Puente than to her visitors. Her cheek was propped on her hand, black hair cascading to the marble tabletop. Her eyes were locked on the agent.

Now we are getting somewhere, Méndez thought. This U.S. angle was powerful new ammunition against Mauro Fernández Rochetti and the Ruiz Caballeros. Things were moving fast. Araceli would be elated.

Most of the kid's story sounds true, Méndez thought. But he had his doubts about certain aspects. Pescatore's depiction of himself as a dupe seemed convenient and exculpatory. This was no time to give anyone, much less a Border Patrol agent, the benefit of the doubt.

"Listen, let me say I appreciate the fact that you are telling us this now, just after it has happened," Méndez told Pescatore. "I am happy you were not hurt. I do not want to sound macabre and congratulate you, this is not appropriate. But obviously you are a professional or you would not be alive."

Pescatore tried to restrain a grin.

"One thing, if I may," Méndez said softly, sipping coffee. "I am thinking the Mauro mentioned by Garrison was the homicide comandante. Was it your impression when Garrison said this name Mauro on the phone that he spoke to him or about him?"

Pescatore retreated into his head-against-the-wall pose.

"I think he was talking to Mauro," Pescatore said.

"Why?"

"When the shooters were gone and Garrison finally came down to the beach to help with Dillard, I went off. I screamed at him, I told him he was a chickenshit asshole, almost got me killed. Garrison just shook his head and said: 'Fucking Mauro, what a mess, fucking Mauro,' like that."

"I see. What did Mauro tell him on the phone?"

Pescatore enunciated as if he were speaking to a simpleton. "I just said. I don't know. Garrison didn't tell me."

"I'm sorry. What do you think Mauro told him?"

"I don't know."

"Where did the Colonel intend to go? Los Angeles, perhaps?"

Pescatore took a bite of pizza and slurped Coke with a straw. He mumbled: "No idea."

You are hiding something, you little punk, Méndez thought with mounting irritation. All the English, combined with the late hour, was giving him a headache.

"I suppose something confuses me," Méndez said. "What you have just told us is not what you tell the investigators a few hours ago, is this correct? You, eh, told them something different, did you not?"

"Well yeah. I wasn't gonna rat out Garrison right there, for Christ's sake. We said we saw these guys coming across and they drew down on us. I figured Isabel was gonna help me straighten things out later."

Pushing a tangle of hair back on top of her head, Isabel Puente said: "I think we're getting off track, Leo. Valentine went with Garrison's story because otherwise he could have compromised my investigation and himself. He made a judgment call in a difficult situation."

Méndez felt bad for Puente, who seemed to think he was leaning too hard on the kid. But Méndez also found her protectiveness annoying and naive. He suspected the agent was working both sides. If that were the case, Méndez wanted Pescatore to know he was not fooling him.

"I understand, Isabel," Méndez said. Then he stuck in the knife. "I just want to be clear that this young man is recounting to us the complete truth."

Pescatore's voice got throatier. "The fuck is that supposed to mean?"

Méndez swiveled his angular profile from Puente to the agent. "I want to assure that, because of the confusion and emotion, or because you wish to protect the investigation, or yourself, or someone, that nothing has been left out."

"Now ain't that a bitch," Pescatore raged. "I just got finished shooting some Mexican cop who blew a PA's head off right in front of me. I didn't particularly like Dillard, but he was a United States Border Patrol agent. And he didn't deserve to get his head blown off by some scumbag Mexican cop. And—"

"I think you should—"

"Now I got another Mexican cop sitting—"

"Make yourself a favor and calm—"

"Sitting here, in U.S. territory, I might add, cross-examining me. Practically calling me a liar to my face. Well you listen up you—"

"All right!" Puente glared at them. "Nobody's calling you a liar, Valentine. I'm sure Leo didn't mean to insult you."

"In fact, you insult me," Méndez told Pescatore. "You are too young and uninformed to comprehend, but my men are in more danger from 'Mexican cops' than you are."

"We about done with this guy?" Pescatore asked Puente, scowling.

Puente spread her hands soothingly at Pescatore and Méndez. Athos slowly mangled his cap on the table, probably imagining that he was throttling Pescatore. Porthos eyed the pizza.

"Let's everybody take a deep breath," Puente ordered. "Anybody want more Coke, coffee, water? Abelardo, do you want some pizza? Sure? Leo, could you and I step into the living room a minute?"

Méndez rose, feeling suddenly like he was about to get a scolding. Isabel Puente slid nimbly past Porthos's oxlike bulk and went into the living room, her jaws clenched.

As Méndez followed, he heard Pescatore whisper to Porthos: "Hey big fella, for real. Go ahead, take a slice, I'm not gonna eat the whole thing by myself. *Ándale, con confianza.*"

It could have been genuine or sarcastic. Either way, it showed a hard-edged composure. Perhaps the agent's tirade had been more controlled than it appeared. And Pescatore's Spanish was better than Méndez had expected.

This kid is hard to read, Méndez thought. I wonder if he'll last long enough for me to figure him out.

7

Pescatore stood in the living room at the door to the balcony, staring through his reflection into the darkness of the bay.

He heard Isabel and the Mexicans in the hall. She was walking with them to their car, probably discussing the less-than-friendly session in the kitchen. Pescatore and Méndez had apologized to each other, but the vibes were still bad.

Fine. Whatever. The hell with Méndez and his stuck-up anti-American make-yourself-a-favor attitude. Pescatore floated in a zone on the other side of exhaustion and fear. He was wide awake, aware of danger all around him, in synch with it. He kept seeing afterimages of Dillard's corpse, muzzle flashes in the rain, Rico going down in a halo of fire. He was focused on being alive. And on the fact that he was in Isabel Puente's apartment at three-thirty in the morning.

After interrogations at Imperial Beach by city homicide detectives, the FBI and the OIG, the station chief had given Pescatore three days off to rest. The chief offered counseling if needed and told him he had done some good shooting out there. Still, Pescatore knew that doubts were hovering. He had never seen so many bosses from so many agencies looking so uptight.

When the chief was done, Isabel Puente had buttonholed him

and told him they would meet secretly at an intersection in Mission Beach. Minutes later, Pescatore passed Garrison lumbering toward the chief's office for his turn to face the music. Garrison said: "Slow motion, Valentine." It could have been an encouragement or a warning. Or both.

In Mission Beach, Puente had him park on a side street. Once he was in her Mazda, she told him they were going to her apartment. They needed a safe place to talk.

While he was getting his mind around that, she dropped another bomb. She wanted him to brief her top Mexican contact, the chief of the Diogenes Group. She gave Méndez a big buildup: the Eliot Ness of Baja, the guy who had busted the Colonel. She steamrolled Pescatore's objections.

Despite Pescatore's dismay when Méndez showed up with two sidekicks, he had to admit they were not run-of-the-mill dirtballs. They didn't have that sleazy strut that comes with years of torturing people and getting away with it. They were quiet and intense. With his sad wolfish face and dry sarcasm, Méndez resembled a streetwise professor in a leather jacket. His comandante in the SWAT gear came off like one of those hardcase old cops who get meaner to compensate for any loss of physical strength. Even the *panzón* with the beard looked like serious business.

But the fact that they were presentable only worried Pescatore more. He could not trust them. It went against all his instincts. The more he talked, the more he decided that Puente had pushed him into a big mistake. Then Méndez had disrespected him.

Puente came back into the apartment talking on a cell phone, which for some reason annoyed him. She hit him with a smile. Her hair was somewhat disheveled. The dark blue of her shirt played into the brown of her cleavage and her slender throat. He liked her even more like this, padding around at home, than when she was all slicked up for work.

He sounded less challenging than he had intended. "Who'd you talk to?"

"The office."

"At this hour?"

"This is a major border incident, Valentine. We're working it around the clock. The Mexicans too."

"Your boy Méndez worked me over, that's for sure."

"Oh, I think you handled yourself," she said, rolling her eyes. "Go ahead and put one of those on if you want."

Pescatore thumbed through a shelf of compact discs containing what appeared to be the collected works of Shakira and Gloria Estefan, some Latin jazz and a lot of Old School soul artists. He selected an Earth, Wind & Fire disc.

"There you go," Puente said. "I wasn't born when that came out, so I know you weren't either."

She lowered herself onto the couch with her legs coiled under her. Pescatore paced, unsure of his next move.

"I thought you said Méndez was cool," he said. "I was waiting for him to shake a Coke can and spray it up my nose."

"He thought you were holding out on him."

"Plus he thinks I'm young and ignorant. That's when I really wanted to slap his face."

"Uninformed, not ignorant. It was your fault, starting off so hostile."

"What did you expect? Can't he leave his boys out in the car or something?"

"Valentine." The wide-set eyes homed in on him. She reached out and patted the couch at a carefully extended arm's length from her. "Take it easy. Sit down for a minute."

He could not gauge her expression. It occurred to him that she might be toying with him. Trying not to seem enthusiastic, he came around the coffee table.

The couch felt like an island. The apartment seemed to recede from them like an image in a wide-angle lens.

Her voice got softer. "I know it's been an awful night. I know it freaked you out talking to Méndez. You have to understand:

Without him there's no investigation, no case, nothing. He's not an informant, he's like my partner."

"You're putting my life in his hands."

"I put my life in his hands all the time. That's why we are shaking things up. Do you understand what kind of individual it takes to run a squad that investigates police corruption in Mexico?"

She had turned so that she was almost kneeling, her left side propped against the cushion. The jeans marked the half-circle of her right hip. Pescatore leaned back to maintain eye contact, reclining thankfully into the plush black fabric. His bones ached as if they had been pounded with rocks.

"The police in Mexico are hopeless," he growled. "They're always announcing some hotshot new chief, some elite unit. They're gonna clean up, the real thing this time. And then the guy gets arrested, or fired, or just sits around getting rich. How many times you seen that, Isabel? You know how you can tell the Mexican cops who really go after the bad guys? They get killed."

"I know a little more about that world than you do. Besides, Leo is an outsider. He was a journalist and a human rights activist."

"Great," he snapped, sitting up. "I couldn't think of anybody who hates the Border Patrol worse. A Communist newspaperman, playing detective. Your partner."

Her face tightened. "So the ideal thing would be if he was a real cop, and honest. Which means he'd have to be dead, right?"

"That'd be perfect."

"Well you might not have to wait too long. Every time I say good-bye to him, I think it might be the last time."

"Oh man. Cry me a river. I'm the one you better say good-bye to, I'm the one who got shot at. Thanks to you."

"Thanks to me?" She grabbed his arm when he tried to turn away. "Thanks to me? Nobody watches out for you except me."

She was in his face, disorienting him. His mind was whirling, soaring. He imagined hitting her. He imagined kissing her. He snarled: "You're about to get me killed, you're all worried about Méndez. What is he, your boyfriend?"

"I don't have a boyfriend." Small steel fingers dug painfully into his forearm. "Watch your mouth."

"Talks that shit to me. Then he turns around all smooth with you. Fuckin' snake."

"You sound like you're fifteen years old." She was up on her knees now, taut and quivering and furious. "Are you jealous of him?"

"Damn right I'm jealous."

A pause. A hint of a grin.

"Oh," she whispered. "Well, we got that cleared up."

Taking advantage of her grip on his arm, he pulled her toward him. She let herself be pulled. He wrapped his other arm around her lower back and nuzzled into her hair, her throat, her face. After a moment, her arms encircled his neck. She pressed herself against him, her breasts full and round against him. His mouth found hers. They slid together down onto the couch.

He didn't know if it was weeks of imagining it or the real thing, but she tasted like cinnamon. Her breath was warm in his ear. Her whisper was close to a sob.

"Don't you worry, Valentine. Nobody takes care of you but me..."

The couch was vast and luxurious. Her body was light and lean and voluptuous in miniature. She moaned softly beneath him. Her eagerness mixed with seeming timidity as she guided him, as he caressed her and pulled at her clothes. She slowed him, controlled him, channeling his desire and rage and fear into a deliberate tenderness.

"Angel face," he murmured, his lips brushing a delicate collarbone.

But the sneaky voice in his head wouldn't shut up. OK, you

finally got her, it said. Or she finally got you. Is she running a game? Does she feel bad because she's about to get you killed? At least you'll die smiling, right?

Eventually, they made their way from the couch to the bedroom. When he finally fell asleep, a long blissful slide into nothingness, the bay outside the window was filling with blue predawn light.

His dreams were demented holograms. He dreamed about her beneath him on the couch, above him on the bed. He relived the feel of her hips in his hands, her eyes blazing into his. The pleasure flooded him so vividly he thought they had woken up and gone at it again. But then he knew it was a dream: She disappeared. He was on the beach in the rain, holding his gun. Méndez and the Colonel and a bunch of bandits wearing ridiculous *sombreros* and bandoliers were stalking over The Line at him, hands by their holsters. Pescatore said, "Don't you mess with me, *hijos de la chingada,* I got Isabel Puente from the Office of Inspector General watching my back." Méndez jeered at him, except it was in his own voice, a snotty Mexican imitation of Valentine Pescatore, saying, "Yeah, Isabel took care of you good, you stupid pathetic pussy-whipped *gabacho.* Now draw . . ."

He thrashed awake like a man being asphyxiated. Isabel lay propped on her side. Her eyes glowed in the indirect light from the bedroom balcony. She stayed in that position with her cheek resting on her hand, watching clinically as he sat up, entangled in sweaty sheets, and figured out where he was. Only then did she reach out for him. They held each other.

"You're like a big teddy bear," she murmured.

He pulled back and touched her face with two knuckles.

"Good morning, *chulita,*" he said. "You surveilling me again?"

"*Chulita?*"

"Uh, yeah." He blinked, feeling a little goofy. "This PA, Galván, he told me that's what Mexicans call a beautiful woman. *Chula*. That wrong?"

"No."

"What time is it?"

"About nine-thirty."

"So now what?"

Puente got up and wrapped herself in a bathrobe. She walked to the doors of the bedroom balcony, her curves encased in black and white stripes.

"Good question, Valentine," she said with her back to him.

He slid out of the bed and gathered her in his arms from behind. She leaned back into him. It was overcast, the kind of California-gray morning that had surprised him when he first arrived in what he thought was a land of nonstop sun. The marina was framed in the window like a painting, the sails sectioning the waters. The only movement came from circling gulls and the wind in the palm trees on the far shore. The giant blue arches of an amusement-park roller coaster interrupted the horizon near the ocean.

"Good question, meaning what?" he asked.

"Meaning I liked what we did. But we shouldn't have done it. Now you've got something on me."

The ice in her voice alarmed him. He tightened his hold on her.

"Oh man, that's kind of a cold way of looking at the whole thing, huh?" he said into her ear. "Huh, Isabel?"

She tossed swirls of hair out of her eyes. He eased her back onto the foot of the bed. They sat side by side for a moment, not looking at each other.

"Hey." He wondered why he was whispering. "I been wanting to ask you. How come you only spent a year in The Patrol? Something bad happened?"

Her eyes got luminous. He thought she was going to pull away, but instead she snuggled closer.

"I guess that's what I like about you," she sighed. "You've got this street act going, but you're sharper than you let on."

In a monotone, she told him she had grown bored studying criminal justice and dropped out of college. She joined The Patrol and got assigned to Nogales, a desert sector with a lot of action. One of her supervisors, a slick mustachioed bruiser, took great interest in her progress as a trainee. He asked her out repeatedly. She declined because she had a fiancé in Miami. But one night, after the unit celebrated a marijuana bust at a bar, she accepted the supervisor's offer of a ride home.

When they arrived at her apartment complex, a dingy place on the edge of the desert, the supervisor killed the engine, turned and, using some lame pretext, asked her to hand over her gun so he could take a look at it. Then he locked the gun in the glove compartment and attacked her in the front seat.

"It was close to midnight." Puente's fingers were laced in Pescatore's. She sounded as if she were describing a crime scene. "We were right in front of my building. We're in uniform. He's tearing my shirt. He's like a dog. I'm terrified. I'm thinking if I could get back my gun. But what would I do, shoot my supervisor? Finally this *viejito* who lived downstairs walks by, thank God. He comes over to the car. And you know what he says? I'm being assaulted, I'm crying, hysterical. You know what this old desert rat says? 'You kids keep it down out here. Take it in the house.' I wanted to shoot *him*."

"Damn. What happened?"

"The supe told me to be a smart girl and keep quiet. He left. Took my gun with him. You can imagine what he said around the station. The other PAs were all laughing and whispering."

"Lowlife scumbag. What did you do?"

Isabel Puente pulled her robe around her. She showed her teeth.

"I bought a mini–tape recorder. I got him into a conversation about the incident, like I was flirting. I recorded his incriminating statements. He had this topless dancer he was sleeping with who was an illegal alien, so I found her. I recorded that interview too. Then I wrote up a complaint and went to the Justice Department. I played the tapes for them. I said I was filing charges and I was going to make a commotion if they didn't do something. Then I went to his house and personally gave his wife copies of the tapes and the complaint. By the time I was done with him, that rapist *hijo de puta* wished he was never born. He was a fool to mess with me. Nobody messes with me."

"Damn," Pescatore said again, wishing he could think of a more sensitive comment.

Tears slid down her face. "Even though I was on probationary status, the bosses cut a deal to keep me quiet. I transferred to the Inspector General. I finished school at night and made supervisor in a couple of years. Happy ending, right?"

"What about the fiancé in Miami?"

"Not so happy."

It occurred to him that for several minutes he had not thought once about the shoot-out or his other troubles. He wrapped her in an awkward hug.

"I'm sorry, Isabel," he said. "I'm sorry."

"You didn't do anything."

"I guess you don't hate the whole entire Patrol though, 'cause otherwise I wouldn't be here, right?" he said, planting a kiss on her forehead.

"Right." She kissed him back with her eyes closed.

She made breakfast. They ate on the living room balcony. She made the jokes about his appetite that had become like a domestic ritual. Backlit by the sun breaking through the gray, she talked about music, movies, her apartment.

He nodded and laughed. He watched the way her hands fluttered up into the recesses of her hair, teasing and fussing with it. He couldn't get enough of her. But it was all forced and unreal. This was somebody else's life: juice, melon and chocolate chip muffins on a Monday morning with a view of boats on the water. As if it weren't a relationship built on suspicion and manipulation. As if they didn't have guns, badges and a border full of corpses and enemies waiting for them. Nonetheless, he did not want the illusion to end. He hoped she felt the same way.

She broke the mood almost without transition. Finishing off her coffee, she told him her task force and Méndez's squad were going to make their move: simultaneous indictments of major players on both sides of the border. She fended off his questions, saying the less he knew, the better.

"OK, Isabel, but what kinda time frame are we talking about?" he asked, nodding as she raised the coffeepot. "Days, weeks?"

"There's still work to do, coordination with Méndez and his people. A week at least."

"Garrison goes down?"

"Oh yes."

"And what happens to me?" He gulped coffee, concentrating. He refrained from asking two other questions that came to mind: What happens to our relationship? And what happens when somebody tries to kill me?

"That's complicated. But you're going to be fine. One thing you need to realize, Valentine. There's people who want you to testify."

"I figured. But what I want to know is how do we play it?"

"We're talking about that."

"It's gonna look strange when I don't get arrested."

"Last night changed some things. I don't have all the answers yet."

"I'm not real comfortable with a buncha prosecutors and supervisors sitting around talking about what's going to happen to me," he said, avoiding her eyes. "I'm counting on you to make sure they don't treat me like a Kleenex."

Her musical laugh made him feel better. She said: "I got your back, Valentine."

She got up, kissed him on the forehead and went inside to get dressed.

He buttoned his uniform shirt, grimacing at the dried bloodstain. He sat in the sun, dozing. A speedboat purred in the distance.

Puente returned wearing the high-powered outfit she reserved for meetings at the U.S. Attorney's office or testifying in court: a suit with a tailored jacket and a short snug skirt. With the outfit and the makeup and the perfume, it was as if she had put on armor and war paint. He told her she looked like a million bucks; he was pleased when the ready-for-business facade dissolved into a self-conscious smile.

They held hands in the elevator. He drifted back into the daydream that they were a couple with a normal life on their way to where normal people went. She drove him back to Mission Beach, cruising once around the block as a precaution, and parked down the street from his Impala. He saw himself in her sunglasses, hesitant and happy. She patted the steering wheel. She was in a hurry.

"Isabel," he said.

"Now is not the time to say anything," she said.

He wanted to tell her he would hold on to the night no matter what happened. He wanted to tell her he trusted her, which was almost true.

"Now is not the time," she repeated.

"Alright then," he said. He heard an echo of that mocking Méndez-Pescatore voice from his dream tell him to shut up and get out of the car.

He turned away, but she caught his arm. She kissed him hard on the mouth before she let him go.

The ride into Pacific Beach reminded him of the light-headed solitude of the commute after an overnight shift. Heading home as everybody else headed out into their day. Hungering to hit the pillow and shut out a world going in the opposite direction. But no overnight shift had left this sweet residual warmth in his belly. He decided he could get used to having an Isabel Puente hangover.

He was grinning like a crazy man by the time he bounded up the outdoor staircase to his apartment. He locked the door carefully behind him.

And he almost had a heart attack when he saw Garrison sitting on the couch.

"There's my buddy." Garrison's voice was toneless. "Welcome home, honey."

"Jesus fucking Christ! You scared the shit outta me!"

With effort, Pescatore pried his hand away from his gun. Garrison slouched in the gloom, his head back and his knees apart. He wore a checkered shirt under a jeans jacket. His hands were clasped behind his neck. He might have been preparing for a nap. Except that his eyes were straining in their sockets.

"Where ya been, buddy?"

Pescatore noticed a suitcase near the couch. "How'd you get in, man?"

"Special Forces teaches you all kinds of interesting stuff."

"That's a good way to get smoked, sneaking around in people's houses."

"Where ya been, buddy?"

Walking off the fright, Pescatore hit a light switch. He poured himself a glass of water at the kitchenette sink.

"Went and saw this chick."

"That's an interesting way to celebrate your first kill. I thought you'd wait around the station for me."

"Man, I was too freaked out. I had to get outta there."

"Which chick?"

"This Angelina lives in Chula Vista."

"The one you met at my party? Anita, with the legs? What're you talking about, she moved back to Jalisco, buddy."

"No, the waitress. From Little Italy."

"I thought she was history."

Pescatore had dated Angelina for a few months. He had lost contact with her after she quit her job. He could not remember what he had told Garrison.

"No, man, you know, she called me finally and we hooked up again," he stammered. He tried to revive his rage from the beach after the shoot-out. "Plus I didn't particularly feel like talking to you, tell you the truth."

"Sit down, Valentine, you're all squirrelly," Garrison ordered. "You still pissed at me, buddy?"

"Yup." Pescatore found a folding chair, opened it and straddled it backwards.

"Well you're gonna forgive me in a hurry." Garrison leaned forward. A silver pistol in a shoulder holster appeared beneath his jacket. There was a tense lethargy to his speech and movements, like he was agitated and willing himself to go slow. "Time to get the heck outta Dodge. We're about to get arrested."

"Arrested?"

"Affirmative."

"When?"

"They're organizing the arrest teams today. They'll serve the warrants tomorrow. Come for you at dawn and haul your sorry butt out of bed."

"Tomorrow? What the fuck?" He no longer had to fake consternation. "Where'd you hear this?"

"My guy at the Federal Building."

"He sure?"

"Sure."

Isabel had told him it would be at least a week before anything happened. It was hard to believe she could be wrong. Unless she had lied. Unless the night had been a scam. He relived the hungry good-bye kiss in the car. Cold-blooded bitch, he thought.

Garrison was saying something about a bag and Tijuana. "Grab your Dopp kit and pack some clothes, buddy."

Pescatore hunkered behind the back of the folding chair.

"Arleigh," he said, the first name sounding peculiar in his ears. "There's no way I'm running to Tijuana, man. I'll take my chances here. What are they gonna charge us with?"

"Federal charges. Maybe homicide too."

"Homicide?"

"Three guys got killed last night. They could say it was in the course of a criminal act. Like if a guy robs a bank and his partner gets killed by the guard."

"Give me a break."

"Listen, that's how they squash you when your time comes."

"I shot a Mexican cop last night. They'd eat me alive down there."

"Don't play stupid. My guys in TJ are gonna look out for us. If they tell the *judiciales* to carry our luggage, they'll carry our fucking luggage. And you know it."

"I don't know. If I run, I'll run to Chicago, Canada or somewhere."

Garrison stood and stretched. The jacket came open so the shoulder holster was plainly visible.

"I'm not asking your opinion, Valentine," he growled. "Police up your situation and get with the program. Enough jiving."

Pescatore's hands sweated as he changed in his bedroom, strapping on his shoulder holster over civilian clothes. He was barely aware of the items he stuffed into a duffel bag. Garrison stood in the bedroom doorway chattering lazily about how this was going to be easier for Pescatore than for him. How Garrison had a five-hundred-thousand-dollar house in Bonita to worry about. How it was a good thing he had money stashed, he had experience shipping out on short notice.

Garrison was keeping an eye on him, hurrying him along. His vigilance opened up an alternate scenario: What if Isabel had told the truth? What if Garrison were lying? Perhaps he knew Pescatore was an informant. Perhaps it was a ruse to lure him down south and whack him.

Hauling the duffel bag into the living room, Pescatore reached for the phone.

"Who ya calling?"

"Angelina, man. I promised to take her to the movies tonight."

He intended to call Isabel Puente and fake a conversation with Angelina in order to sound the alarm. Garrison smothered his hand on top of the phone.

"Negative. Let's go."

Pescatore felt a flash of anger: This is my house you're pushing me around in, you gray-eyed storm-trooping ape.

That's OK, he thought, I still got my cell phone. But then his rage flared again, blending with despair. The cell phone battery was dead. He hadn't charged it because he had spent the night at Isabel's apartment. Now the phone sat in its sheath on his belt, useless. The price of pleasure: He had let down his guard.

They hauled their bags down the stairs. He followed Garrison around the corner to his Cherokee.

"You drive, Valentine."

Pescatore reached to catch the tossed keys. "How come?"

"I got some phone calls to make, buddy."

Yeah right, Pescatore thought, starting the Cherokee with a roar. He wants me under control. He wants my hands occupied. The gloomiest scenario occurred to him: What if his fears about both Puente and Garrison betraying him were correct? In that case, it was just a question of whether he got whacked or locked up. Right now, getting whacked looked like the favorite.

"I'm thirsty, man, lemme get a Big Gulp," he suggested at the stoplight before the freeway ramp, eyeing a 7-Eleven.

"Drive."

He's on to me, dammit, Pescatore thought. I'm DOA.

His hands throbbed from clutching the wheel. Rolling south around the curve of the freeway past the steel ramparts of downtown, past the high slender span of the Coronado Bay Bridge, he remembered the speed trap near National City. On his way to work he often saw a California Highway Patrol car work the area around a viaduct, as busy as a shark at feeding time.

He nudged the accelerator. He turned on the radio as a diversionary tactic.

In a voice both pompous and folksy, a local talk-show host was complaining about Mexicans on weekends: Mexicans at the zoo, Mexicans in Horton Plaza. Can't get away from them. Can't kick them out either, because I guess these are the legal ones.

"Later with that noise," Pescatore scoffed, twirling the radio dial, increasing speed.

Garrison grunted. He was fiddling with his cell phone.

Pescatore tuned to a cross-border bilingual freeway report, then a Tijuana program. An older Mexican woman's amplified telephone voice, kitchen noise in the background, complained about graffiti, tattoos, drug use and other American influences. Decadence, she said. Bad manners. Imperialism.

One side of the border is always bitching about the other, Pescatore thought.

He was going over eighty miles per hour. The speed-trap overpass approached. He left the dial on a *banda* tune, oompah tuba and manic trumpets and rattling drums. It was one of the top Baja stations: X99, *La Que Pega y Mueve.* The One That Hits and Moves.

"*Ah-hiiiiyy,*" he whooped mariachi-style, cranking the volume, edging past eighty-five.

"Hey Valentine, slow the fuck down, what're you doing?"

Too late. Pescatore almost cheered the lights erupting in the rearview mirror, the CHP cruiser swinging into the lane behind him, gathering velocity around a curve.

Your turn to sweat, Pescatore thought. Buddy.

"I do not believe this," Garrison snarled. "A Chippie. You stupid asshole."

"My fault," Pescatore said. He maintained speed in order to irritate the CHP officer and make him suspicious.

"Pull it over right now," Garrison said. "Goddammit. Just take it easy and let's get this done with."

Garrison told Pescatore to get his badge out; they were going to claim to be working plainclothes. Garrison's hand went under his vest. Pescatore figured that Garrison was worried they would run his license and registration. If the feds were getting ready to scoop them up, one thing might lead to another. And if the indictment talk was just a setup to murder Pescatore, Garrison did not want to leave a record that he had been with him that morning.

Pescatore took his time pulling over. The CHP officer got out and approached in the rearview mirror: a black officer in his forties. The strong-legged stride of an aging sprinter, a crisp tan uniform, gold-framed glasses. As the officer came around to the window on the passenger side, keeping the Cherokee between him and the high-speed traffic, Pescatore saw him unsnap the flap of his holster.

Pescatore raised his voice over the drone of passing cars, reaching in front of Garrison to push his badge and license at the officer.

"How ya doin', Officer, Border Patrol, we—"

Garrison blocked Pescatore with his back. He proffered his own badge and declared: "Hi there, U.S. Border Patrol anti-smuggling, sir. We're conducting a surveillance here."

"Wait a minute, one at a time," the CHP officer commanded in a flat voice, examining Pescatore's badge and license. "I don't care who you are, son, you need to slow this vehicle down."

"Yessir, but we got this hot pursuit going," Pescatore said. He winked, grimaced, bobbed back and forth behind Garrison, hoping to catch the guy's attention. The officer's glasses had a designer's logo on the frame and were tinted, impeding eye contact.

"Pursuit? We weren't notified. CHP is s'posed to get notified on a pursuit."

The Chippie's right hand snapped and unsnapped the holster

flap. He stood in a textbook ready stance, knees slightly bent, shoulder pointed forward, front foot aligned with the shoulder.

"Not a pursuit, no sir," Garrison said quickly, anger barely contained. "We've got a load vehicle in our sights. A smuggler. Problem is he's halfway back to The Line by now."

"Goddamn right, this is fucked up, we're gonna catch hell," Pescatore declared.

"Well, wait a minute now..." The CHP officer handed back Pescatore's badge, but kept the license. He craned his neck to peer past Garrison at Pescatore, who made an imploring and terrified face. The officer seemed to realize that something was wrong; even if he thought Pescatore was drunk or deranged, that was a step in the right direction. He worried at his holster, fastening and unfastening it. Snap-snap. Snap-snap.

The officer asked Garrison: "Are you a supervisor with The Patrol?"

A murderous undercurrent built in Garrison's voice. "I'm a supervisor. Sir."

"This a U.S. government vehicle?"

"No sir, my personal vehicle."

"Huh. Why's he driving?"

"I'm directing the surveillance, sir."

"You work smuggling out of Border Patrol sector HQ?"

"No sir, Imperial Beach station."

"So they could verify—"

"Yeah absolutely, they could verify," Pescatore exulted. The station would rush over a carload of supervisors when they heard about them badging the CHP and posing as antismuggling investigators. The day after the shooting on the beach, no less.

Garrison shouldered him aside again.

"Sir, we've got an operation going, couldn't we just—"

"If you got an operation going, where's your radios at?"

Pescatore did not want to look at Garrison in the silence that ensued. He noticed that the CHP officer's nameplate said Boyd.

"I need to see your license and registration documents as well, sir," Boyd said to Garrison, officious and determined.

"Sure, no problem," Garrison said. He did not move. "About the radios, listen—"

"We're gonna lose 'em, we're gonna lose 'em!" Pescatore blurted, playing the loony all out. "This is fucked up!"

"Shut up, Valentine!" Garrison roared, sounding close to the edge.

Boyd took a fast light step backwards, his eyebrows jumping in alarm. His hand was planted on the butt of his pistol.

"I'm calling in," Boyd said. "They'll patch me through to Patrol communications, get this clarified right now."

Garrison cursed under his breath. Pescatore began to see a drawback to his maneuvering: He had laid the groundwork for a confrontation between two frightened men with guns.

8

BY GOD, MAN, DOESN'T anyone in this part of the world wear a suit and tie? I just saw the governor in Mexicali. He was wearing one of those abominable jackets like the baseball players, you know, with the leather sleeves? What a sight."

The Secretary shook his head in a burlesque of despair. His suit was impeccable—pin-striped, three-piece. His tie was mustard-colored. A matching handkerchief poked up out of a breast pocket. A watch chain hung across his vest, an affectation acquired during an ambassadorship in Europe with which he had been rewarded years earlier for perilous government service. His long white fingers tapped a cigarette over an ashtray.

"Well, it's a curious thing, Mr. Secretary," Méndez said. "There was some interesting research done on that here at the university. Our scientists determined that wearing a tie constricts the flow of ideas to the brain. A very serious condition, we call it *chilanguitis.*"

The Secretary bent forward in silent laughter, holding up a hand as if asking for mercy. He seemed unfazed by the stuffiness of the cramped second-floor office that had been hurriedly cleared for their meeting. Aviation manuals were stacked on the desk behind the Secretary. A glass wall beyond the desk overlooked a private hangar.

Méndez was not in the mood for banter, not even poking fun at *chilangos,* natives of Mexico City. He wore the same leather jacket and jeans he had worn the day before at the prison. He was unshaven. His eyes were red from a night without sleep; he had replaced his contact lenses with glasses before coming to the airport. Méndez was not in the mood, but it was a ritual: The Secretary liked him because Méndez was not one of the obsequious, humorless sycophants who infested the ministry. The Secretary prided himself on his sense of humor. And he expected Méndez to play the irreverent maverick.

"Very good, Méndez. Your wit prevails even when you are exhausted."

Despite his nattiness, the Secretary's pallor, pinched face and stooped posture reminded Méndez of a priest. The Secretary had no vices or pastimes other than clothes and books. He lived alone in a cavernous apartment full of bookshelves in a less-than-fashionable neighborhood of the capital. He had a reputation for integrity and bureaucratic infighting skills. As Araceli Aguirre never failed to point out, he was also a true-believing loyalist of the ruling party.

"I imagine you don't have much time to read these days," the Secretary said. "Have you read Castañeda's new one? It's about aging warriors of the left, like you. I must say it is excellent."

Another ritual. The Secretary had utmost respect for writers and liked to talk about books. During the gilded exile of his diplomatic post, he had written erudite essays that were published by scholarly journals and, reportedly, plays that he kept to himself.

"I haven't had a chance, Mr. Secretary. I've been trying to finish a book about the mafia judges in Sicily."

"By God, man. That's not exactly escapist fare. You should clear your head. Take refuge in a bit of Borges, I don't know. Reread 'El Quixote.' How is your family?"

"They seem fine. My wife is treated well at the university,

thanks to my friends there. It's hard to tell how they are from this distance, of course."

"Of course, that must be difficult." The Secretary nodded primly.

Méndez handed the Secretary a manila envelope containing photos and a ten-page memo. Opening the envelope, the Secretary swiveled toward him in the chair. The office was so narrow that their knees almost touched.

"The report on the Colonel's murder, sir."

"No doubt that it was a murder?"

"None. The final pages review the larger investigation and lay out what we intend to do. The moment has arrived to act on our work of the past year. The Americans agree. Frankly, I don't think we have a choice."

"Why?" The Secretary extracted reading spectacles from a pocket.

"If we don't act now, they will know we are frightened or unwilling. It would be dangerous after the events of last night."

"I see."

"This was an escalation. A provocation. By no means did the Ruiz Caballeros have to kill the Colonel the way they did. There were opportunities in the prison. But they waited, aided his escape, then orchestrated everything to be messy and spectacular. The finishing touch, the signature, was killing him at the border. Involving the Border Patrol, doing it under the noses of the Americans. Telling them, and us, that they can do what they want to whom they want."

Although he was speed-reading the report in his lap, the Secretary was listening. His smile uncovered nicotine-stained teeth.

"You have always had a flair for interpreting the semiotics of organized crime. Even in your columns. I used to tell my intelligence analysts: Read everything Méndez writes."

Méndez nodded his thanks. "Politically, it's important to emphasize the American involvement. They will make big arrests of their own functionaries: Border Patrol, inspectors. Even DEA."

"Good. The last thing the presidential palace wants to hear is more howling from the troglodytes in Washington about corrupt Mexicans. If we do nothing, they howl. If we attack our problems, instead of congratulating us they have new examples to howl about."

"No, this will be about a dangerous criminal network that functions on both sides and is being confronted on both sides."

The Secretary fingered an odd prow of black hair that jutted from the center of his receded hairline. He thumbed through the photos.

"And these unsavory-looking gentlemen?" he asked.

The surveillance photo had been taken by U.S. agents in the Gaslamp district of San Diego and supplied by Isabel Puente.

"The older one is known as Ibrahim Abbas. He has ties to terrorist cells in Paraguay and Brazil, according to the Americans. He has bought guns from a Border Patrol agent. He is an emissary of the mafias at the Triple Border. The others are his Brazilian bodyguards. They are brothers: Mozart and Tchaikovsky Moreira. Real names, not aliases."

"Mozart and Tchaikovsky? Marvelous. Totally Brazilian."

"If they are in the area and the timing permits, we will nab them too."

The Secretary resumed reading. Méndez spun half-circles in the rolling chair. He had composed the memo at dawn. He had outlined the strongest possible case, building to the list of arrests on the final page. The names would not surprise the Secretary, but Méndez still found it hard to believe what he was proposing.

Méndez had been a journalist when he had first met the Secretary, at the time an intelligence official leading an anticorruption campaign in Mexico City. Despite the man's genteel ways, he scared people. Méndez had decided during their first interview that he had to cultivate him as a source. And the Secretary had cultivated Méndez: from favored reporter to discreet unpaid adviser to overnight troubleshooter. The government had convinced the Secretary to take a key security job, hoping his reputation would improve its dubious image. Creating the Diogenes Group had demonstrated the Secretary's flair for bold moves.

The Secretary made a ruminative sound, as if acknowledging the weight of the document in his hands. "Impressive. And ambitious."

"We have an entire room filled with evidence files. If it were anybody else, we would have acted long ago."

"Essentially you want to charge Junior Ruiz Caballero with being the boss of organized crime in Baja California and beyond. Are you satisfied that you can prove that?"

"Absolutely. As I explain, he has decapitated the different border mafias and consolidated them into a single structure. All the evidence puts him at the top."

"I know he's heavily involved, but I still see him as too young and deranged to run something so massive. What is he, twenty-five?"

Méndez was getting nervous; they were going over old ground. "Twenty-nine. He might be deranged, but he's not stupid. Look at how well he's done in legitimate business, thanks to his late father's fortune. Not that it is an enviable gene pool."

Junior's father had been a famously sleazy power broker. He had died in a mysterious kidnapping attempt while awaiting trial for a scandal involving embezzlement and murders for hire.

"I suppose a childhood spent following his mother to resorts and detoxification centers in San Diego and New York didn't help Junior's personality," the Secretary said. "And the Senator is not the ideal role model either."

"No. Junior grew up on both sides of the border and absorbed the worst of both worlds." Méndez gestured at the memo. "As you can see, we are not going to charge the Senator for the moment. We could make a strong case that he provides political cover for his nephew and participates directly on the financial side. But I thought it best to hold off."

The Secretary cupped his chin in his right hand and his right elbow in his left hand. "On a legal level, Leobardo, I'm concerned about the weakness of our organized-crime laws. You'd really have to catch Junior in the act to make charges stick."

The Secretary had raised this objection before. Méndez thought he had dealt with it.

"Yes, Mr. Secretary, but the new laws on money laundering and drug trafficking will help. We have proof of specific crimes. We have well-documented connections to Multiglobo Productions and Junior himself. And the direct testimony of the Colonel."

"Which you yourself told me was limited. The Colonel is dead."

"What we know about his murder strengthens our case."

The Secretary stubbed out his cigarette, a chess player's pause. "When do you and the Americans hope to act?"

"We were talking about a week from today," Méndez said, his voice wavering. More resolutely, he added: "It's the right moment."

The Secretary smiled patiently. "I'm afraid that crosses the border between ambitious and reckless."

"Why?"

"Arresting Junior is not just a judicial matter. It is a political bomb. Whether or not you charge the uncle, it is an attack on him and his political group at a delicate moment. You and I understand what monsters these people are, but as far as the public is concerned, the Senator is an elder statesman. And his nephew is a playboy who manages very popular singers and boxers."

"In my humble opinion, none of that makes a difference. We are being pushed by events."

"Before anything happens, I have to consult at the highest levels. This is a question of state."

"We have been discussing this for months."

"Only now is it a concrete possibility. Only now can I approach the people who must be approached."

Méndez cleared his throat. Very quietly, he asked: "How long?"

"More than a week, certainly." The Secretary's long fingers pried his handkerchief from his breast pocket, dabbed at his forehead and his upper lip, then replaced the handkerchief. He patted Méndez on the knee. "Listen, Leobardo, think for a moment. This is a very dangerous step for you."

"As I said, the dangers are worse if we back down."

"It is my duty to protect you and your boys. I know something about the codes of the underworld, too. It is one thing to catch the Colonel red-handed. Those are the risks of battle, they can't really take offense. But now you have the temerity to attack the very top. My God, man."

Méndez plowed on, imagining Araceli's scorn.

"We can't sit and wait. What if we make all the arrests—except Junior? We go after the organization: Mauro Fernández Rochetti and the state police, the smuggling bosses, Multiglobo executives, American accomplices. Kill the body. Then we decide when to chop off the head?"

The Secretary shook his head with finality. "It will be clear that Junior is the target. The impact is the same."

Méndez ran his fingers slowly down the lines in his face.

"There's another problem," he said. "As you know, Araceli Aguirre is deeply involved in the investigation. The human rights commission has been invaluable."

"A dynamic young woman."

"Exactly. She's dismayed. She thinks the Colonel's death could have been avoided."

"It's fascinating to me how the human rights fanatics are ready to throw legal niceties out the window if their agenda is affected. As I told you, the prison transfer was difficult because of cases against the Colonel here in the state system. This is a nation of laws, of institutionality. No matter what Araceli Aguirre thinks."

"Nonetheless, another delay will convince her we are not serious. She may turn her back on us."

The Secretary dabbed fastidiously with the handkerchief again. "Well, only you have control over that."

"I'm not sure I do."

"You are her friend and mentor."

"She might go public. In her position, that's what I would do."

"I can only urge you to ask her to be sensible, consider her political ambitions and refrain from something that could have unfortunate consequences for everyone."

His chin cupped in his hand again, the Secretary was retreating behind a bureaucratic shield. And Méndez sounded to himself like a timid ruling-party lifer. Enough genuflecting, he thought.

"Mr. Secretary, I have to speak frankly," he said. "Until today I had few complaints. You have backed the Diogenes Group with great strength. Thanks to you, we have done marvels. But now, forgive me for telling you, I am worried. If you want me to wait, if you have to make consultations, I must respect that. But I have to ask you: Do you still want me to do the job? Or is this as far as the thing goes?"

The Secretary leaned back. He looked undersized and frail in the formidable suit, like a photo of a face superimposed onto someone else's body.

"Ah, Méndez. An elegant way of asking if I will betray you." He raised a hand to cut off the protest. "Please. You are in the line of fire. I admire your courage, your commitment. Nothing would make me happier than seeing Junior Ruiz Caballero in handcuffs. But I have to worry about institutionality. About questions of state."

Méndez leaned forward, his forearms on his thighs, feeling as if he were in a confessional.

"Fine," he said. "But when you talk to the presidential

palace"—the Secretary grimaced—"tell them this. If we don't stop these people now, it may come back to haunt us. As you know, there is a worrisome political dimension."

The Secretary's eyes widened expectantly. Méndez went on in a low voice: "If the Ruiz Caballeros sustain this alliance with the South American mafias, they will have enormous resources flowing in. This goes beyond the border. The Colonel is just the latest example: They are using murders of politicians and policemen to send terroristic messages. I think the Ruiz Caballeros are moving on two tracks. The presidential elections will be next year. The Senator's group already has a preferred potential candidate, does it not?"

"Absolutely."

"So you have the Senator operating at the political level. And Junior on the mafia level, supplying money and firepower. All that money, all that firepower. They could overwhelm everyone: here and in Mexico City. That is a real question of state."

The Secretary interlaced his fingers on his midsection with an expression that combined discomfort and paternal approval.

"A gloomy and paranoid analysis," he said. "But I happen to think you are right."

They spent another twenty minutes talking. A waiter from the airport restaurant appeared with tea for the Secretary and coffee, which revived Méndez, though a hot drink was not ideal in the sweaty confines of the office.

When they descended the circular metal staircase to the floor of the hangar, they were met immediately by Athos and the Secretary's personal assistant, Gregorio. A subtle young man with silver-rimmed glasses and a gaunt scrubbed face, Gregorio had a knack for gliding ahead of the Secretary and anticipating his wishes. Gregorio was usually as stolid as Athos, but both of them looked preoccupied. The Secretary's bodyguards and aides milled around whispering.

"What's up?" Méndez asked Athos, who deferred with a raise of his goateed chin to the Secretary's assistant.

Gregorio spoke in a breathy Mexico City accent full of rising *o*'s and *a*'s. "Mr. Secretary, I'm sorry but this is really peculiar. While you were upstairs, an individual who works for Senator Ruiz Caballero presented himself. He said the Senator happened to be at the airport and heard you were here. He said the Senator apologizes for the imposition, but he would appreciate it if you could make time for him to invite you to lunch."

"He happened to be at the airport?" Méndez asked Athos, who had a battle gleam in his eye.

Athos's airport sources had told him the Senator and his nephew had showed up earlier in the morning to fly to Nevada in their private jet.

"Then they delayed the departure," Athos said. "This monkey, eh, their people started nosing around asking when the Secretary was expected. The Senator has been sitting in the VIP lounge waiting for you to finish. Junior drove off somewhere."

"What do I tell the man, sir?" Gregorio asked anxiously.

The Secretary lit a cigarette with studied nonchalance. He glanced at Méndez, who shrugged. There was no doubt that the Ruiz Caballeros knew the Secretary was meeting with Méndez. It was a typically brazen gambit. Méndez remembered what Araceli had said the night before: The enemy weren't taking him for granted. They were worried.

"Tell him . . ." The Secretary took a drag on the cigarette. "Tell him I don't have time for lunch. I'm hurrying back to the D.F. But with great pleasure I can say hello to the Senator on the way to my plane. If he'd like."

Gregorio dispatched an emissary. The Secretary blew a stream of smoke from his nostrils. Méndez decided that he looked pretty tough for a bookworm in a fancy suit from the Distrito Federal (Mexico City).

"You will accompany me to the plane," the Secretary told Méndez.

"Very well." Méndez wished he weren't so grubby.

"If I say no outright, it might look like we are hiding," the Secretary said, eyes narrow against the smoke. "Moreover, I've known the Senator, on the inevitable level of government affairs, for twenty-five years. Your presence sets the right tone."

"I leave the political nuances to you, sir," Méndez said. He thought he detected a smile on the corners of the bloodless lips. This wily old bastard is enjoying himself, he thought.

"Shall we, fellows?" the Secretary said.

Men in suits picked up briefcases and radios. The Secretary dropped his cigarette and stepped on it. He frowned at Athos.

"Is it necessary for the commander to carry that elephant slayer?"

Athos looked chagrined, cradling the AK-47 protectively.

"You know something, sir?" Méndez said, giving the Secretary an unintentionally broad smile. "Usually I'd be the first to agree. But right now, I think it helps set the tone, as you put it."

"Very well. The gangster semiotics I leave to you."

The sun fell hard on the tarmac. The Secretary's jet, guarded by uniformed officers of the Diogenes Group and the federal police, was half a soccer field away from the hangar. The Ruiz Caballeros' Learjet was to the right of the Secretary's plane. Beyond the planes was the fence separating the airport from the border highway and the border fence.

The group strode across the tarmac: Méndez and the Secretary accompanied by Athos, Gregorio on their heels, and a loose diamond of bodyguards and aides around them.

Two GMC Yukons parked near the terminal came to life and glided forward. They stopped about halfway between the two planes. Two men got out of the lead vehicle and approached briskly.

Méndez had interviewed Senator Bernardo Ruiz Caballero

several times, but he had not seen him up close for years. The Senator was in his early sixties, his face froglike and dissipated beneath shiny, well-coiffed white hair. He looked chesty in a black linen suit with an open collar that revealed gold chains and medallions. He walked with a horseman's roll, elbows wide. The heels of his black boots banged the tarmac.

Méndez recognized the other man, a portly sweating flunky in a *guayabera* shirt, as the Senator's administrative assistant.

"My dear Luis," the Senator said. It was the first time Méndez had heard anyone call the Secretary by his first name. It reminded Méndez that, though Senator Ruiz Caballero might come off as a crude clown, he had converted provincial power into exponentially greater national power without losing his provincial ways. He was one of the select old hands who controlled their political party's ancient and arcane machinery.

Méndez watched in alarm as the Senator opened his arms for a hug. The Secretary thwarted him adroitly; he transformed the greeting into a handshake in which their free hands patted each other's biceps.

Disconcerted, the Senator regained composure with a volley of words. His voice was croaky and weathered by tobacco and alcohol. "You must come to Baja more often, my friend. I was set to invite you to lunch, I dropped everything and made reservations. Let me know next time and we'll go to Las Leñas. We haven't been there in years, eh?"

Senator Ruiz Caballero spent a lot of time under sunlamps. His skin was overcooked, wrinkled, mottled under the eyes with deep horizontal dents in the forehead. He chewed a mint, his teeth gleaming white in all that brown.

"Senator, what a pleasure, I'm sorry I'm in such a rush," the Secretary said mildly, his body turned as if he would resume stride at any moment.

Then he paused, as if he had remembered something. He clapped Méndez on the shoulder.

"You know Licenciado Méndez of the Diogenes Group, don't you, Senator?" the Secretary said heartily. "One of the finest public servants in one of the finest police agencies in the country."

The Secretary was laying it on thick. Senator Ruiz Caballero looked at Méndez reluctantly. His mouth twisted and the loose folds of skin on his throat quivered, as if he were barely able to control his revulsion. Méndez shook the plump, ring-filled hand as briefly and unenthusiastically as possible. The flinty eyes skittered over Méndez and quickly back to the Secretary. Senator Ruiz Caballero told the Secretary again how good it was to see him. The Senator was on his way to Las Vegas to watch a rookie boxer from his nephew's stable. But he would return to Mexico City in two days and wanted urgently to get together.

Three more vehicles approached from the terminal at high speed: a convertible Mercedes with the top down, trailed by a chrome-studded Buick Regal and a red Suburban. The trailing vehicles were full of men. Funk music boomed out of the Mercedes, organ and bass arpeggios, raucous voices. Three women sat in the backseat of the convertible, clouds of hair streaming. The vehicles skidded to a stop near the Ruiz Caballero jet.

Athos took two steps to position himself between Méndez and the vehicles.

"There's the young man," Senator Ruiz Caballero declared. "Always rushing. Junior! Come here a moment."

Junior Ruiz Caballero was in no rush. Nor was he listening. He emerged in stages from the passenger door on the far side of the Mercedes. The wind ruffled his hair, which had grown long. He took a couple of somnolent, stiff-shouldered steps toward the Regal, elaborately ignoring the little crowd around the Secretary and the Senator a hundred feet away. Junior had been doing some sunlamp time of his own. He wore a blue T-shirt with short sleeves exposing broad fleshy arms. His jeans were low-slung and oversized in *cholo* fashion.

He looks like a wannabe gangster, Méndez thought. Except

that a wannabe with a billion dollars and a vicious disposition becomes the real thing.

"Over here for a moment, Junior," his uncle called uneasily across the tarmac. "Look who's here."

Junior paid no heed. He was talking to a mustachioed man who had gotten out of the Regal, the only other passenger in the caravan to get out. The second man was a behemoth in black. He looked lethal, his bearing almost military. Méndez recognized him from a photo and remembered the street name: Buffalo. The heavy hitter from Los Angeles, the chief of Junior's imported *pocho* triggermen.

The Secretary took it in impassively. There they are, Méndez wanted to say. The enemy. Look at what we are up against. You better crush them before they crush us.

Junior rested a hand on Buffalo's ridge of a shoulder, their heads ducked close together as they talked. Junior sneered, obviously enjoying this bit of theater.

"Junior, please," Senator Ruiz Caballero rasped. Méndez could not tell if he was truly embarrassed or just playing his role in a scene for the Secretary's benefit. "Come say hello to the Secretary . . . And the Licenciado."

The shaggy head turned toward them. Buffalo looked over as well. Junior made a derisive, incredulous face. He said something unintelligible. Buffalo smiled.

Junior Ruiz Caballero raised a fist and, by way of a sardonic greeting, pumped it in their general direction. He looked directly at Méndez.

Méndez returned the stare with a tunnel vision that blotted out everything else. Despite the presence of Athos, the bodyguards, his own officers, he felt utterly alone. Sweating, haggard, unsteady on his feet, he returned that stare for all he was worth.

Junior's pudgy features grew bored again. He gave Buffalo a quick hug and walked toward his plane. Young drivers unloaded luggage, but the other passengers remained in the vehicles.

"That boy." Senator Ruiz Caballero got throaty with facile emotion. "But who can blame him? After what he's been through. All the ghosts, all the crosses this family has had to bear."

The Secretary made a sound that might have been sympathetic. He had clearly had his fill of Tijuana fauna in the sun.

"Very well, Senator, what a pleasure to have seen you if only for a moment," he began.

But now Senator Ruiz Caballero and every other male on the tarmac were watching the second act. A driver held open the doors of the Mercedes. The women who got out were instantly recognizable: three members of Las Chicas Ringside from Multiglobo Arena, fixtures in Junior's entourage. During boxing matches, their job consisted of strutting around the ring in bathing suits, holding up signs that indicated the number of the next round. One was Latina, one was black, one was Anglo. They had big hair, big sunglasses, big bodies fortified by silicone and aerobics and encased in leather and Spandex, straps and buckles. Amazon caricatures on towering heels. Eminently aware of their audience, heads high and shoulders back, the women strode to the plane.

"*Híjole.*" The Senator leered, his teeth crunching the mint. "If I had known those three were coming along, I would have brought my mountain boots."

"We are leaving," the Secretary said.

Amalia Aguirre, age three, was getting sleepy. She climbed around in Méndez's lap making herself comfortable. She put her round face close to his, her ringlets pulled back by a barrette. She clenched his cheeks in her hands and said, "Chubby-chubby. Chubby-chubby."

"Amalita, please, careful with Leo's face," Araceli Aguirre said, putting two glasses of orange-papaya juice on the white patio table. Watching her daughter curl up in Méndez's arms, she said: "My love, why don't you go inside and lie down? Tell Papa to tuck you in."

"It's fine," Méndez said. "Let her be."

He shifted the girl gently to his left shoulder and drank juice. Amalia was so much lighter than his son, who was five. When they were preparing for his son's birth, Méndez and his wife had bought a stack of parenting books at a café-bookstore in San Diego where they liked to spend weekend mornings. The books had been moderately helpful and written in a strangely robotic tone. Any Mexican parent could tell you how important it was to shower a child with hugs and kisses—without citing academic studies showing the negative impact of insufficient affection later in life. Patting Amalia's back, Méndez thought that someone should do a reverse study to measure the negative impact on fathers deprived of contact with their children.

"So it was a grotesque episode," Aguirre said.

"Absolutely. Psychological warfare à la Ruiz Caballero. The Secretary held his own. He treated the Senator like a shoeshine boy."

"And that gave you a good feeling about the Secretary," Araceli said bleakly. "You are convinced that he's totally behind you."

Méndez sighed and held Amalita a little closer. "Basically yes, Araceli. Though I'm sure you are about to explain with great vehemence how mistaken I am."

"With or without vehemence, I think he treated the Senator like that for your benefit. Consolation for the fact that he's not going to indict them next week, or next month, or ever."

They were sitting on the patio of Aguirre's house on a low hill in Colonia Juárez. The patio was cozy: trees, plants, a stone fountain painted with pre-Columbian figures. The white walls had small alcoves in them containing statuettes—a Virgin of Solitude with a high ornate crown, a sweet-faced female saint in a penitent's habit—by Oaxacan artists whose work Aguirre collected.

Méndez felt soothed by the gurgling water, the greenery, the warmth of Amalia. The girl had fallen asleep, her curls in his face, her breathing soft. His eyelids drooped. He did not want to have this conversation. But after the Secretary left, Méndez had felt honor-bound to visit Araceli and deliver the bad news. He found her at home preparing for lunch. When she opened the door, she told him he looked like a zombie.

"I'm disappointed," Méndez said, adjusting his arms to cradle the sleeping girl. "But I don't think his position is unreasonable. He has never let me down."

"You give him the benefit of the doubt regarding the Colonel, then." Aguirre's short hair glistened, still wet from a shower. She wore a white cotton sweater with the sleeves rolled up, her long brown forearms extended on the round table.

"Let's keep in mind that the Secretary created the Diogenes Group," Méndez said. "Without him we wouldn't be having this conversation."

"Don't exaggerate."

"It's true. We'd be sitting in some pathetic rented office like that one you had behind the supermarket ten years ago. Smelling truck fumes. You'd be begging yanqui foundations for grants, feeding me futile human rights reports for my column about how someone should maybe investigate the Ruiz Caballeros one day and—"

When Araceli Aguirre got mad, it was like someone flicked a switch, a current that sparked through her. She became baleful and hyperarticulate. This served her well in a job that called for public displays of indignation.

"Do you want to know what your problem is with the Secretary, Leo?" Aguirre demanded.

"Not especially, but please enlighten me."

They were interrupted, perhaps intentionally, by Rodrigo, Araceli's husband. He walked onto the patio, smiled at Méndez and put a hand on his wife's shoulder. She squeezed the hand without looking at him. Rodrigo gently lifted his sleeping daughter off Méndez's chest and carried her inside.

Rodrigo was bearded and distracted, a biologist of great intellect and serenity. His detachment from the harsh realities with which his wife dealt was the key to their marriage, Méndez believed. He liked Rodrigo, but felt uneasy around him. Rodrigo seemed to have no problem with his wife's friendship with Méndez. And Méndez assumed Rodrigo knew about Méndez's brief romance with Araceli when they were all university students — a topic no one ever mentioned.

Aguirre chewed a fingernail.

"The problem," she said, "is that the Secretary was your source. A very good source. He was an official in this foul system who actually told you the truth now and then. So you idealized him. Journalists do that. And when he put you in charge of the Diogenes Group, you idealized him more. He takes advantage of that. He's manipulating you. He doesn't deserve your trust."

"The fact remains that thanks to him, I'm inside. *We* are inside. We have the power to do something. It's easy to sit on the outside and whine."

"We've had this argument before. Until the Colonel died, I would have said you might be right. But this spectacle at the airport is revolting. A cabinet functionary in charge of upholding the law chatting with the worst gangsters in the country? While a bunch of murderers and goons and floozies stand around smirking? Please. If he had any pants, he would have had you arrest them on the spot."

"A childish fantasy, Araceli."

"You have used up all the power they are going to give you on the inside. Unless someone pushes from the outside."

"Like you?"

"Like me."

"What are you going to do?" He felt defeated. He had known it was coming.

"I'm working on that."

"He told me to appeal to you as your 'friend and mentor,' to be sensible."

"How pompous."

"As your friend and mentor, can I please ask you to wait and see what he says next time I talk to him?"

"I'll wait one more week and that's it. And only because I'm your disciple, or acolyte, or whatever it is mentors have. I'm not going to wait long."

"Thank you."

"You really look terrible. Drink juice."

The fountain gurgled. Birds chirped. A grumble of traffic floated up from downtown. The sound of his cell phone startled him awake.

It was Athos calling from headquarters. He said Isabel Puente wanted Méndez to call her immediately on a secure line.

"It seems you are a good judge of character, Licenciado," Athos said. "Concerning that young man we discussed recently. The one in green."

"You don't say."

"He shot a policeman on the freeway in San Diego this morning and disappeared. They are looking for him. They want our help."

Méndez felt vindicated. He also felt sorry for Isabel. He imagined that she was so distraught over her pet informant's debacle that she could not bring herself to call Méndez directly. His wavering about Pescatore was over. Pescatore had hurt Isabel. He was a sneaky little thug.

"Athos, I hope we find him," Méndez said. "I'm in the perfect mood for a conversation with that young man."

9

BLOOD SEEPED OUT OF Garrison's sleeve onto the cell phone. The phone slid out of his hand into his lap. He fumbled to retrieve it.

"Buffalo," he groaned. "Talk to me..."

Garrison slumped against his door. He was fading fast. But his left hand jabbed the silver Beretta into Pescatore's ribs.

Cursing, Pescatore skidded up to a red light. Drivers honked behind him. The traffic circles in Tijuana were brutal. He didn't understand the rules: The boulevards emptied into the circle and drivers just blazed on into the slalom—battleship Chevys, rattletrap Volkswagens, rust-eaten pickups—somehow knowing when to go and when to yield.

"Come on, Arleigh," Pescatore implored. "Point that somewhere else."

"Shut up and drive you motherfucking wussy," Garrison gasped, an ugly gurgle in his throat.

"We gotta get you to a hospital, man. Let me talk to him."

Pescatore reached slowly for the phone. He encountered no resistance. He pried the phone out of Garrison's hand, recoiling at the sticky smeared blood.

"Buffalo?" Pescatore said, making sure the phone didn't touch his mouth.

"Valentín. That you, homes?" Buffalo sounded unperturbed. In the background, water splashed and a child's laughter echoed. Buffalo said: "How is he?"

"Hurt bad."

"Where?"

"Couple of impacts in the chest up near the throat."

"And you?"

"No damage."

"Where you at?"

"Going up a hill. Coming up on that big boulevard, Agua Caliente?"

"Turn left on the boulevard. Tell me what you see."

"Shit, I don't know..."

The vehicle and foot traffic was oppressively dense. In San Diego you could drive for blocks without spotting a pedestrian. When he had first arrived in Southern California, he had wondered where all the people were. It turned out they were in Tijuana.

"Valentín?"

"Big Boy. I just passed a Big Boy sign. Some kinda stadium on the right. Smells like cows."

"El Toreo. *Está bien.* I got you." Buffalo was walking with the phone, giving orders to someone. Pescatore heard the static of a police-type radio in the background.

"OK, Valentín, *tu tranquilo,*" Buffalo told him in a take-charge rumble. "You just kick it behind the wheel. Kick it stone cold, homes. You're out for a cruise, that's all."

"Alright." Pescatore felt the gun slip down along his side. Garrison's eyes clouded over. A police car passed in the opposite direction.

"Couple of municipal cops just gave me the eye, goddammit," Pescatore said.

"Uh-huh."

"They're turning around. They're comin' after me. Holy shit."

"Easy. *No seas pendejo.*" His voice muffled, Buffalo spoke Spanish into the radio.

By now the CHP had spread the alert to police on both sides of the border, Pescatore thought. Surely someone had seen the gunfight on the freeway. Pescatore had been terrified that a quick-thinking commuter with a cell phone would be their undoing. But Garrison had called his buddy Nacho, the Mexican customs supervisor, who had waved Valentine safely across The Line into Tijuana, bloody passenger and all.

The squad car trailed Pescatore at a distance, no lights or siren. After a few minutes listening to Buffalo alternate between the radio and a second phone, Pescatore asked: "Now what, Buffalo?"

"Nothing. The *municipales* are on the home team. You just listen and I'm gonna talk you in, *cabrón*."

The boulevard curved along the base of hills. He reported landmarks: a twin-towered hotel, a racetrack, a golf course. Buffalo told him to take a right. The street rose into a neighborhood with less dust and more shade. The houses were bigger and nicer. A grass median divided the street. The Cherokee bumped over cobblestones past well-scrubbed children carrying backpacks and wearing blue private-school uniforms.

He heard the roar of a motorcycle. It zipped downhill toward him on the other side of the median, a high-powered beast. The driver crouched in a black ninja helmet that obscured his face. When he came even with Pescatore, the motorcyclist braked into a controlled hotdog skid. He maneuvered up and over the grass median, the bike roaring and jouncing, and turned onto Pescatore's side of the street.

The officers in the municipal police car behind Pescatore did not react to the flagrant traffic violation. In fact, the squad car reduced speed.

The motorcycle overtook the Cherokee on the passenger side. The motorcyclist rose nimbly off the seat to peer at the inert Garrison. Sunlight glinted off the helmet.

"Guy on a motorcycle buzzing around," Pescatore said.

"I know," Buffalo said. "You got a Suburban behind you too. In a minute it's gonna pass you. Follow the Suburban."

Pescatore saw the red Suburban in his rearview mirror. Two men were inside, the passenger talking into a walkie-talkie. At a circular intersection with a fountain in the middle, the Suburban sped up and led the way. The police car had disappeared.

The street got steeper, winding among full-fledged mansions. The high walls were topped with spikes, sentry turrets, encrusted broken glass. The sidewalks had emptied to San Diego–style barrenness save for the occasional security guard, pushcart vendor or uniformed maid. Tijuana seemed a long way below.

"You're almost here," Buffalo told him. "I'm hanging up. No fast moves, you'll make the *vatos* nervous."

The motorcycle whined around like a bumblebee. The motorcyclist appeared to be making sure they had not been followed. He hung back, zoomed in and out of side streets, reappeared right behind Pescatore.

Pescatore saw with grim satisfaction that Garrison had stopped moving. He scooped the supervisor's pistol off the floor and stuck it in his belt. Steering one-handed, he reached roughly into the pockets of Garrison's vest and liberated an ammunition clip, a wad of bills, a cell phone and a USB flash drive.

Garrison had done his best to get him killed, but it hadn't been good enough, Pescatore thought. His voice shaking, he hissed: "That's right, asshole. Hurry up and die. Hurry up and die."

That was real cold, and so was his methodical looting of the wounded man. But he remembered something Garrison had once told him about gunfights. When the shooting starts, you stop thinking, Garrison had said: It's all instinct and reflex. Well, Garrison was dying. And Pescatore was obeying his instincts and reflexes. He was doing everything he could to stay alive.

The Suburban stopped at a violet-colored wall at the crest of a hill. Someone looked down at them over a rampart. The passenger of the Suburban got out: a young man with short hair holding a Tek-9. He was met by a man who came out of a sentry box. A gate slid open.

Pescatore entered a wide driveway between two sprawling houses. Two lots had been combined, forming a compound around the mansions. Buffalo's Buick Regal was one of the half-dozen vehicles in the driveway.

Pescatore got out slowly. The young man with the close-cropped hair stalked up to him. He pointed the Tek-9 at Pescatore's shoes.

"Hey, how you doin'?" Pescatore said, affecting earnest relief. "My man here ain't doing good, I'll tell you that. Where's Buffalo at?"

The gunman answered by scratching his stubbled chin and appraising Pescatore at an angle. He was Pescatore's age. His oversized white T-shirt, "Pacas" tattoo on his bicep and *cholo* scowl behind Ray-Bans recalled the gangbangers Pescatore had arrested at The Line.

The biker joined them, pulling off his helmet. Pescatore saw a small microphone for a two-way radio rigged inside the face shield. The biker had a shaved head, a rugged, narrow-waisted build and a Zorro mustache. His eyebrows arched high, giving him a diabolical aspect.

The biker grunted and got to work frisking Pescatore, who spread his hands wide. He felt desperation as the biker yanked his Glock out of his shoulder holster and Garrison's Beretta out of his belt. The biker relieved him of his phone and Garrison's phone as well.

Pescatore's hosts turned their attention to the Cherokee. When they opened the passenger door, Garrison flopped heavily sideways; the seat belt prevented him from falling into the driveway.

"Damn," the shaven-headed biker said. "*Puro fiambre.*"

Pescatore heard Buffalo's voice approaching from a backyard where a swing set and pool deck were visible. Buffalo wore jeans and a sleeveless black undershirt on his massive torso. His hair and down-turned mustache were spattered with droplets of water. He held hands with a sturdy little boy of about seven who wore swim trunks and carried an inflatable green sea horse. The boy was deep in an animated monologue that had Buffalo enthralled. He held the boy's hand with great gentleness and ceremony.

Buffalo's contentment evaporated when he saw Garrison. With the linebacker quickness that Pescatore had noted before, Buffalo moved between the boy and the Cherokee. He crouched, tousled the boy's wet hair and spoke in his ear. Then he sent him trotting toward a side door of one of the houses. A woman in a maid's uniform stood behind the screen door.

"Yolanda, take Ivan inside," Buffalo ordered in Spanish, his eyebrows low and dark. "Now."

The maid yanked the boy through the doorway.

Buffalo squatted next to the Cherokee, his girth supported easily on his haunches. He studied Garrison with the air of a mechanic looking under a car hood.

"You want me to call Dr. Guardiola?" the gunman muttered.

"Nope," Buffalo said, intent on the corpse. "*Este cabrón ya se fue a la chingada.* Sniper, have Lucho deal with it when he comes back."

The tall homeboy who had driven the Suburban nodded. His stiffly combed hair flared out at the back of his neck. His half-closed left eyelid had probably inspired his nickname.

Buffalo straightened with a finality that suggested that the late Supervisory Agent Arleigh Garrison of the U.S. Border Patrol was no longer an issue.

"Va-len-tín," Buffalo said, drawing out the syllables.

"How you been, man? We made it, huh? Thanks for talking me in." Pescatore offered his hand to Buffalo, who gripped it mechanically.

"What went down, Valentín? *La placa* pulled you over and then what?"

Pescatore told the story largely as it had happened. The sun beat down, the four *cholos* listened. To his alarm he found himself improvising his way into another risk: He implied that both he and Garrison had shot the highway patrolman.

"You definitely smoked him?" Buffalo asked.

"We didn't exactly stick around to take his pulse, but he didn't get up. I just thank God he missed me. It was a miracle."

In fact, Pescatore had not drawn his gun. He had been about to yell a warning to the CHP officer and grab Garrison when the supervisor made his own move. Garrison had slammed Pescatore across the side of the head with his left arm as he drew on the Chippie with his right. By the time Pescatore had shaken off the blow, the Chippie was down. And the wounded Garrison was pointing the smoking Beretta at Pescatore's face and ordering him to drive.

With his thumb and forefinger, Buffalo touched the ends of his thick mustache.

"OK, wait here with Momo and Pelón," Buffalo said. He went into the house.

Momo, the gunman, and Pelón, the motorcyclist, smoked cigarettes and eyed Pescatore like leashed Dobermans. Momo's gun stayed pointed at Pescatore's feet. Pescatore stretched, yawned and sat down on a ledge jutting from the wall of the second house. He played sleepy and disinterested while imagining escape plans. All of them ended with Momo cutting him in half with a burst from the Tek-9.

The blood dripping onto the driveway from Garrison's outflung arm was driving him crazy. The corpse entangled in the seat belt gave him the sensation they were at a twisted crime scene where Pescatore was the suspect and the homeboys were the law.

Finally, Buffalo sent his cousin Rufino to get him. The chunky yokel from Guanajuato looked eager to please. Momo and Pelón ignored him. They think he's a rinky-dink border brother, but he's related to the boss, Pescatore thought.

"Come on, Valentín, my cousin Omar wants to see you," Rufino declared, his shy and friendly tone giving Pescatore a moment of hope.

Pescatore followed him into the house. A hallway and swinging door led into a high-ceilinged living room dominated by a glass chandelier the size of a monster truck tire.

"What a palace, eh?" Rufino whispered. "Don't worry, Omar will take care of you."

The living room was busy with furry sofas, thick rugs and velvet curtains. There were crucifixes and religious art. A life-size painting depicted a kneeling Virgin Mary at prayer, the mournful elongated face encircled by a shawl. There were reliefs and statuettes of Greco-Roman gods, wrestlers, nymphs. Isabel had once raided a gangster's apartment that she described as "narco-chic"; Pescatore had an idea that this was the kind of decor she meant.

Pescatore saw a framed sketch near the well-stocked bar. The sketch was done in black and white: In the foreground was the tear-streaked face of a lovely Latina. Behind her rose a prison wall, a gun tower with a searchlight, the moon among clouds. At the top was the word "*Esperándome*" and below that "Mule Creek SHU."

Mule Creek was a prison in Northern California. SHU stood for "Security Housing Unit," the cell blocks reserved for gang chiefs, hit men and other problem inmates.

Pescatore turned when Buffalo came in.

"Hey, you drew this?"

"Uh-huh." Buffalo sank into an armchair.

"It's great."

"Thanks."

"Nice crib."

"My boss gave it to me a while back. Wedding present. Have a seat, Valentín. *Oye,* you been busy, eh?" Arms folded, Buffalo cracked his piratical, teardrop-decorated smile. "Last night on the beach. Goin' at it with the CHP today, this and that. To the curb, *cabrón*."

Buffalo's demeanor had changed. He looked comfortable, the man of the house at home.

"So in case you wanted to know, that highway patrolman is in intensive care and don't look like he's going to make it," Buffalo announced jovially. "He had your driver's license in his pocket. Every local, state and federal po-lice in San Diego County is looking for you. Your story checked out fine."

"Jesus."

As devastating as the news was, Pescatore was chiefly affected by the realization that the change in Buffalo's manner was due to relief. Pescatore's story had checked out, so the big man would not have to kill him. Pescatore wondered what turncoat U.S. law enforcement source had relayed the information so fast.

"What are you gonna do?" Buffalo asked.

"I don't know, tell you the truth."

"You need a place to hide out," Buffalo said. "You can stay with us."

"Yeah?"

"It's fucked up, Garrison getting popped. But it woulda been a pain in the ass if he turned up *en El Otro Lado.* Lotta questions, federal heat, this and that. Instead, he disappears. You did us a favor gettin' here, even if was too late to help 'im. Showed me some heart."

"Thanks, Buffalo."

The big man's forearms were interlocked in bands of tendon and muscle and tattoos, the Virgin of Guadalupe obscuring a name that ended in *ita.*

"Plus I ain't forgetting you helped Rufino. But you gotta earn your keep. I know you can handle a *cuete.* You can do a little work for me."

"Really?"

Buffalo made a laughing sound deep in his chest. "Ordinarily

I'd say we, uh, ain't acceptin' applications right now. But we'll find something."

"OK. Thanks." Pescatore wished someone would offer him something to eat.

"Let's get you rested. You look torn up."

"Want me to bring in my stuff?" Pescatore rose, glancing appreciatively at the circular stairway past the chandelier.

"What, you think you're staying here?" Buffalo sounded offended and amused. "Fuck that. This is *my* crib, *ese.* You crash next door with the *vatos.*"

They returned Pescatore's duffel bag to him, but not the guns or the phones. Buffalo took him across the driveway to the second house. The living room smelled like a giant ashtray. It looked like a frat house, a crack house and a barracks after a mutiny. The wall-to-wall carpet was a swamp of bottles, pizza boxes, fast-food wrappers, cigarette butts, newspapers, porn magazines. Pelón, Momo, Sniper and two other hard-core gangbanger-looking guys lounged on three couches arranged in front of a giant television in a wall entertainment center. A coffee table held two bongs that were in active use, judging from the aromatic haze of marijuana smoke, as well as a large round mirror.

"Welcome to the sleazoid dive," Buffalo growled. "Maybe you're not a slob like these youngsters. In that case, I feel bad for you. Hey, listen up."

The homeboys slowly separated their attention from the television, which was showing a horror movie about underground creatures chasing people in the desert and erupting out of the sand to chomp them. Buffalo made introductions.

"So this dude was in the *Migra,* huh?" Pelón said. "*La pinche Migra.*"

Pelón stood in front of Pescatore. His hands drummed idly on his whip-tight gut. His glassy-eyed and malicious smile indicated that he had nominated himself to mess with Pescatore, a kind of jailhouse welcoming ritual.

"Now he's wanted," Buffalo said. "He just shot a cop."

"No shit."

"Cut on the news, you'll see."

Somebody worked the remote. Eventually, the big hair and sloe eyes of a Mexican anchorwoman filled the screen. The volume came up during a succession of images: police vehicles, yellow tape and traffic jams on the freeway. ID photos of the CHP officer, Garrison and Pescatore.

"That's him, *güey!*" Pelón whooped.

The anchorwoman said the words "armed and dangerous." They cut to Méndez talking to reporters by an open car door. Méndez needed a shave. He said: "No matter who is protecting these renegade American agents, we will track them down like the killers and cowards they are."

You better bring a whole lot of backup, you conceited Mexican jackass, Pescatore thought, feeling a chill of hate.

There were more howls from the homeboys. Pelón turned back to Pescatore. "Better stay in the house, *cabrón.* Diogenes is comin' to getcha!"

Pelón took a long swig from a beer. His eyebrows angled upward. "Now let me get this straight, *güey:* You're in the *Migra,* right? You're a cop?"

"That's right," Pescatore said. He adopted the icy tonk-thumping face he had used in confrontations with groups of aliens at the levee.

"But today, you shot a cop?"

"*Así es.*"

"*Chinga.*" Pelón surveyed Pescatore and then his audience. "I guess you sure enough joined the other patrol now, eh? *Ya entraste en la otra patrulla, güey.*"

The others broke up, whooping and chortling. Buffalo allowed himself a smile. Pescatore wondered what was so fucking funny.

Buffalo enlightened him.

"In TJ they got a nickname for us, Valentín," he said. "I'm

surprised you never heard about it. They call us La Patrulla de la Muerte. The Death Patrol."

His room was in the servants' quarters.

It was on the third floor in the back of the L-shaped mansion. The room was dim and the walls and floor were bare: a near closet made more claustrophobic by the slanted ceiling. But he saw no sign of rodents or insects, and the mattress in the corner was clean.

The door had no lock. When Rufino left, Pescatore took the lone chair and wedged it under the doorknob. He placed his keys on the edge of the chair so they would fall with a clatter if anyone tried to enter. He sat on the mattress, his back propped on the pillow against the wall. Closing his eyes, he reviewed options.

Ever since the shoot-out on the beach, he had whirled helplessly among people and events. It was like a merry-go-round cranked out of control. No one would be inclined to show mercy to a rogue Border Patrol agent on a cop-killing beef. Law enforcement and migrant advocates, Anglos and Mexicans and African-Americans, they would be elbowing one another aside to fry him, and the hell with annoying details like the truth. He had to get in touch with Isabel Puente and try to convince her of his innocence. He wanted to figure out his next move with her help. On the other hand, he did not want the Death Patrol thinking he was anything but guilty. He wondered whether Puente would believe him and how much she could do for him.

Thinking about her was painful. He had a fleeting erotic flashback of Isabel unleashed that night in her apartment: her voice hoarse and urgent in his ear, her brown body coiled around him. Hard to believe it had all been an act. He wanted desperately to think that Garrison had lied to him in order to get him across the border. But what if Garrison's information on the impending arrests had been accurate? What if that was the very reason he wanted to whack Pescatore? In that case, Isabel had lied about the timing of the arrests for sure. He could only think that meant she had planned to double-cross him and have him arrested too.

Pescatore got up and went to the narrow window. The walls of the compound below were high and coated with jagged glass. There was at least one sentry he knew about, probably more. If they caught him escaping, he was history. No talking his way out of that shit. If he succeeded, the run to San Diego would be dangerous. He could find the Diogenes Group and surrender to them. But he would have to get past all the law enforcement agencies in town that were nothing more than branches of the Ruiz Caballero organization. And another problem remained: During his obnoxious little TV appearance, Méndez had called Pescatore a killer and a coward. He had sounded like he really meant it. Like he looked forward to questioning Pescatore, Mexican-style, when he got his hands on him.

Pescatore flopped facedown onto the bed. He heard faraway music, a bass line throbbing up from the living room. He remembered his first night at the Border Patrol academy in Artesia, New Mexico. The far side of the moon, as far as he was concerned. The dormitory rooms plastered with class schedules and posters of bikini babes draped over Harleys. The legions of trainees from Texas, Arizona, California. There had been Mexican-Americans, Anglos, a few Cubans and Puerto Ricans mixed in. Even a contingent of Portuguese-Americans from Rhode Island and New Jersey. But nobody from Chicago or anywhere near his world. That night had been the most alone he had ever felt in his life. Until now.

Pescatore fell asleep. He sank in a bottomless black ocean. He dreamt repeatedly about waking up, the doorknob turning, the keys clattering, glass shattering, shots, blood, Garrison's eyes bulging upside down. But Pescatore slept regardless. He slept and slept and slept.

* * *

Over the next couple of days, Pescatore fell into the rhythms of life in the gangster house. He stayed indoors, mainly in the living room in front of the TV, where at least a couple of homeboys could be found watching and partying at all times. Pescatore had rarely smoked marijuana. While working hotel security he had marveled at how the doormen and bellhops he got mixed up with started their mornings with a joint. Reefer didn't get him going; it submerged him, staggered him. But when Sniper passed him a joint on his second night in the mansion, Pescatore got with the program. He felt anesthetized, the world pushed to a safe distance. He sucked down beers too, hoping to ward off paranoia about the fact that he was hanging out with couchfuls of *cholos* who were the stuff of every PA's nightmares. This house was the equivalent of being thrown into an immigration lockup or a county jail. Yet the gangsters accepted him nonchalantly. If Buffalo said he was cool, he was cool. And if Buffalo told them to torture him to death for the sole purpose of seeing him get that look on his face, they would do that too.

So Pescatore smoked and drank. He sleepwalked in a realm of dread and wonder. He watched himself on television. The Mexican news gave a lot of coverage to the freeway shooting. Pescatore and Garrison were the chief suspects. The news flashed an academy photo of him, heaped abuse on the Border Patrol, and reported that the Diogenes Group and Mexican federal police were hunting all over the state of Baja California. A breakthrough was imminent. Contemplating his clean-shaven smile in the photo, Pescatore decided to grow a Buffalo-style mustache. Next to him, Momo spoke up with unexpected words of support.

"Don't even worry about it," Momo told him, giving Pescatore his raised-chin, slit-eyed stare. "That's a lotta hype about *la federal. Puro pedo.* Long as you're with us, they ain't gonna sweat you."

If Buffalo was the commander of the Death Patrol, Momo was his lieutenant. The stone-faced Momo partied as hard as anyone else, but he was a stern taskmaster. Buffalo rarely visited the house; only Momo and Rufino visited Buffalo. The driveway was a strict border between the houses. Buffalo's family kept to their side of the line as well. Pescatore glimpsed Buffalo's wife on the third day, climbing out of an Escalade. Rufino helped her carry fistfuls of shopping bags—Neiman Marcus, Saks Fifth Avenue, Nordstrom—into the house. She was statuesque in a long summer dress, a bit of a belly, sunglasses propped in rich black curls. Her face had the weary beauty of the sketch on her living room wall.

Sniper and Pelón were the sergeants. The enlisted men were a shifting cast of a dozen youths, mostly gang members from California in their late teens and early twenties. Pescatore got the impression they were an all-star team of prospects recruited from a variety of gangs. They spoke the fractured Spanglish of penitentiaries, jails and juvenile lockups on both sides of the border. Instead of killing each other over street corners, they were killing together and living large. Their days started about noon when they drifted downstairs to the large modern kitchen. They ate steak, eggs and *chilaquiles* at the kitchen table or hunched on stools around a butcher-block island in the middle of the black-and-white tiled floor. A matronly woman named Doña Marta cooked for them and cleaned up once in a while. Tent-shaped in a brown dress, she moved in her own universe, her flat face wrinkled in disapproval, groaning periodically with exertion. She talked to nobody and saw nothing.

On the third day, Pescatore felt safe enough to start looking for a telephone he could use to call Isabel. Even if he made just a short call, he wanted her to hear his voice, to let her know he was alive. But he had already determined that the house had no land lines. The only homeboys he saw using cell phones were Momo, Sniper and Pelón. He knew the organization was careful about communications. Isabel had told him they had sophisticated intercept technology and countersurveillance techniques. Once he got his hands on a phone, it would be like carrying a time bomb. He would have to dispose of it or risk somebody finding it on him.

Pescatore spent the morning sneaking around rooms and hallways in search of a stray cell phone. No juice. He set himself up in front of the TV, hoping a *vato* might leave a phone unattended while getting wasted. It didn't happen. The next morning, Momo, Sniper and Pelón left early. That night, the news reported that a Mexican federal prosecutor had been machine-gunned in his driveway after his retirement party; Sniper and Pelón reached over and slapped each other five. The TV news showed a quick image of Méndez walking into a building past cameras. A voice-over explained that the Diogenes Group was on the case.

"That *cabrón* right there needs to get got." Pelón gestured at Méndez, his bald profile making him look like a warrior-monk. "Fuck sending messages. If we're gonna do 'im, let's do 'im, homes. Boo-ya, boo-ya"—he pantomimed the recoil of a shotgun with both hands—"*y se acabó.*"

Momo took a swig of beer, wiped his mouth, and without looking at Pelón told him to shut the fuck up.

At breakfast the next day, Buffalo appeared in the kitchen. Without preamble or explanation, he handed Pescatore his Glock. Pescatore nodded, exhilarated but trying to come off like it was all business. Buffalo did not give him back his cell phone or mention it. Pescatore thought fast and made a decision on impulse: If they trusted him enough to give him his gun back, a phone was maybe not that big a deal.

"Thanks, Buffalo," he said. "Think I could get my phone too?"

Buffalo's expression made him wish he had stayed quiet. "Who you gonna call?"

"Nobody!" Pescatore looked shocked at the notion. "Nobody. It's just I had a lotta numbers stored in there for people, family back home, you know."

Buffalo's forehead furrowed. "I don't think I gotta explain why it's not a good idea for you to call anybody right now, Valentín."

"Yeah, I know, I sure wasn't—"

"You're a fucking fugitive. Murder One. Low profile, *silencio radio,* this and that."

"Sure, you got it, man, of course," Pescatore said. Now I'm fried if they even catch me looking at a phone, he thought. Nice work, Valentine.

"Anyway." Buffalo brightened. "Remember what I said about earning your keep? I got a *chamba* for you."

They drove out to Junior's ranch on the road to Tecate. Pescatore squinted, unaccustomed to daylight. At the target-shooting range they met a handful of youths, a mix of U.S. gang members and Mexicans. Like motley soldiers, they stood at attention as Buffalo told Pescatore to instruct them in rudimentary pistol technique—loading, cleaning, handling—then lead close-range target practice.

"Introduction to guns, man, basic basics, like they don't know a fucking thing," Buffalo said. "These youngsters, they're always wavin' *cuetes* around, but they're ignorant. They're lucky they don't shoot themselves or each other. Me, I don't have the time or the patience."

The assignment surprised Pescatore. But he warmed to the task. His pupils were diligent and respectful. He gave the demonstration in Spanish and English, improvising, mimicking his Patrol instructors from the academy days. Buffalo nodded approvingly. During the next week, they came back three more times and Pescatore led more sessions of target practice. Buffalo sat on a picnic table, watching intently. He looked grim.

About two weeks after Pescatore's arrival in Tijuana, the house had visitors: Moze and Tchai, the smooth cheerful Brazilians from the night of the arms deal. The word was that they were waiting for a kingpin named Khalid to visit from South America. They sat in lawn chairs by Buffalo's pool, listening to Brazilian party music on iPods plugged into a little speaker.

Isabel Puente would be interested in this development, Pescatore thought. He was still undercover, recording details, writing reports in his head. But he was starting to feel cut off. Like the Imperial Beach station, Puente seemed to belong to a remote and improbable previous life. He still thought about her, especially when he was high. But it was as if she were becoming unattainable again: a fantasy as much as a memory.

That evening, the Death Patrol stood guard at a restaurant. The operation reminded Pescatore of the precautions the U.S. feds took before a visit to the border by the attorney general. At dusk, he walked through the restaurant with Buffalo, Momo, Pelón and Sniper. They checked entrances and bathrooms, frisked waiters and cooks. More gunmen arrived: homeboys, Mexican gangsters, state police detectives in cowboy boots, stiff-legged slacks and leather jackets. They deployed sentries with radios on rooftops and corners, on foot and in cars.

Buffalo and Momo left. Pescatore waited with Pelón and Sniper in the entrance vestibule. He was excited about the action—and about the fact that they had brought him along. Once he started getting access to the street, an opportunity for escape could develop. At least he might be able to slip off somewhere for a couple of minutes and find a way to call: maybe a pay phone, or he could buy a cell.

The restaurant was decorated like a *hacienda,* long tables, white lace and dark wood, vegetation around an indoor waterfall. A trio strummed guitars in a corner. The place was all fancied up for a Friday night, but bereft of customers. It stayed empty until 10 p.m., when the dignitaries arrived.

First came Mauro Fernández Rochetti, commander of the Tijuana homicide unit. He looked grayer than on television but easily recognizable: withering stare, strong-boned profile, womanly mouth. He was escorted by a chubby-cheeked bodyguard in a cowboy hat. Then came the Brazilians. They held the doors for Mr. Abbas, their sharp-dressed Arab boss. Abbas hovered in turn around an older Arab in metallic eyeglasses who carried himself like an ambassador. Khalid, Pescatore thought. A nervous maitre d' in a tuxedo led them to a long table off by itself.

A few minutes later, the walkie-talkies chattered. Sniper straightened and told Pescatore to look sharp. "*El jefe. Aguas, ponte truchas.*"

Momo glided into the vestibule. He held the Tek-9 under a jacket draped over his arm like a Secret Service agent. Buffalo filled the doorway, looking the place over. Pescatore felt a rush of expectation.

Junior Ruiz Caballero's swagger verged on a waddle. He was built wide and thick. A two-tone leather jacket exaggerated his shoulders. His brown hair was shaggy, with blondish sun streaks. The word that occurred to Pescatore was "user": the tanned face had the strained mouth and charged-up grimaces of a cokehead. The features were handsome, almost pretty, a broad nose and sullen lips. But a layer of jowl spread on the sides and below the chin like a balloon inflating. His belly bulged in a shiny silver shirt. Junior was a user, if not an abuser, and getting sloppy.

Junior's green eyes glistened. He walked stiff-armed and bowlegged. He swept into the vestibule and gave Sniper, Pelón and Pescatore an unexpected sleepy grin. Pescatore, feeling the same flunky's smile on his face as on everyone else's, wondered if the guy knew who the hell he was.

Junior pointed two fingers at them extended out of a fist, mimicking a gun. He made playful popping sounds, his thumb moving like the hammer of a revolver. Then he went inside.

10

THE BISHOP ARRIVED in an ancient Eldorado driven by a slim young priest with wet-combed hair. A nun with goggle-sized spectacles accompanied them.

Méndez watched from the window of his office. Athos greeted the bishop in the courtyard below. Diogenes Group officers assembled.

"His Eminence," Méndez said. "Here to inflict another Ash Wednesday on us."

"You do not sound grateful or respectful," Araceli Aguirre said.

The bishop's belly strained his black soutane. His smile was unctuous. He handed out his trademark laminated cards, decorated with images of the Virgin of Guadalupe, to the officers. There were rumors the bishop would soon leave Tijuana for a big job at the Vatican.

"The bishop has gotten fat and rich baptizing the children of the fat and rich," Méndez said, slumping into his chair.

"All children have a right to be baptized, Leo," Aguirre said, taking a drag on a cigarette.

She should stop smoking, she's too thin, Méndez thought. Her cell phone rang and she answered: a reporter, as usual. The Tijuana correspondent of a national newspaper was on the line, apparently complaining that Aguirre was interfering with his vacation plans. She told the correspondent that he would look like the biggest cretin on the planet if he did not postpone his trip to Mexico City to attend her press conference the next day. She scolded him for daring to ask if she had called the press conference to announce her gubernatorial candidacy and ordered him to keep his frivolous political speculation to himself. The human rights commission was dealing with very grave, very delicate matters that required her full attention.

"A sneak preview?" she declared. "What do you think this is, a striptease? No special privileges for *chilangos.* You change your flight and you be there tomorrow like everybody else, my little friend. Have I ever let you down? I'll make a hero of you yet."

Méndez touched the plane ticket in the breast pocket of his sport jacket. He had bought the ticket two days earlier. Instead of locking it in his desk, he realized, he had carried it around with him, even during the predawn drive to Ensenada with a federal police informant who swore that Pescatore was holed up in a hotel near the port. The raid had turned up addicts, whores, two-bit hoodlums, illegal immigrants from China and Bangladesh. But no trace of the fugitive Border Patrol agent.

Méndez made sure the ticket was secure in the pocket. It was a San Diego–Oakland round trip, departure scheduled for Friday with the return Sunday. He wondered if his failure to remove it from his pocket was Freudian. Maybe the lapse reflected his eagerness to see his wife and son for the first time since November. Or maybe he had a subconscious desire to lose the ticket because he was apprehensive about the reunion.

Aguirre hung up.

"I suppose it would be useless to ask you to postpone this a few days," Méndez said.

"If it were for you, I would give you all the time you want," she said. "But it's the Secretary. You have run out of explanations for his behavior. It's clear he doesn't want to do anything. He doesn't even want to catch these Border Patrol agents."

More than two weeks had passed since the Secretary had rejected Méndez's request to make arrests, forcing the Americans to postpone their operation as well. Convinced that the Secretary had let them down, Araceli had decided to make good on her threat. She was going to hold a press conference to discuss the Colonel's murder and the circumstances and the individuals behind it.

"I told the Secretary that finding Pescatore and Garrison would be a perfect way to help the Americans and make them look bad at the same time," Méndez said. "That seemed to catch his interest. He promised to put the federal police at my disposal, but they are just going through the motions."

"Do you think the yanqui informant is alive?" Aguirre said.

"We heard a rumor that Pescatore was with the *pochos* and that Garrison is dead. Nothing solid. Isabel thinks Pescatore is alive. She also refuses to believe that he was involved in the killing of the highway policeman. Despite the evidence to the contrary."

Aguirre made a derisive noise with her lips. "She acts so high and mighty. Then she has a fling with this little murderer and turns to mush."

"I don't know with certainty they were having a romance, Araceli, I only told you I suspected that," Méndez said uncomfortably.

"It seems obvious to me."

"Isabel is loyal to her informant, though I won't defend the wisdom of her personal choices. She got upset when I told her my men have orders not to take chances with him, given that he's been involved in two killings that we know of. In any case, I think the mafia is hiding Pescatore, dead or alive. He's not smart enough to stay underground in Mexico on his own."

"And there is no way they can give you the yanqui and leave it at that," Aguirre said. "He opens the whole Pandora's box: Garrison, the Colonel. No wonder the Secretary won't take your calls."

"He takes my calls. But he says it's a very delicate political moment and he doesn't know when he'll have news."

"Have you heard anything more about the South American connection?"

"No. You're not going to get into that with the press, are you? I've reached the point where I don't trust them anymore."

Isabel Puente had recently passed on a tip: U.S. wiretaps had picked up talk that heavy hitters from the Triple Border had been in town. The intelligence suggested that the South American visitors and Junior had discussed an "operation" targeting Méndez.

"A traitor to your profession. You've really taken this police secrecy thing to heart."

"The media in this town have too many agendas. Too many spies. Too many of them working for Junior or terrified to cross him."

Aguirre smiled benevolently.

"No, Leo, I'll do my best not to compromise your case. I will focus on the Colonel: He filed a human rights complaint which I investigated. It pointed me at the Ruiz Caballeros, and everything else developed from there. I am going to make it clear that the federal government has a responsibility to do something, to back up people like you. This state has become an empire of impunity."

She was rehearsing lines for the news conference. She had a talent for it; she charmed, entertained and browbeat journalists into submission.

"Araceli, this is going to be a bombshell," Méndez said.

"I'm just trying to help," Aguirre said. "I hope it doesn't cause you too many problems with the Secretary."

"That should be the least of your worries." Méndez got up, his shoulders hunched in the sport jacket, and looked out the window again.

Porthos and Athos talked to the bishop in the courtyard. The priest and the nun were organizing objects on the hood of the Eldorado. Athos shaded his eyes, looking up at the second-floor window. He waved at Méndez, holding his arm up a couple of extra seconds to denote urgency. Méndez waved back. They were waiting for him.

"To be frank, I have done as much as I can do," Méndez said. "The indictments are ready. My officers are ready. If the Secretary tells me to bring him Junior's head on a platter, I'll do it. And if he says it's time to resign, I'll say thank you very much, sir. At your orders. With great pleasure."

Aguirre blew smoke at the ceiling. "I have trouble imagining that."

"I'm serious, Araceli. I am ready to walk away. And it's basically your fault."

"Why?"

"You kept harping on me to talk to Estela. So we finally talked. For hours; I don't want to see the phone bill. We talked and talked. About Juancito, us, and frankly, a lot of trivialities. But I can't wait to see them. I can't believe how I've neglected them."

Her dark eyes softened, scrutinizing him. She spoke with a bit of difficulty.

"How nice, Leo. It turns out you were listening to me."

He turned back to the window, collecting himself. "So if your show tomorrow is successful, the Secretary will relent and we go to war with the Ruiz Caballeros. Once and for all. Jihad. If not, you will have saved my family and cost me my job. Either way, it's your fault."

"Leo..."

"Who knows, maybe I'll just stay in Berkeley and do nothing. I understand they treat bums very well, even Mexican ones. I could give seminars. The progressive gringos up there can't get enough of the human rights song and dance."

Aguirre looked as if she wished he hadn't broken the moment

so abruptly. But she played along. "What an image, the stern Mr. Méndez on campus. You wouldn't last a week. You'd miss the violent emotions."

"You'd be surprised at my capacity for sloth."

"We should go downstairs, the bishop is waiting."

"Let the old bastard wait."

"Leo, please!"

It was a perennial point of conflict with them: Except for a few scrappy Jesuits and liberation theology types, Méndez could not stand the church. And he could not understand how Aguirre could be so tolerant of the clergy.

In the courtyard, the officers of the Diogenes Group had lined up as if they were on parade. Their solemn, absolute engagement in the ritual made Méndez feel ashamed about his snide comments.

The bishop moved along the row of officers. The nun accompanied him, holding the plate of blessed ashes. The bishop smeared ashes in the shape of a cross on the forehead of each officer and murmured a blessing.

Aguirre stepped to the end of the line, straightening her jeans jacket and pulling it close over her white blouse. She grinned at Méndez. She gestured at him to join her. He shook his head.

The bishop reached Aguirre. He marked the cross on her forehead. He blessed her in a resonant tenor he had cultivated on his weekly television show.

"*Memento, homo, quia pulvis es, et in pulverem reverteris.*"

The bishop hesitated, looking expectantly at Méndez. Aguirre made an insistent face, enjoying Méndez's discomfort. Now all the officers were looking at him.

Méndez relented and stepped forward.

The bishop beamed and reached for the plate held by the nun. The well-manicured fingers made gentle contact with Méndez's forehead. Méndez gritted his teeth.

"*Memento, homo, quia pulvis es, et in pulverem reverteris.*"

And it was over. The bishop shook hands with Méndez. They murmured pleasantries at each other. The officers milled around, their crucifix-marked foreheads making them look like members of some kind of urban tribe.

Araceli Aguirre appeared in front of Méndez. Her eyes were bright and amused, her smile half mocking, half tender. She kissed him on the cheek.

II

THE MOOD IN THE HOUSE changed after the Brazilians left.

Momo woke the homeboys up early on Tuesday, banging on doors. He warned them to keep a lid on the partying and be ready to work. They watched TV and waited for orders. The next day they remained at battle stations. The TV showed images of Ash Wednesday Mass. Buffalo visited briefly, glowering, his mood foul. Momo handed out radios, black bulletproof vests with the word POLICÍA stenciled on the back, and heavy weapons. Pescatore received an AK-47 to complement his pistol.

More waiting, television, lassitude. Nobody knew the details, but a big job was in the works.

It rained that night, pattering on the roof that sloped down just above Pescatore's bed. Thursday was clear and felt like summer.

In the morning, Momo ordered Pelón, Sniper, Pescatore and two others to bring their stuff into the driveway, where Rufino sat at the wheel of a brown Chevy van, wearing mirrored sunglasses. They loitered in the shade, weapons piled nearby. They gorged themselves on takeout from McDonald's.

At about 11 a.m., Buffalo came out of his house carrying a sawed-off shotgun. He wore a black turtleneck under a police flak vest and fingerless leather gloves. He got into the van next to Rufino.

The others strapped on their body armor and got in back. The interior had been cleared out to leave only a bench seat along each wall, as in a helicopter or a cargo plane. There were no side windows.

"Right now we're Plan B," Momo explained by way of a briefing as the van whizzed east along a highway into the factory district. "We're backup. But let's be ready. Everybody stay awake, you understand what I'm sayin'? If we give the word, you jump out and shoot whoever I tell you to shoot."

That's it? Pescatore thought. That's all the intelligence you're gonna give up? He was disturbed by the thought that he did not know how he would respond at the moment of truth. Kill for the Death Patrol? Turn his gun on them? He cursed himself: He had not succeeded in making a break or calling Isabel. He had bided his time, playing it slick. Now things were moving too fast.

Feeling bulky and cramped in the bulletproof vest, the weight of the body armor digging into his thighs, Pescatore leaned forward to look past Sniper at the windshield. He caught glimpses of Otay Mesa, the arid industrial lowland interspersed with shacktowns where the factory workers lived. The van rolled along a ridge between urban valleys formed by the *colonias,* a low patchwork skyline dominated by homemade television antennas and blue water drums on rooftops.

The van slowed and turned. They rumbled off cement onto an unpaved, jaw-jarring road that dipped steeply. It was the main entrance to a *colonia*. Rufino cursed at the mud and rocks, swerving back and forth.

"*Cuidado,* Rufi," Pelón jeered. He sat across from Pescatore, legs akimbo, steadying the butt of an assault rifle on his knee. "They got them Godzilla potholes around here. Eat you alive."

The going was slow. Rufino skirted swamps and craters left by the night's rain. The wheels whined and churned up mud. The windshield acquired a layer of grit. Through it flashed images: an aerial spaghetti of electrical cables. Grocery kiosks with hand-painted signs. Walls of brick, wood, sheet metal, cardboard. Listless dogs, shirtless kids, a white horse pulling a cart. A banner on a peaked red roof proclaimed the arrival of the Jehovah's Witnesses.

The street rose to reveal a smokestack horizon: an industrial complex on a nearby hill. There were Asian insignias on a wall. The van rolled downhill again past a junkyard fence plastered with hubcaps, then snaked among low, closely packed houses.

The van stopped. Buffalo told Rufino to honk the horn. Buffalo checked his watch.

"Don't tell me this lame-ass *naco* overslept," Buffalo snapped. "Can you believe that shit?"

Buffalo and Momo got out. A dog barked shrilly.

Rufino turned on the radio. Over an opening salvo of drums and horns, a disc jockey declared: "We're off to Sinaloa."

The sliding door of the van rattled open. Momo ushered in a short dark youth wearing a navy-blue canvas windbreaker with a turned-up collar. The kid had slicked-back hair, a smudge of a mustache and an earring. At first he looked to Pescatore like another *pocho.* But then Pescatore changed his mind: The guy seemed Mexican in the way he shook hands with each passenger, muttering a deferential "*Buenos días*" with each handshake.

The newcomer sat next to Pelón, who made a production of clapping his shoulder. Pescatore recognized him. He had been at the shooting sessions that Pescatore had led at the ranch. Pescatore remembered his tense, short-armed stance on the target range. His name was César; somebody had said he was a fugitive. César's gaze met Pescatore's, lowered without acknowledgment.

The van did a U-turn and picked up speed. César leaned his head back against the metal, seemingly unaffected by the bouncing and shaking. His eyes closed, as if he were dozing off. But he chewed gum at a rapid pace. His small fists clenched and unclenched. A cowboy ballad came on the radio, a *corrido,* and he mouthed the words.

The ride back to the city center took about twenty minutes. They parked on a tree-lined side street in the Río Zone. Momo told them to get their weapons ready.

Buffalo turned off the music and produced a walkie-talkie. He talked and listened for a few minutes. He rose and made his way into the back among knees and gun barrels. He hulked in a crouch in front of César, smiling tightly.

"All right, champ," Buffalo said, his hand on the youth's knee. "Everything good?"

César chewed gum and nodded. He fiddled with a short black necklace.

"Your *placa.*" Buffalo gave César a wallet-style case containing a police badge. "Clip it on your belt like the *judiciales.* By the buckle. Lemme see the pistol."

César handed over a .38 revolver. Buffalo examined and returned it. César stuck the gun in a side pocket of the jacket.

His voice low, Buffalo told César it would be a walk in the park. Buffalo told him to do it just like they had rehearsed. Head shot if he could get close enough. If not, the body mass. Shoot until the target is down.

"And then you go out the way you came. Arturo Ventura and El Bebé will be waiting for you in the parking lot. Like we planned. Fast and calm. They get you out of there before anybody knows what the hell is going on."

César nodded. He worked open his dry, cracked lips. He asked, apologetically, what would happen if he fucked it all up.

Buffalo gritted his teeth. "Don't worry. That's why we're here. If we have to, we come in and finish the job. Fire up the whole place, put on a real show, this and that. But I know you're not gonna need us. Right?"

César mentioned a bank account and his uncle who would take care of things if needed.

"Just in case, sir," César said. "You know? Sir?"

"Sure," Buffalo said. "But there's nothing to worry about. You're playing in the major leagues now, little brother. Pure professionals. Stick with the plan and everything will be fine."

César accepted Buffalo's vigorous street handshake, complying uncertainly when Buffalo bumped fists with him above and below. Pelón patted César's shoulder again, this time with great solemnity.

Pescatore saw that the object on César's necklace was a small crucifix made of black thread. Pescatore's hand rose involuntarily to the similar crucifix at his own throat. Pescatore was sweating profusely, his mind racing. Something was about to go down. He couldn't just sit and watch.

César crossed himself once, twice, three times—forehead, mouth, chest. He raised the crucifix to his lips.

Momo opened the door. Sunlight slanted in, made them grimace. Pescatore tensed forward, his feet poised, knees bent.

Chewing hard, his right hand jammed in his jacket pocket, César rose unsteadily.

Pescatore slid off the seat and followed César toward the door. He had no real plan other than to reach the street and figure out what was happening. To his dismay, he realized that no one else had budged. He had barely advanced a step when Momo grabbed him by one bicep and Sniper by the other. Momo yanked him back off balance, making him stumble sideways against the wall in the heavy vest. Momo's furious, red-streaked eyes seared him at close range.

"Where you goin', *güey?*"

"Aren't we gettin' out?" Pescatore stammered, as the homeboys jammed him roughly back into his seat.

César hesitated in the doorway, glancing wide-eyed over his shoulder.

"Sit the fuck down." Momo spat the words at Pescatore through clenched teeth. "And stay the fuck down."

Pescatore felt a spasm of rage and frustration. He had a vision of opening up with the assault rifle right then and there, going nuts, spraying everyone in the van.

Not much of a strategy, he told himself. That's gonna get you nowhere. The energy drained out of him. He stayed down.

The distraction dealt with, Momo put a hand on César's back and propelled him gently out of the van. Momo reached for the door handle. The door slid shut with a thump.

12

On Thursday, Méndez took a morning off for the first time he could remember. He ran errands related to his trip. He wandered stores in search of a gift for his son. A book, a toy, a compact disc? He agonized over every option, afraid of making a bad choice and showing how out of touch he was with Juancito's life. He abandoned the quest, empty-handed, for an appointment at federal police headquarters.

Afterward, Méndez, Athos and Porthos went across the street for coffee in a little glass-walled café that was on the ground floor of an academic think tank. The café provided a view of the headquarters of the federal police and prosecutors. The new attorney general's delegate had just been assigned to Tijuana. His handling of the hunt for Pescatore had been so desultory that Méndez had decided he was either an idiot or on the mafia payroll.

"Every day they have another sighting of the gringo in Mexicali or Ensenada or Sonora," Méndez said. "Next will be Chiapas. Is there any doubt in your mind that Pescatore is right here in Tijuana?"

"If he's alive, he's here, Licenciado," Athos said. "That's what our best informants say."

"We don't have the manpower to raid every safe house in the city on our own."

"I almost prefer dealing with the state police, Licenciado. At least I know they work for Junior. With the federales you have different commanders connected to different narcos. You have chiefs transferred from the army who don't know police work or Baja. Young officers out of the academy who don't know anything. A mess."

"Listen, did you send a car to Araceli's press conference?"

"Of course."

Méndez turned up his radio and contacted the officers reinforcing Araceli's bodyguard at the city's Cultural Center, where the press conference was to be held at 1 p.m. They reported that a group of protesters from the "pro-police" association had shown up and installed themselves next to the press corps, apparently intent on heckling Aguirre.

"It looks a little complicated over here, Licenciado," the officer drawled over the radio. "Strange characters. *Orejas, aspirinas,* you know."

Méndez was not surprised that the press conference had attracted spies and para-police operatives. But he had not calculated that the group associated with the fired police officers would show up. Harassing Aguirre on camera would not help their cause.

As Méndez listened to the radio, Athos touched his forearm and gestured at the federal police headquarters across the street. Two Suburbans drove up the ramp out of the basement garage. The Suburbans sat at the top of the driveway with their motors idling. The vehicles were full of federal officers in brimmed uniform caps.

"We are right around the corner," Méndez said into the radio, looking at the Suburbans and quizzically at Athos. "Should we drop by?"

"That's up to you, Licenciado... Might not be a bad idea," the voice on the radio said.

The Suburbans departed at a good clip. They turned north in

the direction of the Cultural Center. Méndez did not like Athos's look as he watched them go.

"I guess we'll head over there," Méndez said to Athos, who was on his feet, slinging the strap of his assault rifle over his shoulder.

Méndez and Aguirre had agreed it would be best for him to keep his distance from the press conference. Already, the fact that Aguirre had a full-time bodyguard from the Diogenes Group had brought both of them flak.

Athos sensed Méndez's reluctance. As the Crown Victoria covered the few blocks to the Cultural Center, he said: "If you prefer, Licenciado, stay in the car. We will take a look."

Méndez sighed. He had been focused on the aftermath of the press conference, on anticipating the reactions. And on his trip to Northern California.

"No, I'll go with you," Méndez said. "We hang back unless they pull something. At this point, Athos, I'm not going to worry about appearances."

"Very well—Abelardo, stop here!" Athos growled. "We'll cut across the plaza on foot. Take the car around to the parking lot. Keep your eyes open."

Athos rarely raised his voice. Méndez felt his stomach tighten.

Aguirre had convened the press conference on the concrete esplanade outside the Cultural Center, a massive construction in the center of downtown. Its most distinctive feature was a theater shaped like a giant golf ball. The Cultural Center was a good TV backdrop, and its proximity to the border was convenient for American journalists who didn't want to venture too far past the border.

Méndez and Athos walked briskly across the concrete expanse toward the multisectioned complex. They came up behind cameramen and reporters gathered in front of a row of glass doors at a side entrance. A podium and folding chairs for reporters had been set up outdoors. To the right of the journalists, near the shadow of the towering ball-shaped auditorium, were about twenty-five demonstrators. A few uniformed city police officers held them back.

Méndez caught up with Athos. They paused at the back of the press corps. Everyone's attention was on the glass doors. Méndez put on his sunglasses, wanting to avoid eye contact. But sure enough, a veteran newspaperman materialized next to him and gave him a friendly, furtive elbow in the ribs. His name was Dionisio. He was short, wore a brimmed cap and leather coat no matter what the weather, and chewed incessantly on sunflower seeds. Méndez knew him as a solid, well-sourced reporter.

"What a pleasure to see you, Licenciado," Dionisio said sotto voce. He popped a mouthful of seeds, staring straight ahead at the empty microphone. "Will you be participating in the event with Doctora Aguirre?"

"Absolutely not," Méndez muttered, feeling unexpectedly guilty about stiff-arming a former colleague. "Give me a break, maestro. Let's wait until afterwards, OK?"

Athos interrupted, his radio held to his ear. "Here comes Carrasco."

Carrasco, the Diogenes officer assigned to guard Aguirre, emerged from one of the glass doors and propped it open. He wore a floppy button-down shirt with the sleeves rolled up and the tails out over his holster. The protesters started chanting slogans and waving signs.

The glare of the sun on the glass made it difficult to see inside. Méndez spotted Araceli Aguirre approaching inside the lobby, framed in the doorway. She walked deliberately, straight-backed in a wine-colored dress with a silk scarf at her throat. She carried a sheaf of papers in her right hand. An assistant trailed her. The photographers and cameramen outside prepared for action.

"There she is," shouted a protester.

A crescendo of whistles and chants: "Aguirre, traitor! Human rights for police!"

The protesters surged forward, driving back the municipal cops. Aguirre's bodyguard grappled with a pudgy protester who held a picket sign.

Stupid assholes, Méndez thought in alarm, what do they think they are going to accomplish?

The first gunshot sounded like a door slamming.

The shot came from behind Aguirre. It came from inside the building. It hit her just before she reached the doorway. She stumbled forward and sideways against one of the glass doors. The papers jumped from her hand, fluttering in an arc of white.

Another shot: Aguirre banged hard into the door and collapsed, red streaking down the glass.

Méndez comprehended the full horror of what was happening now, reaching for his gun. The screams started.

More shots. Méndez heard himself scream too. He could feel the veins and tendons stand out in his neck.

Méndez saw the assassin: a diminutive silhouette in blue. The assassin crouched a few feet behind Aguirre in a straight-armed, wide-legged, two-handed stance, head low behind the pistol. A robotic, almost ridiculous stance. He fired down at her, the recoil making his stubby arms jump.

"They're killing her!" a woman shrieked. "My God, they're killing her!"

The lethal apparition was obscured by pandemonium. Protesters and reporters fled, dropped to the cement, fell over chairs and one another. But the photographers and TV crews obeyed their reflexes: They rushed toward the doorway of the lobby where Aguirre had fallen, cameras held high.

Méndez heard Athos bellowing, saw him slashing through the melee with the rifle butt. Méndez staggered in his wake, hyperaware of the pistol in his hand, pointing it down for fear that it would discharge into the crowd.

Scrambling around a cameraman entangled in a cable, Méndez lost his balance. He fell heavily and scraped open his left hand on the cement. He struggled to his feet in time to see Athos pursuing the assassin through the doors on the other side of the narrow lobby.

Aguirre lay crumpled on her stomach. She was motionless. Méndez wished at that moment that he had not seen so many corpses and crime scenes. He shouted her name, shouted for an ambulance, knowing it was futile. Then he heard more shots and screams from the direction where Athos had run. Araceli no longer needed him; Athos still did.

Méndez sprinted across the lobby through the doors and an interior patio. He careened through the Cultural Center's bookstore, knocking over a book rack, and down an outdoor pedestrian ramp to the parking lot.

At the bottom of the ramp, Méndez came upon Athos holding two prisoners at gunpoint. Athos sighted down the barrel of his AK-47 at the men, who knelt with their hands above their heads. Their pistols lay on the pavement in front of them, where they had been dropped at Athos's command. The two men had badges on their belts; they were obviously policemen unaccustomed to begging for their lives with a rifle pointed at their faces.

Athos roared: "Sons of bitches, don't move! You're dead, sons of bitches, fuck your mothers."

"State police," one of the officers implored. "He was armed. Commander Rojas, we are police!"

"Shut up, shut your fucking mouths, fucking criminals." Athos coiled gracefully behind the weapon. He spotted Méndez and barked: "Licenciado, are you all right?"

Méndez did not answer. He took in the inevitable sight of the dead assassin: a dark blue heap on the sidewalk. Nausea jolted through him. Araceli and her killer both gone, the crime signed, sealed and delivered. A textbook, prime-time assassination. Méndez knew who the enemy was, how they operated. He had been there to stop them. They had slaughtered her in front of him.

"All of them," Méndez snarled. "They're all in on it."

Porthos appeared, his belly heaving. He moved efficiently as he manacled the state police detectives with their own handcuffs. They complained loudly. Exhibiting strength and a vast wingspan, Porthos slammed the prisoners down on their faces. He looked at Méndez.

"Doctora Aguirre?" Porthos asked, flinching through his black beard.

Méndez shook his head.

Athos toed the assassin's corpse thoughtfully.

"It's that kid from the prison," Athos said. "The Colonel's *chalán.*"

Méndez turned back into the building. He brushed past men with cameras and men with guns. Guns and badges everywhere: federal, state and municipal police, uniform and plainclothes. They had arrived with impossible speed, how quickly the bastards had arrived to oversee the slaughter, Méndez thought. They're all part of it, one way or another.

Araceli was still facedown. Her arms were beneath her, as if she were hugging herself against a chill. Her assistant and her bodyguard knelt beside the body, a ring of bystanders, journalists and police around them. The photographers and cameramen were at work, on automatic, hovering over the carnage. There were scuffles, curses, sobs.

The blood spread beneath Araceli, a crimson darker than her dress, which had ridden up one of her bony legs to midthigh. Méndez wanted to pull the hem of the dress back down, but he was frozen in place. The side of her face that he could see was unblemished, the long jawline, the short sculpted hair around the moon-shaped earring.

They were her favorite earrings, the sun and the moon. She had worn them the night a year ago when she and Méndez had dinner and Méndez confirmed the rumors: He had been named chief of a new special police unit. And he had recommended that the legislature appoint her human rights commissioner to replace him. She had laughed with delight and triumph. She told him they would be unstoppable. They would make Tijuana tremble. That night was the closest they had come in years to talking about their romance in university days. The closest he came to telling her that he still felt something for her that he felt for no one else, including his wife. But he hadn't said it. He had never said it.

Carrasco, Aguirre's bodyguard, approached Méndez. Carrasco had a cut over one eye, his shirt was torn and his knees were drenched in blood.

"Licenciado, I'm so sorry," Carrasco blurted, his face wrenched and tearstained. "It's my fault, I should have watched her back."

Méndez wanted to comfort him, but he found it impossible to speak. The bodyguard seemed far away. Méndez was thankful for the refuge of his sunglasses. He was overwhelmed by the madhouse sounds racketing off the glass walls of the narrow lobby: crying, running feet, reporters yelling into phones, the click of cameras and the jabber of police radios. Porfirio Gibson's nasal voice chattered somewhere behind him.

All the vultures, he told himself.

Méndez stuck his gun in his belt. He took off his sport jacket, remembering that the plane ticket to Oakland was still in the pocket. He knew now that he was not meant to use the ticket. He was meant to be alone.

Méndez crouched and spread the jacket carefully over Araceli Aguirre, shielding her, too late.

Part Three

REASONS OF STATE

13

PESCATORE HAD NEVER BEEN so high in his life.

It was the next afternoon. They staggered back into the house from the van. They flopped onto the couches, shedding their weapons and body armor. The television blared. Beer cans popped. Joints changed hands. Pelón and Sniper huddled over the mirror on the coffee table, chopping out lines of cocaine.

Pescatore had been drinking around the clock. But he wasn't sleepy anymore. The pills that Sniper had handed out at the ranch near Tecate that morning had cranked him into tooth-gritting, lip-licking alertness. By then, the girl was gone. She left him inert on a bench. Said she was going to the bathroom and never came back; must have caught a ride home. Somebody told her something that freaked her out.

What did he remember about her? Her name: Marisol? Soledad? The tops of her breasts swelling out of a leotard. Extra heft in the hips and thighs. Turning, posing on the dance floor, swaying against him in knee-length leather pants. Marisol-or-Soledad was from Calexico. Said his accent in Spanish was cute, reminded her of this South American singer on MTV Latino. She was one of the platoon of women waiting when the homeboys arrived at the ranch. The place was fancied up for a party: mariachis, an outdoor bar, a disc jockey on the gazebo spinning tunes. Oldies for *cholos:* "Always and Forever," "Who's That Lady?," "Lean On Me." But the mood was less than mellow because Pelón wandered around firing one-armed volleys at the stars with his AK-47.

Time for the Death Patrol to celebrate. Mission accomplished. But nobody bothered to tell Pescatore what the mission had been. Soon after César had gotten out, the van had left the Río Zone and headed for the ranch. Riding silently, the homeboys heard traffic on Buffalo's police radio. César had used the gun on somebody important.

Marisol-or-Soledad was curious too: What are you guys celebrating? Pescatore just mumbled and poured rum in her Coke. He did not want to think about it. Marisol-or-Soledad was all over him and he responded in kind. He pulled her close on the dance floor by the gazebo, hungry for her. He pawed at her leotard, her rum-and-Coke-and-nicotine taste filling his mouth. He tried to coax her into the darkness beyond the firing range. Let's go see Junior's zoo: He's got ostriches, kangaroos, a big ol' Galápagos turtle. She nuzzled him, toyed with him, told him he was too drunk to be trusted. As they lurched toward a bench, she said, "*Oye, que borracho estás, no?* You going to vomit?"

She kept asking what they were celebrating. What a pain in the ass. Somebody must have told her. Or told her to stop asking questions, bitch. That was what had freaked her out.

Time moved in freeze-frames. Pescatore contemplated strange things. The way Pelón's eyebrows climbed his scalp. The way Pelón's lips strained back from a startling outsized mouthful of teeth. Pelón and Sniper sat across the coffee table from Pescatore, laughing at the screen.

"Aw, ain't that a fuckin' pity," Pelón whooped. "Served her right."

Pescatore found himself suspended head down over the mirror, homing in on the white lines with a plastic straw. A sour stream blazed up through his sinuses. He snuffled and spluttered, turning away from the mirror. It was the first time he had done cocaine. It felt like a noseful of chlorine. He slumped miserably, trying to play it off, hoping the others were too wasted to notice.

Then a flash of awareness cut through the fog in his head. Amid the clutter on the table—pistols, ammo, keys, cigarette packs—he had spotted a cell phone. The phone was silver. It was decorated with a red-green-and-black decal: an image of a skeleton wearing a wedding veil and holding a Grim Reaper's scythe. Santa Muerte, the patron of the *narco-pistoleros.* Sacred Death. Pescatore believed it was Pelón's phone; he had seen the shaven-headed homeboy fiddling with it. Pescatore calculated the distance to the phone. More than an arm's length. Closer to Pelón and Sniper than to him.

The shouting got really loud. Pescatore looked up. The TV showed a corpse. A woman sprawled in a red puddle among cops, bystanders, discarded paramedic's gloves.

Cut to indignant politicians. Cut to tearful relatives. Live shot: a funeral. A coffin on a lawn.

A familiar face: Méndez. Unshaven, gray-flecked stubble, red-streaked squinty eyes. Open-collared striped shirt under his leather jacket.

Méndez walked among mourners. He carried a little girl in a black dress with a frilly white collar, her curls held back by a black headband. The faces around them were anguished, distorted. Méndez and the toddler were not crying. Méndez held the girl high on his chest. Her arms encircled his neck. They both looked as if they were staring at a door that was about to open onto something hideous.

"You're next, *güey!*" Pelón hooted. "You're next, Méndez. Gonna kill your ass!"

Oh God, Pescatore thought. The image of Méndez and the girl hit him like a punt in the gut. That's what we're celebrating. César killed that lady. Who was she, Méndez's wife? Oh fuck.

What did they do? What did we do? The camera zoomed in on a bearded professor-looking guy behind Méndez. The man was crying so hard his whole body convulsed. Mourners held his arms, practically carrying him.

"*Cállate, maricón!*" Pelón made a whimpering noise. Sniper echoed him, egging him on. Pelón took a long hit off a joint, threw his head back and wailed like a coyote.

The television showed file footage of the dead woman: Araceli Aguirre. Talking into microphones, a Mexican flag behind her. A big shot. Cute in a skinny, retro-hippie kind of way. The newscaster spewed words: assassination, human rights, crisis of government.

Pescatore tried to concentrate on the phone on the table. He scanned the mess frantically, shaking his head to focus, until he located the phone again. But then he saw Buffalo appear behind Sniper and Pelón.

Buffalo had been drinking whiskey all night, brooding and unapproachable. He held the bottle now. He still wore the fingerless gloves. The sleeves of his turtleneck were rolled up over his bulging tattooed forearms. His mouth was slightly open, the lips curled tightly inward. He watched Sniper and Pelón cackle and howl on the couch.

"Good idea," Buffalo said, just loud enough to be heard over the blaring television. "That's nice: Disrespect the dead. Disrespect their families. You two oughta shut the fuck up."

Sniper felt the edge in Buffalo's tone; he quieted down. But Pelón chortled obliviously. Pelón threw Buffalo a delayed-reaction glance over his shoulder, not quite making eye contact.

"We just havin' some fun, man, *qué onda contigo?*" Pelón scoffed. "Why you wanna make a issue out of it, Buffalo? Damn."

Buffalo's face contorted. Three steps brought him around the couch. With his left hand, he grabbed the remote control off the table, killed the sound on the television and hurled the remote across the room.

"What'd you say, *puto?*" Buffalo's bass voice reverberated. "Now you're disrespecting *me?!*"

There was sudden silence. The grip of Buffalo's right hand on the bottle had shifted. He held it straight-armed and thumb down, around the neck, as if it were a club. Someone's about to get their bald skull tonked, Pescatore thought, watching Sniper sidle away from Pelón. Pescatore felt himself cringe as if he were the imminent victim beneath the two-hundred-fifty-pound shadow.

Pelón glared up at Buffalo through a cloud of disbelief, coming to grips with the reality of the confrontation.

"Disrespectin' me," Buffalo repeated in a choked voice. "Talkin' shit. 'Cause you sat in a van while César shot that lady. Sat in the van with your hand on your dick. And that makes you a big mafioso. Not a little faggot punk bitch."

Pelón stiffened. His eyes jumped to a pistol lying next to the mirror, then away, terrified by the impulse.

Buffalo followed the look with grim satisfaction. His grip tightened on the bottle. His upper body tilted forward.

"That's right, Pelón," Buffalo said, savoring the words, delivering them like blows. "Make a move. Reach for that *cuete* so I can bust your face open. No, wait, let's get Veronica first. That skank *haina* you call a girlfriend. She can watch."

Pelón made a strangled noise. He did not budge. An invisible force pinned him to the couch. Pescatore remembered one of the homeboys telling him how Buffalo had stabbed to death an inmate in Mule Creek with a blade fashioned out of a toothbrush.

Buffalo grunted.

"You ain' shit," he said. "Now get outta my sight. *Fuera, ya!*"

Pelón rose, keeping a careful distance from the pistol on the table. No front, not a shred of attitude left. He tripped over someone's outstretched legs. At a glance from Buffalo, Momo got up fast and followed Pelón out of the room with a gun in his hand.

Pescatore decided that he'd never get a better opportunity to grab a phone. He hunched forward as if contemplating the cocaine traces on the mirror. Arm extended, he palmed Pelón's cell phone without looking at it. He reclined and slipped it into a pocket of his jacket. His head whirling, his heart hammering, he stared at the television.

The news program repeated the image of Méndez holding the little girl. Pescatore felt his stomach tighten. His eyes burned and blurred.

Perfect, Pescatore thought in a panic. I'm gonna start bawling. Crying like a bitch in front of everybody. And Buffalo's gonna crush my skull. And then he'll find the phone.

"Where you think *you're* going, Valentín?" Buffalo snarled after him.

"Throw up," Pescatore gasped, stumbling, eyes averted.

By the time he reached the hallway, it was no longer a lie. All the tastes of the night, of the past two weeks, heaved up inside him: liquor, reefer, pills, coke, Marisol-or-Soledad. What are you celebrating? What did we do?

He caromed down the hallway into the kitchen and retched into the sink. Clinging to the faucet, he drank from the tap. The water spattered his hair and face and jacket. Camouflaging his tears, swirling them safely down the drain.

For a moment, he saw only blackness. He coughed, gulping air and water alternately. The blackness was disintegrating when he heard the voice behind him.

"Makes me sick too, homes."

Pescatore saw Buffalo indistinctly among floating silver spots. Buffalo had propped himself against the butcher-block counter in the middle of the kitchen. His feet were spread wide. He swigged from the bottle. Pescatore realized how drunk Buffalo was. Slow-motion drunk, stealth drunk. His voice and face seemed steady. But he teetered. His head nodded in little flurries. His breathing was agitated.

Pescatore put a hand on the pocket containing the cell phone, making sure it was still there. He mumbled apologetically about how that cocaine had gotten all on top of him. Buffalo did not seem to hear.

"Makes me sick, Valentín."

"What?"

"What happened to that lady. Them braggin' about it."

Mystified, Pescatore wiped a sleeve across his mouth. Buffalo's black eyes glittered, unfocused.

"I told Junior: I vote no," Buffalo said hoarsely, slurring. "Hell, no. I told 'em, wanna do somebody, do Méndez. He's askin' for it. Not that lady, *por Dios.* You don' do that. That's fucked up."

"Yeah."

"Junior's all geeked up. Khalid's encouragin' him, like darin' him. Junior wants Khalid to know he's the *chingón* around here, and he respects Khalid's advice. Junior's partyin' all night, this and that. He won' listen. I told him and I told him. But he hadda make a example of the human rights lady. So Comandante Mauro and me, we set it all up."

Pescatore heard himself say: "How come you did it, if you were against it?"

Buffalo did not look at him. His bandit mustache sagged. His voice had dropped; he could have been talking to himself.

"Tha's what I do. Tha's my job. *Así es la onda.* You seen my house, my cars—he gave me everything. I stayed in fuckin' Colonia Libertad when I was a kid, Valentín. We didn' even have a toilet. We went north, my *viejo* moved around working *los* fields. We stayed in the projects in Pacas. Had a toilet there. But you know what? We had the *pinche mayates* waitin' outside to kick our asses every day. Every day." Buffalo grinned blearily, humorlessly. "Back then the projects was still wall-to-wall *mayates,* and they didn' like the Mexicans moving in. You had to be ready to throw down. Do something for your race. Like in the joint. Except funny thing is, when I was locked up I met some of those same brothers we use to fight back in the projects. And we got along OK."

In a rush of images, Pescatore saw the Taylor Street of his childhood, the barred Italian shops and restaurants facing the low-rise housing project where the blacks lived across the street. That was a border, he thought. That was a serious border. He said: "Where I'm from was kinda like that too."

Buffalo was adrift in his own words. "Never had shit till I hooked up with Junior. I'm down with Junior, all the way, to the curb. But yesterday was bad, Valentín. Real bad."

Buffalo sounded strangely nostalgic talking about his house and cars, his voice full of loss. It went beyond remorse. He seemed convinced that the murder of Araceli Aguirre had a whiff of doom about it for all involved.

"The AFI gonna come after us?" Pescatore asked.

Buffalo puffed dismissively. "We own the federales. All we gotta worry about is the Diogenes Group. *Pinche* Méndez. Thinks he can sweat Junior. It's all his fault, really. He was the one pushing the human rights lady."

"That motherfucker."

"Motherfucker is right. And he wants you bad."

"Me?"

"Our friends in *la federal* say the Diogenes Group is huntin' for you and Garrison overtime. Spreading around *lana* to informants. They say Méndez isn't particular, long as he gets you. Dead or alive."

Pescatore shook his head. He would have thought the Americans wanted him alive, cop-killer or not. Did that mean Isabel had given up on him and told Méndez to do his thing? Or that Méndez decided he'd handle Pescatore any way he wanted on Mexican turf?

Buffalo looked directly into Pescatore's eyes for the first time since entering the kitchen. The sudden clarity of the stare surprised Pescatore. "You're not used to gettin' high so much, huh, Valentín?"

Pescatore shook his head. Buffalo continued: "Stay away from it, then. You got more discipline than these youngsters, your training from the *Migra. No seas pendejo.* You come with Momo and Sniper and me. We're gonna stay close by Junior. Get yourself cleaned up now, drink some coffee. *Órale.*"

Buffalo turned away, focused again, his moves brisk. Pescatore regarded his own haggard reflection in one of the kitchen windows. He shook his head. How about that, he thought. I made supervisor in the Death Patrol.

"One thing." Buffalo paused in the doorway. "You be sure an' look sharp around Junior. Last week he told me we should cut you loose, give you up to *la federal.* Throw 'em a bone for the *americanos.* I said no, you handle yourself good, you helped us out with Garrison, this and that. I vouched for you, homes. Don't make me look bad, you understan' what I'm sayin'?"

Back in his third-floor room, Pescatore wedged the chair against the knob. He put the keys on the chair. He crouched in a corner holding the phone, the gun within reach on the bed. He dialed Isabel's apartment. She had told him to call land lines whenever possible. The Santa Muerte skull leered at him from the decal on the phone.

"Puente."

She sounded like she was in a bad mood. He imagined her just home from work, sitting at her kitchen table over a cup of Cuban-style coffee the way she liked it, strong and sweet. He closed his eyes.

"Hello?" she demanded.

He whispered: "Isabel."

Silence. She spoke finally in Spanish, voice trembling, her Cuban accent fierce.

"What did you do? For the love of God, what did you do? What have you done, crazy imbecile? Are you all right?"

He clung to the emotion in her voice, the purity of it. No way she was good enough of an actress to fake that on the spot, right?

"I'm OK," he whispered more softly, his eyes on the door. "Isabel: I did not shoot that highway patrolman. It was Garrison. He damn near shot me too. You gotta believe—"

She switched back to English. "I believe you. Is it safe to talk?"

"No. But I had to call you."

"Valentine, I thought you were..." Her voice broke. Then her tone changed, like she was getting control of herself. "Listen. Can you tell me where you are?"

Pescatore's grin was triumphant. "I don't know if you're gonna believe me."

The boxing ring was in a private gym that took up a wing of the Ruiz Caballero family compound at the crest of Colonia Chapultepec. One wall was mostly glass, offering a view of the brown beehive hills of Tijuana in the afternoon, the Pacific streaked purple and crimson.

Junior was turning purple and crimson himself. Sweat leapt from his hair mashed beneath the helmet. Sweat cascaded from the flab wobbling over the waist of his baggy trunks. He breathed arduously through the mouthpiece, making a distressed humming sound as he threw punches. But there was power in his wide, round-shouldered frame, judging from the sledgehammer sound of the impacts.

His sparring partner was Kid Avila, the rangy pro from Northern California who had defended his championship title a month earlier at Multiglobo Arena. Kid Avila patiently withstood Junior's flailing and lunging. Kid Avila moved now and then, catching blows on his forearms and gloves. He threw periodic measured punches to sustain the illusion of combat. He allowed Junior to connect, reacting with theatrical grunts and headshakes.

"There you go, *jefe,* way to stick!" Avila said.

Buffalo, Momo, Sniper and a half-dozen men lounged outside the ring on bleachers and folding chairs, echoing him.

"*Muy buena,* Junior."

"*Dale duro.*"

"Get it on, get it on."

Mr. Abbas did not participate in the commentary. The gangster from South America sat on the other side of the ring in a folding chair by the glass wall. He drank from a tall glass and checked his watch periodically. He was alone; Moze and Tchai had left with Khalid before the assassination.

Judging from what Pescatore had seen on the way in, the Ruiz Caballeros lived and did business in a complex that was a hilltop fortress done in red-roofed hacienda style. The well-guarded walls enclosed buildings on terraced levels connected by wooden decks and walkways. There were corporate offices, a recording studio, the gym, separate residences for Junior and his uncle. Statues of cavorting cherubs filled a fountain in the middle of the circular driveway. There was a barn-sized garage with rows of antique cars under plastic covers.

Pescatore sat miserably on the low bleachers. He was drinking Coke from a can, hoping to get hydrated and alert. Despite the air-conditioning, he was perspiring. His head throbbed. He felt uncomfortably well armed with the pistol in his shoulder holster and the AK-47 by his side.

Buffalo's comments in the kitchen had amped Pescatore's paranoia to full volume. So Junior had wanted to give him up to the Mexfeds as a fall guy. But Buffalo had made it sound like he had stood up for Pescatore. Buffalo was his protector, believe it or not. Not totally reassuring after seeing him go off on Pelón, who had disappeared. Had they whacked Pelón just for talking shit? It made things easier for Pescatore as far as hanging on to the cell phone.

Junior's voice startled him; Junior stood at the ropes shouting. Except for the swear words, his Spanish sounded different than that of the homeboys or the aliens at The Line. More Mexico City than TJ, ideal for bossing around servants. Between croaks for oxygen, Junior berated an older Mexican bodyguard for bothering him. The bodyguard extended a phone at him plaintively, saying it was the third time the Senator had called long distance from *El D.F., urgente.*

Junior spat out his mouthpiece, extended his arms to his sides and waited. He gave Mr. Abbas a frown that said: This is the kind of shit I put up with from these mopes. Mr. Abbas nodded sympathetically.

A hunched trainer in a warm-up suit scuttled through the ropes and set to work removing Junior's gloves and helmet. The bodyguard clambered up to hold the phone to Junior's ear.

Once the gloves were off, Junior roamed the ring with the phone. Pescatore caught fragments of the conversation, mainly Junior cursing and telling his uncle to calm down. At one point Pescatore understood him to say: "Everything's fine here. Stop whining and handle your part. And tell those guys to stop worrying like little sissies. I don't care. Reevaluate the relationship? That's funny. Tell them careful or *we* reevaluate relationships. One by one. No, that's exactly what you tell them. Stop calling me every five minutes."

End of conversation. Sitting near Pescatore on the bleachers, Buffalo sighed heavily. Junior tossed his head, geysering sweat. He pasted his hair back with his fingers and leaned on the ropes.

"Yo big man, whassup?" Junior's English had barely any accent at all. Pescatore remembered that he had spent time at colleges in the States. He sounded like a frat boy talking street.

"This and that, you know," Buffalo said.

"What's the matter? Still pissed at me?"

Buffalo seemed both proud of and uncomfortable with Junior's public admission that Buffalo was authorized to get pissed at him.

"You know I ain't," Buffalo said. "You know I'm just watchin' out for you."

"Enough. My uncle is whining like an old woman. I know what I'm doing."

"OK."

"The bitch wanted drama, Buffalo." Junior cocked back his head to squirt water into his mouth from a plastic bottle. He spat emphatically onto the canvas. "We gave her drama."

Buffalo nodded.

"You should think like Khalid," Junior said. "He understands this stuff. Psychology. He said, it's your territory, you make a statement—"

"I heard what he said," Buffalo grumbled. He eyed Abbas, who had perked up at the mention of Khalid.

Junior noticed Pescatore.

"Who's this *vato?*" he asked.

Pescatore got up.

"This is Valentín," Buffalo said.

"The *gabacho* who was in the *Migra?* Who smoked the highway patrolman?"

"*Simón.*"

Pescatore made his way down the bleachers. He thought to himself that it gets to a point where fear becomes comfortable, like a coat you never take off.

He went up on tiptoe to shake a thick and extremely wet hand. The agitated eyes regarded him from within layers of chin and cheek. From this angle above Pescatore, Junior looked like a malevolent man-child appraising a small animal.

"Valentín used to do some boxing hisself," Buffalo said.

"Really," Junior said. "The pride of the Border Patrol. You want to go a couple of rounds? How long you think you'd last with me? How long you think you'd last with *him?*" He jerked his head at Kid Avila, who lounged in the far corner. "Thirty seconds? Fifteen seconds? That would be the last Mexican you ever chase, my friend."

There were chortles. Pescatore remained soldierly, remembering Buffalo's admonition.

"Ready to go a few rounds?" Junior insisted.

"Hey, you're the man." Pescatore imagined himself flattening the tanned nose, which looked like it might have gotten a tweak from a plastic surgeon, with a short straight right. "You're the one helped me when I needed it, you and Buffalo. Say the word and I'll get in the ring with you, him, Julio César Chávez, you name it."

Junior's smirk, and Buffalo's body language, made him think that it had been a good answer.

"Maybe later," Junior said. "I'm still giving the champ his workout."

Junior tossed the phone in the general direction of the older bodyguard. The trainer came forward to gird him into the mouthpiece, helmet and gloves. This time, Kid Avila played punching bag. Junior went after him like it was Round 12 in Madison Square Garden.

Pescatore drank deeply from the ice-cold Coke. He shivered in the air-conditioning. He wondered if he had a fever. He was woozy, but seeing things with febrile clarity. Here he sat a couple of yards from the boss of the organization Isabel had assigned him to infiltrate. You couldn't get closer to the fire without getting burned. The murder of Araceli Aguirre had jolted him awake. It was like coming out of anesthesia. And his call to Isabel had given him purpose. No more cringing and getting high, no more scheming about escape. He was on a mission.

He imagined Isabel waiting for his next call. He saw her on the balcony where they had eaten breakfast, staring out at the lagoon, worrying about him. He had to hear her voice again. Now that she was looking out for him again, he felt ready to take on fat-ass psycho Junior.

Pescatore chafed and brooded. He listened to the leather thudding in the ring, the chorus cheering Junior. He watched Junior bulling Kid Avila back into a corner. Junior built up a windmill rhythm. His furious staccato humming punctuated his punches.

This guy is bad news, Pescatore thought. He belongs in the zoo. But for the time being, I better look like I'm getting with the program.

"That's it," Pescatore called. "Use that right. Way to hit, homes, way to hit!"

14

THE NIGHT AFTER THE assassination, Mauro Fernández Rochetti gave Porfirio Gibson an exclusive television interview.

It was a live feed to Mexico City to start the nightly national news. The homicide chief wore a gray suit and navy-blue tie. His silver hair was combed in crisp waves and ridges. He sat in a high-backed leather chair with his hands laced together on his desk. He looked grave and in charge.

"This individual who is our deceased suspect, César Oscar Ontiveros, worked for the Colonel in the prison," Fernández Rochetti said. "A flunky. A servant. And a thug of the lower depths. Arrests for drugs, petty offenses. When the Colonel escaped from the prison, he brought César with him. César was as devoted as a dog."

Gibson hunched earnestly in front of the desk. "And isn't it true, Commander, as we reported exclusively today, that César Oscar Ontiveros blamed Araceli Aguirre for the Colonel's death? That he had become obsessed with her?"

Watching television in the Diogenes Group headquarters, Méndez slouched in his chair. Porthos and Isabel Puente slumped as well, as if weighed down by so much deceit and perversity. Athos sat with his forearms on his thighs, his cap in his hands.

"Absolutely correct, Porfirio," Mauro Fernández Rochetti said.

"Araceli Aguirre had given the Colonel the strange, unrealistic impression that her human rights commission could somehow save him from the very serious charges against him. The Colonel believed her. When he was killed, César was heartbroken. He felt Señora Aguirre's betrayal set in motion the events leading to his boss's death."

"So it was revenge. The classic motive of the underworld."

Puente, her ankles crossed in suede boots, crossed her arms as well. She gave Méndez a quick look and said: "What a duo."

Mauro Fernández Rochetti narrowed his eyes. "I think that's a very accurate analysis. And don't forget César was a violent young convict, unbalanced. He had drugs and alcohol in his system at the time of the murder."

Gibson asked why the Diogenes Group had arrested the two state police detectives who had killed the assassin.

"My officers have been kidnapped by the so-called Diogenes Group," Fernández Rochetti said tightly. "They intervened heroically and killed the assassin when he confronted them. They deserve medals, yet the Diogenes Group has put them in custody for some bizarre reason. It is an aberration. They are political prisoners."

Gibson referred to a notepad. "I'll read you what Licenciado Méndez, chief of the Diogenes Group, said yesterday: 'The state police will never solve this murder. They will never investigate the only two places they should investigate: the office of the chief of their own Tijuana homicide squad and the headquarters of Multiglobo Productions.' What is your comment about this very serious insinuation, Commander?"

Fernández Rochetti squared his shoulders and showed a flash of tongue.

"Two points, Porfirio, if you please. Number one, it's easy to make accusations without proof. There is proof for everything I have told you. Second: I have been a policeman for thirty-seven years. Not one or two years. Thir-ty se-ven." Soft pats on the table accompanied each syllable. "I've never been a newspaperman or a political agitator. Only a policeman. And I have learned that police work is bittersweet. I always try to emphasize the sweet and eliminate the bitter. A real policeman can't afford to get hysterical at a moment like this. That's my advice to Mr. Méndez."

After the interview, the anchorman and anchorwoman in Mexico City made comments about how bad things were at the border. How all Mexicans hoped the authorities would pursue the case to its ultimate consequences. Then they moved on, having dedicated an entire seven minutes to the assassination without once mentioning the name Ruiz Caballero.

The phone rang. Méndez mouthed the words "The Secretary." The man in Mexico City had seen what he needed to see of the evening news.

"That Mauro Fernández Rochetti is certainly a foul specimen, is he not, Leo?" the Secretary said.

Vivaldi was audible in the background. Méndez imagined his boss sipping a brandy in his study. Getting no response, the Secretary continued: "I am working hard for a decision at the highest levels to remove the case from the state police and designate the federal police and the Diogenes Group as the investigative agencies on the assassination."

"The federal police? You would trade one traitor for another."

"I thought the federal police had been comparatively neutral."

"Only more passive."

"In any case, I'm afraid it may take a while. The Ruiz Caballeros are spreading around money and pressure. The Senator's allies are protecting Junior and the state police. Any progress with your prisoners? I'm feeling heat to surrender them."

"No. I don't think there will be unless we use old-fashioned methods. But our northern friends"—Méndez glanced at Isabel, who nodded—"are still ready to move forward with the indictments. And any technical assistance we need. I think there's no doubt we can establish that the state police engineered the assassination and then got rid of the assassin. It's not a question of proof. It's a question of political will."

"For the moment, Leobardo, I can only repeat how important it is to keep a cool head. Go slowly. Start at the bottom and work our way up. It's a delicate moment."

"Yes sir," Méndez said, bridging his eyes with a hand to his forehead. "Slowly. Start at the bottom and work up."

"Exactly," the Secretary said. He hesitated. "I'll be in touch as soon as I can. Take care of yourself."

Méndez hung up and sipped coffee. He asked Athos: "Do we have a surveillance team on Junior?"

"Yes."

"I want to be on top of his movements at all times. Review the plans for capturing him."

Puente sat up and said: "Leo, did I hear you talk about going slow?"

Méndez patted the phone as he would a pet. He gave her a ragged smile. "I was imitating the Secretary, actually, and lying through my teeth. I have no intention of waiting any longer. Maybe if I had lied sooner, Araceli would still be alive."

Athos and Porthos looked pained. Méndez raised a hand, cutting off Puente.

"I'm serious," he said, hearing his voice shake. "I miscalculated badly. I was wrapped up in my own fuzzy ideas. I thought I would be the target. I never thought they would go after someone so popular, a human rights official, a woman. It's a barbarity, it violates all the codes. But I should have seen it coming."

"Licenciado, all of us were caught off guard," Athos said.

"It won't happen again. We have our arrest warrants, signed by a brave federal prosecutor in Mexico City, and our evidence. As soon as you say the moment is tactically sound, Athos, we grab Junior."

Athos nodded contentedly. Porthos's grin was awed. Puente looked preoccupied.

Méndez regarded her deadpan. "What? You think it's impossible?"

"No," she said. She took a deep breath. "I want to tell you something. It complicates the situation, but it could help. Valentine finally made contact. He's OK."

"Ah."

"He's inside, Leo. He's with Junior's entourage and he's ready to help us any way he can."

Puente went on to explain the series of events that had propelled the fugitive Border Patrol agent into a position of trust with the Ruiz Caballero triggermen. Méndez leaned back in his chair, his eyes almost closed, trying to appear impressed. He didn't trust Pescatore. He thought Isabel's faith in him was naive and risky. He didn't understand whether it was hidden talent or clumsy gringo luck that kept the young agent alive.

"Isabel, that's all very interesting," Méndez said when she had finished. "But you'll forgive me if I have grave doubts. The fact that Pescatore has fallen in with Araceli's murderers does not change my opinion of him."

"He has taken an incredible risk in reaching out to me, Leo," Puente said. "Don't you think that proves his credibility?"

"Not if it is a trap."

"I know him. He's not that slick an operator. Not with me."

"Don't misunderstand me, I am very happy for you that he—"

"Happy for me?" Puente leaned forward combatively, her stare hardening. "What do you mean? It has nothing to do with me. You should be happy for all of us."

Méndez raised a hand defensively. This was no time to get into a battle. They needed each other too much. "That is what I meant. I am happy he has stumbled into the right place at the right time."

Later that night, Puente let Méndez listen in on Pescatore's next call. Pescatore was apparently hiding in a bathroom, whispering into the cell phone. The details convinced Méndez that the kid really was inside Junior's entourage as he claimed. Pescatore sounded sincere, for whatever that was worth. Puente kept the conversation brief, telling Pescatore what they needed. But there was an undercurrent of intimacy in the way she talked to him: her eyes down, her mouth close to the phone, her voice husky. There is no doubt whatsoever that something happened between these two, Méndez told himself. Let's hope for the love of God that it hasn't affected her judgment.

The next day, a team of undercover Diogenes officers shadowed Junior. He rode in a five-vehicle caravan to have lunch at his favorite seafood restaurant in a mini-mall in the Río Zone. He stopped afterward for drinks in the lounge of a twin-towered hotel. He was showing himself in public, making a statement that he had nothing to fear.

But Junior stayed home that night. While they waited for a call from Pescatore, Méndez dozed at his desk with his head propped on his arms. A disc on his computer soothed him: Billy Strayhorn playing solo piano. Méndez had insisted that Puente rest in the adjacent sleeping quarters. At 3 a.m., she hurried into his office, shirttails out of her jeans, hair tousled, listening to her phone as she snapped her fingers to get Méndez's attention.

After she hung up, Puente briefed Méndez. Pescatore had reported that Junior's people had relaxed. The word had come from Senator Ruiz Caballero in Mexico City not to worry. The heat would be off soon.

"Really," Méndez growled. "That might explain why the Secretary didn't call tonight."

Puente stifled a yawn. "Valentine said Junior's in a terrible mood. A woman wanted him to see her. Natalia?"

"Natasha," Méndez said. "Did he say anything else?"

"Buffalo convinced Junior it was better not to go. And Junior didn't like it. Who's Natasha?"

"The wife of an old man with money."

"Pretty?"

"She was Miss Rosarito or something. Junior has a house in Colonia Postal he uses for their get-togethers."

"How romantic."

Méndez knew the rhythms of Junior's moods and appetites. From the moment he heard the name Natasha, Méndez had the instinct that he was going to get his chance. The next morning, Méndez ordered Athos to plan the operation for Colonia Postal, a quiet neighborhood in the hills east of the San Ysidro Port of Entry. Athos established a command post in a house across the street from Junior's love nest. The owners were out of town; Athos took over the house in the name of police business. He persuaded the maid to spend the night elsewhere. He gave her money for expenses and sent her off with a chaperone, a female officer of the Diogenes Group.

The message from Pescatore came Sunday evening: "Natasha tonight."

Méndez and Puente hurried to the command post. To reach it they parked on a street downhill and crept through an alley and the backyard.

"A good location for what you have in mind," Puente said, peering out of the darkened living room window. Lined with stucco houses, the long street curved up a hillside. It was not an ostentatious neighborhood; Junior's hideaway was one of the larger homes. The feebly lit street seemed particularly lifeless on the weekend. Crickets creaked in purple ivy.

"Almost too good," Méndez said. "Let's hope your young Valentine isn't luring us into an ambush."

"He's not *my* young Valentine."

Méndez shrugged. He pointed his flashlight at the diagram Athos had spread on the dining room table. Athos had deployed an inner ring of officers, the arrest team, in the command post house and outside on foot and in vehicles. Another group was backup. There were two snipers on the roof of the command post.

"How does it look?"

"All right, considering our limitations," Athos said drily, puffing on a cigarette. His black cap was turned backwards like a baseball catcher's. A dagger in a leg scabbard complemented his usual outfit. "We're not exactly the Delta Force. But we'll fight with what we have."

At about 10 p.m., the surveillance team reported that Junior had left his home in his Mercedes with one security car.

Athos joined Méndez and Puente at the window. He delivered orders into his radio. When the report came in that Junior had picked up Natasha, Méndez clapped Athos on the shoulder.

Half an hour later, headlights rounded the hill and grew rapidly.

"There's your boy," Isabel Puente whispered in English. "Buffalo Mendoza riding backup."

The Mercedes and the Buick Regal disappeared into the garage.

During the next hour, Méndez, Athos and Puente drank bottled water, ate peanut M&Ms and talked in whispers. Méndez thought about writing a note to his family in case he was killed. Everything he composed in his head sounded melodramatic. He always agonized when he tried to write something personal to his wife. He thought back to his most recent conversation with Estela. They had wept together about Araceli. Then he had told her that there was no way he could go to Berkeley for the time being. Her tone turned cold. She told him that, now more than ever, it was time to drop everything and visit his family. While he still could.

He was reaching into his jacket pocket for a notepad and a pen when Athos said it was time. They slipped out and crept across the street. Silhouettes moved around them as officers surrounded the house, taking aim from behind vehicles, trees, fences. Méndez, Athos, Puente and half a dozen agents crouched next to an intercom set in a low brick wall. Athos took a breath and pushed the buzzer.

The deep voice that answered spoke with a *pocho* accent; Méndez thought it might be Buffalo Mendoza. "Who is this?"

"The Diogenes Group," Méndez said, feeling vaguely ridiculous. "We have an arrest warrant for Mr. Hugo Ruiz Caballero."

There was cursing, a mutter of voices, a long silence. Méndez was about to push the buzzer again when a new voice surprised him. It was snotty and unmistakable.

"Méndez," Junior said. "Trying to fuck me, as usual."

"Time to behave like an adult, Junior. You are surrounded. Surrender quietly." As he spoke, Méndez felt his cell phone buzz on his hip.

"I am the one who gives the orders, you idiot," Junior responded. "If you don't believe me, answer your phone. It's important."

"For the sake of the young lady, stop playing the hard-ass and come out," Méndez snapped. But his phone buzzed again, disconcerting him. He checked the number display: the Secretary.

Aware of Athos staring at him, Méndez turned away from the intercom and answered his phone.

"Méndez, have you taken leave of your senses?" The connection with the Secretary in Mexico City was faint but clear. "I have just received a call from the highest possible level"—Méndez calculated that could be only about six people in Mexico—"informing me that the Diogenes Group is arresting Junior Ruiz Caballero. That you have him surrounded. Have you completely lost your mind?"

"I am doing my job, Mr. Secretary."

"I want you to withdraw immediately from that absolutely intolerable situation you have created. Before you cause another tragedy. I am giving you a direct order."

"Impossible," Méndez said, with more resolve than he felt. He was aware of Athos muttering into his radio.

The Secretary enunciated with frosty precision. "Think of your agents, if not yourself. Those who survive will go to jail, I assure you of that. Their lives will be ruined. All of them."

Méndez's thin features twisted. Athos grabbed him by the shoulder.

"Licenciado," Athos hissed, his breath all tobacco and coffee. "We are setting up a barricade at the end of the block. There's a caravan coming up the hill. Fifteen vehicles full of federal police."

"Not state police?"

"No, federal for sure. Armed for war. Twice as many as us. Someone tipped off Junior." Athos's voice was steely. "Do we hit the house or not?"

"No..." Méndez broke off. He raised the phone, unable to look Athos in the eye, and said to the Secretary: "Why is a federal police contingent on its way here?"

"They have orders from the attorney general to make you withdraw. They will open fire if you do not."

"And you endorsed that order."

"Calm down."

"You would allow them to fire on your own agents."

"Institutionality, Méndez. Institutionality above all things. Someday you will learn that."

"Someday I will tell you face-to-face exactly what I think of you and your fucking institutionality," Méndez said. He hung up.

Officers ran through the shadows to reinforce the barricade. Another vehicle sped downhill. The officers around the house remained in position.

Puente was on one knee, holding her gun in both hands and pointed at the ground. She had dropped all pretense of respecting the rules against American agents carrying weapons south of the border. She stared at the house. Worrying about Pescatore, Méndez thought in spite of himself. Puente gave him a brief smile.

"Leo," she said. "It looks like the bad guys are winning."

"We have to get you out of here," Méndez said.

The federales would have a field day if they caught an armed U.S. agent with the Diogenes Group. He told her he would have an officer sneak her away, get her to San Diego or the U.S. consulate in Tijuana.

She shook her head. "Negative, Licenciado. I'm in this all the way."

Resisting an urge to kiss her, Méndez hurried downhill. The three-car roadblock overlooked a steep section of the tree-lined street. At least the high ground gives us a good firing position, Méndez thought. He stood among his officers, watching the column of Suburbans and Jeep Cherokees climb the hill, the boxy shapes glinting in the glow of the streetlights. The caravan stopped about fifty feet away. Lights went on in houses.

"Easy now," Méndez told Athos. "We don't shoot first."

Federal police officers spilled out of the vehicles. Most of them were youthful, trim and close-cropped, soldiers transferred from the army to the police as part of an anticorruption campaign. They fanned out in combat stances.

A flashlight beam waved back and forth. Three men approached in the middle of the street. Méndez recognized the new Tijuana delegate in charge of the federal attorney general's office. His name was Peralta.

"Diogenes Group," a voice called. "Licenciado Méndez?"

"At your service," Méndez said. He stepped forward. He and Athos walked toward Peralta. Toward the gun barrels pointing at them. Too many to count.

As he walked, he flashed on a childhood memory. His father had once taken him to see an adventure movie: *Khartoum.* Charlton Heston was Gordon Pasha, the British general who holds Khartoum against Sudanese hordes. After a long siege, his troops are overrun. Gordon stands on a balcony above the invaders charging into his ruined fortress. He goes down a staircase into a sea of enemy guns and lances. He stops and gives them a smile. The mob grows quiet. Then the moment passes. Someone throws a spear that kills Gordon; the movie ends with his head on a pike.

It was the first film Méndez had ever seen. The final scene had blazed itself into his memory. As a college student years later, he had seen *Khartoum* again. He had been disappointed. He had been forced to conclude that the film was imperialist, wrongheaded and cheesy. Gordon was a colonial aggressor. Nonetheless, one impression did not change. Méndez had been fascinated once again by the way the soldier smiled at death, welcomed it, embraced it. A very Mexican attitude.

As he advanced, the breeze caressed his face and ruffled the trees overhead.

The federal police were nocturnal creatures. They waited for dark to conduct raids, escort drug shipments north, prowl the border preying on migrants and smugglers. So the chiefs flanking Peralta, a pair of gnarled warhorses, seemed alert and composed.

Their boss, the top federal official in Baja, did not. Peralta's hair was matted and puffed up unevenly in back, clearly the result of a recent and rude awakening. He wore a blue T-shirt under a wrinkled yellow dress shirt and a rumpled tweed jacket. He squinted painfully through gold-rimmed glasses that, like his attire, contrasted with his outsized jaw and the physique of a nightclub bouncer.

"Licenciado Méndez, good morning," Peralta said. He was in his thirties. He spoke with formal courthouse diction, but his voice trembled.

Méndez felt morbid satisfaction. He's shitting in his pants. He thinks I'm on a suicide mission and I'm going to take him down with me.

"Licenciado," Méndez said.

"Lamentably, as you may know, we have been instructed to take charge of the people in the house," Peralta said, swallowing. "I would appreciate your cooperation."

Méndez did not plan to make it easy for him. "I have an arrest warrant. In fact it was prepared by a federal prosecutor like yourself. I propose we arrest them together."

"Lamentably, those are not my orders."

"It's the logical thing to do. We hold them until this gets resolved in Mexico City."

"No sir. I was ordered to escort the young man wherever he needs to go. I hope you understand."

"Yes." Méndez felt a shudder of rage. "Congratulations."

"For?"

"You only arrived a month ago. And today you'll make a million dollars."

Peralta's head tilted as if he had been slapped. One of the chiefs dropped his hand toward his holster, grunting, "Enough of this crap."

Méndez reached across his body for the pistol in his belt, already imagining the sound and gore it would make if they shot each other at this distance. Athos's rifle lowered to chest level. Metal echoed up and down the block as both sides racked ammunition clips to firing mode.

"Gentlemen, please!" Peralta smothered the chief's arm, preventing the gun from clearing the holster. Turning, he raised his hands wide in a restraining motion directed at the officers behind him. He remained that way a moment, silhouetted against headlights.

Peralta turned sorrowfully back to Méndez. He said: "Are we really going to kill each other right here in the street?"

"That's in your hands." Méndez had the gun at his side, pointing at Peralta's belly.

"You are outnumbered," Peralta said. "I have no quarrel with you. I have no desire to be here, believe me. But I will carry out my orders."

Anything else would have driven Méndez over the edge. But Peralta, to the evident disdain of the chiefs accompanying him, had shown a shred of humanity. He actually seemed ashamed of being a lackey to criminals.

Méndez knew he had lost. There was nothing left to do, unless he wanted to sacrifice dozens of lives for a gesture of defiance. He put his gun back in his belt.

The prosecutor nodded several times with relief. His voice stayed soft.

"Do I have your word that you will stand aside and let us proceed, Licenciado?"

"Do your duty."

In the weak light, Méndez could not tell if Peralta's eyes were sleepy or had tears in them. Méndez turned away. He heard the prosecutor say he was sorry.

Trudging uphill, Méndez thought: That man is in the wrong line of work. Like me.

15

He saw Isabel only for a moment, but he was sure she had seen him too.

Pescatore was in the front passenger seat of the Buick Regal with his AK-47. Sniper drove. Ahead of them in the Mercedes were Momo, Buffalo, Junior and Junior's gorgeous chick. Pescatore could see Natasha's shiny golden-brown hair snuggled close to Junior's curls in the back window. Either she was cowering or she had fallen asleep.

The caravan rolled slowly uphill. Federal cops perched in the open doors of the moving vehicles. Federal cops on foot lined the street. They were bulky with weapons, flak vests and ammunition clips.

The Diogenes officers were spectators on the sidewalks. Sniper bared fangs at them from behind the wheel. "That's right, *putos.* Get back. We got a po-lice escort."

Pescatore spotted Isabel on the sidewalk. Ponytail, boots, the denim shirt and jeans she had worn that night at her apartment. The night he wished he had appreciated more, because he would never be that happy again. Isabel had her thumb against her teeth, which meant she was thinking hard or in a bad mood. Next to her were Méndez and the old comandante named Athos. Their glares tracked the Mercedes like lasers.

Pescatore made eye contact with Isabel. Obviously she wasn't going to wave at him, but he still didn't like what he saw. Her face didn't flicker. Hello and good-bye. As the Buick accelerated, she rested a hand on Méndez's shoulder. A comforting gesture, easy and affectionate. Pescatore felt hollow to the core. He felt bereft of everything except the conviction that he had seen her for the last time. And his final memory would be of Isabel playing cuddly sidekick with Méndez.

The caravan gathered speed. The Mercedes followed a Cherokee carrying the federal chiefs and their civilian boss. They topped the hill and descended into the pale brown expanse of Otay Mesa.

Sniper mumbled something about the Diogenes *pendejos* following them.

Pescatore thought about how close he had come to turning the AK-47 on Sniper during the frantic scene at the house when he had been expecting the Diogenes Group to bust through doors and windows like badass commandos.

The caravan hit the asphalt at hot-pursuit speed. The few cars on the road got the hell out of the way. Pescatore looked back. A half-dozen Diogenes sedans—old and ratty compared with the federal fleet—trailed at a distance.

The airport was more crowded than he had expected. Travelers gawked when the police battalion pulled up to the terminal with rifles sprouting out of the vehicle windows.

Buffalo emerged from the Mercedes, eyebrows and mustache set in full glower. His shotgun was in plain view, the stock cupped in his elbow. A police badge was pinned to his belt. He hacked at the air impatiently; Sniper and Pescatore scrambled out. Buffalo leaned back into the Mercedes and consulted with Junior. Buffalo ordered them back into the Regal again.

The police Cherokee led the way past gates, parking lots, guardhouses. Guards and guys with clipboards approached them, fell back like targets in a pinball machine. The caravan circled the terminal and drove directly onto the tarmac, bearing down on a section reserved for private aircraft.

"Whose plane is that?" Pescatore asked.

"Mr. Abbas."

Abbas seemed to be in charge of the operation. He escorted Junior aboard the plane immediately; Natasha remained in the Mercedes. In the doorway of the plane, Abbas huddled with Buffalo and a pilot. Ground personnel swarmed the Learjet, getting it ready. The federal police set up a perimeter. The Diogenes Group was nowhere in sight.

"Hurry up, *cabrón.*" Sniper grimaced at Pescatore through the open driver's door.

Pescatore wrenched himself up out of the seat. He trotted to the plane. Buffalo stood at the top of the stairway leading to the entrance. Pescatore paused, one foot on the stairs, one still on the tarmac.

"Whatsa matter, Valentín?"

Pescatore opened his mouth. Here's the problem: The last thing in the world I want to do is get on this plane. Because I'm actually an undercover U.S. operative, you see. I'm the guy who almost got you busted just now. Frankly, I'm afraid you're going to find out. And kill my ass.

"Uh, nothing," Pescatore said. "I just hope I don't need a passport, 'cause I ain't got mine with me."

"*Órale, güey.* Where we're going, only passport you need is that *cuerno de chivo.*"

The takeoff over the Pacific revealed a panorama of the lights of San Diego to the north: the suburban lowlands, the ribbons of freeways, the rampart of the coastline and the glowing cluster of downtown domes and towers. Then they were into the clouds and away.

Pescatore huddled against the window, pretending to doze. His mind was in threat-assessment mode. Overloaded. Clicking out of control. OK, the plane has two single-seat rows in the back half of the cabin. I'm in the front seat, right side. Buffalo's in the front seat, left side. Sniper and Momo behind us. Junior and Abbas sitting at a bolted table in big executive swiveling seats. A flight attendant pouring orange juice. Two pilots. Destination unknown.

Junior used his cell phone to bang out absentminded rhythms on the table. He was smoldering. Sweat had formed horseshoes under his armpits. A dark *V* spread down the front of his floppy blue shirt, which he wore with the tails out. He swiveled back and forth, a leg curled up under him. His free foot jiggled in a basketball shoe. He tossed his head back, turned and spat noisily. Disgusting, Pescatore thought. But Abbas did not protest about the carpet stain.

We definitely scared the shit out of Junior, Pescatore thought, closing his eyes. Ever since his phone call to Isabel, he had felt sharp and clean and good about what he was doing. They had been a team again. They had communicated so well: wasting no words, all business, but he heard the pride in her voice. He had called the shots, guided her and Méndez toward the showdown. It had all fallen into place. When he entered the house in Colonia Postal, knowing that Isabel and the Mexicans were concealed outside, he experienced a rush that made his own survival seem trivial. Time to throw down. One way or another, it was going to be over.

But Junior started getting phone calls. Junior went nuts, thundering downstairs bare-chested and coke-addled, Natasha hanging on him, looking like a frenzied colt. Pescatore thought Buffalo was going to slap her to shut her up, slap her and Junior both so Junior would explain why they had to get out of there right away.

But then the Diogenes Group had made its move. Pescatore, playing the dutiful henchman, didn't know what to do. Start shooting? Tell everybody to get up against the wall? What if he messed it all up? All he wanted was someone else to fire the first shot. He didn't want to take the lead, ruin everything.

Now he couldn't shake the suspicion that he had ruined everything anyway. No showdown, no closure. He was trapped on this plane with his pathetic daydreams. He had imagined it so differently. Unscathed or dying, he had imagined it ending in Isabel's arms, her whisper warm in his ear.

He awoke flailing at invisible assailants. His neck ached. His mouth was rusted shut, his eyes crusted over.

Buffalo regarded him from across the narrow aisle. He was listening to an iPod.

"I put it up for you," Buffalo said as Pescatore groped around for his rifle in a panic. Pescatore scanned the overhead rack and the floor: The AK-47 was not in sight. He realized there was no engine sound. He saw Abbas in conference with the pilots in the open door of the cockpit. Sunlight was visible beyond them. The plane had landed. But no one looked ready to get off.

"Where we at?" Pescatore rasped. Give me back my AK, you bastards. Please.

Buffalo slipped the headphones down around his trunklike neck.

"Quito," he intoned, eyebrows raised, savoring the exotic syllables. "Just a pit stop. You go back to sleep."

Pescatore refrained from asking where Quito was. His panic at the loss of the rifle was tempered slightly by Buffalo's easy rumble, his comfortable slouch.

"Whew, I was crashed," Pescatore said. "That was rough last night."

"*Simón.*" Buffalo leaned confidentially toward Pescatore, who followed his glance toward the rear: Sniper and Momo looking out their windows, the flight attendant in her galley, the closed bathroom door. "Didn't I tell you about Méndez, *cabrón?* Didn't I tell you that fucker was gonna sweat us?"

Pescatore nodded.

Buffalo muttered: "*Eso si,* he's got some *cojones* on him."

"Somebody really saved our ass, huh?"

"Mexico City *chingones,* man. Junior got a tip, called some big shot and they showed Méndez who runs the fucking show once and for all."

Pescatore wanted to know who the Mexico City *chingones* were. How much they knew. Why Junior was on the lam if he ran the show. But he did not want to push Buffalo; he had learned to pass up obvious opportunities and circle back later to ask questions. He gestured at the iPod. "Whatcha listening to?"

"Oldies, this and that. Santana. Plus this song they wrote about me in the *pinta.*"

"Everybody likes Santana, man. They should make him president of the world."

"He's *el mero mero.*"

"What's a *pinta?*"

"The penitentiary in TJ."

"A song about you? By who?"

Buffalo looked sheepish, but he was enjoying himself. "A *banda* group who was locked up at the time. Back when Robustiano Moran was in there. You heard of him?"

"Uh-uh."

"This capo from Sonora. They used to call him Cirujano: He was like a surgeon with a gun, his aim was so good. Anyway, I was working for this other capo who hated his guts. I got in a big shoot-out with Moran and two of his *cuates. Puro desmadre.* Chasing all over. *Cabrones* threw a grenade at me."

"In a prison?!"

"Hell, in that *pinta* they got every kinda weapon there is. Except bazookas. I was bleeding all over. But I did the two guys, wounded Moran. I ran outta ammunition. Hadda finish him with my hands."

"Damn."

Buffalo chuckled, pantomiming. "I'm pistol-whippin' him, whaling on his skull, this and that. It was pretty funny. The whole yard is watching, I'm poundin' on this dude way after he died. Some wiseass yells out: '*Ya está bien, Búfalo! Ya lo mataste bien muerto, cabrón.*' I fell down and lay there for a while. A couple days later these guys in the band made up the song. A *corrido.*"

"What's the name of it?"

"'La Ley del Búfalo.'" He lifted off the headphones and passed them across the aisle. "Wanna hear it?"

"Yeah."

"This band's got talent. I helped them get a contract with Junior's label last year. I owed them. A song, that's special. Something for my son to remember me by."

Pescatore looked appropriately reverent as he slipped on the headphones. The introduction was a sweet three-voice harmony, then drums kicked in like a call to battle.

But he didn't hear much else. There was movement in the back of the aisle. A blast of cologne preceded Junior as he appeared between the seats, faked a punch at Buffalo and then pivoted and fired a fist at the center of Pescatore's forehead. Pescatore flung up a block, flinching badly, the headphones askew. The full force of the odor nauseated him: Junior's cologne interspersed with waves of vomit, sweat and alcohol. Junior grinned; he was just horsing around.

"Think fast, *gabacho,* I got you now." Junior thumped Pescatore's biceps and forearms, nothing playful about the pain searing through his arms. Junior drummed the tops of their seats. "*Qué onda?* Everybody good?"

"Oh yeah," Pescatore stammered, hating himself. "Kicking it in the Learjet. First class all the way."

Junior looked revived. His skin-straining grin was back. He cupped his belly where it pushed at the buttons of his shirt. His words slid over each other. "I know Buffalo is mad because we didn't smoke Méndez last night, no?"

"*No señor,*" Buffalo said. "You handled it just right, *patrón.*"

"*Pinche* Méndez. He thought I don't have no psychology."

Junior put a finger by his temple. "But we played smart. Checkmated him. He looked like a *maricón* last night. And he signed his death warrant, didn't he?"

"*Así es.*"

"*El Buf* will take care of it," Junior exulted. "Will you waste that motherfucker for me? Cut off his ears and make him eat them?"

"*Con mucho gusto, jefe,*" Buffalo scowled.

"How about you, *gabacho?*"

"*A todo dar,*" Pescatore drawled in his best Tijuana cadence.

Buffalo winked at him behind Junior's back. Pescatore grinned.

Mr. Abbas and Junior resumed their places at the table. Abbas told him they had reached Khalid by radio; everything was arranged. Another refueling stop and they'd be there soon.

"Khalid looks forward to returning your hospitality," Abbas said in a proper accent that sounded British and French at the same time. He crossed his legs in the swivel seat. "He is delighted to have you as his guest. You may stay with us as long as necessary."

Junior studied the bearded man with sudden wariness.

"Khalid is a gentleman," Junior said slowly. "A wise man. That's why we work together so well."

"He has the same sentiments about you."

Junior leaned across the table, not listening, eyes wide and finger jabbing. "But I do not want you to have the wrong impression. I could turn around and go back right now, Abbas."

"Of course, I—"

"I appreciate Khalid's help. But I am not running. I have no need to run."

"Good heavens, no."

"My uncle and me have the situation under control. I *want* to make this trip. Lower my profile at home. Spend time with Khalid, develop our projects. That's what this is about. A business vacation. Am I clear?"

Junior was getting wound up. Abbas pacified him with some supersmooth ass-kissing. He waved over the flight attendant and had her pour drinks.

Pescatore lost interest. Through the window he could see a corner of an airport terminal in the early morning light. It looked like a glorified bus station. A Jeep with four helmeted soldiers, maybe military policemen, guarded their plane. Beyond the Jeep, a crowd of people behind a chain-link fence. Could they be here for Junior? Did people know who Junior was in Quito?

Pescatore decided they weren't interested in the Learjet. Their attention was focused on the runways where commercial planes maneuvered. Pescatore first thought they were travelers, but there wasn't much luggage in evidence. He saw women with big goofy hats, bowler and stovepipe contraptions. The women ambled like wrestlers, fireplug builds beneath wool sweaters and petticoats. Except for some vendors and street punks, the men were old and grave; they wore suits the color and texture of cardboard. The children had flat, sun-blackened cheeks. They slept, played, chewed mechanically on pieces of bread and fruit that the adults handed them. The gathering seemed ritualistic, unhurried, as if these people came to this fence often and planned to spend the day there. Compared with Mexicans, the people were pure-blood-Indian-looking. But the faces and the stances, the strength and patience and wariness, reminded him of The Line.

"Fucked-up country," Buffalo muttered, leaning over him toward the glass.

"What're they doin'?"

"Some of 'em are saying good-bye to relatives. Some of 'em are getting ready to go themselves. Probably where we came from. Or Europe. Looks like half the country's gettin' outta Dodge."

Pescatore remembered that Quito was the capital of Ecuador. It occurred to him that the fence was a place to hook up with smugglers, buy documents, arrange trips. He spotted well-fed hustler types, distinguished by sunglasses and cell phones on the hips of designer jeans, working the crowd.

Pescatore said: "I once caught some Chinese guys in Imperial Beach. They came up from Quito. There was intel about whole neighborhoods of Chinese in Ecuador getting ready to go to the States. And we were catching Ecuadorean aliens too. Going to New York, New Jersey, paying fifteen to twenty thousand a head. That must be what a house costs around here."

"Yeah," Buffalo said. "Those are hill and mountain people, look at 'em."

Pescatore decided Quito was a hub in the OTM smuggling racket Junior ran with his South American partners. The Learjet's destination was no doubt the Triple Border Isabel talked about so much, somewhere in Brazil or Paraguay.

The long-haired flight attendant hovered over him in a cloud of coconut perfume, offering a cup of orange juice. He accepted, and nodded again when she raised a vodka bottle over the cup.

"Thanks," he mumbled. "Any chance of breakfast? Or lunch?"

She told him she would serve food once they were airborne. Her heavy makeup creased into a pained smile. She moved on quickly, thigh flashing in the short skirt. She didn't seem too comfortable with the clientele. Hard to blame her, what with Junior ranting and spitting and everything. Though she no doubt encountered her share of lowlifes working for Abbas.

Pescatore tried to calculate how long it had been since his last bona fide meal. Isabel would have given him all kinds of shit: You're surrounded by bad guys. You're on a one-way flight that could be your last. And you're worried about stuffing your face.

Yeah well, gotta keep my strength up, baby. The vodka and orange juice gave him a tangy jolt. Breakfast of Champions, he thought, and drank more. He tried to catch the flight attendant's eye, maybe score a bag of peanuts or something. He raised his cup in a silent toast to the Ecuadoreans pressed up against the fence. Go with God, folks. Right now I'm stuck with the devil.

16

THE SMELL IN HIS HOUSE had gotten worse.

The smell was moldy and dank. Méndez had noticed it the last time he was home. But he hadn't had the time or inclination to investigate. At first he had thought the smell came from outside, from the construction site of the high-rise that would soon obstruct the last vestiges of his view. When the Méndez family had moved into the narrow town house in Playas de Tijuana, the front windows offered a panorama of the ocean. Five years had brought an eruption of mini-malls, narco-mansions, half-empty condominium towers built to launder money. Now Méndez had to stand in a corner of his second-floor balcony and lean to the left for a glimpse of the surf.

Méndez watched Porthos reach a prodigious arm across the kitchen table and refill his mug with exaggerated care. Méndez, Porthos and Athos were drinking from the only clean glassware he had found: three of his son's mugs. Méndez's mug was decorated with a killer whale from SeaWorld.

No, the smell definitely came from inside the house. Probably a burst pipe. Another sign, like the grime illuminated by sunshine on the Formica table, the stacks of dishes and glasses in the sink, that the house had gone to hell in his family's absence. The house and everything else had gone to hell.

Méndez raised his mug.

"To Junior," he said. "To Junior and his uncle, and Mauro Fernández Rochetti, and the state police of Baja California Norte, and the federal police of the United States of Mexico. Fuck all their mothers."

"Amen, Licenciado," Porthos said, and drank.

Athos's pointy, nicotine-stained teeth appeared inside his goatee as he raised a Snoopy mug.

A flame of tequila expanded in Méndez's chest. They were sitting around the kitchen table. They were still wearing their raid jackets.

After Junior's getaway, Méndez had stayed away from headquarters. He had ignored the messages from the Secretary, turned off his radio and cell phone. He intended to communicate his resignation from government service only when he was good and ready.

"Junior surprised me," Méndez said, staring at the killer whale. "He knew the state police would have started shooting, fucked up everything. So he brings in Peralta and the federal police. And the Secretary and the attorney general drop their pants."

"What I want to know is, who tipped them off?" Porthos said.

"If you ask me, the gringo," Méndez said. "Isabel says that doesn't make sense. She says it had to be someone in our unit."

"A traitor?" Porthos said.

"Isabel says the Secretary must have gotten word of the operation before we started. She has a point, the *federicos* showed up very quickly."

"Maybe Mexico City called Junior to warn him, not the other way around," Athos said.

"Maybe." Méndez thought about working up the energy to pull off his bulletproof vest. "I still think the gringo played both sides. Isabel is not objective when it comes to Pescatore. Her only weak spot, as far as I am concerned."

"She looked good out there last night," Athos said. "A real lioness."

That observation amounted to an outburst for Athos. It was perhaps the only sign that he had been drinking. Along with the repeated tapping of his fingers on his temple beneath his receding hairline.

"A very attractive lady, Agent Puente," Porthos said in his earnest proclamatory way. "I was surprised about her and Pescatore. I thought she didn't... I thought she preferred... well, you know."

"What?"

The big man rubbed his beard uneasily. "Well, Licenciado, I thought she had an, eh, alternative lifestyle."

"*Epah,* maestro," Athos said, raising his eyebrows. "Where did you learn that term?"

"In a debate on the radio, I think."

"A complicated way to say she likes women."

"I know it's difficult for you to comprehend, Commander, but I was being delicate."

"You're delicate all right. Listening to radio shows like a *comadre.*"

Méndez reached slowly across the table for the bottle and filled their mugs. When Athos and Porthos went into their put-down ritual, they were like bears taking lazy swipes at each other. They were performing for his benefit, trying to cheer him up.

"Her lifestyle is perfectly normal—except she has the bad taste to prefer that yanqui hoodlum to one of us," Méndez said. "In any case, she never quits. She went back to San Diego because she thinks the task force can track the destination of the plane."

"South America, no?" Athos said.

Méndez stared out the window, feeling the tequila rekindle his anger. "We had him, Athos. I hesitated. I let you all down."

"No sir."

"Once the federal police showed up, I..." The alcohol was

jumbling Méndez's thoughts. "Even if we had held them off, what would we have done? I thought..."

"You protected your men," Athos said. "You let no one down."

"That's right, Licenciado," Porthos said.

"There's only one thing I regret," Athos said, the lines around his eyes crinkling mischievously. "I wish you had let Porthos lead the charge. I really wanted to see him knock down the door with that big fat gut of his."

"As you bravely gave orders from the rear," Porthos growled.

They chortled and drank, comfortable with the silence and one another. Méndez considered Puente's theory: If there was a traitor inside the Diogenes Group, Athos and Porthos were the only ones he could trust. Here we are, on our own at last. The Three Musketeers.

"What really infuriates me is Mauro Fernández Rochetti," Méndez said after a while. "The jailbreak, the Colonel, Araceli. He has manipulated everything."

"What he did to Doctora Aguirre is the ugliest thing I've seen in seventeen years as a policeman," Porthos declared. "And I've seen ugly things, believe me. Ugly ugly ugly."

Athos nodded.

"Repugnant son of a bitch," Méndez said, sipping from his mug.

"A real beast," Porthos said.

Méndez bit his lower lip. "After what happened with Junior this morning, Mauro thinks he owns this town."

"He's probably sitting in Café Bumpy right now," Athos said quietly. "Laughing about it."

"Now?" Méndez reached for his mug.

"He has breakfast at El Bumpy every morning."

"He thinks our arrest warrant is worthless, we'd never dare touch him," Méndez said, draining the tequila.

"Probably he thinks that."

"I'd enjoy wiping that smile off his face."

"Me too, and how," Porthos said, polishing off another drink. "Abuse his human rights for a while."

"That would be something, Licenciado."

They looked at one another.

"In fact, I'm tempted to go pay him a visit right now," Méndez said. He knew when he said it that it was going to happen.

Athos wiped a hand thoughtfully across his lips. He put on his cap. Porthos gave a soft whoop. Méndez resisted an urge to laugh out loud.

He was surprised to find that he felt steady on his feet. Steady, warmth rushing through him, ready for combat. D'Artagnan goes out hunting for his nemesis, Rochefort, the Man of Meung, the Cardinal's ace swordsman.

"Very good," Méndez said. "Let's get going, then."

Café Bumpy was a diner off Boulevard Agua Caliente. In recent years it had lost clients to the new coffee-shop franchises in town that offered glossy menus, big parking lots and gleaming interiors. El Bumpy was older, ricketier, greasier. But it survived thanks to cops, journalists, government officials and other old-school clients of dubious repute.

Porthos circled the block once. They spotted Fernández Rochetti's Suburban in the gravel parking lot. They saw the homicide commander at his usual window table with his cowboy-hatted bodyguard, Chancho.

The three men had barely spoken during the ride over. The odds were bad. The Musketeers pick a fight with the Cardinal's Guards, the Musketeers challenge a regiment, an army. Look at me, Méndez thought: an amateur cop to the end. A second-rate writer with a gun, reeking of tequila.

Porthos stopped in the alley behind the diner. Méndez and Athos got out of the car, slipped through a gap in a wooden fence and crossed a patio containing Dumpsters. As Athos opened the back door to the kitchen, he gave Méndez a fierce grin over his shoulder.

"Total suicide, Licenciado."

"Absolutely."

"What do we do after?"

"One thing at a time."

Athos told Porthos over the radio that they were inside.

They stalked through the restaurant kitchen. The cooks froze at the sight of the guns. At the swinging doors to the dining room stood an assistant manager who knew Athos and Méndez. She was heavyset in a green uniform, her hair arranged with ribbons. She blinked rapidly, dismayed, and said, "Oh no, Comandante, please, what?"

Athos put a finger to his lips.

Past the swinging doors, Méndez took the lead. He stormed down a narrow aisle between crowded booths, turning a corner, his jacket knocking over a ketchup bottle on a table. Méndez homed in on Fernández Rochetti in his booth: natty in a blue blazer and red tie, intent on his breakfast. Fernández Rochetti's bushy eyebrows were raised in concentration as he cut steak, holding the knife and fork with his hands close together.

Méndez had the arrest warrant in his left hand and the gun in his right. He had intended to announce the arrest with by-the-book language. But all the rage and liquor bubbled up in his throat; he managed to roar Fernández Rochetti's name before slamming the warrant onto the table. The homicide chief reared back, sputtering in surprise.

Méndez grabbed the tie and yanked Fernández Rochetti out of the booth. He clubbed him once across the head with the gun barrel. He was aware of Athos pointing his rifle at Chancho's chest, exclamations from nearby tables, Porthos's voice booming from the front entrance: "Police, stay down, nobody move or I blow your heads off."

Méndez clung to Fernández Rochetti's tie. He hauled him along the row of booths. Fernández Rochetti staggered and choked. Méndez gave him another swat with the gun, the metal thunking against the back of his skull. Méndez wondered if the gun would go off by mistake. Dragging Fernández Rochetti toward the front entrance. Giving the tie a savage twist and yank. Fernández Rochetti on one knee, gagging.

So this is the real way to arrest someone, Méndez thought. This is what I've come to, Mauro, right down to your level.

Mendez realized that the warrant had remained on the table, a discarded facade of legality. At the front door, Athos covered the room with the rifle. Porthos grabbed the prisoner, pawed inside his blazer and relieved him of his gun. They stumbled down steps into the parking lot, where Porthos shoved Fernández Rochetti face-first onto the hood of the Crown Victoria and handcuffed him.

"I'll kill you all, sons of bitches," Fernández Rochetti gasped as they crammed him into the backseat, Porthos hustling around to the driver's side.

"Shut up, asshole," Méndez growled, hearing the shriek of brakes.

A blue Dodge Charger skidded into the parking lot, clearly a state police car. Perhaps the detectives inside the car had seen the commotion as they approached; perhaps they had been called from the restaurant. Méndez scrambled back out of the car and started to take aim over the roof.

Athos was way ahead of him. He had been backpedaling toward the Crown Victoria in rearguard mode, his rifle aimed at the diner. Now he pivoted smoothly toward the new threat. Two officers emerged from the Dodge Charger, drawing pistols.

Athos did not wait for them to announce their intentions: He opened fire. He raked the rifle back and forth, bullet holes spattering a long *X* across the windshield, splintering glass, shredding metal: the bodies jerked and shuddered.

One detective toppled facedown in the gravel, his pistol clattering beside him. The other detective staggered on the far side of the car, wounded but still on his feet, trying to return fire.

Athos sprinted forward, his cap flying off. He veered left, shooting on the move, shooting from a crouch, shooting down into the body of the second detective.

"Let's go let's go let's go," Porthos bellowed from behind the wheel. Somebody was coming out of the front entrance of Café Bumpy and Méndez hunched, anticipating fire from that direction. He jammed his gun into the base of Mauro's skull to keep him on the floor. Athos swung into the front seat. The Crown Victoria lurched and roared, spraying gravel, fishtailing into Boulevard Agua Caliente. Porthos snarled behind the wheel and tromped the accelerator, in the clear.

Athos turned up the volume of the police radio on the dashboard. A report was coming in already on the state police frequency: Shots fired. Officers down. Commander Fernández Rochetti abducted by assailants.

"Where to, Licenciado, our headquarters?" Porthos bellowed.

"The Line," Méndez said, dialing Isabel Puente's number on his phone. He felt a rush of euphoria and disbelief.

"Forgive me, Licenciado, The Line?" Athos asked.

Although Athos's thinning hair was disheveled, his goateed face was like stone. He just killed two men and he isn't even breathing hard, Méndez thought. Nonetheless, the old cop looked like he would prefer a faceful of bullets to running to San Diego.

"I don't have any other ideas," Méndez exclaimed, strange half-choked laughter welling up in him. "Do you propose we barricade ourselves in the headquarters? Who's going to help us?"

"Yes, but..."

Athos was making the same calculation: There was nowhere else to go. Certainly nowhere Athos would be safe after killing two state police detectives.

They headed east past the Cultural Center and City Hall and turned north. They stopped on a side street long enough to gag the semiconscious Fernández Rochetti with a rag and stuff him into the trunk. Fernández Rochetti's eyes had the dull glow of a dying animal's. He was silent.

Méndez told Puente over the phone that he had an urgent package for her. He asked her if her friends in blue at San Ysidro could help him make the delivery before the competition caught up. She told him she would handle it.

The traffic in the twenty-four-lane northbound approach to the San Ysidro border crossing was backed up for a good half-mile, a sea of vehicles, exhaust fumes, vendors and pedestrians. Porthos followed ramps and bridges to a separate Mexican-run lane for VIPs east of the port of entry. A Mexican immigration officer sat outside a guard shack by a gate like those at railroad crossings.

Athos concealed the rifle. Porthos nodded at the approaching green-uniformed figure.

"Run him over if necessary," Méndez whispered, forcing a smile.

But the officer recognized them, saluted and raised the gate. The VIP lane descended a gentle incline and curved left, emptying out at a spot that was still in Mexican territory but put them near the front of the lines waiting to enter the U.S. inspection lanes.

"Go to Lane One, Leo," Isabel told Méndez over the phone. "They know you're coming."

Porthos sped toward the first three lanes, which were empty because the inspection booths were closed. The Crown Victoria crossed over a yellow line into U.S. territory, which began several hundred yards south of the inspection stations.

On his left, Méndez saw four U.S. Customs and Border Protection inspectors hurrying toward them through the sea of cars. One inspector held a lunging German shepherd on a leash. They were one of the roving teams that walked the vehicle lanes sniffing out drugs and illegal immigrants. They were jogging, hands on their blue caps.

"Here come your dogs, Isabel," Méndez said into the phone.

"You're OK. Just hurry up and get across before we have another diplomatic incident."

The inspectors encircled the car and escorted it on foot, glancing south.

"Say so long to our lovely and beloved Mexico for a while," Méndez told his men, sinking back in the seat. "This mess will take a while to clean up."

In the shadow of the port of entry, Méndez remembered an article he had once read about a Mexican performance artist who portrayed different characters of the border: a lowrider, a Tijuana yuppie, an indigenous shaman. The artist "baptized" each character by dressing in full costume and crossing through the U.S. border station on foot to see how the inspectors reacted. Every crossing is like a rebirth, the artist had said, a transformation of the individual and of the world he enters.

Méndez thought to himself that the idea of birth was only half-right. Crossing was also a kind of death.

Part Four

TRIPLE BORDER

17

THE PLANE DESCENDED OUT of fields of clouds over the jungle. The treetops were dense and unreal and interminable, a green reflection of the clouds above. The plane descended and descended and there was no break in the sea of vegetation. Just as the plane seemed about to scrape its belly on the trees, the jungle gave way to a landing strip.

It was a tiny airport. A low control tower, a deserted shed of a terminal. But the runway was long enough to accommodate a 747.

Wet heat washed over Pescatore as he stepped stiff-legged from the plane. The force of it made him blink. The worst heat he had ever experienced had been when he worked a detail at the Border Patrol station in El Centro. The Imperial Valley desert was like a furnace. You felt permanently singed, even at night.

This was worse. This was brutal: a swamp of humidity that smothered motion and thought. Pescatore started to take off his jacket, but remembered his shoulder holster. He wiped at the sweat blossoming on his unshaven upper lip. He noticed a hangar near the tree line where a barbed-wire fence enclosed the airstrip. There were KEEP OUT signs in Portuguese. The hangar was freshly painted in camouflage colors. The doors were padlocked.

A Brazilian doper airport, Pescatore concluded. Probably guns too. Plus the occasional VIP fugitive.

Moze and Tchai waited by the runway with a crew of thuggish Brazilians attired like them: black lightweight vests with multiple pockets over their guns, wrists and chests heavy with gold chains. Moze and Tchai exchanged hugs with Abbas and handshakes with Junior, who looked queasy.

Pescatore ended up with Momo in the far backseat of a sport utility vehicle. Junior and Buffalo were in the middle, Abbas by the driver. The road led out of the jungle into the outskirts of a city.

"That is the Syrian-Lebanese club, you remember we took lunch there with Khalid," Abbas told Junior, indicating the arched wall of a country club on the roadside. "He would like to give you that stallion you fancied."

Junior grunted. He reclined behind big bug-eye sunglasses, a bronzed arm draped over the top of the seat. His cologne blended with the smells of upholstery and air-conditioning.

They entered the city. The buildings were taller and more modern than Pescatore had expected: high walls, barbed wire, guardhouses fronting condominium complexes. The people were a spectrum of colors and races. Palm trees shaded the business district. A sign bore the words FOZ DO IGUAÇU. Pescatore remembered a map Isabel had showed him: Foz was the Brazilian city at the Triple Border.

Although Junior had been here before, Abbas kept up a tour-guide banter. Abbas enjoyed the cultured inflections of his own voice. "That department store is new... splendid growth in construction and investment... City Hall over here... do you see the mosque, the minaret there? Khalid is a very generous benefactor."

Past downtown, open-fronted luncheonettes and flophouse hotels mixed with automotive shops, truck depots, storage yards. Traffic thickened. Trucks, buses, minivans, columns of pedestrians. The road curved along a canyon. Flags fluttered over a bridge.

"That, gentlemen, is the Paraná River. Ciudad del Este on the other side."

Abbas put some ceremony into the announcement, but Junior did not react. Junior had fallen asleep. His chins nested on his chest, his lips puckered. Pescatore saw an *R*-shaped diamond in his left ear.

Abbas examined Junior. He continued mechanically. "The Paraná River. Could we call it the river of dreams?"

The muddy stagnant waters at the bottom of the canyon did not look like a river of dreams. But Pescatore realized he was seeing an international border: the line between Brazil and Paraguay. All his Border Patrol instincts kicked in.

The pedestrians swarming off the bridge from Paraguay carried bags and backpacks. Two youths trotted by: dark-skinned with blond-streaked nappy hair, sinewy in shorts, T-shirts and thongs. Strapped on their backs were colossal cardboard boxes swathed in black duct tape. The youths covered ground with the stamina of marathon runners, drenched in sweat, bent beneath their loads.

"Tripped out," Pescatore whispered to Buffalo. "What's in the boxes?"

"Contraband," Abbas said. "Mostly cigarettes."

"Cigarettes?"

"For the Brazilian black market. Paraguay imports enough cigarettes for every man, woman and child to smoke a pack a day. We call the smugglers *formigas:* ants."

Pescatore was aghast and amused. His fingers cupped an invisible radio. He wanted to call it in: Hey, Brazilian Border Patrol, there's like five hundred smugglers coming across. You slugs gonna respond or what?

It was ridiculous. No one made a move to check the vehicles entering and departing the jam-packed two-lane bridge. At the

Brazilian customs station, a green flag depicted a yellow diamond enclosing a blue globe. Sturdy mustachioed cops in gray uniforms and laced boots stood around a lone truck in the inspection area, arms folded, just watching the parade.

Reaching the bridge, Pescatore felt the vertigo he always got at The Line in San Diego: simultaneous fascination and apprehension. Amplified now by a brand-new border and the craziness that had brought him here.

A group of smugglers crouched on the walkway of the bridge. They raised hands to shield against the sun, scouting the Brazilian cops. The smugglers started forward, retreated a few yards. They removed the boxes from their backs and hefted them to a large, jagged hole in the chain-link fence.

"What's up?" Pescatore said. "They're tossing their stuff in the river."

"It is quite organized, believe me." Abbas yawned. "Their people down there will retrieve everything."

Figures at the riverbank below waded knee-deep toward floating boxes. Near them, another line of backpackers climbed a steep path toward Foz, unmolested.

The bridge had only one lane going in each direction. Like the roads on the riverbanks, it was woefully out of date for all the vehicles and pedestrians. Traffic crawled, stopped, lurched. A line of armored trucks passed in the opposite direction, yellow beasts with elongated snouts and slitted rectangular eyes. Pescatore counted six.

"We prefer cash in these parts," Abbas chuckled. "That lot is freshly washed. On its way back to the politicians and gambling barons of Brazil."

Halfway across the bridge, two policemen had a smuggler backed against the fence. The Paraguayan cops wore Foreign Legion–style caps and oversized fatigues. The cops were practically teenagers, closely shorn with prominent noses, scrawnier and shabbier than the Brazilians. The smuggler's ponytail sprouted beneath an Orlando Magic cap, his duffel bag stuffed to the bursting point. He yelled at the cops, jaw to jaw. Other smugglers trudged by, ignoring the confrontation, probably figuring it had pushed the odds a bit more in their favor.

One of the officers set himself with a lazy wriggle of his shoulders. He gripped his nightstick with both hands. Pescatore flinched; the cop whacked the man in the knee. The blow, combined with the weight of the duffel bag, toppled the smuggler. As the other cop raised his stick, traffic obscured the scene.

Ouch, Pescatore thought. Real professional. Thumping tonks in broad daylight.

The bridge reminded him of training films of the border in El Paso. Except it was much smaller and it crawled with these backpack smugglers instead of illegal aliens.

Craning forward, Pescatore said: "Uh, excuse me, Mr. Abbas? I thought they called it the Triple Border. These are just two countries here, right? How come the Triple Border?"

He was aware of Buffalo's eyes on him, no apparent disapproval. Pescatore felt emboldened: just another gangster, making conversation.

"The border of Argentina is nearby. There is a point where all three borders come together. And our business community mixes together all three countries."

The final stretch of the bridge took forever. Ciudad del Este inched closer: a forest of midsized buildings on the bluff overlooking the river. Walls and roofs were plastered with billboards and banners — pink, yellow, purple — announcing products and stores. Pescatore saw smugglers clustered on the riverbank with loads of cigarettes. And other items: He spotted a guy stuffing a plastic bag down the front of his sweatpants.

Ants, Abbas had called them; the action on the riverbank resembled an ant colony.

No one checked papers at the end of the bridge. In Ciudad del Este, the traffic churned up red dust. Crowds spilled into trash-lined gutters. Vendors' tables and booths choked the sidewalks in front of stores. A vast tapestry of merchandise: flowers, diapers, watches, onions, cassettes, compact discs, leather jackets of every hue, nets bulging with soccer balls, stacks of stereo and computer components.

"*Cuanta mierda venden,*" Momo muttered.

Buffalo laughed in his throat. "You can buy anything, homes, long as it's fake."

Pescatore saw banks, currency exchanges, more armored cars, omnipresent security guards with shotguns. Itinerant money changers in orange vests clutched rolls of bills, worked calculators, leaned into car windows. Pescatore saw signs in Portuguese, Spanish, English, Asian languages, a warning about product piracy, a shingle that said ALI BABA AND CO. Women in Muslim veils passed a man arranging pornography on a rack. A contingent of shaven-headed Asian monks went by. They wore sandals and billowing brown robes; they seemed to float through the melee of buying and selling, loading and unloading, everyone jabbering into cell phones and radios.

The scene recalled Avenida Revolución in Tijuana, but much denser. And Pescatore didn't see any restaurants, bars, nightclubs or hotels. Just hundreds and hundreds of stores. It was like TJ stripped down to its core. A demented bazaar.

Ten minutes later, it ended abruptly. A fast avenue took them out of crowds and dust and high-rises into parkland. Houses dotted a semicircle of hills around a lake.

They approached the walled, palm-shrouded entrance of a hotel: El Naútico Resort. A police van was parked in the driveway, surrounded by officers who resembled the soldier-boy thumpers on the bridge. They carried short machine guns on straps.

"Your security force," Abbas told Buffalo. "We will also leave you Mozart and Tchaikovsky."

The hotel was built onto a hillside and slanted down to a man-made lagoon in back. Abbas supervised the check-in with ostentatious commands. He shook hands and hurried off, promising that Khalid would be in touch soon.

The El Naútico Resort had flower beds, a discotheque, a multilevel pool, tennis courts, a playground. But nothing appeared to have been refurbished — furniture, wallpaper, carpets — since the 1970s. A smell of insecticide hung in the halls. The air-conditioning clanked and groaned deep in the bowels of the place. Long-faced bellhops in pillbox caps escorted the group, who had no luggage — except for a golf bag Abbas had provided for the weapons — to a floor two levels below the lobby.

Their rooms faced directly onto the lagoon. Despite high ceilings and dance-floor dimensions, the rooms were dank. Patches of humidity bubbled on the walls and fogged the mirrors and bay windows. Beyond the glass, a lone rowboat sat at the dock.

Junior stayed awake long enough to have a tantrum when the faucets in the presidential suite spurted rusty brown water. He spat something in Spanish that Pescatore translated to himself as "What a fucking dump." Then Junior went back to sleep.

Buffalo handed out two-way radios to Momo, Sniper and Pescatore. He organized a schedule for sentry duty.

Before his shift, Pescatore napped in his room. Then he called room service and ordered macaroni with meat sauce, a jumbo salad, a strawberry milkshake with a little caramel in it, apple pie and a small pot of espresso. And then another shake. The meal made him feel better, though the pasta was overcooked and the espresso was watery.

Pescatore's watch started at 4 a.m. He picked up his radio and resumed his masquerade as a henchman. He prowled like a phantom. He climbed stairs to a gym littered with dusty barbells. The black-and-white weight-lifting diagrams in a glass case on the wall had been clipped from an American muscle magazine from 1973. He padded through a ballroom with cracked mirrors and apparitional white sheets over tables. He wandered long dim halls to the lobby. A desk clerk watched him furtively, looking cadaverous in the greenish glow of the mahogany-framed reception area.

As he made his rounds, Pescatore came across hotel security men and uniformed policemen. He greeted them in Spanish. To the Brazilians stationed near the suites, he repeated the phrase that Moze and Tchai used: "*Tudo bem?*" Everything good?

He counted a dozen sentries, plus the police van at the entrance. It would be hard to get in or out unnoticed.

Pescatore made his way down to the dock. He stood listening to the thrum of insects and the burble of the lagoon.

Everything good? Oh yeah. He was marooned thousands of miles from the United States of America in a godforsaken hot-ass smugglers' paradise. A forced recruit in a traveling gangster circus led by a crazy cokehead billionaire woman-killer.

Pescatore realized he was mumbling to himself. Glancing around in the dark, he sank into a deck chair. It was too risky to call Isabel Puente; the hotel phones were not secure. Pelón's cell phone was useless here. What if he found a U.S. consulate? He imagined himself knocking on bulletproof glass, flashing his Patrol badge at a marine. By the way, I'm wanted for a cop-killing, but I'm innocent, really. This chick at the Justice Department I slept with one time, she can vouch for me. Her and her Mexican friend, who'd just as soon shoot me as look at me.

He needed a smart plan. He feared that word would eventually get back to Junior about his turncoat calls to Isabel. By now, he had no doubt that the Ruiz Caballero organization had snitches in law enforcement all over the hemisphere.

He dozed. He watched the sunrise over the lagoon. The air was already burdened by heat. At 10 a.m., he returned to his floor for the changing of the guard. As he reached Buffalo's door, Junior's voice froze him.

"Hey *gabacho*. You play ball?"

Junior stood barefoot and shirtless outside his room, hand on gut as usual. His torso was an epic battle between fat and muscle. His bushy hair looked electrified. His eyes were red and shiny. He licked and tightened his lips rhythmically. Pescatore suspected that he had just had a morning pick-me-up.

"Do you play ball?" Junior repeated, nasal and imperious.

"Ball?"

"Speak English, *güey?* Hoops. Basketball. You play?"

"Little bit."

"There is a court here. I want to play. Get the *muchachos.*"

"I gotta tell you, it's hot out there. Real toasty."

"*Y qué?* Find somebody in this shithole to get us clothes."

With Junior mouth-breathing over his shoulder, Pescatore rousted Momo and Sniper. Junior told them to let Buffalo sleep. Pescatore harassed various hotel employees until they came up with T-shirts, shorts and a red-white-and-blue basketball.

Half an hour later, the foursome trotted through a rippling haze onto the basketball court, where they smoked a joint. In the distance, a pair of elderly golfers shuffled off the links. Guests occupied one table on a second-floor terrace of the hotel. Otherwise, Junior's boys appeared to have the El Naútico Resort to themselves. Momo wrapped their pistols in towels and placed the towels behind the base of the basketball pole.

"Two on two," Junior ordered. His shorts and T-shirt were too big for him; they made him look even more like a powerfully built, foul-tempered child. "Me and Sniper against Momo and the *gabacho.*"

Pescatore stood at the top of the key facing Junior, who was the same height but a good thirty pounds heavier. Junior whipped the ball at him and grinned, squinting against the harsh pale sun.

"Check."

As a kid, Pescatore had not been the most impressive player on the playgrounds of his neighborhood. His repertoire consisted mainly of a jump shot that was accurate on the rare occasions that he got the ball.

On the court at El Naútico, though, he was Michael Jordan in the land of the gumps. He wanted to laugh at the TJ mafiosos, the *pinche* Death Patrol. They were scrubs. Like sorry-ass girls. Look at droop-eyed Sniper, tall but hopelessly gawky with a shot that came from behind his ear to clang off the rim. And muscle-bound Momo: stiff, strictly horizontal. Pounding holes in the blacktop when he dribbled. Momo didn't even try to shoot.

Junior was better. As in the boxing ring, he gave signs that he had once been quite an athlete. But he was desperately out of shape. He refused to accept his limitations. He played TV ball: fancy drives, behind-the-back passes. He crashed around like a runaway tank. Within minutes, his breath came in heaves and his moves in slow motion.

As for Pescatore, he was in great shape after two years of training, chasing and brawling in the nonstop nights of Imperial Beach station. He shot every time he got the ball. If he missed, he swooped in for rebounds and hit layups while the others flailed like men in quicksand. For the first time in a long time, he was having fun.

Junior offered grudging compliments at first. But his mood darkened as the score grew lopsided. He berated Sniper. "Help me out, *pendejo, qué te pasa?*"

Pescatore blew past them and banked in a reverse to win the first game. Junior declared a rematch. He lost the second game too. Before the third game, Junior mopped his puffy face with his T-shirt and caught Pescatore trying to restrain a grin.

"This time," Junior grunted, showing the whites of his eyes, "I shut you down."

Pescatore passed to Momo, who promptly passed back. Pescatore caught the ball going into his leap, released with a smooth follow-through and swished the jumper. On the next possession, he drove. Junior clouted him, staggering him; Junior still had his strength. Pescatore did not call a foul. He did not call fouls when Junior yanked his shirt, shoved and slapped him, banged him with elbows and hips. Pescatore kept scoring, and Junior kept hitting him. Finally, Junior swatted Pescatore's hand so hard that he had to walk off the pain, wincing, pulling at jammed fingers.

Junior snapped: "Play ball, bitch."

"You're hacking all over the place."

"*Cállate, puto.*"

Pescatore cupped the ball in his wrist and returned the glare. Sniper and Momo looked worried. By now they were just going through the motions. They caught Pescatore's eye, signaling him to take it easy. A voice in his own head told him to back off, cool down. But his fingers burned. The pain had spoiled his buzz. His thoughts spiraled. Fuck it, he told himself. I don't care how pissed he gets. I'm gonna make him look bad.

He scored baskets, fending off blows, slashing back as good as he got. It had become a street fight. He ached all over. They were dripping as much as if they had fallen into a pool. Junior tottered, ranting bilingually.

"Keep talkin' that shit," Pescatore grumbled.

Momo interrupted plaintively: "*Oiga,* Junior, maybe let's take a break, eh? *Nos tomamos una chela o algo.*"

Junior paid no attention. His face, neck and arms had acquired a cherry-colored flush. He gave Pescatore a twisted smile. "You're hot shit, eh, *gabacho?* Eh, *chingón?*"

"Game point," Pescatore said, tossing him the ball. He wanted to finish it fast, escape this trap, this stupid duel on oven-baked blacktop. It occurred to him out of the haze that Junior was capable of having the homeboys cut his throat over a game of basketball.

Junior returned the ball and set himself. Knees bent, hands wide. He growled: "Think you're something"—Pescatore faked, drove right, ball shielded by his hip—"but"—Junior scuttled crablike, arm windmilling—"I'm gonna"—Pescatore left the ground, propelling high, Junior barreling toward him—"smack your *shit!*"

It was a near shriek. Pescatore lowered a shoulder as they slammed together in midair. Junior's fist caught him across the brow. He tumbled, rolled, ended up on his knees. He touched the blood on his forehead.

Junior had reopened the cut that Pescatore had suffered chasing Pulpo across The Line, long ago, in another life.

"Junior, *estás bien? Qué pasó?* Help him!"

Buffalo's voice approached from the hotel. They gathered around Junior beneath the net. Pescatore realized that the second impact he had heard, an echo of the collision, had been Junior hurtling backwards into the pole. Junior flopped on his side like a landed fish, making strangled noises.

Buffalo cradled Junior's head and roared orders. "Get some water. Do something, *mamones!*"

"*No te enojes,* Buff." Sniper's voice shook. "He just got the wind knocked out of him. Look, he's opening his eyes. Ain't he?"

Buffalo slung Junior over his shoulder, waving off help, and carried him to his suite. Pescatore trudged behind. He told himself that Buffalo was even stronger than he looked, because Junior hadn't missed a meal in a long time.

Junior lay motionless. The hotel nurse arrived. Buffalo called Abbas, who sent a doctor.

The doctor had a pencil mustache and black-framed glasses that dwarfed his bald head. His diagnosis was exhaustion, dehydration and a near concussion. He took Buffalo aside and stammered about blood pressure, cardiac issues, drug abuse. He recommended repose and a number of tests.

Buffalo handed the doctor a wad of cash and told him to go away. He fired off phone calls to Tijuana and Mexico City. Junior's eyes had opened only for a moment. Except for the fact that he was breathing, he looked dead.

"What did you fucking do?" Buffalo hissed at Pescatore between phone calls.

"Nothing." Pescatore sprawled in an armchair with a towel

pressed to his cut, more disgusted than afraid. "He wanted to play ball."

"You played too fucking hard, *ese!*"

"Man, he was outta control. Look at my head."

"Just chill and let him win, understand? Don't you see the shape he's in?"

"The other day he was goin' at it in the ring, looked good to me."

"He's hittin' the coke twenty-four-seven, Valentín. And—" The phone rang. Long-distance from Tijuana. Buffalo told Pescatore: "You just fucking do what I say...*Sí,* Dr. Guardiola? *Bueno? Me oye?*"

Buffalo turned away with the phone. Pescatore dabbed at sweat and blood. He listened to the quaver in Buffalo's voice.

Outside, the big man had seen Junior was down and gone into action with paternal reflexes, effortlessly in charge. But now, pacing by the bed, Buffalo looked lost.

18

It's all very ironic," Méndez said. "Maybe it's poetic justice."

"What is?" Isabel Puente swept back her tresses with both hands. The plane tickets were fanned out on the table in front of her like playing cards.

"The last thing I ever wanted to do was work for the American government. Long ago I saw Barbara Walters interview Fidel Castro. She asked him a question. He avoided it. She insisted. Finally, Fidel said: 'I won't answer that. The CIA would love to know the answer. And I don't want to work for the CIA. *Ni pagado, ni gratis.*' That's how I have always felt. *Ni pagado, ni gratis.*"

Puente left her hands up in her hair for a moment and said with mock indignation: "I know what you are doing, Leo. You are trying to goad me with that Castro stuff. Playing the *mexicano zurdo resentido.* Right?"

Méndez allowed himself a smile. The other Americans at the table watched blank-faced, probably perplexed—if they even understood that she had called him a resentful Mexican lefty. It was strange having this conversation with Isabel in front of an audience. He enjoyed watching her in action. Although her agency did not have the clout of the FBI and DEA, Isabel was running the Ruiz Caballero case. Her bosses on the task force knew she had the best rapport with Méndez.

"I can't blame you," Puente continued. "It's an unorthodox situation. Let's be clear: You are *not* working for the USG. We talked to the Secretary: As far as he is concerned, you are still an employee of the Mexican government. Even though you said you resigned."

"The Secretary may say what he wants. I have cut all ties to him and I do not wish to speak to him again."

"But you are still technically on the public payroll unless they remove you. You are only on loan to us. We'll provide the resources and the logistics, but you will lead the operation. With my assistance in an advisory capacity."

She slid three of the four plane tickets across the table to him. Above her on the wall of the conference room was a bulletin board with photos of suspects, drug busts and confiscated vehicles. A federal agent with artistic talent apparently had sketched the in-house insignia: a puma, crossed pistols, a silhouette of the border fence under ornate letters: BAMCaT. The Border Area Multi-Agency Corruption Task Force was housed in a discreet office park in an industrial zone near Chula Vista.

Méndez sighed. "Fine. I have already made my commitment. But I would like to discuss the implications in private with my comandantes. I have dragged—"

Athos stirred on Méndez's left. Méndez paused and Athos said: "It's fine, Licenciado. I'm with you. After all, I'm a fugitive."

Méndez had expected nothing less. But he knew Porthos had domestic entanglements: four children, a new house, a bakery owned by his in-laws in La Mesa. The bearded commander was examining his slablike palms.

"Porthos?" Méndez said. "You could take time to think..."

"No, Licenciado, please," Porthos drawled softly, head low. "I spoke to my old lady already. She'll be fine. Who could pass up a chance to see the world?"

That drew a smile from Balmaceda, the DEA representative, a rowdy cowboy who spoke Tejano Spanish. Like Isabel, he seemed to relish the uproar set off by the transborder abduction of Mauro Fernández Rochetti: the media assault, the arrests and indictments that had finally taken place on the U.S. side. The Americans had charged several border inspectors, a Border Patrol agent, an ICE agent and a recently retired DEA supervisor. They had also indicted Garrison, who was missing and presumed dead, and Mauro Fernández Rochetti. They had said nothing publicly about Pescatore.

Two days earlier, Balmaceda had been there in the garage of the task force when Méndez had opened the trunk to reveal Mauro Fernández Rochetti in his inert handcuffed disgrace. The DEA supervisor had thrown a bone-crushing arm around Méndez's neck and whispered: "They should give you a medal, man. They should make you the fucking president of Mexico just for taking that animal off the street."

"So now what?" Méndez asked.

"Now we go after them," Isabel said.

"What about the informant?" Balmaceda interrupted. "The inside guy. He alive?"

Isabel kept her eyes on Méndez. She looked annoyed; she was so leery about burning Pescatore that she avoided mentioning him in group settings.

"We haven't heard from him," she said. "We believe he was on the plane. The plane belongs to Khalid and we tracked it only as far as Quito. But thanks to the FBI, and other agencies that will go unmentioned, we now have a precise location. Leo, you are familiar with Dr. Guardiola?"

"The narco-doctor. Junior's personal physician."

"He just left for Paraguay. Buffalo Mendoza called. Junior is not well."

"Too much coca and drinking?"

"That's not clear from the intercepts. But the doctor left quickly. He took a commercial flight. Junior must have used a clandestine airfield. Argentine intelligence says the smugglers have lots of them at the Triple Border. Anyway, we know where Junior is."

"And?"

"You and I will do our best to catch him."

Méndez shook his head. "I don't know. Certainly, I'm impressed. If I had known I could get so many Americans indicted, I would have put Mauro in a car trunk a long time ago."

Another fire-eating smile from Balmaceda, who said: "We'd been sitting on the indictments forever. Now we've got the Mexicans excited about corruption on our side—instead of how Mauro Fernández Rochetti ended up in San Diego. Or the *judiciales* who got so nicely popped at Bumpy." He gave Athos a fraternal nod, one *pistolero* to another. Athos nodded back hesitantly.

Méndez had never been fond of the DEA supervisor; he had assumed that Balmaceda regarded him as a sneaky Mexican wannabe cop. Now it occurred to him that this was a potential ally he had failed to cultivate. Méndez said: "You handled the Secretary well by leaving Junior out of it for the moment. But listen: Do you really think we can walk into Ciudad del Este and put Junior in a trunk too? Isn't this Khalid like an emperor down there?"

Daniels, the Justice Department boss from Washington, cleared his throat. He sat sideways, elbow on the table, sipping a glass of water. His demeanor had suggested he was not part of the proceedings, merely a thoughtful listener. Now he slid around to face Méndez.

"If I may," Daniels said, straightening his tapered back in a wide-lapeled, double-breasted suit that looked as if it had been sewn onto him. He was African-American, late forties, hair and mustache sprinkled with gray. Isabel had confided that he was a high-level boss, smart, a real politician. His voice was resonant and mannered and he made no effort to pronounce Spanish words correctly.

"Khalid is powerful, Mr. Méndez. The Triple Border is a prototypical base for bad guys. That's one reason we are so very keenly interested in this case. Khalid has connections to terrorism, hostile intelligence services. He moves dope and guns to South America, Africa and Europe. We don't want him protecting Junior. We don't want him doing business with the Ruiz Caballeros. We don't want Islamic groups, Venezuelan and Iranian operatives, narco-guerrillas, developing a direct pipeline to Mexico and California."

"I would say this pipeline already exists."

Daniels's refined ways reminded Méndez vaguely of Duke Ellington. "You may be right. Yet and still, Khalid is not the only force at the Triple Border. We will have a number of agencies supporting you. Full engagement. We intend to pressure him. See if we can push Junior into the open."

"And if we actually put our hands on him? Do you think Senator Ruiz Caballero and his political friends will tolerate that?"

"Junior is more vulnerable than he seems," Isabel said. "Thanks to you. You made him run."

"I wonder," Méndez said. "Let me remind you that my government still has not said Junior is a suspect."

"There is a strategy there," Daniels said. "The Secretary doesn't have the wherewithal to confront the Ruiz Caballeros. Not publicly. But we think the political dynamics have changed. Your warrants have not been countermanded. If you catch Junior outside Mexico, if it's a fait accompli, we think the Secretary would be willing to take the credit."

"What courage."

Daniels raised his hands and shoulders in a worldly, that's-how-it-is gesture.

Méndez said: "Why the charade? Grab Junior yourselves, put a bag over his head and bring him here. You do it all the time with Muslims."

"Not an option," Daniels responded, ruffled, momentarily a bureaucrat on the defensive. "For one thing, it's difficult to prove up crimes by him in the United States."

"Even with Fernández Rochetti and the American officers you have detained? They worked for the Ruiz Caballero mafia."

"Yet and still. It's not a viable option, bilateral relations being what they are. This needs to be a Mexican operation. This needs to end with Junior Ruiz in a Mexican prison."

"He will go into the front door and out of the back."

"Leo." Isabel Puente's determined grin softened the snap in her voice. "Aren't we getting ahead of ourselves? You haven't caught him yet!"

There were chuckles. Méndez leaned back. He looked at Athos and Porthos. Patient, loyal. Ready to follow him to the lair of Cerberus and back.

"And listen," Isabel added. "I think we should get going soon. The trail is hot. Besides, with all the yelling and screaming in Tijuana about the Mauro Fernández Rochetti incident, now is a really good time for you guys to take a long trip."

Enough talk, Méndez decided. He had set this wild ride in motion on the morning they invaded El Bumpy. Now they had to hang on and keep going.

Méndez said in Spanish: "Well, boys, what do you think? Do we catch a plane?"

Los Angeles, Miami, overnight to Buenos Aires. There was a three-hour wait for the flight to Puerto Iguazú. While Athos and Porthos wandered duty-free shops in the Buenos Aires airport, Méndez and Isabel Puente sat in a restaurant reading classified briefings about the Triple Border. The dossier had been provided by the U.S. government, but was written in Spanish. Méndez assumed the original source was Argentine intelligence.

The report opened with a bang:

> The Triple Border has become a focus of destabilization in South America. The legal order in the region has been substituted by institutionalized disorder. This involves the most varied forms of illicit activities, including money laundering, drug trafficking, arms trafficking, contraband, product piracy and fraud. American credit-card firms report the loss of millions of dollars from cloned and stolen cards in the region last year. A more profound concern is the presence of financiers, operatives, recruiters and spiritual figures of terrorist groups such as Hezbollah, Islamic Jihad, the Muslim Brotherhood, al-Qaeda and others.
>
> These illicit activities generate as much as $20 billion a year and have overwhelmed the governments of Brazil, Paraguay and Argentina, creating important pockets of corruption and attracting an increasing variety of international criminal networks and espionage services from Latin America, Asia, the Middle East and Eastern Europe. The new influx combines with the longtime presence of mafias in the historic merchant communities from Taiwan and Lebanon. This globalization of crime has become a political and economic threat for the region and, potentially, the hemisphere.

"Sounds like we are going to feel right at home," Méndez told Isabel. He read through an economic analysis, a list of recent arrests and murders, and an intricate breakdown of which businesses were suspected fronts for criminal or extremist organizations. Most of the Middle Eastern figures were aligned with the kingpins known as Abbas and Khalid: Junior's partners.

The blond waitress returned with another pleasantly strong coffee. She was slinky in a way that suggested outdoor exercise and harsh dieting. He found her tone and manner cheerful, but excessively informal.

"Surrounded by Argentines," Méndez said as she walked off. "My God."

"Do all Mexicans hate Argentines?" Isabel asked.

"Schopenhauer said: 'Every nation mocks the other nations, and they are all correct.' It's not just us: Everyone dislikes the Argentines. They're the yanquis of Latin America."

"If you say so. I don't have a problem with them."

Méndez could see why. A table of airport employees, wavy-haired young men with radios, ties and white shirts, were glancing their way. They appraised Isabel, who was radiant despite a day of travel, a catwoman in dark blue leggings. Her sleeveless top displayed well-made shoulders the color of her coffee with milk. He wondered idly if the Argentines thought he and Isabel—leaning toward each other, murmuring behind their cups—were lovers. Or did they think she was too much for a thin, graying, sad-faced Mexican?

"Our Argentine at the Triple Border comes highly recommended," she said. "They say he freelances for the Israelis too. He must have his hands full."

Méndez nodded and toyed with his ham and cheese on toast.

"Isabel," he said slowly. "Let me ask you something."

"OK."

"Please tell me if this is intrusive or inappropriate."

"OK."

"Are you still worried about Pescatore? Are you hoping that we will be able to rescue him? I have the impression, if you'll forgive me, that you're fond of him."

Her thumb rose to press against her teeth. She cocked her head. "What are you trying to say, Leo?"

"That I am concerned. You care for him a great deal. No?"

She looked away. "That's my business."

"Of course. But I fear it's inevitable you'll be hurt. He's not to be trusted. I still think he tipped off Junior that night in Colonia

Postal. I think he has deceived you. And if you'll forgive me, there's a good chance he's dead."

She seemed to force herself to meet his eyes. Her coffee cup hovered; she sipped slowly, taking refuge. He regretted what he had started. But he was also relieved. Part of him wanted everything in the open.

"I'm doing this because it's my job," she said. "The biggest case of my career. Because you are my friend"—he started to thank her but she plowed on—"and because I hate Junior and what he stands for as much as you do. And I feel awful about Araceli. Even though I know for a fact she didn't like me. No, let me finish. As for my personal life, I'm not going to hide my feelings for Valentine. You're wrong about him. You judge people too quickly. But none of that is relevant to our mission."

"Isabel..." He reached for her hand. She withdrew it in a cold fury. "I'm sorry."

"What is your problem with Valentine?" she demanded. "Is this about me? About you?"

Let it go, he told himself. Remember it as a moment of weakness. Concentrate on the job. Nonetheless, the idea that Isabel could be infatuated with a punk like Pescatore infuriated him.

"Don't worry about it," he said.

"This is a strange time to get complicated with me, Leo."

"My wife tells me I'm overprotective. Araceli complained too. But neither of them is around. I suppose I end up overprotecting you by default."

"If that's true, I appreciate it," Isabel said, her tone softening. "But I don't need it."

The waitress saved him by appearing with the check. They paid. Méndez, eager to change the subject, asked Isabel the name of their contact at the Triple Border.

She checked a notepad, avoiding his eyes. "They call him Facundo the Russian."

* * *

Facundo was not Russian.

He was Argentine. He looked Turkish or Middle Eastern. Heavily stubbled jowls, a prowlike nose, black mustache. He was tall, big-bellied and jaunty. His base of operations was Puerto Iguazú, Argentina, a town of about thirty-two thousand that in the better neighborhoods seemed Southern European, despite the jungle setting, and once prosperous. But the streets were full of shuttered and boarded-up storefronts. Dogs slept on the sidewalks.

His walk stooped and shambling, Facundo led the way through a compound filled with black Mercedes sedans, apparently a hired-car service. The name of his business was Villa Crespo Autos and Security. Facundo ushered his four guests into an office, banged on a cantankerous air conditioner, distributed cool drinks, transferred a snub-nosed pistol from his belt to his desk. He did all this without interrupting an epic monologue that he had begun at the airport when he picked them up and continued as he got them settled in the officers' quarters of a base of the Gendarmería, the Argentine border police. A Gendarmería chief had welcomed them to the base, but deferred quickly to Facundo again.

"What heat, no?" Facundo thundered. "What a sauna. This is nothing, believe me. This is child's play. This is a crisp fall day in the jungle of the north, ha ha. You must be exhausted, Dr. Méndez. All of you. Let's have our discussion and you can get some rest. So many hours traveling. And on top of that, this heat. It's a sauna, I tell you. Nooo, this is too much, who can withstand this? Noooo. Can I offer you coffee as well as the lemonade? Myself, I'll stick to this horrid concoction. It's the national vice, I'm afraid. Well, one of the national vices."

Méndez noticed two portraits on the wall behind Facundo: Evita Perón and Moshe Dayan. At first, Méndez had thought that Facundo was hard of hearing. He bellowed like a man in a windstorm. But soon Méndez decided that his decibel level was simply well above normal. When Facundo finally paused to sip *mate* tea from a gourd, Méndez, feeling he should make conversation, said he hadn't realized there were many Russians in Argentina.

Facundo performed a circular gesture of assent with one hand. "Few Russians in the literal sense, Dr. Méndez."

"Actually, it's not 'Doctor.' Please call me Leo, at your orders."

"We Argentines have terrible title-itis. We call lawyers 'Doctor.' We call doctors 'Doctor.' All these doctors, but if you break your leg, don't count on them for help!"

During this exchange, Méndez watched Facundo's eyes: bemused, intelligent, detached. Méndez wondered if he was really a vintage Argentine blowhard. Méndez suspected that the barrage of words was a diversion, a facade behind which Facundo sized up his listeners. Méndez spotted a printout of a Tijuana newspaper article on the desk; the photo of a smiling Araceli Aguirre jarred him. The neat stack of Mexican articles had apparently been pulled from the Internet. Facundo was in his fifties; he came off as distinctly pre-cyberspace with his beige linen suit, pointy brown shoes and operatic manner. But he had done some homework.

Facundo explained that his full name was Facundo Hyman Bassat.

"Argentines call Jews 'Russians,' you see. Argentines call Arabs 'Turks.' And Argentine Jews call Sephardic Jews 'Turks.' If you wanted to take the national idiosyncracy for ethnic nicknames to the extreme, I would technically be Facundo the Turkish Russian. Absurd, eh?"

"Are you from around here?"

Facundo faked a shudder. "No sir. Buenos Aires. Born and raised, body and soul. I moved to Israel as a young man. Military service, had adventures, saw the world. My Spanish-language skills were in demand. Then I came back to Buenos Aires. Hard times. A friend talked me into buying this taxi service up here on the frontier. Drivers pick up a lot of information out on the street all day. I realized there was a market for investigations, security work. There was this community of merchants, especially Taiwanese and Lebanese. Many hardworking folks, but many scoundrels. Chinese extortion. Arab feuds. Brazilian bandits. Islamic fanatics. Companies and governments needing eyes and ears. So we evolved. But enough about me: Let's talk about young Mr. Ruiz Caballero."

"Good idea," said Isabel, whose foot had jiggled throughout the autobiography.

"We will operate from here in Puerto Iguazú, the smallest of the three border cities. The most controlled as well. You may know about the anti-Semitic terrorist bombings in Buenos Aires some years ago. The terrorists had their support cells in this area. So the Argentines finally began enforcing the border. That doesn't mean there isn't still corruption, identity documents for sale, stolen cars departing, cocaine and marijuana coming in. But it's better than Foz. The Brazilians are friendly, wonderful music and what have you, but too relaxed for my tastes. And the Paraguayan side... well, Paraguay is the belly of the beast."

"Which is why Junior holed up there," Isabel interjected.

"Yes, Miss Puente. I'm coming to that." Facundo the Russian beamed chivalrously. "Your Mr. Ruiz is Khalid's guest at the El Naútico Resort in Ciudad del Este. Perhaps you'll recognize these faces."

They moved closer as the Argentine opened a folder. The photographs had been taken with a long-range lens. They showed men getting in and out of cars, leaving an airport terminal.

"There's Buffalo and the *pochos* from Los Angeles," Méndez said.

"And Dr. Guardiola," Porthos said. "That's Rufino, he drives for them. I wonder if Junior's going to bring his girlfriends."

"He has a taste for the ladies?" Facundo said.

"Quantity and quality," Méndez said. "And he's crazy about sports, especially boxing. Hyperactive. If there is a gym, he'll go, either to box or to watch. But he's sick, no?"

"The word is that he's recuperating from, eh, overexertion."

"Too bad. He also collects exotic animals, by the way."

"We have plenty of those. Four-legged and two-legged. Our information is that a lot of cash arrived with the second group from Mexico. Police chiefs and intelligence officials in Foz and Ciudad have received down payments for protection. The Mexicans brought goodwill gifts to Khalid and his friends and colleagues too."

Méndez grinned. "Some things are the same everywhere. Junior is paying tolls."

"How many gunmen with Junior?" asked Athos, producing a cigarette.

"Oooof." Facundo offered Athos a lighter, then leaned back in a mastodonic executive chair and sipped pensively at his *mate*. "Eight Mexicans. Ten Brazilians: Mozart and Tchaikovsky's crew, and let me tell you, those fellows are tigers. Give them an Uzi and they'll paint you a picture on the wall. And the Paraguayan police, at least twenty-five. Nooo, Comandante Rojas, unless you brought the U.S. Marines, we will not be reenacting the raid on Entebbe. Not right away, at least."

Méndez said: "You sound like you might have a few ideas on how to proceed."

Facundo's bushy eyebrows danced. "Well, one or two, Doctor. As I told you, the Gendarmería will give us their base. Infrastructure. Muscle if we absolutely need it. But the Argentine border police are not supposed to operate in Paraguay. There are certain interests they prefer not to offend. That's why they do me the honor of utilizing my humble services... Excuse me, are you looking for something, Miss Puente?"

Isabel was on her feet rummaging through photos. She

stopped, leaned forward, and put both hands on the table, her bare triceps tensing.

"Are you all right, Miss Puente?" Facundo asked, his eyes wide with concern. "This heat, my God. Some more lemonade?"

Isabel Puente sat down abruptly. A woman in love, Méndez thought.

"No," she said. "I'm fine. Thank you."

The photo on top of the stack showed a group at the portico of the hotel. In front was Buffalo Mendoza with the pointy-bearded gangster known as Abbas and a Tijuana flunky with a suitcase. Bringing up the rear was Valentine Pescatore. He had acquired a mustache. But there was no mistaking the bantam build, the curly head ducked slightly, the big and skittish eyes.

"Look, it's the Border Patrolman," Porthos said. "He's alive. And it looks like he got a new job."

19

HIS PHOTO STARED BACK at him above his new name.

"Lookit you, *ese,*" Momo rasped over his shoulder. "*Puro paraguayo.*"

When asked what he wanted his name to be, Pescatore had improvised. He fused the names of his father's favorite boxers: Ray "Boom Boom" Mancini and Roberto Durán. Now he had a Paraguayan passport identifying him as Raymundo Durán, born in a place called Encarnación. New passport, new clothes, new mustache: He was traveling farther and farther away from himself.

He was in Galerías Alhambra, a vertical warren of stores in downtown Ciudad del Este. Pescatore and Momo sat in the fifth-floor waiting room of a travel agency that was a front for a fraudulent passport operation. Posters of Cairo and Casablanca decorated the walls. Clients filled ratty sofas, next in line to become overnight Paraguayans with bona fide, if illegally obtained, identity documents to prove it. Young tattooed Asians. Long-bearded Arabs with wives in black gloves, despite the heat, and full veils covering all but the eyes. Bull-necked Eastern Europeans. A regal Nigerian.

Buffalo strode out of the office, monster biceps bowling over invisible obstacles. He said: "All set, let's hit it."

They walked one flight down a broken escalator into a musty, block-long gallery as dense with shoppers as the streets outside. Once again, Pescatore found it hard to believe that he was in a Spanish-speaking country. Half the time he didn't understand the babble around him. The shoppers were mostly Brazilian. The merchants in the stalls and glass-walled shops spoke Arabic and Asian languages among themselves and Portuguese-Spanish patois with customers. And there was also the Guaraní Indian language of the Paraguayan security men, the maintenance workers, the cooks at the indoor lunch counter where Pescatore stopped to buy fries and a Coke to go.

Brazilians sat at the counter surrounded by bundles destined for the contraband markets of São Paulo and Rio de Janeiro: two-bit smugglers bent over paper plates in the fluorescent light, watching grease sizzle on the skillet.

"Eatin' again, Valentín?" Buffalo shook his head. "We just had breakfast."

Pescatore grinned sheepishly. The vibes with Buffalo were better now that Junior had recovered. Pescatore's standing had improved with Momo and Sniper as well; he thought they had secretly enjoyed seeing him knock heads with Junior on the basketball court.

The city was full of shopping towers like the Galerías Alhambra. Too dingy to be considered malls, they did not have movie theaters, food courts or anything else that got in the way of buying and selling. Each tower was a castle of one of the Arab clans who divided up the business sectors under Khalid's orders — a citadel defended by cameras, bars, security guards with shotguns at every turn. Mr. Abbas owned Galerías Alhambra. It specialized in electronic products. The cacophony changed with every shop: disco, *ranchera,* tropical, rap, samba. Video-game explosions. Giant TVs flashing images of George Clooney, Jennifer Lopez, Jackie Chan. All the newest latest stuff, the top brands — at least according to the labels.

Buffalo stopped to buy himself a new iPod. Sniper picked out a cigarette lighter shaped like a Luger. Pescatore paused in front of a screen showing soccer highlights. The Argentine accent of the announcer was instantly familiar. It reminded him of his father: Spanish that sounded like Italian. The lithe, long-haired players on the screen wore blue-and-white-striped jerseys resembling the triangular Argentine pennant that had dangled from his father's rearview mirror when Pescatore was a kid. He bought a key chain decorated with the Argentine flag.

"Let's go," Buffalo said. "Khalid's waitin' on us."

For their first sit-down since Junior's arrival, both Khalid and Junior turned up in safari-style outfits. Junior wore baggy khaki shorts and Timberlands; Khalid sported a guayabera shirt with epaulets and clip-on shades over his steel-framed glasses.

Pescatore had only seen Khalid for a moment at the dinner in Tijuana. In the sunlight he was rotund but solid, a well-preserved sixty-year-old with coppery skin. His demure smile came and went with all the warmth of someone flicking a light switch.

The homeboys and the Mexican henchmen who had arrived with Dr. Guardiola distributed themselves with the Brazilian entourage in four vehicles. The convoy drove across the river into Brazil and through Foz to the Bird Park, a sanctuary for jungle birds and butterflies. Shaded pathways wound among giant cagelike enclosures that contained a collage of tropical colors.

Khalid paced with manicured fingers laced behind his back. Junior hovered around him. One minute they were deep in conversation, patting each other's shoulders, nodding gravely. The next minute Junior was practically climbing the mesh walls. His trunklike calves pumping, he hurdled a wood rail to frolic among the flamingos. He leaned back, perilously off-balance, mesmerized by hawks and owls in the treetops. He spread his arms and turned circles in a cloud of butterflies that spattered bursts of violet, black, yellow, orange. Khalid watched with a mix of indulgence and impatience.

"Junior digs this kinda shit," Buffalo said, leaning on a bench. "A real nature lover."

Medicines and rest had restored Junior's color. But his grimace had become perpetual, like that of a man staring into the sun.

Pescatore saw a tourist couple in white hats pose for a guide snapping photos. The guide was a no-necked Brazilian with Popeye forearms. Pescatore had seen him at the wheel of a dark Mercedes taxi in the parking lot outside. Was it his imagination or were the tourists taking a lot of pictures with Junior and Khalid in the background?

Leaving the bird sanctuary, the caravan took a highway that led toward Argentina. They exited before the border and entered a jungle park abutting the Iguaçú Falls.

The falls announced themselves with billows of white foam steaming up out of a lush gorge in the distance. Then came a hissing crescendo of sound. The convoy stopped at a colonial-style hotel on a plateau overlooking the spectacle: a miniature mountain range alive with waterfalls. Rows of waterfalls, hundreds of them. Mile-long curtains of water thundered and churned and poured into multileveled lagoons. The play of light and water constructed rainbows everywhere, interlocking archways of color. On the far side of the gorge, visitors walked on a network of catwalks and bridges among dancing waters. Pescatore leaned on the rail of the observatory platform, enjoying the moisture on his face, a respite from the heat.

"We can take a helicopter if Junior wants," Buffalo told someone. "They only let helicopters fly on the Brazil side. That part over there, that's Argentina."

There was no discernible boundary, but Pescatore had finally seen his father's country. He remembered arriving in San Diego, confronting The Line and the knowledge that those were his mother's people on the other side. Isabel was the only person to whom he had ever described that moment. Once again, as far as he had strayed from home, there was something familiar here.

Some part of him, buried deep, connected with this place. Like it or not.

Junior ruined Pescatore's private moment by getting into an argument with Dr. Guardiola. Junior didn't want to hire a helicopter. He wanted to ride one of the tourist speedboats that were skimming in and out of the falls in the gorge below. Dr. Guardiola said it wasn't a good idea. What if the boat capsized and Junior had to exert himself? Junior bitched and raged until Abbas intervened, suggesting they take pictures.

Somebody produced a Nikon and the photo session began. Brightening, Junior cleared everyone aside to get a shot alone with Khalid, arms around shoulders. Junior clowned and choreographed: me and all the Brazilians, now just Mexicans, wait, let me suck in my gut. Pescatore edged away. He wanted no part of the picture.

Khalid clapped his hands ostentatiously and announced that it was time for lunch. They entered the paneled dining room of the hotel. Junior, Buffalo, Khalid, Abbas and Dr. Guardiola occupied the table of honor in a corner by bay windows with a view of the falls. Pescatore and the homeboys were assigned to a small round table directly behind Junior where they could watch the entrance.

Champagne arrived. Junior proposed a toast.

"Partners and friends," he said, tossing the hair out of his eyes with a flourish.

Khalid bowed, raised his goblet and responded: "Friends and partners."

Khalid spoke impeccable Spanish with a refined accent from Spain, full of crisp *s*'s and lisping *z*'s. He said he had a villa on the Costa del Sol. Although Khalid was playing the generous host, it looked to Pescatore as if Junior were trying to sell something that Khalid hadn't yet bought. The older man's left eye was disconcertingly out of synch behind thick glasses, so it was hard to tell where he was looking or what he was thinking. Khalid reclined, his movements deliberate, scrutinizing the young Mexican. Junior strained forward into his monologue, laughing raucously, going off on tangents.

Pescatore caught bits and pieces. Junior crowed about how much money they were going to make, how lucky they were to have teamed up. Khalid agreed. Khalid mentioned that Brazil had the fifth-biggest population and the eighth-largest economy in the world. He said something about how fortunate he was to have relatives, and therefore trusted business partners, from Côte d'Ivoire to Turkey to Australia.

"It all comes together right here at this table," Junior declared. "This is the future we are making, Khalid. The crossroads of the twenty-first century. Who can stop us?"

"You are young and strong and you want the world," Khalid said, adjusting his glasses. "I admire that. No one can stop you but yourself."

Pescatore didn't get a chance to hear Junior's response because Khalid declared that the *rodízio* had begun. The *rodízio,* to Pescatore's delight, turned out to be a hell of a meal. Waiters trooped in, slicing strips of lamb and veal and steak off skewers, shoveling salads and breads and drinks onto the table nonstop. Pescatore pounded champagne and *caipirinhas,* a lime drink with a bittersweet punch. Soon everyone except Khalid was stuffed, drunk and boisterous.

The louder Junior got, the quieter Khalid got. He was practically murmuring, but it sounded like they were talking about Mexican politics. Khalid wanted to meet someone personally. Junior said that would happen soon enough, but not to worry, he spoke for his uncle. The candidate would appreciate a sign of commitment from Khalid and his associates, Junior said.

"Of course, of course," Khalid said. "Which reminds me, we have to take care of Mr. Fong. He speaks for the most serious Chinese interests in town. They feel neglected."

Junior complained about people coming around with their

hands out. "It's getting ridiculous. I'm supposed to be your guest."

Khalid smiled expansively. He urged Junior to dig into the dessert tray, the specialty of the house.

On the way out of the hotel, Pescatore spotted the tourist couple and brawny driver from the Bird Park. They were near the observatory platform, but they had their backs to the falls. They seemed more interested in the hotel. Both the guide and the husband had cameras, and they snapped away as the convoy passed. Pescatore felt a twinge of hope and dread. There was nothing unusual about seeing the tourists again: The Bird Park and the falls were the standard tourist attractions. On the other hand, the tourists looked a bit too goofy to be true. Perhaps the U.S. feds, the Mexicans, or both had caught up to Junior. Even if they really were undercover good guys, even if this meant the cavalry was coming, Pescatore wasn't sure that improved his chances of surviving—or staying jail-free. It would not help his case to be seen riding around fat and happy like one of the boys. He would be asked why he had not tried to escape. The only response he could think of was: Escape to where?

The convoy was within sight of the bridge to Ciudad del Este, mired in stop-and-go traffic, when they pulled over onto the shoulder of the road. Buffalo hurried from one vehicle to another. Moze and Tchai conferred with him and yammered into phones. Buffalo jogged through the traffic to the window of the car in which Pescatore sat.

"*Aguas,*" Buffalo told them. "Be ready. Big problem. The Brazilian po-lice got a roadblock goin' on the bridge."

"I thought this border was wide open," Pescatore said, his heart thumping. "I thought they didn't do that."

"Fuckin' Abbas says they check papers once in a while, special operations, but they always tell him first. Nobody told him shit today. Khalid's tearing him a new one."

Pescatore squinted at the bridge. Traffic was frozen in both directions as far as he could see. There was a cluster of uniforms and police cars with whirling lights at the bridge entrance, engulfed on both sides by lines of pedestrians.

"What do Moze and them say they're lookin' for?" Sniper said, his droopy eyelid open as wide as it would go.

"Us."

20

Although he took grim pleasure in the hunt for Junior Ruiz Caballero, Méndez had all but abandoned hope of seeing him behind bars.

After Junior's escape from Tijuana, Méndez had concluded that he had blown his best chance. He decided that the hands-on satisfaction of capturing Mauro Fernández Rochetti was the most he could expect. Yet he had accepted the offer to continue the pursuit into South America. Rather than lofty notions of justice, Méndez was driven now by a more basic impulse. Even if he couldn't catch Junior, he could hound him, haunt him, make his life miserable. Remember the Count of Monte Cristo, Méndez told himself: Don't underestimate the power of hate.

Méndez kept those sentiments to himself as he enjoyed the spectacle of Facundo the Russian making the rounds of his contacts. Like a seedy Santa Claus, Facundo dispensed bribes to an assortment of police, prosecutors and notable citizens in the three border cities. The cash came from the U.S. taxpayers by way of Isabel Puente. Nonetheless, Facundo's methods made Puente nervous.

"It's the only way, Miss Puente," Facundo said. "Justice is expensive around here. How do you think the big corporations deal with product piracy? It's the biggest industry in town. They have to pay the judges and the customs people, just like the pirates. Basic market economics."

"I'm sorry to hear law enforcement is for sale around here," Puente said.

"Oh, that's not completely true," Facundo boomed. "There are honest chiefs and prosecutors too. In their case it's easy: I simply tell them a bit about who Ruiz Caballero is and they are happy to help."

Facundo's voice strained over the *bandoneón* and strings wailing from his car radio. He steered carelessly, one-handed, half-turned in his seat. He crooned along with the tango, which was about an Italian immigrant drowning his sorrows at the Buenos Aires waterfront. When the singer broke into the refrain from "O Sole Mio," sustaining it at full volume, Facundo matched him note for note, shaking his head fervently.

Méndez saw Porthos elbow Athos. Puente scrunched down behind her sunglasses. She had been quiet and pensive since she had seen the photo of Pescatore a week before. And her rapport with Méndez hadn't quite recovered from the Buenos Aires airport. They were acting self-conscious, overly polite with each other.

"Marino, Marino, what a voice...," Facundo murmured, wrenching the wheel just in time to avoid colliding with a yellow armored car backing out of a driveway. "How does our city compare to Tijuana, Doctor, if I may ask a connoisseur of borders?"

"Impressive." Méndez was still flinching from the anticipated impact. "It's like Tijuana all right." Also the Casbah, Hong Kong and Tepito in Mexico City."

"I've never seen so many Mercedeses," Isabel said.

"Stolen, stolen, stolen," Facundo clucked, gesturing at vehicles with his head. "Half the cars are stolen in Argentina or Brazil. There was a time when thieves preferred Mercedeses. The president drives a stolen Mercedes. But these days minitrucks are more popular, Jeeps, Suburbans, that kind of thing."

Porthos chuckled. "Just like home, eh, Licenciado?"

Trailing them was a second Mercedes, carrying three of Facundo's men. The crossing from Puerto Iguazú through Foz had taken half an hour. The crossing of the bridge between Foz and Ciudad del Este had taken a full hour because of the swarm of Paraguayan riot police and Brazilian military patrols. For the third day, the security forces were engaged in activities that Facundo said were extremely rare: checking papers, stopping smugglers and confiscating contraband.

Downtown Ciudad del Este was a storm of humanity. In addition to commercial traffic and the vending stands that occupied every free inch of sidewalk, idle smugglers were everywhere: napping by their bales, squatting forlornly at the riverfront. Hundreds of demonstrators milled in the streets near the border crossing. The marchers carried Paraguayan and Brazilian flags. Their picket signs denounced the crackdown and demanded that they be allowed to earn a living. Protesters tossed firecrackers from the beds of pickup trucks, blasted music from boom boxes and chanted through bullhorns.

"What a sight," Facundo said, admiring the results of his handiwork. "What an upside-down world. Crooks defending their right to break the law."

"Who are all the demonstrators?" Puente asked. "Smugglers?"

"And taxi drivers, money changers, vendors, shopkeepers. Anybody who makes a living connected to smuggling."

"This should give Khalid the idea that Junior is bad for business," Méndez said.

"I think so. Forty thousand people cross that bridge every day. Whenever the Brazilians decided to check papers, it's a guaranteed mess. That's why they don't do it often."

The Brazilian immigration sweep at the border bridge had been their first breakthrough. The roadblock netted hundreds of illegal immigrants, a good many of them entrepreneurs commuting from homes in Foz to their stores in Ciudad del Este.

After visits from Facundo, the Brazilian Army garrison had deployed patrols to harass the backpack smugglers as well.

Facundo's operatives reported that Junior, who was on the Brazilian side of the bridge when the roadblock began, had retreated to Khalid's mansion in Foz. Khalid had provided a helicopter that flew Junior and his crew back to the hotel in Ciudad del Este. Paraguay was their best refuge.

"That's fine," Facundo said. "Right now we just want to keep them off-balance, stir up confusion."

"This fellow we are going to see can help?"

"Munir? He runs the chamber of commerce. A very important crook. That's where he lives, that new building just there. He works a few doors down."

The ten-story tower at the end of the block was still wreathed in construction dust. Gaudy arches and columns flanked the entrance. A guard in paramilitary attire sat in a sentry box beneath a sign that announced the grand opening of the Al-Andalus apartment complex. The windows on the lower floors were covered by metal shutters, giving the place an uninhabited look that contrasted even more with its surroundings. The rest of the street was a row of storefronts with names like Aleppo, Faisal and Mokhtar: cell phone shops, groceries, a green-shingled *halal* butcher shop with Arabic script in the window.

There was activity outside the butcher shop. Young Arab men congregated in front. They were lean and stern. A few wore skullcaps, beards, *kaffiyehs* around their necks. Méndez watched them exchange kisses on cheeks, press their hands to hearts, their air of idle menace melting into affectionate smiles. They filed into the doorway of the butcher shop, pausing deferentially to greet a long-bearded, wrinkled man in a *dishdasha* who sat in the shade, barely awake.

"The *shabab,*" Facundo muttered as he backed into a parking spot. "There's a little mosque on the second floor. A prayer room, anyway. I can assure you they don't preach tolerance and brotherhood up there. In fact, they raise money and recruit for the training camps."

"Which camps?" Puente asked.

"Wherever there are camps. Depends on their inclination. Lebanon. Iran. Pakistan. Perhaps Venezuela, but I have heard that at the level of comments, not hard intelligence. There are more Shiites here, but they get along with the Sunnis. They are united against the common enemy. That is to say, you and me. Especially me."

Facundo killed the engine. He observed the Arabs, drinking in details with professional relish. He waited until the sidewalk had cleared, the last men helping the bearded codger fold up his chair and shuffle inside. Finally, shaking his head as if coming out of a trance, Facundo turned to Méndez. Facundo smiled crookedly.

"Listen, Dr. Méndez, Miss Puente. I will not be talkative. I make the introduction, I turn Munir over to you and that's it."

"Why?" Puente asked as they got out.

Facundo pulled a briefcase from the trunk and slammed the lid. "We, eh, have conflicting opinions on a number of political questions."

A hoarse cry greeted them from the rear of the store. "The Zionist dog! And his friends. Come in, come in."

In Tijuana, Méndez had seen many shops like Chez Munir. A classic border store. The goods lining the high shelves had no discernible organization or presentation: liquor bottles next to vacuum cleaners next to Barbie dolls next to alarm clocks. Dust motes floated in sunlight that was chopped in rows by the burglar bars in the front window. Children could be heard playing somewhere.

Munir received them at the end of the center aisle. He sat precariously on a stool behind a little three-legged table covered with plastic coffee cups, a plate of cookies and cell phones. He did not get up; he had one leg thrust out at an angle that suggested it was of little use to him. His small round belly protruded in a striped short-sleeved shirt. His wire-rimmed glasses adorned a bulbous face with a chiseled nose. His white-gray hair stood and fluttered in the breeze of a fan, giving him the wind-tossed aspect of a broken-down pirate at the helm. Mouth-breathing asthmatically, he ordered a young woman in a head scarf behind the cash register to bring coffee.

"You represent the Zionist-controlled American government?" Munir said to Puente. "A pleasure. What a charming young policewoman. Facundo usually brings me grouchy lugs who think they are Clint Eastwood. And that I am the chief of Hezbollah."

"Nice to meet you," Puente said, blank-faced.

Apparently Munir amused her even less than he did Facundo. Puente declined the stool the young woman brought for her. The tableau was uncomfortable: They stood around looking down at Munir and hoisting thimble-sized plastic cups of very hot coffee.

"I always tell the Americans and the Argentines the same thing," Munir said. "No terrorists here. Hardworking wretches trying to make a living, that's all. We don't have any extra money for political causes. We are starving. Even Facundo will agree with me there. Am I right, my Zionist friend?"

"Oh absolutely. Wasting away in front of our eyes," Facundo said in a monotone. He was behind Méndez.

"No terrorists," Munir puffed. His unwavering glee gave a mocking quality to everything he said. "No Hezbollah, no al-Qaeda. And even if there were, they wouldn't be terrorists. Because they are freedom fighters. They would be our George Washingtons, our Thomas Jeffersons, young lady. Where are you from, originally? With your lovely coloring, those big dark eyes, you might have ancestors from my part of the world."

"The United States of America," Puente said.

"Ah. Well then, you know what I mean."

One of the cell phones on the table rang. Munir answered. He put a hand over the phone and announced that a radio station wanted to interview him about his leadership of the protests against the border operations.

"Please forgive me," Munir said to Puente. "As executive director of the chamber of commerce, it is my duty to attend to the professionals of the press. Very important talk show. A television crew is coming later."

Munir raised a hand in a one-moment gesture; it hovered for the rest of the telephone interview. With labored breathing, he railed against the Brazilian, Argentine, Paraguayan and North American governments for strangling the economic lifeblood of the border community with their search for drugs, guns and terrorists.

"What nonsense. The guns come from Miami. The drugs go through the ports of Santos and Bahia. The terrorist bombings were in Buenos Aires, why bother us here? The only terrorists in this town are the Mossad. They kidnap our sheikhs off the streets, they take them God knows where to do God knows what. As executive director of the chamber of commerce..."

Méndez looked at Facundo, who gave him an I-told-you-so shrug. Munir made a reference to "foreign thugs" coming into town and causing trouble. "We don't have any use for outsiders. We have problems of our own. If the police want to get tough, let them get tough with the Mexicans and the other riffraff who come around giving our community a bad name."

A slap at Junior, Méndez thought. As if in confirmation, Munir flashed him a roguish grin, finished the conversation and hung up. Munir addressed Isabel again.

"Oh, the ignorance, young lady," he exclaimed. "The sheer ignorance of the press and so many others. They talk about terrorism financing. Nonsense. Drivel. They don't understand basic concepts of Islam. Have you ever heard of *zakat,* young lady? It's charity. Good Muslims have a sacred duty. We give to charities, mosques, social organizations in our homelands. We contribute to distinguished religious personages who do us the honor of visiting us. And there's such a thing as Muslim hospitality, my dear. If a brother comes to my door, I give him meals and a bed for three days. No questions asked. Then someone dares to accuse me of harboring a terrorist."

Munir spoke in a jumble of accents and inflections. His Spanish had an Argentine intonation, but many words were Portuguese. He said "*zakat*" in pure Arabic. His English pronunciation was good as well. Two toddlers came into view around one of the shelves, little boys in sweat suits. They drove toy tanks back and forth on the scarred wood, making a huge racket.

Facundo stepped forward, patting one of the boys on the head. He told Munir that his friends hadn't come all this way to listen to this warmed-over radical nonsense. It was time to get down to business. He put the briefcase in front of Munir and made a move to open it. Munir stopped him with a look that combined gratitude and annoyance.

"Thank you, thank you," he murmured, pressing his right hand to his heart.

"We can be sure the protests and problems will continue, then?" said Méndez, realizing that Puente just was not cut out for negotiating over briefcases full of cash. She nodded, seeming grateful for his help. "It's very important to us."

"Of course they will continue," Munir exclaimed. "Of course. As executive director of the chamber of commerce, I can assure you the hardworking people of this city will not stand by while the Brazilian and Paraguayan governments do the dirty work of the Zionist Americans and take bread off our table!"

"Will Khalid interfere?"

Munir snorted. "No one can stop the merchants and working people of the border community from expressing their rightful grievances. Khalid has his business and we have ours. He doesn't bother us, we don't bother him."

"The point is, we need things to stay hot and agitated,"

Facundo said. "Are you listening, you damned old rug merchant? The hotter and more agitated, the better."

"Don't worry. The voice of the people will not be stifled."

Puente looked as if she could think of a voice that needed stifling. She asked: "Is Khalid still committed to Ruiz Caballero? Will he protect him?"

Munir regarded her shrewdly over his glasses. "Yes. But Khalid cannot neglect the difficulties of all of us who have known him for so long. Those of us who have been in this town since it was just a few shacks in the jungle. Who have made it what it is today."

What it is today: a den of thieves, Méndez said to himself. The trick is to get them fighting among themselves. As thieves will.

21

THE DEATH PATROL ROLLED on Munir right after breakfast. Buffalo didn't let them in on the details until they had left El Naútico. Too late for Pescatore to do anything but nod in glum obedience and listen to the big man give the lowdown.

The night before, Abbas had met with Junior by the hotel pool. Abbas brought news: His spies reported that Munir Khoury, a leader of the business community, had gotten a visit from American and Mexican cops, one of them a woman.

"Had to be Méndez and them," Buffalo said, pulling on his fingerless black leather gloves. "This Munir, he's some kinda *chingón,* he's the one organizing the marches. Abbas says ordinarily they could just work it out with the Brazilian po-lice and army. But it ain't happening. This Munir's fuckin' with Khalid because Méndez is givin' Munir and the police and the army money to keep the border checks goin'. That means Khalid's hittin' on Junior for more *lana,* and you know Junior don't like it."

"Junior mad again?" Momo asked. He was in the front passenger seat of the Suburban. He cranked the volume on a Daddy Yankee song.

"*Así es.* Spittin' nails. Abbas told him let it be, they was going to have a serious talk with this Munir. But after Abbas left, we was watching the news. Munir comes on talkin' shit about

Mexican gangsters ruinin' business. Junior lost it. To the curb." Buffalo imitated Junior's bratty Mexico City accent: "*Salgan y maten a ese pinche árabe de mierda ahora mismo! Ya! Que lo maten ya! Chinga su madre,* this and that... Turn that shit down, would you? Where the fuck are we?"

Pescatore and Sniper were in the backseat with Buffalo. They had brought handguns; they wanted Moze and Tchai's men to think they were just going for a ride. The problem was that Buffalo had only been to Ciudad del Este once before. He had just a vague idea of how to get to Chez Munir. The Suburban slogged through traffic. Buffalo peered at storefronts and street signs, giving uncertain directions to Rufino. Buffalo glowered when they got stuck behind a fleet of clothing racks being pulled by Asians in the middle of the traffic. After forty-five minutes of meandering, they arrived in a block of Arab-owned shops in an area with less pedestrian activity.

"OK." Buffalo checked and slapped home the clip of a semiautomatic. "Keep it running, Rufi. Sniper, you got the front door. Keep an eye on them *vatos* with the beards next door. Momo and Valentín come in with me."

Why didn't he give me the front door? Pescatore thought.

The heat felt like a faceful of steaming Jell-O. The moment had arrived: Pescatore was going to have to pull a trigger for the mafia. Or come up with Plan B real quick.

Nothing occurred to him. Buffalo led the way through multicolored plastic streamers hanging in the shop doorway to dissuade flies. Rotor fans on the ceiling churned up the air, but had little effect on the temperature.

Buffalo's cowboy boots were loud on the floorboards. He hadn't drawn his gun yet, so Pescatore didn't either.

The old man sitting at the end of the aisle raised and then lowered his head deliberately, appraising them over spectacles. Pescatore noticed a cane propped in a corner.

"Gentlemen?" the old man said.

"Munir?" Buffalo demanded.

"That's me, sir, at your service." Munir spoke in the Portuñol that Pescatore was getting used to.

Momo shuffled slightly to the right and Pescatore mirrored him, sliding to the left. Not that Munir was running anywhere. He had a gimp leg. His breath rattled noisily. He looked to Pescatore like a sick aged bird of prey, not much fight left except in his eyes.

Great, for my first hit I get to smoke a cripple, Pescatore thought.

Then there was a rumbling sound and peals of laughter. A boy on a Big Wheel came rolling out of a side aisle. He ran into Munir's little three-legged table, rattling together a coffee cup and several cell phones.

"Boom!" the boy shrieked delightedly.

Another boy ran up and started tussling with the boy on the Big Wheel, chattering away. They were both Middle Eastern with very curly hair. Neither of them looked over five. They paid no attention to the newcomers.

"Easy, boys," Munir said tenderly. "Grandfather has visitors."

Buffalo's scowl wavered. He was standing over Munir like a human hammer about to pound. But still no gun appeared. Maybe the kids'll make him back off, Pescatore told himself desperately. Buffalo wouldn't do a guy in front of his grandkids. Would he? Would he do the grandkids too?

"Where are you from, gentlemen?" Munir asked. His Adam's apple swelled for a moment, but otherwise he put up a pretty cool front. "Mexico?"

Buffalo might have nodded.

"Friends of Mr. Abbas, no?"

Buffalo's chin moved again.

Munir spoke quickly and ceremoniously: "Ah well, it so happens I just had a long telephone conversation with Mr. Abbas this morning. I assured him we could resolve any misunderstanding that may have . . ."

Buffalo shook his head.

"No, I assure you," Munir said. "Mr. Abbas called me and we agreed that..."

"That doesn't have anything to do with me."

The words were hard and final. Munir made a little sound as if the air were being let out of him. He knew exactly what time it was. But his manner stayed courtly. He put a hand on the head of the smaller boy, who was gnawing on a cell phone. Munir held Buffalo's gaze as he raised his voice.

"Fatima," Munir called.

A woman with a head scarf came out of a back room. Momo swiveled quickly toward her with his hand in his vest. She looked at the visitors and then at the floor. Her body seemed middle-aged in the lumpy smock. But her plump face, encircled by the dark purple veil, made her look no older than Pescatore.

"Fatima, please take the boys next door," Munir said. His expression turned from hopeful to grateful when Buffalo nodded. "I have business with these gentlemen."

Hissing in her language, the woman got hold of one boy. She pried the cell phone out of his hand. But the older one clung to his Big Wheel and started whining, which agitated his brother. Wrestling for the handlebars, they banged into the little table. A phone fell to the floor with a thump. Wheezing in distress, Munir patted his brow with a handkerchief.

"Valentín." Buffalo's voice was barely audible. "Help the lady."

The woman looked sharply at her father. Munir gave his daughter a smile so radiant and reassuring that Pescatore himself believed for a moment that everything was going to be alright.

Pescatore squatted next to the squalling boy with the Big Wheel, trying to shush him.

"Come on, little guy," Pescatore implored. "Hey. Come on. I'll give you a push."

The Big Wheel had a long handle in back that rose waist high. Pescatore clutched it, inspired. He made loud engine noises.

The kid stopped in midwhimper. He got with the program. He climbed aboard and started pedaling down the main aisle. Pescatore trotted behind him, vroom-vrooming half-heartedly, steering with the handle. The mother hurried alongside with the smaller boy in her arms.

Sniper, on guard just inside the doorway, looked at Pescatore as if he were crazy. Pescatore lifted the boy off the Big Wheel, catching a momentary smell of orange-scented shampoo. He fought down an impulse to hug the kid to his chest and run like hell.

Instead, he handed the boy over to the mother. She hoisted a brother under each arm, like sacks of groceries. Halfway through the plastic streamers of the doorway, she stopped. She looked back. Horror twisted across her face.

"Run, lady," Pescatore rasped in Spanish, his mouth tasting like steel wool. "Run and don't come back."

Silently, she took his advice. The streamers were fluttering in her wake when the shooting started.

Sniper shouldered roughly past him to check if the sidewalk was clear. If the dudes at the butcher shop had heard the shots above the snarl of traffic and chatter of commerce, they had prudently retreated.

Buffalo, Momo, Sniper and Pescatore trotted back to the Suburban. A couple of street peddlers, Brazilians in sun hats with multicolored blankets and hammocks piled on their arms, backed out of their way. Nobody on the street made a move. This was not a town where people were in the habit of calling 911.

Buffalo rode in front. Not far from the hotel, he turned to look behind them. Pescatore managed to catch his eye.

Pescatore blurted: "That was fucked up."

Buffalo faced front again. He was seething. Pescatore thought for a moment that the big man was going to ignore him and make him look bad. But he could not restrain himself.

"That was fucked up, with the kids there and everything, huh?" Pescatore said.

Buffalo did not turn around. He spoke through tight lips.

"It was his own fault. He talked too much. Broke the rules. Somebody talks too much, that's what happens: You shoot him in the mouth. Somebody double-crosses"—Buffalo used his hand to mime a gun pointed at himself—"in the back of the neck. A spy, in the ear. It all means something. It's for a reason. I don't do this shit because I like it. If people would act right, follow the rules and shut the fuck up, I wouldn't have to."

The Death Patrol reported to Junior. He was getting ready for a massage on a second-floor veranda. He lay on his stomach wrapped in towels that were soaked with sweat. A radio played Paraguayan harp music.

There was a distraction: Two masseuses arrived. They looked like Brazilian beauty queens. They wore flimsy silk wraps over bathing suits. Thick, shiny, African-style braids cascaded down their long slender backs. They walked with throwaway grace, completely comfortable with their bodies and the reactions of the men in the room. One of the women—upturned nose, shimmering eyes, golden-brown skin—met Pescatore's stare and returned it, smiling with easy intimacy.

Junior greeted the women with a sleepy kiss each. Time for a freak show, Pescatore thought. This *cabrón* better be careful or he's gonna have a heart attack.

Facedown in his towel pillow, Junior asked Buffalo what he wanted.

"All set, *jefe,*" Buffalo said. "Just took care of that Munir asshole for ya."

Junior's head came up slowly. His fingers pried apart a curtain of hair. His eyes searched through cobwebs and fog. He focused finally on Buffalo.

"Munir," Junior said.

"Yeah. All taken care of. *Un buen jale, bien limpito.*" Buffalo's head was bowed. His hands were crossed one over the other on his Harley belt buckle.

"Who? Did I…"

"*Sí señor,* last night. Sure did." Buffalo looked crestfallen. "The one was talking that shit on TV, remember?"

Junior shook his head.

"*El canijo árabe?*" Buffalo said. "*Viejo, con lentes?* Mr. Abbas told us about him?"

"Oh. Yeah. OK." Junior didn't sound convinced. But he made a languid thumbs-up sign. Then his eyelids and his head succumbed blissfully to gravity.

"*Muy bien, muchachos,*" he mumbled into the towel.

As the Death Patrol descended a long staircase to the lobby, Sniper whispered to Momo: "Just like that time with the lawyer up in Montebello, you remember? Same thing. He was all wasted, yellin', givin' orders. Next day he was like, 'Licenciado who? What you guys talkin' about? I said to pop the lawyer?' Didn't remember jackshit…"

22

THE DRIVEWAY LEADING INTO the courthouse compound was guarded by a line of riot policemen. Chest-high Plexiglas shields, helmets with visors, blue overall-type uniforms. And oversized clubs that were almost as tall as the boy-cops holding them.

From his vantage point at the courthouse entrance, Méndez looked over the gleaming helmets at the protesters on the edge of a shantytown outside. They chanted at the policemen and waved signs protesting the border blockade. Their jeers turned to cheers when a cow wandered out of the shantytown among them.

The cow was black and white, gaunt, heat-stunned. Protesters slapped and pushed its haunches, urging it forward. Tail switching, trailing flies and dust, the cow meandered toward the police. It gathered momentum. The police braced visibly at its approach. Méndez wondered if they would use their batons or, if they felt insulted enough, their guns.

The cow nosed around at the boots of the cops. The cheers increased. But the cow seemed to lose initiative. It turned in a slow circle and tottered back from where it had come.

"What?" Isabel Puente asked, hearing Méndez chuckle.

"Nothing. It reminded me of a book, *The Autumn of the Patri-*

arch. There's a part where cows invade the presidential palace: 'A cow on the balcony of the palace, what an awful thing, what a shitty country.' "

"Oh," Puente responded. She didn't have much time for his literary references.

Facundo returned a few minutes later. He strode through a hallway lined with statues of bearded national heroes.

"If we could only get that guy in a room with Junior, he'd talk him to death," Puente muttered.

"I have to say I kind of like Facundo," Méndez said.

"I thought spies were supposed to be quiet."

"I don't care if he calls himself Russian, Jewish, whatever: He's a first-class Argentine big mouth. But I like him."

"He gives me a headache," Puente whispered.

Facundo looked grimly triumphant.

"The prosecutor came through," he said. "He's serious about the Munir case."

"He's not scared of Junior or Khalid?" Puente asked.

"The prosecutor has a brother who is a general in Asunción, so he has strong protection. He works with military intelligence rather than the police. And frankly, this particular prosecutor is kind of a madman."

"Is he honest?"

"Not at all. When I showed him your warrants and told him the Americans want Junior, his eyeballs turned into dollar signs." Facundo produced a cigarette and handed another to Athos, who lit them both. Facundo savored the smoke. "Oh, you can be sure he is going to cause trouble. It's like firing a human missile at Junior."

"Greed works wonders."

"Not greed alone. The prosecutor is indignant. We can't have foreigners coming into town and knocking off the director of the chamber of commerce. It is unacceptable. It isn't done."

Méndez appraised Facundo, whose usual sarcasm appeared to have deserted him. "I thought you despised Munir."

"A strong word, Doctor: 'despised.' "

"You said he was a gangster, Facundo. A financier of terrorists."

"Oh, he was. A scoundrel. Absolutely without morals. Also anti-Semitic."

"So?"

Facundo avoided eye contact. He spoke in a mumble. "Well, what can I tell you? For years I had many dealings with him. I'd go in the store. He would call me a Zionist dog. I'd call him something equally nasty. But he would give me coffee. Always coffee. And we'd talk. Many insults, arguments, but we talked. It was business. He was a grandfather, I'm a grandfather. Who knows, Dr. Méndez? They say hate is closer to love than indifference."

Wiping a sleeve across his forehead, Facundo turned and led the way down the stairs. Méndez winked at Puente. Surprise: The big brassy Turkish Russian was a softy at heart.

In an attempt to tighten the noose around Junior, Facundo's men had set up surveillance on the El Naútico Resort. Athos and Porthos took turns overseeing the operation. But they had had no luck intercepting phone calls, leading them to think Junior was using an encrypted satellite phone. Today, however, Facundo announced that a "friendly government" wanted to share information with them.

Their destination was the consulate of Taiwan. It was located in a mostly residential hillside neighborhood overlooking the lagoon and Junior's hotel. The street was blocked off by a Paraguayan police checkpoint backed by an armored vehicle. Before entering the brick guardhouse, Facundo explained that the consulate worked closely with a few other governments — Argentine, U.S., Israeli — that monitored the Triple Border.

"They have had access to a wiretap of Junior's phone calls

from the hotel. Mr. Han was kind enough to let me know right away. Always a good man to trade information with."

The consulate was a hilltop fortress complete with gun towers. They climbed a steep outdoor flight of concrete steps and passed through more checkpoints. Mr. Han received them in a high-ceilinged, highly refrigerated conference room. He was in his thirties, sleek and athletic in an off-white designer suit that had to make him a contender for best-dressed diplomat in town. His slicked-back hair and gold bracelet gave him a touch of street-cop flair. He told them he had become interested in Junior Ruiz Caballero after Junior's emissaries had entered into a major deal with a Chinese network, brokered by Ibrahim Abbas, to smuggle immigrants into California.

"The Asians and the Arabs usually do not do business together," Han said, in solid Spanish. "Frankly, it is not my priority. I spend eighty percent of my time on the mainland gangs. Big Circle Boys, Fuk Ching, you name it. I have to worry about them shaking down and killing Taiwanese businessmen. But anybody they get involved with, I want to know all about it."

"The Tijuana smuggling connection is booming," Méndez said.

Mr. Han nodded. "The Asian criminal organizations know a moneymaking opportunity when they see it. But here in this country they mainly keep to themselves. They have many rules. They rarely go out except at night: a few restaurants, stores, the casino. They only deal with certain people in certain ways. If they want money from an Asian shopkeeper, they do not need to spell it out. They just send him whiskey. One bottle means forty thousand dollars, two bottles mean eighty thousand. Good luck proving extortion. Everybody understands. Or else. Here, let me show you something."

Han led Méndez and Puente from the conference table where they'd been sitting to a window. It overlooked an internal patio.

There was an Asian garden with rocks, sculptures and an ornamental footbridge over a little brook. On the lawn, a middle-aged Asian in a black outfit was immersed in a martial-arts exercise. His salt-and-pepper hair and thick-backed physique suggested a military background. He swiveled, changed stances, threw slow kicks. He was absolutely absorbed in the workout.

"That is the biggest money man in our community," Han said softly, his tone clinical. "He came here a year ago to build a plastics factory. This crazy city, everybody sells every kind of junk. But nobody *makes* anything. Unless you count the warehouses that do pirate videos and CDs. We need bona fide industry."

"Is he a diplomat or something?" Puente asked.

"No. Private sector. He showed up from Taiwan, started building the factory. The boys came around asking for money. But he would not pay. They firebombed his site, harassed his workers. They killed his business partner. But he was stubborn. He got it into his head that he was not going to pay. One day two guys came to see him. They told him it was his last chance. Started pushing him around. Rubbed him the wrong way. So he pulled a gun: bam-bam-bam. Cleaned them up." Han fanned his palm over an imaginary gun hammer, Wyatt Earp–style, surprising Méndez with the pantomime and the Argentine street slang.

"Quite a story," Puente said.

Han turned back to the table; the show was over. Méndez took a last look at the industrialist-gunslinger on the grass. The man's eyes were half-closed in a kind of rapture. His body coiled and unfurled as he engaged invisible enemies. Méndez saw that his feet were bare.

"So now he has to live with us, here in the consulate," Han said. "He sent his family to Buenos Aires. The Paraguayan police take him to his factory every day. And there is a new lottery in Ciudad del Este: People bet on when the gang will eliminate him."

They sat back down. A Paraguayan woman entered carrying

a tea tray. Han waited patiently for her to fill and distribute cups and leave.

"The point is," Han said, leaning toward Méndez, hardly any trace of the diplomat left now, "the Asian gangs do not mess around. When they do business with an outsider, it is always a risk. This deal with Ruiz has been lucrative. But frankly, I do not think it will last. As long as he was far away, fine. But now he is here. Throwing his weight around. Making enemies. It is not their style."

"He lacks discipline," Méndez said. The word caused Han to nod deeply.

"Exactly. That is good for us, bad for them. So everybody's watching him." Han reached at last for the digital recording device that his visitors had been eyeing since their arrival. "These calls were recorded during the past two days and provided to us, to our great surprise, by a well-informed source. We'll give you the whole recording. You are the experts."

Méndez wondered about the provenance of the wiretap, whether the Taiwanese were working with the Americans. It all seemed very roundabout to him. But then the tape started and he recognized Junior's voice immediately. It sounded thick and slurred. The phone call had clearly awoken his uncle, Senator Ruiz Caballero.

SENATOR: What? What time is it, for God's sake? What's wrong?

JUNIOR: I don't know. I don't care. I've stepped in a ton of shit and it's your fault.

SENATOR: My fault? What's the matter with you?

JUNIOR: I thought you said your people put a muzzle on Méndez. The son of a bitch is down here. He's fucking things up with Khalid.

SENATOR: I told you, that's the Americans. If Méndez is there, he's freelancing for that Cuban woman I told you about. We don't have any control over that.

JUNIOR: You do too. You talk to California, or Wash—

SENATOR: Careful, careful on the phone, Hugo!

JUNIOR: These fucking Arabs don't stop asking for money. They say they're getting heat because of me. They're feeding off me, what the fuck is this? I'm thinking about going back to Baja.

SENATOR: That would be problematic right now.

JUNIOR: So you haven't done a thing. You haven't taken care of those warrants yet!

SENATOR: I'm working on it. I can't guarantee there wouldn't be inconveniences, legally speaking, if you came back right now. Especially in this mood you're—

JUNIOR: All right, that's it. Now you have to get up off your ass and lend a hand.

SENATOR: How?

JUNIOR: First you send me a contribution for Khalid—

SENATOR: It's not like you don't have the dough—

JUNIOR: A contribution! And help me set him up with that man from Monterrey. He's interested in contributing. He's breaking my balls about a trip to meet the candidate—

SENATOR: Careful!

JUNIOR: And find out exactly what the fucking gringos are doing down here. And then get your supposed American friends to make them disappear. Because if I do it, there will be a bloodbath like you can't imagine, do you understand? Get moving, you stingy old bastard. I will not stand for this shit.

SENATOR: Calm down. And listen carefully. You may need to do some housecleaning. Our friends say you may have picked up an undesirable employee.

Han's cell phone rang on the table next to his elbow. He glanced at the display, grimaced apologetically and stopped the recording.

As the diplomat murmured into the phone in Mandarin, Méndez realized that all of them had been straining toward the recording device as if on leashes. Isabel's thumb had gone to her teeth early in the conversation; she had started biting it after the reference to "that Cuban woman."

It did not concern Méndez that Junior knew they were on his heels. That was part of the strategy. But who were the Ruiz Caballeros' friends in the United States?

23

Junior had no attention span. He didn't listen. Twice within the space of fifteen minutes, he had asked Pescatore what kind of name Valentín Pescatore was and where he was from.

Junior was acting friendly. Too goddamn friendly. It was their first real conversation. It worried Pescatore more than the confrontation on the basketball court. Pescatore was still trying to understand how exactly he had ended up in the presidential suite with Buffalo and Junior. Just the three of them kicking back in front of the television. Pescatore spoke when spoken to and puffed on the joint when it was handed to him.

"Chicago, huh?" Junior mused, spewing a jet of smoke. "Never liked it. Too cold."

Junior had stretched himself out on the couch. He sniped at the television with the remote control, jumping between MTV Latino, a sports channel and a nature channel showing cheetahs and buzzards. His T-shirt was decorated with a picture of one of his company's Mexican bands, a dozen *norteños* in feathered cowboy hats and outlaw leather coats. A room-service cart gave off a smell of leftover steak and vegetables that mingled with the reefer and Junior's atomic cologne.

"Italiano-Argentino-Mexicano, eh? And you end up with the *Migra*. Check that out."

Junior's eyes stared out of puffy purplish circles. He made strange noises when he breathed, as if he had excess phlegm or saliva in his nose and throat. Whatever the problem was, it made him snort and spit a lot. He had developed an ugly cough too.

Buffalo, sitting on an armchair near Pescatore, passed the joint without sampling it. Buffalo had barely said a word.

"Yeah, I didn't fit in with those good ol' boys and Tejanos and everything, I'll tell you that," Pescatore said.

"Uh-huh." Apparently losing interest, Junior coughed and pawed around on the carpet for his drink.

Through the tall windows, Pescatore saw Moze on the dock with a machine pistol over his shoulder, a lean silhouette against the dusk. The day before, the team of Paraguayan cops guarding the hotel had pulled out without explanation. Moze and Tchai had intensified their vigilance. And Junior hadn't stopped all day: phone calls to Mexico City, e-mails, couriers, conferences with Abbas, more phone calls. Abbas had taken them to visit a warehouse Junior had invested in, a depot for contraband software, videos and compact discs: boxes of swag as far as the eye could see. Khalid had been supposed to come along, but he had canceled at the last minute. As far as Pescatore could tell, the vibes between Junior and Khalid were getting worse.

Junior flipped through two Arabic-language channels: a guy in desert headgear reading news, a dark-eyed woman ululating to a disco beat in front of minarets. A Brazilian news program showed a prison riot: Buffed convicts on a cell-block rooftop waved clubs and shanks, shirts furled over their heads for masks. A police helicopter banked through a column of smoke. Bare-chested inmates, hands behind their heads, filed through a gauntlet of helmeted storm troopers.

"Valentín," Buffalo said.

Pescatore turned in slow motion, realizing that Junior had produced a paper from somewhere and was poking it at him. Like a camera zooming in for close-up, Pescatore focused: It was a photo of Isabel Puente.

The photo was posed, face front. It looked like a Department of Homeland Security personnel photo, which was theoretically not an easy thing to get your hands on if you weren't in the government. Puente's hair was up, making her seem stern and vulnerable at the same time, Pescatore thought fleetingly, as fear smothered him. What was this about?

Junior propped himself on an elbow. His casual tone wasn't altogether convincing. The paper trembled in his hand. "You know who that is, *gabacho?*"

Pescatore took the photo, actually a computer printout of a photo, and glanced rapidly at Buffalo. The big man looked ominously sad.

"Sure," Pescatore said. "That's Isabel Puente, from OIG. Inspector General. It's like internal affairs."

Buffalo turned to Junior with satisfaction, the gesture saying: See, my boy tells it straight up, he's got nothing to hide.

"That's right," Junior said slowly. "We been doin' some research. This is the boss of the operation against us. With Méndez. *La muy puta.* She's fucking Méndez too, did you know that?"

Isabel and Méndez. It made sense. It confirmed Pescatore's worst suspicions. Junior hawked and spat in the direction of an ashtray.

"No," Pescatore said. "How'm I supposed to know that?"

"Well, you were fucking her too, right?"

Pescatore fought down panic. "Jeez. That's a real personal question, you know?"

Buffalo slapped him without getting up. He simply reached out and slammed a planklike hand across Pescatore's face.

Pescatore had been leaning forward. The impact knocked him clean out of the chair. He found himself facedown on the coffee table.

Junior giggled and rumpled Pescatore's hair. He let his hand linger in the curls. The caress terrified Pescatore more than the slap. Images spattered his brain, memories of every war story, intelligence report and newspaper article he had ever seen or heard about what the Mexican cartels did to traitors before granting their most heartfelt wish: letting them die.

Buffalo stood over him. His voice was hoarse.

"Next thing comes outta your mouth better be yes or no, and it better be the truth. Otherwise I take a lamp and I rip out the wires and I light you up like a fucking Christmas tree. Understand, youngster?"

Pescatore hauled himself back into the chair, an ocean roaring in his head.

"Were you fucking her?" Buffalo said.

"Just one night I did," Pescatore muttered.

"What was going on between you two?"

"Why didn't you say nothing, *canijo?*" Junior was sitting up now. "We got sources everywhere. You gamin' us?"

"Hell no. You never asked me, right?" Pescatore gathered himself, put on his best head-busting, mob-defying PA face. And plunged over a cliff. "Garrison knew all about it. I figured you guys did too."

"Garrison knew?" Buffalo asked.

"That's right." Pescatore told them about the Pulpo episode, being summoned to the Inspector General's office, Isabel's recruiting pitch. Good lies build on the truth, he thought desperately. "So I told Garrison she was snooping around, cuddling up to me and whatnot. He said go ahead and play along. Find out what the task force was up to, you know."

"And you got yourself some leg on the side," Buffalo said.

"Garrison didn't tell you about it?" Pescatore demanded.

Junior's greenish-gold eyes flickered wetly in the light of the television. Pescatore thought about his empty shoulder holster under his jacket, which he had put on to withstand the air-conditioning that Junior had cranked into arctic overdrive. Pescatore's gun was on a table somewhere behind him. Or maybe on a shelf.

"Look, man, you guys are treating me like some kinda rat. It ain't fair." Pescatore's indignation felt surprisingly genuine. "Back in Tijuana, I brought you Garrison, Buffalo said that was totally clutch. And—"

"*Ya basta,* Valentín," Buffalo snapped. But then he gave Junior a reproachful look that made Pescatore want to hug him, in spite of the throbbing left side of his face. "Junior knows you got heart. You been earning your keep. But this is serious business, *cabrón.*"

Junior took a gulp of rum and a hit off the joint. He raised his chin petulantly and kept it there, his voice shrill with rage.

"Méndez and that Cuban bitch think they can sweat me. Me. *Te imaginas?* And you worked for them. *Pinche* spy."

"No way, man," Pescatore exclaimed. "I got nothing to do with Méndez. He's a scumbag. He hates my fucking guts. You know that, they were hunting me all over Baja for shooting that cop."

Junior crushed the joint into an ashtray.

"Now I am going to ask you another question," he said, his voice getting louder and slower. "And remember this: If you give me the wrong answer, I'm gonna have Buffalo cut off your ears and make you eat them. So listen carefully: When was the last time you talked to Isabel Puente?"

It was the make-or-break question. The rest had been a warm-up. Buffalo was too close and too fast—going for the gun would be suicide. Buffalo seemed to be sticking up for him, which made Pescatore think that Junior could be swayed. Either they knew the truth or they didn't. Either they had decided to waste him or they hadn't.

In a way, he was relieved. The waiting and cringing were over. He had expected this moment ever since he had started this masquerade. The biggest, and probably the last, masquerade of his short and confused life.

24

THAT'S WHAT I CALL A FIRST-CLASS errand boy," Méndez said.

Albino Losada, until recently the deputy attorney general of the state of Baja California, sat in a room on the other side of the glass that separated him and his interrogators from Méndez, Puente, Porthos and Facundo.

Losada sweated profusely. His side-combed haircut was mussed, his mustache wilted in the heat. He was manacled to his chair. Although Losada was a long way from home, he contemplated his dimly lit surroundings with a mute horror bred by familiarity. As a prosecutor in Tijuana, he had seen and done things — memorable, unspeakable things — in rooms like this. But he had never seen this kind of room through the eyes of a prisoner contemplating a prosecutor: a bald, bull-shouldered Paraguayan with rolled-up sleeves. An ornery Paraguayan who did not seem inclined to go easy on a member of the Latin American judicial fraternity.

"A Mexican success story," Méndez continued, leaning closer to the glass. "From attorney general to bagman. And the *chilango* bootlicker for a sidekick."

Manacled in the chair next to Losada sat Senator Ruiz Caballero's pudgy private secretary, whom Méndez had last encountered on the tarmac at the Tijuana airport. His name was Rogelio Aragón. He looked as if he wished he had never been born.

The prosecutor and a Paraguayan military intelligence agent in fatigues and cowboy boots stalked back and forth in front of the prisoners, barking questions. Another military man with a towel around his neck recorded the answers on a dinosaur typewriter, flailing at keys that echoed like rifle shots.

There was a computer, dusty with disuse, on a table next to the typist. The table also held a suitcase that had been confiscated when Puente, the Mexicans and Paraguayan intelligence agents, acting on information from a wiretap, had arrested Losada and Aragón. The capture had taken place on a highway from the Asunción airport to Ciudad del Este. The Mexican functionaries had flown in from Mexico City with two bodyguards, off-duty Baja state police detectives who had resisted arrest and were now in the hospital.

The suitcase contained a million dollars.

"What a haul, Leo," said Isabel Puente. She paced in time with the interrogators beyond the glass. She turned to Facundo, who was reclined on a couch, a forest of black and gray chest hair blossoming out of his tropical shirt. "You think we can use some of that money to buy more enemies for Junior?"

"Oh, I think so, Miss Puente," Facundo said, fueling himself from his *mate* gourd. He lowered his voice with a nod at the interrogation room. "Once we subtract the prosecutor's, eh, expenses. In any case, we are chipping away. My men report that the police platoon has been removed from guard duty at the El Naútico Resort. The police don't like Junior's antics."

"Good." Méndez took a sip of foul coffee. He was pushing Junior in the right direction. He wanted to keep up the momentum. He picked up a notebook confiscated from Losada that contained a number for a satellite phone Méndez believed to be Junior's. "I think the time has come to harass Junior more directly."

"Meaning what, exactly?" Isabel asked, warily, in English.

"As the great Tijuana journalist Fernando Romero once said, 'When in Rome, *ponte cabrón*.'"

Minutes later, Losada and the Senator's secretary had been transferred from the interrogation room. They sat on the couch, looking a bit less miserable. Porthos handed the phone to Aragón.

"Have you got it?" Porthos growled. "Tell him what happened: You are in custody. Then hand the phone to the Licenciado. Is that clear?"

The prisoners nodded.

"And stop cringing like little girls. Nobody has laid a finger on you. Yet."

Isabel leaned against a wall, thumbs hooked in the belt of her jeans. Méndez gave her a conspiratorial wink as Aragón babbled something into the phone about bad news and heartfelt apologies. He held out the phone to Méndez.

"Hello? Aragón you idiot, hello?" Junior's mouth was too close to the phone. His voice sounded like it had during the recorded phone call: distorted, dazed, sick.

"This is Méndez."

Silence. He was starting to think Junior had hung up when he heard a cough.

"Méndez," Junior said.

"That's right."

"Am I supposed to be impressed?" Junior's tone was whiny and mocking. His breathing was noisy. "You expect me to piss myself?"

"Not unless you do that routinely."

"What do you want?"

"I want you to stop prolonging the inevitable. Surrender. Turn yourself in."

Méndez saw Porthos flash a surreptitious thumbs-up at Isabel.

"Very funny. Stop fucking around. Send me Aragón with my money. You've got nothing on him."

"Oh yes I do. I want to see the look on your uncle's face when he hears."

"Aragón is an employee of the Mexican Senate. You can't hold him."

"Watch me. This is going to make a stink in the D.F."

"No one would print it. No one cares what happens in Paraguay. You're dreaming."

"In any case, say good-bye to Aragón and his suitcase. Say good-bye to your Paraguayan police escort. You are losing friends fast."

Another silence. Méndez thought he heard the clink of ice cubes in a glass.

"Fine. Keep him. Keep the fucking money."

"I think I can find a worthy purpose for it."

"Fucking Diogenes. Nobody likes your attitude. Nobody will come to your funeral."

"Calm down. Take a Valium. I've got a proposition. If you want Aragón, I'll consider a trade."

"Trade?"

"Give me Buffalo Mendoza. And Pescatore, the yanqui. The cop-killer."

Isabel bounced off the wall and gestured incredulously at Méndez. He turned away.

"You think you have real big balls, talking to me like that," Junior said.

"I'm serious. It will buy you time with your uncle. He's had about enough of you. Give me those two, something to show the Americans. Enjoy your last vacation a bit longer."

A snort. "Listen, Méndez, it's been an immense pleasure, but that's about enough."

"Think about my offer."

After he hung up, Isabel pulled him aside. Her eyes flashed. "What in God's name were you thinking about with that offer for Valentine?"

"Perhaps it is a way to get him back, which I assume is what you want. At the least, it sows dissent, keeps them guessing."

"Or they could decide it's not worth sheltering a cop-killer, which he's not, by the way, and get rid of him."

"Isabel," Méndez said gently, "I think it's time you accepted that Pescatore has gone over to the other side."

"You don't know that. He's undercover, trying to survive."

"It may be too late. That comment the Senator made about housecleaning makes me think they have found out on their own that he worked as an informant for you, even if his heart was not in it. And the point of this whole complicated exercise, I am afraid to tell you, is not to rescue Valentine Pescatore."

25

ON THE LOOSE AT LAST, Pescatore headed straight for the border.

He bought a chocolate bar and a Chicago Bulls cap from a street vendor. He wolfed down the chocolate bar without really tasting it.

The cap was a pirated imitation. The bull looked more like a goat. He pulled the brim low. He walked fast.

The sidewalk was a tunnel formed by shops on his left, vending stalls on his right. He threaded through a manic crowd. He flinched every time someone jostled him. He imagined spies and pursuers everywhere, braced himself every time he saw a cop or a security guard. He got spooked by the drivers cursing in the congealed traffic, by eruptions of metal against metal as merchants yanked down burglar gates over storefronts. Ciudad del Este started closing early, no doubt for good reason.

The street dipped. The human current pushed him faster. The street emptied into a road that ran along the riverbank. Pescatore turned left toward the border crossing.

He heard an amplified guitar echoing among buildings, probably from one of the high-rise shopping galleries. Carlos Santana playing "Europa." The sweet sustained wail tugged at him. He knew that guitar solo note by note, like the words of a song. A wave of melancholy and nostalgia made him close his eyes momentarily. But then the music was swallowed up by a guttural symphony of motors, car horns and radios. And the sounds of another protest at the bridge: chants, a siren, an amplified voice. A tear-gas gun thudded; smoke billowed in the afternoon sunlight.

Pescatore zigzagged across the road into the weeds of the riverbank. He came to a kind of lean-to with a wood roof and an open front. It faced onto the border canyon and the torpid waters of the Paraná River below.

The structure resembled a bus-stop shelter, but three times as long. It was a way station, a loading depot for smugglers. And it was packed. An assembly line of shirtless men removed cigarette cartons from crates and wrapped them into bales. They sealed the bales with black tape and attached straps for backpack-style carrying. They helped smugglers hoist the prepared bales onto their backs. Once outfitted, however, the smugglers didn't go anywhere. They removed the packs and fiddled with them. They smoked cigarettes in the shade. They surveyed the Paraguayan riot police at the bridge and the Brazilian soldiers patrolling the opposite riverbank. They dozed.

Pescatore made his way into the shelter. He felt invisible. The smugglers all but averted their eyes as he passed. He assumed they were reacting to his vest: In the fashion code of the Triple Border, the vest labeled him as a Man With a Gun.

Pescatore found a spot next to a group of diminutive backpackers with straight black hair. They wore long-sleeved shirts despite the heat. He nodded and got polite nods in return. He wasn't an expert, but they looked to him like Bolivians. He had a flashback to that night in San Diego when Vince Esparza had complained about having to process "Bo-livians." If Pescatore could have rewound his life back to that moment, he would have made some different choices. Definitely different.

Crouching, he saw the wooden wall was smothered with graffiti. Knives and pens had scrawled profanities and boasts. But there was also political philosophy in multicolored spray paint: "*Viva El Jinete y los generales.*" "*Muerte al Jinete y los generales.*" "*Viva la democracia.*" "*El Jinete, los generales y la democracia son todos la misma mierda.*"

What now, Valentine? He calculated angles. They had taken away his new Paraguayan passport. He had no vehicle. No one he could trust. On the positive side, he had a couple of hundred dollars and a pistol. Also tucked into the pockets of his vest were Pelón's useless cell phone and Garrison's USB flash drive.

Otherwise, Pescatore had nothing. He was your basic undocumented alien. A tonk. What a joke on him.

Squatting on their haunches or sitting cross-legged in the dirt, the possible Bolivians listened to a man in a brown hat. The man apparently held rank in the microsociety of the loading depot. His seat of honor was an empty crate. His bony knees protruded from cutoff canvas shorts. His hat was a wondrous thing: a jaunty shape that evoked Fred Astaire or Frank Sinatra, but corduroy, decrepit, too small. It perched on lank gray hair. Tropical feathers poked out of the band.

"You're not getting across today, *compañeros,*" the man said. His age was indeterminate, but they had clearly been hard years. His rust-colored, nearly toothless face collapsed from his cheekbones to a pointy chin. Though he spoke Spanish, he sounded and looked Brazilian: a pretty even mix of European, Indian and African. "Another damned riot at the bridge. Might as well get some rest, get out of the sun. This mess won't clear up for a while yet."

Someone asked why.

"Politics." The man rubbed stubble, a street sage with skeletal wrists and elongated, misshapen fingers. "Politics. A big fight going on. Some Mexican mafiosos trying to take over. The Chinese are against them. The Arabs are divided. The police in the middle. And us little working people suffer. You try to earn a living..."

Pescatore scanned the slope leading down to the water. He could swim for it. He could find someone with a raft and pay his way over. Maybe there was a way to fly out. The place was full of secret landing strips. But he'd have to wait for nightfall. It was risky. If he got caught, chances were he'd get handed over to Junior's people or to Méndez's people. If he actually escaped, he'd have no control over what happened between Méndez and Junior. And he would break his word to Isabel one last time. Though that didn't mean much now that he knew about her affair with Méndez. Who really deserved his loyalty at this point: Isabel or Buffalo?

"And you, *argentino?*" The man in the hat gave Pescatore the once-over. "What's your story?"

"I need to cross," Pescatore blurted instinctively, affecting an Argentine accent.

"No papers?"

"No."

"You are Argentine, yes?"

"More or less."

The toothless mouth masticated that response. "Just you? No packages? Nothing complicated?"

Pescatore nodded, the flat eyes of the Bolivians on him. He felt a rush of hope. Maybe Mr. Hat could get him across. Pescatore needed a coyote.

"I can pay, no problem," Pescatore said.

"Well, that's good. You can pay. Congratulations." The man in the hat sneered, aware of their audience. Pescatore had breached etiquette, gone too fast. The man made a face as if preparing to sniff him. "You wouldn't be some kind of *milico,* would you? Snooping around?"

Milico, Pescatore figured, meant "cop" or "spy." He heard muttering. The unloading and loading had come to a stop. People were listening.

"Not me, man," Pescatore said, as nastily as possible. He

reached into his vest and gripped the butt of his holstered gun. He left his hand there. "How about you?"

He got a rise out of the way the man in the hat faltered, the sneer wilting. Pescatore considered drawing down on him, jamming the Glock into his ear just for fun. Pescatore no doubt looked as mean and desperate as he felt. The heat alone made him want to shoot somebody.

Macho thrills aside, he had worn out his welcome. Nobody here was going to help him.

"A very good afternoon to you, friends," Pescatore said. He straightened out of his crouch and left the shelter, ignoring the chatter in his wake. "Buncha criminals."

Pescatore advanced toward the bridge, scanning the river for smugglers on the move. Nothing. The Brazilians and Paraguayans had shut the line down cold. No wonder the citizens of Ciudad del Este were rioting. No wonder Junior was getting a bad rep. But still, how hard could it be to get out of town? Pescatore was an expert on border-crossing, wasn't he? In San Diego, he had seen it all. He had seen people use tunnels, speedboats, car trunks, human pyramids, truck-borne ramps that sent load cars soaring right over the fence.

The bridge to Brazil was guarded by a contingent of gas-masked riot cops who checked the endless single-file traffic and tossed occasional tear-gas canisters at the rock-throwing demonstrators. He caught a whiff of the stuff. That was all he needed. He reversed direction. He was in way over his head; too far to escape now.

He retraced his steps uphill. He couldn't spot anyone tailing him in the crowds. The *locutorio* was on a street corner near Galerías Alhambra, the shopping arcade where he had gotten his passport. The *locutorio* was a public-phone business. The red letters on the barred front window advertised cheap calling rates and wire transfers all over the Americas, the Middle East, Asia and Africa. There was a counter in front and six glass-partitioned cubicles with phones.

It was his third visit of the day, but the dour Asian lady behind the counter gave no sign that she appreciated his business. She handed him a slip of paper with the number of a phone cubicle on it.

The air-conditioning was not getting the job done. In the solitude of the cubicle, Pescatore dried his sweaty hands on his jeans. He wiped his upper lip with his sleeve. If he lived through this, the mustache was history. He closed his eyes and held his head in his hands. The pulse in his temples drummed against his palms. He pursed his lips and blew hard a couple of times. He remembered what Buffalo had said on the day Pescatore drove Garrison's corpse into Tijuana: Kick it. Kick it stone cold.

Pescatore placed a collect call to San Diego, California, USA. By now, the operator at the task force knew exactly who he was. She had been prepped for the call.

"Mr. Valentine, right?" she chirped. "Have you connected in a jiffy."

This time, the triangular patch-in to Isabel Puente back in Ciudad del Este took less than a minute.

"There you are," Isabel said.

"On time, right?"

"Ready?"

"To see you, yeah."

"Where?" He could tell she was wound up, forcing herself to go soft and smooth.

"There's a little department store. Minerva Mall. The only swank place in this sleazoid town. You know it?"

"Yes."

A tingle of confidence: It was the first time he was calling the shots. "Alright then. Let's say the fourth floor. Where the pianos are at."

"What time?"

"In an hour."

"OK."

"Just you and me, right?"

"We went through that already."

"I don't surrender to anybody but you."

"OK."

"What I'm saying is, I know your precious Méndez has got your back. I know that fucker don't trust me. But you keep him away until you and me can talk. I ain't talkin' to him. If him or his dirtbag *judiciales* get in my face, it's not gonna be pretty. You understand?" Pescatore fought the tremble in his voice.

"Just you and me, Valentine." He wanted to think he heard a glimmer of warmth when she said his name. "I hope I can trust you."

"Like old times, huh?"

"Six-thirty p.m.," she said. The line went dead.

Pescatore hung up. He picked up the receiver again. He punched out another number. It was difficult: His hands were out of control and tears blurred his vision.

26

ISABEL PUENTE ENDED THE argument by getting out of Facundo's car and marching toward the Minerva Mall.

Méndez regarded Porthos and Facundo. They looked like uneasy witnesses to a domestic dispute. Méndez lifted his narrow shoulders.

"What can I tell you?" Méndez said. "In the final analysis, she's the boss. What do you think of the setup, Facundo?"

"My men walked the store, top to bottom," Facundo said, shifting a toothpick rapidly from one side of his mouth to the other. "Seems clean. Could be worse."

"We could check it once more," Porthos said, glancing at his watch.

"The Minerva Mall is supposed to be neutral territory," Facundo said. "A gentlemen's agreement. The bosses want a place where they can take their mistresses without walking into a massacre."

"So you don't think Khalid would pull anything in there."

"Not Khalid. But I can't answer for young Mr. Ruiz."

"Or Pescatore," Méndez said, turning to Porthos. "He has a talent for catastrophe. If he so much as blinks, we shoot to kill, Comandante."

"With pleasure, Licenciado," Porthos said.

"Stay in constant touch by radio or I'll get neurotic," Facundo said. "Let's be quick about this."

Méndez adjusted the gun in his belt as he and Porthos hurried after Puente.

"It would be nice to have Athos here," Porthos said.

"Someone has to watch the hotel," Méndez said. "It's a calculated risk, I know. But Isabel is right: If Junior moves, we want to be on top of him."

Porthos glowered in a way that indicated he had had enough of Puente giving the orders. And I'm the one he expects to take control, Méndez thought. The apprentice pseudo–police chief.

The Minerva Mall was an apparition. A rectangular six-story salmon-walled alien spaceship. A cosmic joke plunked down in the middle of Ciudad del Este. The revolving door whisked them out of the rowdy streetscape into a marble-and-glass refuge. A pair of security guards, one male and one female, flanked the inside entrance. They resembled mannequins in crisp blue uniform suits. Their wet-look hairdos seemed frozen into place by the air-conditioning.

A multiscented blast of perfumes assaulted Méndez. The ground floor was devoted to cosmetics; the sales pods had neon-strength signs spelling out brand names in pink-and-white script. Like the security guards, the salespeople were young, well-scrubbed creatures from a different planet than the mob of peasants, merchants and pirates outside. Members of a Korean tour group were the only visible customers. They wore yellow visors and T-shirts adorned with the name of a Christian fundamentalist church in English and Spanish. They clutched thin bricks of cash.

Méndez caught up to Puente on the escalator. He felt the same flustered anxiety he had experienced once when his wife had blown up and walked away from him in public. He thought: What fun is a lovers' quarrel if we aren't lovers?

"Have you seen the prices in here?" he said. "The stuff must be real. They'd get shot selling fakes for that much."

When Puente turned, she was under control. The knuckle-biting, wet-eyed, name-calling fury had been wiped away. They glided onto the second floor: designer watches, jewelry, pens.

"I feel bad about losing my temper," she said.

"Me too."

"You admit that if we get Valentine back he's an incredible witness for us."

"Theoretically, yes. I'm just concerned about your safety."

"As usual. But you seem to have forgotten who's in charge."

"I remember being told this was a Mexican operation."

She snorted. "First, that doesn't mean you get to tell me what to do. Second, don't always believe everything they tell you in San Diego."

The third floor offered men's and ladies' garments and fur coats. Piano music got louder and closer above them.

"So in the final analysis," Méndez said, "you are an American."

"And proud of it."

He stumbled when the escalator reached the fourth floor; she deftly adjusted her feet to negotiate the landing without breaking eye contact.

There was a real live pianist. He was playing "Take the 'A' Train." Ordinarily a tune Méndez liked, but the interpretation was full of cheesy flourishes and rococo ripples. The pianist sat at one of six grand pianos arranged in a circle at the center of a marble mezzanine. The music echoed upward in an atrium topped by a skylight two floors above.

"So that's what gangsters buy for their mistresses," Méndez said. "Pianos."

"I wonder if anyone has ever bought one," Puente said.

The pianist was a senior citizen with a somewhat mildewed dignity. His backswept gray hair aspired to a Beethoven-like mane; he shook it occasionally for emphasis. His three-piece suit had a velvety sheen and looked no younger than him. A placard in Spanish, Portuguese and English informed shoppers that the pianist's name was Johann and that he gave private lessons, tuned pianos, performed at weddings, baptisms and funerals, and offered "musical consulting services" in all three border communities.

"Licenciado, Miss Puente, I'm going to take my position," Porthos said. "Where do you plan to meet... the young man?"

"I'll wait in that coffee bar. There's a wall to cover my back and it has a view of the escalator," Isabel said, indicating half a dozen tables and a counter.

"We'll monitor you from the fifth floor," Porthos said.

"Fine."

Porthos hurried off. The pianist segued into "The Man I Love."

"I had better get out of the way too," Méndez said.

Puente did not seem in a hurry to sit down. She looked exhausted. Méndez thought: After all that arguing, she's got doubts too, I know she does. She's afraid Pescatore will let her down once and for all.

"Isabel, do you believe him?" Méndez blurted. "You still trust him?"

She sighed. "His story is credible."

"So you think he managed to escape from Junior's entourage, just like that, and spend the night in hiding? And call you repeatedly without being detected?"

"That's not so hard to believe."

"You don't think Junior and Khalid could find him if they wanted to?"

"Maybe they aren't that interested. Junior's a wreck, we know that. And Khalid is keeping Junior at arm's length."

Méndez nodded dubiously.

"Good luck," he told her.

"This is about work," she murmured, eyes roving the atrium. "This is about the operation. My personal feelings are secondary."

Méndez covered his radio with his hand. He said: "Look,

we're here because I lost a friend. I don't want to lose another. Please be careful."

She nodded, wide-eyed.

Méndez rode the escalator up to the fifth floor. He positioned himself at the railing near the down escalator, overlooking the pianos. Porthos was in place at the opposite railing. Méndez checked in with Puente, Porthos, and Facundo on the radio. He raised Athos, who was camped out at his surveillance post outside the El Naútico.

"Signs of movement here, Licenciado," Athos reported. "They brought vehicles in front, ready to go. Whether it's the fat boy or not, if they proceed in your direction, I will too. We are only five minutes away."

"No," Méndez said. "You stay on the fat boy. Don't let him out of your sight, whatever happens."

Méndez watched the woman behind the counter bring Puente a cup of coffee. Puente stirred it without drinking.

The pianist had stopped playing. The silence in the atrium was startling.

The pianist sipped water. He stretched his arms, shooting his wrists out of frayed sleeves. He did a little head roll to work the muscles in his reedy neck. He gave a ceremonious nod and smile to Isabel, who was sitting about twenty-five feet away from him.

Hair bobbing and shining, the pianist hunched back toward the keyboard and got back to work. He played the opening bars of "Hello, Dolly."

27

As PESCATORE STEPPED OFF the escalator in the atrium of the Minerva Mall, the first thing he saw was a weird geezer at a piano playing "Hello, Dolly" and making a real racket.

The second thing he saw was a guy who looked like Méndez at the railing one floor above, pressed into the shadow of a pillar.

Which didn't surprise or bother him, because the third thing he saw was Isabel Puente. She wore tight leggings and a loose shirt. Her hair, black and abundant, was arranged with a barrette, bringing out the cheekbones that he remembered caressing once with his knuckles.

As she rose behind the table, it struck him how small she was, a tiny thing, really. And young—even though she always acted like he was the kid. She looked pale and unnaturally bulky; he spotted the outlines of a bulletproof vest under the shirt. Her right hand hovered near a shirttail, ready to draw. She was taking no chances with Valentine.

Nice reunion, he thought. Real touching.

When he embraced her, though, it blotted out everything else: Méndez above them like an ill-fed vulture, the images of Junior and Buffalo, the terrible things that had happened and that were about to happen.

Her left hand planted itself on his chest as if to fend him off.

But she kissed him back. Her mouth hot, her teeth gouging his lip. He held her close, dizzy with the cinnamon taste, her vest hard against him. He heard and felt her sobs. He clung to her, and the moment, as long as he could.

"I'm sorry," he whispered. "I'm sorry."

"Easy," she said, giving him a sweet final kiss. The small hand riding his chest propelled him backward. She disengaged. "Enough."

"Isabel, I never wanted to hurt you," he said. "I never ever had a choice. You just gotta trust me."

"Are you alright?" she asked curtly, still in a stiff-arm tactical stance.

"Isabel, we gotta get out of here. It's all gonna hit the fan."

"What do you mean?" She reached back, the moonlike eyes drilling him, and picked up a two-way radio from the table.

He improvised wildly, remembering bits of what he had scripted in his head. "On my way in I saw some of Khalid's boys in a vehicle. I think they saw me. We don't got much time."

Glaring at him, she spoke into the radio. The radio gave off agitated voices, street noises. He saw Méndez moving along the railing above, radio at his ear, and on the other side of the atrium the bearded *judicial* he had met in Isabel's apartment. The beefy cop had a gun in his hand, apparently not giving a shit about what anyone in the store might think. The piano music was driving Pescatore crazy.

"Facundo? Facundo, what's going on?" Isabel demanded.

An extremely loud voice echoed over the radio. Pescatore heard the faint but unmistakable crack of gunshots in the background. The Mexicans above sprinted for the escalator. Puente cursed.

"Come on! This way!" Pescatore exclaimed. He bolted, running past the pianos, hearing "Hello, Dolly" falter and finally come to a stop.

Puente called his name and gave chase, as he had known she

would. A saleswoman in blue pitched backwards out of his way. He blazed over marble past a row of female mannequins in bridal and communion gowns.

If there was one thing Pescatore was good at, it was running. He took sprint-relay strides, hands half-clenched as if pulling down strings, head pumping, back straight, despite the prospect that someone was about to put a bullet in it.

He rounded a corner hard, knocking a pile of boxes off a table, throwing a glance over his shoulder. Isabel pelted after him with Méndez and the big man well in the rear.

Pescatore found the freight exit by the elevator, just as they had planned it. He slammed through double swinging doors, skidded to a stop in front of a dank freight elevator fronted by cagelike mesh. He turned and drew his gun.

Seconds later, Puente kicked through the doors. She came in low and fast in a shooter's crouch. Pescatore made no move to raise his gun. His eyes locked on hers as she drew a bead on his chest. Right on the ten-ring. The best thing that could possibly happen would be for her to pull the trigger.

She didn't get a chance. Momo and Buffalo jumped her from either side of the doors, where they had been hiding.

Buffalo hadn't told Pescatore exactly where they would be. But his orders had been clear: Don't worry about us, we'll be there. You just lead 'em where I say. They'll be expecting a bunch of us outside, so we set up a diversion in the street. Meanwhile me and Momo sneak in and do our Delta Force thing.

The problem was that Junior had ordered them to capture Puente alive. So Momo grappled with her gun arm. Buffalo, holding his sawed-off shotgun, tried to help as he kept watch for the pursuers. She ducked and twisted, resisting furiously. She turned Momo in a circle. She headbutted him under the chin, driving him up and back.

Puente's gun hand pulled free. She shot Momo twice in the belly at flesh-scorching range. Buffalo slammed a fist on her head as if he were pounding a table. Puente and Momo went down together. Her gun clattered away on the floor.

Pescatore rushed up and got her in a chokehold. He backpedaled toward the elevator, dragging her. Buffalo bent quickly over Momo, who was motionless on his back. Buffalo rose and trained his shotgun on the swinging doors.

"You did good, homes," Buffalo rasped at Pescatore. "*Aguas,* they're comin'."

When Méndez and the other Mexican appeared beyond the swinging doors, advancing behind their pistols, Buffalo cranked off a shotgun blast that shredded wood and eardrums.

"That's as far as you get, *cabrones,*" he snarled. "Or we blow this lady's brains out. No closer."

Puente stirred and wriggled in Pescatore's grip. He put his mouth against her ear and hissed: "Just trust me. Hold still and don't do nothing."

Incredibly, Méndez showed himself in the doorway, straightening, his gun pointed down at the floor. He's got a death wish, Pescatore thought.

"Wait!" Méndez called in that schoolteacher tone that Pescatore hated. "Don't do anything stupid. I offer myself in exchange for her."

Lame dumbshit wannabe hero, Pescatore thought. Sacrifices himself for his chick.

"You're in no position to negotiate, motherfucker!" Buffalo retorted in English, his Spanish deserting him in the heat of the moment. "She just killed one of my boys. I oughta smoke her and you both."

Pescatore flinched, thinking the big man would turn the shotgun on Puente. But that wasn't the plan, and Buffalo knew it.

"You know what will happen if you kill an American agent," Méndez said. "Listen to me."

Pescatore could feel Isabel reviving, her small hard muscles bunching, elbows jabbing him. His mouth was full of her hair.

Her shoes scrabbled for leverage, planting her weight to unleash some kind of martial-arts move on him. Pescatore yanked her savagely up and back. He tightened his forearm against her throat. She gagged, a sound that made him feel as if he were being torn in half. Fighting down shame and revulsion, he put the barrel of his pistol alongside her head.

"Méndez," Pescatore heard himself shout in a faraway nightmare voice. "You want Isabel to live so damn bad, you shut up and do what we say."

28

PORTHOS IMPLORED HIM NOT to do it.

The stucco walls of the service hallway beyond the double doors created an echo. It was hard to hear. Pescatore and the massive *pocho* shouted threats and commands simultaneously. The radio on Méndez's belt gave off the frenzy of a gunfight in the street: Facundo's men versus a swarm of adversaries. He could hear Athos on the radio as well. And through it all, the gentle husky voice behind him begged him to stop.

"Please, Licenciado," Porthos said from behind the pillar where he had taken cover. "It's suicide, Licenciado."

But there was no doubt in Méndez's mind. It was his duty and his punishment. He had put too many others at risk. He stooped and laid the gun on the linoleum. The doors settled shut behind him, leaving Porthos on the other side.

"Now kick it over! Hurry up and kick it over!" Pescatore's face emerged from behind Puente, his gun arm stiff and shaking. He appeared to be choking her into unconsciousness.

Méndez put his foot on the gun and sent it skidding toward them. Buffalo roared at Porthos to keep back or he would blow a hole in his boss. Buffalo reached out, grabbed Méndez's shoulder and yanked him forward in a single motion that sent Méndez running-stumbling into the room-sized, roofless freight elevator.

They dragged Puente inside. The cage clanged shut. The elevator began to descend.

Watching Pescatore dump Puente into a corner, Méndez said: "Look, let her go while you can, before it's too late."

Pescatore whirled. Their faces were inches apart. Pescatore shifted his gun to his left hand, opening himself to attack, silently taunting Méndez to try something. Pescatore was half a head shorter than him; the young man's eyes strained up in their sockets.

"The fuck you think you're giving orders to, asshole?" Pescatore said.

Pescatore hit Méndez with three whip-fast punches that bounced Méndez off the wall. Méndez swung back feebly and Pescatore sidestepped. Still using only one arm, the agent delivered a methodical barrage of blows, chopping and pounding through Méndez's defenses. Pescatore was brutally strong for his size.

Méndez didn't remember falling. But the fact was that he was lying on his side. The floor smelled: grease, cigarettes, ammonia, work shoes. Blood filled his mouth and seeped from the back of his head. He was coated in sweat; the elevator was an oven. He saw Puente huddled in the corner, her knees drawn up, hair disheveled. Buffalo stood guard over her with the shotgun, legs planted like columns. A spectator to Pescatore's business with Méndez.

Méndez pointed up at Pescatore and spat blood. He enunciated carefully: "Fuck your mother, yanqui, traitor —"

Pescatore kicked him in the belly, cursing in Spanish and English. He was wearing hiking boots. The impact ignited a flame of pain that spread until Méndez's torso was a single fire. Méndez croaked, mouth open wide.

The lights of the elevator shaft starred and blurred above him, the way lights did when he wasn't wearing his contact lenses. Maybe one of his lenses had slipped off. He was going to need a new contact lens. Now that's a real problem, he thought.

Méndez started shaking his head and found he couldn't stop. Gears clanked and scraped as the elevator descended. A private rectangular hell.

"Valentín, that's enough." The big *pocho*'s voice was obscenely calm. Méndez saw the legs shift, the shotgun barrel dig into Puente's neck. Buffalo said: "Hey lady. Don't you get slick or it's over, understand?"

Puente sagged back in the corner. She had been watching from under her lashes, bracing for an opportunity. Buffalo said: "You beat him down good, Valentín. Like you wanted. Now finish him."

"Fuck that." Pescatore's boot lashed into Méndez's chest. He thinks I'm a soccer ball, Méndez told himself. Do I look like a soccer ball to you, *gabacho?* Méndez wanted to say, his jaw working against the filthy floor. He couldn't get enough wind.

"Come on, *ese,* Rufino's got the car waiting. The fellas got their hands full out in the street. Let's finish it. What're you doin', Valentín?"

The elevator groaned to a sudden stop. Pescatore's doing, Méndez assumed.

"You heard Junior," Pescatore declared. "Junior said he wanted us to cut off Méndez's ears. Cut 'em off, and make him eat them. And he said to call so he could listen while we did it."

29

THE ONE THING PESCATORE hadn't counted on was Buffalo punking out at the moment of truth.

Not Buffalo: the mechanic, Junior's pet robot killer. Now look at him: disobeying orders, hemming and hawing. Talking about let's just shoot him and get it over with.

Pescatore stood so he half straddled the prone Méndez. He looked incredulously at the big man, who had the shotgun trained on Puente.

"Whattaya mean, Junior won't care?" Pescatore demanded. "He said he was gonna make me eat my own ears if I messed up."

"Junior says a lotta crazy shit," Buffalo muttered.

"He was real clear about it. He said we keep Isabel alive. She's our insurance, a bargaining chip."

Pescatore glanced at Isabel. Her shirt top was askew, her cleavage swelling out of it just to torture him. Her eyes were luminous, implacable.

"*Cuanto te odio,*" she spat. How I hate you. A spear right in the heart, but it only took Pescatore a second to shake it off.

"Shut up, bitch," Pescatore retorted. He turned back to Buffalo. "And then Junior said we do the thing with the ears. On the phone, give him the play-by-play. Remember?"

Buffalo glowered. Méndez moaned at Pescatore's feet. The

Mexican had sure fooled him. In San Diego, Méndez had come off so cool and mean that Pescatore assumed he could handle himself. But it was a front. Méndez was a wimp. He probably hadn't been in a fight since the eighth grade, and lost every one before that.

Pescatore noticed that the knuckles of his own right hand were torn and bloody. The after-jolts of the beating he had administered to Méndez were still tingling through him. It occurred to him that it wouldn't take more than another round or two of punishment to finish off Méndez.

"Look, Valentin, it ain't personal for me," Buffalo said. "Maybe for Junior. For you because of the girl. For me it's just work. *Otro jale mas.*"

"But Junior said—"

"I know what he said," Buffalo snapped. "We can tell Junior Méndez got shot and we couldn't do nothing, this and that. No ear cutting. I hate that psycho shit."

"*You* want *me* to lie to the man?" Pescatore whooped shrilly, sounding to himself like Junior.

"No but..."

Pescatore was awed by his own recklessness. He was mouthing off to Buffalo a day after the big man had been on the verge of wasting him. Pescatore had turned the whole thing upside down. Buffalo put up with it only because the thought of lying to Junior tied him in knots.

"All I'm sayin' is, I think we better get with the program. Do what we were told."

"All right." Buffalo's face twisted in disgust. "You're right. Shit. Fuck."

"You got a knife, right?"

"Yeah. Here. Wait."

30

Méndez's palms were flat on the floor of the elevator. He pressed down as hard as he could. He got no results, like a man who has done too many push-ups.

He had decided to work up the strength to attack, force them to shoot him. He did not intend to provide Junior with any telephone-sadism thrills. And, a journalist to the last, Méndez did not want his son to grow up one day and read the stories about the way they had killed his father. Juancito's life would be hard enough without that kind of crime-tabloid indignity.

"Cover the girl, Valentín," Buffalo said, his voice floating somewhere above.

"I am. You gonna call Junior?"

Méndez couldn't get his body to cooperate. His mind either. He was having trouble staying focused on the duo of subhumans discussing the barbarity they were about to inflict on him. One too many blows to the head; he was drifting off.

An image took shape. From about a year ago: He had just been named chief of the Diogenes Group. He had kept an overdue promise and driven with his son to an empty beach near Ensenada. They had kicked around a soccer ball on a warm overcast day. Nothing elaborate, they hadn't even played that long. But his son had talked about it for weeks afterward.

Méndez was back on the beach now. But the memory slipped and mutated in ways he didn't like. The beach was no longer idyllic and solitary. It was crowded with strangers and people he knew. Instead of playing, Méndez was fretting. He scanned the crowd for enemies. He warned his son about getting too close to the water. He glared at all the idiots ruining his beach.

His son watched quizzically. Finally, Juancito trotted up to him with the ball under his arm.

"Don't worry so much, Papa," the boy said. "Just play."

Méndez laughed with relief. The boy tossed the ball. Méndez caught it on his foot. He started juggling, enjoying the simple pleasure of it. They headed the ball to each other. They kicked harder and harder, spreading out. His son's sturdy brown feet slapped the wet sand as he ran. They played and played until the beach emptied out and it was just the two of them again.

"Was he laughing just now?" Buffalo said.

Méndez wasn't sure what Juancito had really said. The ache of regret was so acute. The sensation that he had kicked the ball too far, that the game was over, was so real. Now he wasn't sure if the visit to the beach had really happened at all. If it was a memory or a dream.

"He ain't laughing. Look at 'im, he's crying," Pescatore scoffed. "Least he will be in a minute. When he's chewin' on them ears."

31

PESCATORE WATCHED BUFFALO lean the shotgun against the wall. He watched Buffalo pull a hunting knife and a cell phone from his belt. Time to call the boss, as ordered.

Buffalo squinted at the phone. He pressed numbers one-handed. He made a quick pass with the flat of the knife on his denim-clad thigh, wiping both sides of the blade.

That was when Pescatore extended his gun arm full-length. He opened fire from a distance of two feet. Maximum. So easy. Nothing to it.

The shots were explosions within explosions within explosions. The echoes were magnified hugely by the elevator shaft. The bullets spun Buffalo around and slammed him into the wall. Pescatore fired and fired, feeling the sound vibrate in his teeth and bones.

Buffalo shuddered and twitched. He slid down the wall. He came to rest in a slump, his weight on one knee. His thick, muscular haunches and legs bunched under him, forming a fulcrum that kept him upright.

His eyes full of smoke and his ears full of pain, Pescatore counted nine discharges. He stopped shooting. Buffalo stayed where he was. Half on the floor, half against the wall.

Pescatore stepped close and inspected him, gun at the ready. There was no doubt the big man was dead.

Even though he hadn't really fallen. Even though his face was pressed up against the metal as if he were listening intently to something on the other side. As if he were taking a quick breather before getting back to work. He was suspended in time and space forever.

Nobody's badder than Buffalo, Pescatore thought. Dead, but not down.

Pescatore reached into his own shirtfront with his left hand. He extracted the woven jailbird crucifix he had bought from the old Maria at the border crossing in Tijuana. He ducked his chin and worked the black necklace up over his head. Gingerly, he draped the cross over Buffalo's shoulder.

32

THE THUNDER OF THE GUNSHOTS was like another beating, a giant stomping his skull.

When it finally subsided, Méndez opened his eyes. He came slowly to the realization that the shots had not been meant for him.

Porthos saved the day, he thought for a moment. But the elevator was between floors and the doors were closed; no new arrivals.

It occurred to Méndez that perhaps Puente had grabbed a gun. But she was still slumped against the wall. Like Méndez, she was trying to make sense of what she saw: Pescatore standing over the grotesquely crouched hulk that had been Buffalo.

Pescatore turned. He went on one knee beside Puente. He touched her cheek with two knuckles. He whispered to her.

She closed her eyes. She kept them shut tight, tears spilling from beneath the lids.

Pescatore stepped over to Méndez, who cringed. But there were no more kicks or punches.

Pescatore bent close. His voice was almost unrecognizable. It had acquired a fearful serenity.

"See that, Méndez?" Pescatore said. "He looked out for me. Saved my life a couple times. That's what he gets for trustin' me. And I liked him a whole lot better than I like you."

Part Five

IN THE LABYRINTH

33

EVER SINCE HIS DAYS AS a teenager on Taylor Street, Valentine Pescatore had carried with him the foreboding that, despite his hopes for a career in law enforcement, he would one day land behind bars.

Pescatore's uncle Rocco, the Chicago Police lieutenant, had wanted his nephew to be a cop. He had done his best to help him toward that goal. But he often said: "Val, if you don't stop acting like a *stronzo,* you are gonna end up in the joint."

Pescatore's cell wasn't Alcatraz. It didn't have rats or vermin, just wall-hugging lizards. It smelled moldy, but not nasty. You could see palm fronds through the bars, flashes of color as a jungle bird hopped around. Although the holding cell in the headquarters of the Gendarmería, the Argentine border police, was intended for multiple customers, he had it all to himself.

But it was, in fact, the joint.

Pescatore heard the guard approach, keys jangling. The guard was broad-backed and ham-necked in sweaty green fatigues. Pescatore had decided that there were two types of Argentines: the Italian-looking ones and the Mexican-looking ones. The guard belonged to the second category. He sounded relaxed and countrified.

"What's the matter, *caballero?* You don't like the menu?"

Pescatore swung up to a sitting position. "I'm not hungry."

With a grunt of exertion, the guard pulled the breakfast tray back under the bars and carried it away. Pescatore crossed his ankles. His legs felt warm in the square of sunlight that fell through the high barred window. After two days in the cell, he was in no hurry to leave. It was safe. It was calm. He had done a lot of thinking.

He had not seen Méndez or Puente again after the three of them had stumbled out of the freight elevator in Ciudad del Este. Cops and soldiers had swarmed the Minerva Mall. The commanders of the Diogenes Group had handcuffed Pescatore. Athos had killed some guys in a shoot-out outside the mall. A convoy sped Pescatore out of Paraguay and through Brazil into Puerto Iguazú, Argentina, where they questioned him at the Gendarmería base.

To Pescatore's surprise, the Mexican cops had not smacked him around. The interrogators switched off: Athos alone, Athos and Porthos, Porthos and a big swarthy Argentine in plainclothes who had his arm in a sling and resembled a hard-boiled salesman. Officers of the Gendarmería came and went during the interrogations. Athos and Porthos had refused to tell Pescatore what had happened or what was in store for him. They shook their heads when he asked for a chance to talk to Isabel, maybe send her a note.

Nonetheless, Pescatore had answered all the questions: about the assassination of Araceli Aguirre, Junior's contacts with Khalid, what kind of sat phone he had seen Junior use. His answers were clear and detailed. It occurred to him that Isabel might be in the next room, behind the one-way glass, watching. In any case, he had no reason to hold anything back.

He eased himself up off the bunk and did push-ups. The guard returned, this time accompanied by Athos and Porthos.

"Good morning, Comandantes," Pescatore said.

"Good morning, *muchacho.*" Porthos sounded affable but wary.

No handcuffs this time. They walked him to the interview room with the pale green walls and one-way glass on his left. He sat at the weathered white table.

The Mexicans did not sit. Pescatore was not surprised when Leobardo Méndez came in.

"Young Valentín," Méndez said. He carried a coffee cup on a saucer.

"How are you, Licenciado?" Pescatore tried to say the title with grave respect, the way the Mexicans said it. He spoke in Spanish; Méndez answered in English.

"More or less all right."

Méndez settled stiffly into a chair, grimacing. His face had been redecorated by the pounding Pescatore had given him. Yellowish-purple bruises smeared his left cheek and spread up his forehead into the gray-tufted hair. His lower lip was puffy. Stitches peeped out of a bandage stained with dried blood that covered half of his left eyebrow. The nose, big and vulnerable as it was, had survived intact.

"Sorry about that ass-kicking," Pescatore said.

The Mexican's eyes narrowed. "A somewhat peculiar apology."

Pescatore started to answer, but Méndez turned his attention to the other three. Méndez won the telepathic argument: Porthos, Athos and the guard trooped to the door.

"We will be right outside," Athos said, looking hard at Pescatore.

"Thank you," Méndez said.

Pescatore sat up. The last thing he had expected was a one-on-one. He wondered wildly if Méndez was going to take a swing at him, challenge him to a rematch. He wanted no part of it.

Méndez sipped coffee slowly, regarding Pescatore with the cup held aloft.

"I suppose I should thank you," Méndez said. "Of course, it

is a curious way to save someone. Dragging them into a… *emboscada.*"

"Ambush."

"Yes."

"It was the only way to play it."

"I see."

"You don't have to believe me." Pescatore kept his voice even. "But that's the truth. How… Is Isabel OK?"

"Yes." Another long sip.

Pescatore adjusted himself in the chair. He had blamed Méndez for all his troubles. He had been convinced that Méndez hated him right back. But now the Mexican seemed at ease. He wasn't acting like he finally had his most-wanted gringo enemy in his clutches.

Méndez touched the bandage on his eyebrow, the fingers probing gingerly. "The only way. It was all part of your plan, what happened in Ciudad del Este."

"I told your officers already. Junior and Buffalo made me set you up. I didn't have no choice. And it was the only way I could try to stop 'em. They were surveilling me the whole time. I did what they told me. I made my move when they made theirs."

"At the last minute."

"Yeah." Pescatore was grateful for a chance to tell the truth. "That thing with the ears, man…"

"Yes?"

"I did it to get the drop on Buffalo. To get him to put the gun down. You know I wouldn'ta let him do that to you."

"Do you want to know my theory?" Méndez gazed into his coffee cup. "From the beginning, when you start working for Isabel, you improvise. Playing both sides. I think you don't know what you were going to do."

Méndez's fists clenched. Maybe he wanted some physical payback after all. He continued: "You are not stupid, but present-oriented. Reacting purely to the moment. Your life is like this.

Always a double agent. You did not know until you shot El Búfalo if you would help us or kill us."

"Bullshit," Pescatore snapped. He cursed himself for losing control. The truth was he wasn't sure what he had been thinking in the elevator. He had been swept up in his double masquerade, in his fury at Méndez and everyone else who had been messing with him. Though he had known it was inevitable, he had staved off the decision to kill Buffalo as long as he could.

"You don't know me," Pescatore said. "You're a smart guy, I give you credit. But, you don't mind me saying so, you got a problem with me. Maybe that makes you not so smart."

The eyebrows raised unevenly because of the bandage. "Really."

"You look at me, all you see is a Border Patrol agent. The worst kind of gringo. You got these ideas, they get in the way. You don't see *me*."

The silence discouraged him, but Pescatore kept going. "My intentions were good, Méndez. I messed up plenty. But I did the right thing in the end."

Méndez studied him. "What was that you said in the elevator about El Búfalo? You liked him?"

Pescatore spoke carefully, his throat tightening. "He looked out for me. Said he owed me, because I helped out his cousin one time. So I felt like I owed him."

"An assassin. Junior's Doberman."

"He wasn't like Junior: it was just work to him. At least Buffalo had a code. And that's more than I can say about a lotta people I been dealing with. On both sides of the line."

"But you killed him."

"I got a code too, believe it or not."

After a long minute, Méndez shrugged. "Fair enough."

"What does that mean?"

"I am glad you made the right choice, whatever your reasons."

"So you appreciate me saving your life."

"Yes, Valentín. Even if it was an accident."

When Méndez grinned, he looked younger. He had the air of an underfed wolf: graying hair, lined face, red-streaked eyes. The blue sweater and slacks weren't fancy. Méndez was the first high-ranking Mexican cop Pescatore had seen without any flash to him: no Rolex, no gold, no designer labels.

"I guess maybe I was wrong about you," Pescatore said. "Isabel said you were good people."

"You should have listened to her."

"Méndez. You gotta help me out with one thing..."

"*Oye, muchacho.* I am not your sentimental counselor."

"Listen: This is hard for me to say. I know about you and her."

Méndez's lip curled. Pescatore stammered: "I hated you for a while, but not anymore. I'm not jealous. I just want a chance to talk to her, apologize for real, you know?"

"There is nothing sillier than a young man in love, is there?" Méndez growled, switching to Spanish. "A deluded young American."

"I'm kinda embarrassed to get into this now," Pescatore muttered. "But Junior and Buffalo told me about it. They had real good sources, somebody in the USG."

Méndez shook his head. "I am married. I have a family. You have a delusion. Isabel Puente is a marvelous woman. Strong, enchanting"—Méndez relished the words, lording them over Pescatore—"and a true friend. Nothing more. Your problems are your own."

Damned if he's not telling the truth, Pescatore thought. He resisted the urge to look at the one-way glass. Was she on the other side listening?

"Good news for me," Pescatore said weakly, switching to Spanish as well.

"You think so?"

"Will she talk to me?"

"She is busy. And she is less philosophical than me. Mexicans have a lot of endurance. But she wants to give you the beating you deserve." Méndez finished the coffee with a shudder. "Is that all you are worried about?"

"Not much I can do, right? Are they going to keep me locked up?"

"Me, no. I do not presume to speak for the Americans. Probably not."

Pescatore swallowed. "You mean it?"

"In the final analysis, you saved our lives."

"I guess I'm luckier than I deserve."

Méndez raised his hand, palm up, in a you-said-it gesture.

"But listen," Pescatore said. "What about Junior?"

"We raided his hotel with the Argentine Gendarmería. In a helicopter. An outrageous invasion of Paraguayan sovereignty, I must say."

"And?"

"Ruiz Caballero was gone. After he sent you and the *pochos* after us, he ran. My men disobeyed my orders and came to the Minerva Mall to help me."

"But he told us to bring him Isabel."

"A ruse. If you killed us, all the better. But he wanted to be sure the Americans would chase you and Isabel, not him. That is why he told you to keep her alive. He sacrificed Buffalo and the *pochos* in order to ensure his escape."

"Scumbag. What about Khalid?"

"Our information is that he helped organize Junior's exfiltration. He gave Junior a big *abrazo,* put him on a plane and told him to never come back. Khalid no longer finds Junior amusing."

"Any idea where Junior went?"

Méndez grimaced. "At this point I have to rely on your government."

"So what's the deal? Why don't we—uh, you guys get after him and lock him up?"

"Would you like to help?"

"Damn right. I hate that fat psychotic bastard."

Méndez reached into a shirt pocket and pulled out a small USB flash drive. Pescatore remembered that Porthos had found it while frisking him. He spotted a speck of dried blood on it.

"What can you tell me about this, Valentín?"

"It's Garrison's, right? I grabbed it after he got shot. I never got a chance to look at it, tell you the truth. I been carryin' that thing all over the place."

"Isabel and I went through the contents carefully. She almost had a seizure."

"Yeah?"

"It contains a list of Garrison's contacts." Méndez lowered his voice with a touch of sarcastic melodrama. "There are names and numbers and e-mail addresses that are very curious. They do not make sense for Garrison to have. Neither as a Border Patrol chief nor a mafioso. People in government, politics, embassies, names in Washington, Virginia, Mexico, Central America. Also items that appear to be instructions to Garrison, reports from Garrison, coordinates for meetings and communication procedures."

"What's that all about?"

Méndez smiled slyly. "I am just a paranoid leftist Mexican journalist with a gun. But Isabel is a serious, responsible investigator. She is convinced that Garrison was an agent or source for American intelligence."

"Wow." Pescatore scratched his unshaven jaw. "He was always talking about his contacts. He had this reputation in the sector, like he was untouchable. And he was Special Forces way back when."

"Exactly."

"That would explain how he got away with so much," Pescatore said excitedly. "I know you're not a big fan of The Patrol, Licenciado, but the fact is I never met any other agents that did crazy stuff like Garrison and his crew."

"You say you want to help. Fine. I am sure you will make yourself useful."

Pescatore felt overwhelmed. In the space of a few minutes, through some process beyond his understanding, he had gone from being a jailbird to part of the posse. And apparently he had Méndez to thank for it.

34

MÉNDEZ KNEW.

He had known from the moment Puente told him that the Americans had located Junior. Daniels, the Justice Department boss, had told her to come back. Junior was "under control." Méndez knew something strange was going on.

Puente knew it too. But she declined to speculate during a day of flight time: Foz to Rio de Janeiro, Rio to Los Angeles, Los Angeles to San Diego.

The federal complex in San Diego was crowded with lawyers, clients, cops, bureaucrats and criminals. The beauty of the sunny morning made Méndez, still sore from his injuries, especially glad that Pescatore had come to his senses in the end.

"So now all the questions get answered," Méndez murmured to Puente.

"Hope so," she said, leading the way into the lobby. She wore a long tight skirt and more makeup than Méndez had ever seen her use.

Athos, Porthos and Pescatore brought up the rear. As they crowded into the elevator, Pescatore gave Méndez a rueful smile. Although the comandantes had kept him on a short leash, Pescatore was no longer a prisoner. He had been a model of good behavior, Méndez had to admit. The beseeching looks the kid directed at Puente were enough to move a stone to pity.

But not Puente. She had avoided acknowledging Pescatore's existence since they had left the Triple Border. She simply looked through him with an icy composure that made Méndez glad he wasn't on her bad side.

It was eerie to be in an elevator again with Puente and Pescatore. The incident with Buffalo in Ciudad del Este was the kind of experience from which you don't recover in a long time, if ever. The three of them had crossed a blood-drenched border together, a bond uniting them whether they liked it or not. To his surprise, Méndez found he could not work up the energy to despise Pescatore; he accepted the younger man's explanation. When Méndez had mentioned this to Puente during the flight to Los Angeles, she had declared that the beating had scrambled his mind. She said she would never forgive Pescatore for deceiving her.

"The thing is, he wants badly to apologize to you," Méndez had whispered in the darkened airplane cabin. Their faces glowed in the light of the touch-controlled TV screens installed in the seat backs.

"Too bad," she retorted. "He's lucky he isn't going to the penitentiary. He's unstable. He's a childish thug. I'm amazed he gets sympathy from you, Leo."

"Something he said, about my ideas getting in the way of what I see. He's not dumb."

"No?"

"All I am saying, Isabel, is that emotionally it might be good for you to hear what he has to say. To put the thing to rest."

"It would be a sign of weakness. Besides, we have important things to worry about."

Puente emerged from the elevator ready to deal with important things.

Daniels waited in a conference room with an aide. He greeted them with much shoulder-patting and arm-gripping. They sat at tables that were arranged in a square and laid out with coffee and pastries.

"Congratulations, Mr. Méndez," Daniels beamed. "Hell of a job. I'm so glad you're all OK. You folks were great. You thoroughly disrupted and dismantled the Ruiz Caballero organization down there in Paraguay. You have the thanks and gratitude of my government."

In the windows, office towers gleamed. Glass and sun and sky created aquarium hues. The Federal Building made Méndez feel resentful and insignificant, conjuring comparisons to the rickety outposts of justice in Tijuana with their 1970s decor and vague odors.

Daniels fit the view. He wore a charcoal-gray double-breasted suit with a regal white shirt collar and steel-colored tie, reminding Méndez again of a bandleader. Daniels did not appear to have had the misfortune of perspiring in a long time. His supple fingers hoisted a plastic coffee cup with flair. He turned eating a doughnut into a dignified exercise.

Nonetheless, he did not look comfortable. The painkillers and the trip had slowed Méndez's thought process, but also lent it a slow-motion clarity. He realized what was bothering him: He had expected the U.S. Attorney to be there with Daniels. He had expected prosecutors, bosses from Isabel's task force, agents. Anyone who might want a piece of an event as career-friendly as the capture of Junior Ruiz Caballero.

"Thank you for your kind words," Méndez said. "Actually, I very much hope I could congratulate you. I understand you have news about Junior."

Daniels smiled blandly. "I was just getting to that."

A pause. Daniels's smile did not waver. Méndez saw Puente's thumb go to her teeth momentarily. She said: "Where is he, sir?"

"Southern California." Daniels could have been talking about the weather.

Puente smiled uncertainly. Athos and Porthos looked at Méndez, who made a quizzical face. Pescatore sat low in his chair.

"Well, that's wonderful," Puente said. "Isn't it? Is he under arrest?"

"As I told you, we've got him located and under control." Daniels crossed his long arms and leaned back.

Méndez decided he wasn't going to say another word until Daniels stopped his dance. Puente seemed torn between treating Daniels like a boss or a suspect.

"Under control?" Puente asked.

"We know where he is and we're watching him. And he knows it. As a leader of a criminal enterprise, he's neutralized."

"But he's free." Her exasperation overcame her deference. Her voice rose. "Why?"

Daniels made a ruminative noise. He got up, put his hands in his pockets and took a couple of steps into the enclosure within the square of tables. He bowed his head pensively, like a professor or a trial lawyer. It occurred to Méndez that Daniels must have been a wizard in the courtroom.

"Look," Daniels said. "I'd love to pop him. That's why I sent you all after him in the first place. If you recall. And let's examine what you've achieved." He ticked off fingers: "You brought about the arrest, off the record, of the top suspect in Mrs. Aguirre's murder, Commander Rochetti. Buffalo was the other top suspect, and he's dead. You broke up a major alliance in South America that was moving dope and guns and people and contraband all over. An alliance that had terrorist potential. Now the meanest, baddest people in the Ruiz Caballero organization are in jail, dead or running. All that in a few weeks. None too shabby."

He looked at each of them, let it sink in. "But what about

Junior Ruiz? Well, it's complicated. Political. You chased him out of the tri-border region. We were ready to scoop him up. Then red lights start flashing. Big red lights."

"What does that mean?" Puente asked. "Why can't we finish what we started?"

Daniels propped himself on a table. His head went up and his smile disappeared, a boxer coming off the ropes. "Because Washington doesn't want us to."

"Why not?"

"Because Mexico City doesn't want us to."

Méndez smiled maliciously. He searched for the words, wishing his accent weren't so strong. "Since when do you care in the least what Mexico City wants?"

Daniels sighed. "Mr. Méndez. This is painful for me. Your friend was assassinated. You damn near lost your life. You're a brave and honest man. I'm sorry to tell you that the politicians do care, very much, what Mexico City thinks. Back when I organized this, I said it had to be a Mexican operation. The presidential elections are coming up in Mexico. There's instability, economic dynamics. A delicate time. We have to go slow."

Méndez caught Puente's eye, thinking he should cede on her turf, but she nodded.

"So what you are saying, we chased Junior half of the way across the world, and here he is," Méndez said. "Under your nose. And it is finished? All for nothing?"

"You've built a strong case. It's a question of political timing in Mexico."

"Political timing. After the elections, perhaps?"

"Perhaps."

"What if the presidential candidate of the Ruiz Caballeros is elected? What if another candidate is elected and they buy him, or kill him? Will the timing be better?"

"I'm a prosecutor, not a politician. I couldn't answer that."

Méndez turned to Athos and Porthos with a mirthless laugh.

In Spanish he said: "You understand, right? You follow this? Suddenly the big machos are little girls."

"What...," Daniels began, but something had burst inside Méndez. His English started to fail him when he got agitated.

"Isabel, please translate for me," Méndez continued in Spanish. "I want to be precise and clear. Just now you said it was delicate, Mr. Daniels. My ex-boss said something like that a few weeks ago, about Junior. The Secretary is not a criminal. But he is an instrument of the mafia. I was disappointed but not surprised when he let me down. But the one thing, the one thing, I have relied on is you Americans. Your satellites, computers, money. Your ideas of right and wrong. You decided I was a good Mexican. So you did everything to help me catch the bad Mexicans. You were overbearing, you weren't flexible, you stomped around making mistakes. But you were always there, pushing. I never expected you to back down. Now we find out how far the power of the Ruiz Caballeros really extends."

Isabel translated as he spoke. Daniels jammed his hands deeper into his pockets.

"I'm not going to bullshit you," Daniels said. "The Ruizes have contacts in D.C. The uncle lined up a top law firm, one of the best."

"Of course," Méndez said in English. "The Senator made a deal. *Un arreglo.* Imagine all the investments they have in this country. Billions of dollars of business with Americans. Very embarrassing, no? Unfortunate connections, inconvenient friends. Boxing, music, banking, politics."

"All I know is, there have been serious back-channel conversations on Junior's behalf."

"In fact, you don't have him under control. He has you under control."

"Yet and still. There's political timing and there's police timing. Meanwhile, you'll be taken care of"—Daniels gestured at Athos and Porthos—"as far as immigration status, lodging, whatever you need. The Mexican authorities have assured me that the shooting of the state police officers in Tijuana will be ruled self-defense. And Ms. Puente, after your performance on this case, you can pretty much write your ticket as far as your next assignment, city, agency. You name it."

Daniels had praised and tempted her at one stroke. Méndez thought: Can I blame her if she jumps to the winning side?

"That's very nice of you, sir," Puente said. "But I can't focus on that now. We've put Mr. Méndez and his men in a great deal of danger. It looks to me like we did it mainly because we wanted that alliance between Junior and Khalid broken up. Now the dirty work is done, and we abandon him. I feel ashamed of what I'm hearing in this room."

"Now, Ms. Puente, that's not fair," Daniels said, forehead creasing with the first traces of irritation. "We pulled out all the stops to catch Junior down there. That Argentine operative we set you up with is the best intel asset in the region. You can't imagine the interagency hoops I jumped through. He got you real close, didn't he?"

Méndez flashed back to Facundo at the airport, his arm in a sling, teary-eyed, as he bear-hugged them one at a time. He felt a rather Argentine pang of nostalgia.

"I grant you that," Puente said. "But we have to answer Leo's question. What now?"

"We wait," Daniels said. "We hope. This has been a big buildup to a big disappointment. This kind of thing, frankly, makes me think about going back to the private sector."

Daniels straightened, turned and walked back around the table. He sat heavily, his body language announcing that everything worth saying had been said.

Méndez went over to a window. Business suits flowed across a grassy esplanade toward restaurants with the wooden facades typical of the Gaslamp district. Although the Federal Building made him resentful, it had made him feel powerful too. He always had the sensation of feeding off its energy. With the yanquis behind him, his attempt to pass himself off as a policeman could succeed. Now it was over. At the same time, he felt a grim satisfaction. He should have trusted his instincts. There would be no more playing cop. But that didn't mean he had run out of weapons.

"Let me mention something we have not discussed until now," Méndez said slowly. "It has become clear to me that the Ruiz Caballeros have allies inside your government. More than one person. Traitors. We have come across some very explosive information. This should concern you."

Daniels glanced at Puente, who returned the look evenly. Daniels shrugged.

"It does concern me. Look, Mr. Méndez, we all need to calm down. If it's comforting for you to make me the villain, fine. But I am in your corner. I will continue to be in your corner. The problem is that I am just the messenger. And I've said pretty much what there is to say."

35

THEY MET THE REPORTER at a Cuban restaurant on Morena Boulevard.

The five of them crammed into Isabel Puente's work vehicle, a Crown Victoria. Jammed into the backseat between Athos and Porthos, Pescatore noticed Puente glancing at rearview mirrors, scanning the traffic. He felt disoriented. These were Tijuana-style precautions. As if the pursuers had become the pursued. As if the border had been erased.

The restaurant was an agreeable space next to a Latin food market. Family memorabilia—diplomas, passport pages, black-and-white photos—were enclosed in glass cases like a tiny immigration museum. The reporter was waiting at a secluded corner table reserved by Puente. Her name was Steinberg. She wore a sweater and jeans.

Pescatore did not have experience with reporters. Méndez had said this one knew what she was doing. It was clear she took the meeting seriously: Her pale blue eyes laser-focused on Méndez and the sheaf of printed pages he handed her. They both spoke in Spanish.

"For your reading pleasure," Méndez said.

"You want me to read it right now?" Steinberg asked. "I can't have a copy?"

"Unfortunately, not yet. Take your time. Let's order something."

Steinberg barely looked at the menu, ordering a fruit shake and a sandwich. She bent over the pages. One hand pushed her blond hair up onto her head and stayed there.

The rest of them waited, toying with their food. Pescatore watched Puente out of the corner of his eye. She looked tired but beautiful, sunglasses propped in her hair. Her thumb was up against her teeth. She still wasn't speaking to him, except to snap an occasional order. Even then she avoided eye contact, as if the sight of him made her sick. As long as she let him stick around, though, he figured it was a step in the right direction. So Pescatore had acted like part of the team and kept his mouth shut—except when they asked him questions. They had asked him a lot of questions, especially Méndez. He had done his best to answer, just as he had in the jail in Argentina. The setting was nicer this time: Puente's apartment. Pescatore had dreamed about the place for weeks, their Crown Point love nest. But the reality of the return had been depressing.

The reporter finished reading. She smiled uneasily. She's tough but she's scared, Pescatore thought.

"Incredible," Steinberg said, a tremor in her voice. "Does anyone else have this?"

"Only you," Méndez said. "My Mexican journalist friends will never forgive me. But anything like this published exclusively by an American newspaper will have five times more impact than if it appears in both countries."

"Where is Junior exactly?"

"The San Diego area. The FBI and DEA have been shackled by politics. Senator Ruiz Caballero's friends have convinced the Americans that the very stability of Mexico is at stake. If the Ruiz Caballeros fall, they take the country down with them. Nonsense, but there you have it."

"God." Steinberg switched to English. "Um, Ms. Puente. I

know you're already quoted here. But you're willing to be quoted by name, in my paper, as a U.S. official?"

"That's right," Puente said. She had agreed to the sit-down with the reporter, but it went against all her reflexes and training.

"It's extremely important to have American officials on the record," Steinberg said.

"I know." Grudgingly, Puente added: "I can connect you with two supervisors in the task force. To verify the story. No names, just backup."

"Great." Steinberg flipped open a white spiral notebook.

Méndez asked: "Can you publish this in its complete form?"

Steinberg put the pen down. "I have to be honest, Licenciado. My paper isn't going to publish a story by you. They'll want me to write my own article, based on your account."

"That's not the same thing," Puente said sharply.

"I have to recast it for an American audience," Steinberg explained. "A lot of names, connections, it has to be simplified. But I think my paper will publish an excerpt or shorter version. Your story will be the basis of whatever I write."

Méndez looked disappointed. Pescatore knew he had poured his heart into it. After interviewing Pescatore and the others, Méndez had spent the night writing at his hotel.

Méndez said: "In Mexico, it might have been reproduced word for word. But I am sure you will do a fine job."

"I'd really like to know more about Garrison and his intelligence activity. Details."

"We'll see. You always have to hold something in reserve."

"I'll have to ask the U.S. Attorney's office for comment."

"Of course," Méndez said. He reached out and turned to the last page. "Do me a favor: If at all possible, use this section in what you publish."

Steinberg read out loud: "'In Mexico, it is fashionable to talk about corruption, about narco-politics. About how nothing will change until the real bosses fall: the elite who run business and politics with the help of the gangsters. Everyone talks, but nothing happens. I have known for years that confronting men like the Ruiz Caballeros was the true test of Mexican democracy. Only recently did I discover that it is a test of democracy in the United States as well.'"

Steinberg looked up. "I'll use it. Thanks for having faith in me."

Méndez chuckled. "I hope you still want to thank me when it's over."

"After reading this, the person I really need to talk to is Agent Pescatore," Steinberg said. She turned toward him, her pen poised. "I mean, you were on the inside, you saw so much. You'll go on the record too?"

Pescatore glanced at Puente. "Uh, sure. I—"

"We're all in agreement," Puente interrupted, her voice flat. "We're at your disposal."

Pescatore sat up straight. He tried to look respectable and serious. It was showtime.

Méndez startled him by putting a hand on his forearm. "Don't forget, Valentín, you are the most vulnerable of all of us."

"How you figure that?"

"Your age, your rank. You don't have political connections. You were publicly accused of crimes. Your information has been very valuable. But think hard about the risks involved before you speak."

Isabel rolled her eyes. The blonde looked disconcerted.

Méndez sounded reluctantly protective, as if he felt honor bound to speak up. His words warmed Pescatore's heart. They also worsened his fears that these shenanigans would lead to prison. But he wasn't going to bitch out now.

"That's fine," Pescatore told Méndez. He said to the reporter: "It's the least I can do for the Licenciado. He's a stand-up guy."

36

THE CALL CAME ON SATURDAY, the day before the article was supposed to run.

During the week, Puente's friends at the task force had reported that a journalist was sniffing around about the Ruiz Caballero case. Bosses were climbing walls. There were strategy sessions, conference calls, a tense interview.

On Saturday, the five of them were eating a lunch of takeout Chinese food at Puente's apartment when the phone rang. She listened and said "OK" a few times. She wrote something down. She looked at Méndez.

"It's going to happen," she said, her voice close to a whisper.

They drove to a parking garage in La Jolla. The task force had turned the roof level into a command post. Balmaceda, the DEA supervisor, practically sprinted over to their car. He was wearing a DEA jacket, a gun strapped low on his blue-jeaned right leg, and shades.

"We've been saving the champagne for you," Balmaceda exclaimed.

He told them that Junior had spent the afternoon on foot accompanied by Natasha, his girlfriend from Tijuana, and two Mexican bodyguards. "Thinks he's home free. Practically rubbing our noses in it. I'd love to know what kind of deal his uncle cut for him."

"You really have the green light?" Isabel said.

"We're just waiting for the right spot. He's in that restaurant now. Pounding drinks and stuffing his face."

Méndez leaned on the wall of the rooftop and looked down at the restaurant. A Lexus and a Porsche sat at the valet parking stand. Palm trees swayed in the breeze. The ocean shimmered in the distance. Trouble comes to paradise, he thought.

Junior and Natasha left the restaurant an hour later. They strolled, the guards trailing. They stopped in boutiques.

"OK, enough shopping," Balmaceda said. "He spent the equivalent of my yearly salary on her yesterday. Next place where it isn't crowded, we do the jump-out."

It went down fast. Three sport utility vehicles glided up in front of a boutique. Agents in body armor swarmed inside. Within minutes, the radio reported that Junior was a prisoner.

The interior of the boutique was long and sparse and white. Mannequins struck fanciful poses on balconies that lined the walls above the clothes racks. The place was filled with heavily armed agents, laughing and talking, blowing off steam. Junior's two bodyguards were laid out on their bellies. Their shirts had been pulled up over their faces like hoods. A female agent had taken charge of Natasha, who was sobbing hysterically. She was half-in and half-out of a long sleeveless dress that showed off golden flesh.

Advancing through the circle of hulking SWAT agents in body armor, Méndez caught a glimpse of thick legs in baggy shorts and Timberlands. Despite his tan and a new goatee below bloated cheeks, Junior resembled a well-fed cadaver. His arms were pinned to his sides by the cuffs. His bulk was slumped in the armchair, almost horizontal. His eyes were closed. A cup of coffee had spilled across fashion magazines on a table. The agents had rushed Junior as he watched Natasha modeling outfits.

The moment was not how Méndez had imagined it. He tried

to muster triumph, hatred, jubilation. But he felt hollow. Everyone looked at him expectantly. He had the impression he should say something, but he didn't know the policeman's etiquette for the situation.

Junior solved the problem. He yawned. His eyes opened and he croaked: "Méndez."

"At your orders," Méndez replied.

"You are lucky."

"Why?"

"My uncle is getting old. He sold me out. If he were ten years younger, he would have killed you all. The Americans too." Junior's glare rested on Isabel Puente. "But now the bastard's old and tired. So he throws you a bone."

"Maybe times are changing," Méndez said.

"Are they? You think you'll ever get my uncle? Not if you send me to Mexico."

"That's where you are going. And, believe it or not, to jail."

"You are losing an opportunity. My uncle's the top dog and you know it. You think I'll survive five minutes in prison if he doesn't want me to? They'll cut my throat the first night."

"It will be a VIP prison," Méndez said. "You will not even catch cold."

"Listen to me," Junior said, his voice turning shrill. "I'm ready to give him up."

"I'm not in the mood for negotiating just at this moment," Méndez said.

Balmaceda gave an order. Agents hauled Junior to his feet. He roared unintelligibly as they dragged him away.

On Monday, an immigration judge ordered Junior expelled to Mexico. A Mexican delegation headed by the Secretary arrived to take charge of him. The Secretary sent a request through the Americans for a meeting with Méndez. Méndez accepted, mainly out of curiosity.

That was how he found himself in a hotel lounge on the San Diego waterfront, watching the Secretary fiddle with a dish of peanuts. The Secretary looked as clerical as ever. He treated Méndez with wan formality, like a professor with a problem student. He informed Méndez that he would soon resign. With the elections coming up, the government wanted someone more pliable in his post. The Secretary had been offered an ambassadorship in Europe, his second foray into diplomatic service.

"It has been narrowed down to a French-speaking capital," he said. "Everyone tells me to hope for Paris. Frankly, I'd be content with Brussels or Bern. The Parisians are so tiresome, don't you think?"

No longer obliged to come up with responses to such comments, Méndez watched the sailboats on the bay through a tall window.

The Secretary had brought a day-old Sunday newspaper with him. He picked it up from the table and made a show of examining the front-page package about the capture of Junior Ruiz Caballero. Steinberg's article had been diluted by the breaking news, as Méndez had expected. The questions about Junior's presence in San Diego, the political obstruction by the Americans, had been pushed down in the story. Garrison's mysterious connections were mentioned without much explanation. But there was a long sidebar profile of Méndez that quoted extensively from the article he had given her.

"Don Quixote meets Eliot Ness," the Secretary mused. "The Americans turn everything into a movie."

The Secretary nibbled nuts and sipped orange juice. His voice mild, he continued: "I imagine that you are under the illusion that it was the threat of your article that caused the arrest of Junior."

He can't bear the thought that I might have come out on top, Méndez thought. The old snake.

"I try not to have illusions," Méndez said. "All I know is that the American and Mexican governments got together to protect a criminal. And when the press found out, they decided he wasn't worth it."

"Perhaps you want to know what really happened."

Méndez waited.

"You see, a lot of manipulation went on," the Secretary said. "The governments manipulated each other. The Senator manipulated Junior. And the Americans manipulated you."

"How?"

"When Junior got himself kicked out of South America, it was clear to the Senator and his friends that his nephew was a real problem. No matter how much money he made for them, how much he scared their enemies. But they knew Junior's capture would be a disaster. Skeletons spilling out of closets, arrests, killings. So Mexico City convinced the Americans that the Ruiz Caballeros were too hot to touch. The agreement was to park Junior in San Diego, where he would have to restrain himself for the time being."

"The Americans didn't put up a fight," Méndez said. "They had things to hide too."

"You simplify too much. Their agencies were divided, as usual. That is where Mr. Daniels showed he is not the typical American clod. He has more subtlety, more style. Daniels needed leverage. So, I darkly suspect, he told you what you needed to know. Calculating, correctly, that you would get upset and, being a journalist at heart, go to the press."

"Kind of convoluted, don't you think?"

"Your crusade gave him the argument he needed in Washington to force the arrest of Junior down our throats. To beat the media to the punch."

"He could have gone to the press himself."

"Why take that risk? If it didn't work, you were a shield for him. A scapegoat. Are you naive enough to think that the article would have run if the Americans hadn't wanted it to?"

"Although I feel nostalgic for the days when we used to sit around bashing the Americans, I happen to think they have a free press in this country. Despite its many defects."

"In any case, the Senator managed to save himself, his political group and their presidential candidate. 'Jettison that demented sadistic nephew of yours, and we can still do business. At least until the elections.' That was the message to the Senator."

"Lovely." Méndez let the disgust show in his face.

"As a writer, you would have found it instructive. I was dispatched personally to see the Senator at his country house in Toluca."

The Secretary paused theatrically.

"We talked about old times. We drank an excellent brandy. Carlos Primero. I told the Senator, gently, that he had no choice. Junior had to be sacrificed. Do you know what he said? It was priceless: 'That boy has been like a son to me. But he is not my son.' That was it. We understood each other perfectly."

Because you are both foul specimens, Méndez thought. He leaned forward. "Listen, Mr. Secretary: In addition to Garrison, the Ruiz Caballeros had someone inside the U.S. government feeding them information. Someone powerful."

"That surprises you?"

"No. But I would like to know: Who was it? Daniels? Did he double-cross them?"

The Secretary arched his eyebrows. Méndez had little hope for the gambit. But there was a remote chance that sheer smugness might induce the Secretary to answer. Or that he might see a benefit in using Méndez to drop a bomb.

"Let me put it this way," the Secretary said. "If the Senator had an ally in Washington, as you theorize, I can assure you that person would be someone at a level Mr. Daniels is unlikely to attain. Despite his talents and the fact that, I must say, he dresses more elegantly than most American functionaries."

The Secretary removed and wiped his glasses. He shook his head. "*Ay* Leo. I made a mistake with you, I see that now."

"What mistake?"

"Bringing you into government service. I knew about your politics, your anger. But I thought your experiences at the border had made you tough-minded. I'd like to think I was correct, at first. But the pressure, the distance from your family. The Aguirre assassination. Human entanglements. They weakened you. I gave you power, and you made a mess with it."

Méndez narrowed his eyes. "It must be nice not to have human entanglements. I thought that made you different. But you sold out just the same."

"There is no need to get cross."

"Ever since I can remember, I've run around in labyrinths created by people like you. Whether it's street-corner narcos or political assassins, there is always something to hide. I am afraid Araceli Aguirre was right about you. For now, I'm content with Junior. Eventually, the rest of you will end up where you belong too."

The Secretary's face constricted. Méndez wondered if he would get up and walk out. Instead he sighed elaborately, as if Méndez had just confirmed his suspicions. Extending a long pale finger, the Secretary tapped Méndez's photo on the front page of the newspaper.

"Of course, the most incredible thing is that you came out well in the end," the Secretary said. "Who knows? At the rate things are going, we could lose the election next year. God protect our homeland, the reformers and the neophytes and the imbeciles"—he emphasized the word, a final stab—"could end up in charge. And I might come to you looking for a job."

"I know we both look forward to that day," Méndez said.

37

THE HANDOFF TOOK PLACE at The Line in San Ysidro.

Pescatore stood to one side with Méndez, Athos and Porthos. Isabel was busy in the contingent of American federal agents clustered around vehicles. They were all in the restricted parking lot by the border fence.

A Border Patrol custody bus unloaded prisoners nearby. Agents herded the released illegal immigrants back through a gate into Tijuana. On Interstate 5 to the east, the slow steel river of traffic flowed into the Mexican customs station, glass and metal glinting in the sun. Pescatore saw tourists and other pedestrians filing through the turnstile into Tijuana. A Border Patrol Wrangler cruised by. Pescatore thought he spotted Galván driving. He wondered if Galván had ever found a PA boyfriend for his cute cousin from Guadalajara.

It was the daily routine. Except that a federal SWAT team had set up a perimeter on the north side of the fence. A phalanx of Mexican federal police had done the same on the south.

When the Border Patrol bus departed, a black van pulled up. U.S. Marshals piled out. They extracted Junior, who wore a blue prison jumpsuit and manacles on his wrists and ankles. They half escorted, half carried him to the fence, where a contingent of Mexican federal officers wearing ski masks and holding heavy weapons had appeared in the open gateway.

The exchange took place without frills or ceremony. Pescatore barely caught a glimpse of Junior, head down, hair unkempt, eyes closed. Then he was gone.

"So much for him," Pescatore said to Méndez. "I gotta tell you, Licenciado, I'm pretty disappointed with Junior. The way he whined and carried on in La Jolla when they arrested him. A big mafioso like that. You'd think he'd a had some dignity."

"He is not a big mafioso anymore," Méndez said, arms folded.

"How you figure?"

"When you catch someone like Junior, all that is left is a shell. The power has already moved on to some other person."

"Well that sucks." Pescatore shook his head. "How come you bother, then, if it's always too late?"

Méndez clapped him—rather paternally, Pescatore thought—on the shoulder. "A very good question. I suppose you chase them to keep the power on the run."

Méndez said he had to catch a flight to Northern California to see his family. Pescatore told him he hoped things went well.

"What will you do with yourself?" Méndez asked.

The answer came to him with sudden certainty. "Go back to the Border Patrol. If they'll take me."

"Really?" Méndez grinned wolfishly.

"Why not? It's an honest living. Before, I felt like I belonged with the criminals. But then it was the other way around, you know? So I want to give it another shot. For real, this time."

"Good for you, then."

"What about you, Licenciado? You going back to Tijuana?"

"Absolutely. I will pose as a journalist this time."

"Well, you ever need me for anything, you just let me know..."

Looking over Méndez's shoulder at the federal agents dispersing, Pescatore spotted Isabel Puente getting into her car. He hesitated. Méndez followed his gaze.

"If I were you, *muchacho,*" Méndez said softly, "I would give it a try. At the border, anything can happen."

Pescatore nodded, embarrassed. He quickly shook hands with Méndez, Athos and Porthos. They watched as he hurried to the black Mazda. He went up to the passenger side and rapped gently on the glass.

After a moment, the window lowered halfway. Isabel looked out at him.

"Miss Puente," Pescatore said. "Got a minute for me?"

He saw his reflection in her sunglasses. He stayed in his half crouch. The silence lengthened.

"I thought we might go someplace quiet," Pescatore said. "Continue our conversation."

She made him wait. When she spoke at last, her voice was husky and resigned.

"Am I under any obligation to let you into this vehicle?" she asked.

He grinned. "None whatsoever."

ACKNOWLEDGMENTS

Many thanks to:

Mike Connelly for aid above and beyond the call of duty.

My great editor, Asya Muchnick, for making it happen and for making it better; the people at Little, Brown and Mulholland Books; and my agent, Bonnie Nadell.

Carmen for the lovely, lovely editing, and everything else.

Carlo and Sal, brilliant brother-editors.

Valeria, a star-in-the-making.

My parents for years of love, patience and support. And my parents-in-law, always near in our thoughts.

John Malkovich, Lianne Halfon and Russ Smith for the encouragement and effort.

The many men and women in law enforcement north and south of The Line who have given me their wisdom and trust.

The journalists of Latin America, especially my old friends in the Tijuana press corps, for their solidarity and courage.

ABOUT THE AUTHOR

Sebastian Rotella is an author and award-winning senior reporter for ProPublica, an independent organization dedicated to investigative journalism. He covers issues including international terrorism, organized crime, national security and immigration. Previously, he worked for twenty-three years for the *Los Angeles Times,* serving as bureau chief in Paris and Buenos Aires and covering the Mexican border. He was a Pulitzer finalist for international reporting in 2006. He is the author of *Twilight on the Line: Underworlds and Politics at the U.S.–Mexico Border,* which was named a New York Times Notable Book in 1998.